third time's the charm

LIZ TALLEY

Third Time's the Charm
Copyright ©2018 Liz Talley
ISBN-13: 978-0-9985187-3-2

Edited and formatted by Victory Editing.
Cover design by the Killion Group.

dedication

When it comes to book clubs, you can't beat the Bayou Book Bitches.
We drink wine (and vodka), read good books, and laugh A LOT.
I'm so glad you invited me to stick around.
#orangeisthenewzucchini #Marywillnotdothat #ibrokeyourbaseboards
#Denmarkisauscity #guestauthorsseemtostick

And also to my friend Kathy Sikes, who loves dogs as much as I do!

also by Liz Talley

Come Home to Me

Morning Glory:

Charmingly Yours
Perfectly Charming
All That Charm
Prince Not Quite Charming (novella)

Home in Magnolia Bend:

The Sweetest September
Sweet Talking Man
Sweet Southern Nights

New Orleans Ladies:

The Spirit of Christmas
His Uptown Girl
His Brown-Eyed Girl
His Forever Girl

also by Liz Talley

Bayou Bridge:

Waters Run Deep

Under the Autumn Sky

The Road to Bayou Bridge

Oak Stand:

Vegas Two-Step

The Way to Texas

A Little Texas

"A Little Texas" in Small Town U.S.A. with Allison Leigh

A Taste of Texas

A Touch of Scarlet

Novellas and Anthologies:

The Nerd Who Loved Me

"Hotter in Atlanta" (a short story)

Cowboys for Christmas with Kim Law and Terri Osburn

A Wrong Bed for Christmas with Kimberly Van Meter

chapter one

Sunshine Voorhees David wanted to cry, but she wouldn't. Because Sunny didn't cry anymore. Tears never changed a damn thing. They just caused a gal's mascara to run and made her nose clown red. Nope, Sunny definitely wasn't going to cry.

But that didn't mean the hard peach pit of despair sitting in her gut wasn't growing heavier each day that passed. Life felt pretty crappy at the moment, and after changing her mother's diaper earlier, that wasn't just a figure of speech.

"I told you I wanted to watch *CSI: Victims Unit.* This is *Law and Order,*" Betty Voorhees complained from her wheelchair in the living room. "And this chicken potpie's cold."

"Well, it wouldn't be cold if you'd told me you needed to go to the bathroom instead of just... going to the bathroom." Sunny crossed her arms and gave her best Nurse Ratched impression.

She'd known it would be hard taking care of her invalid mother, not just because Betty was disabled but because the woman might as well have been a pit viper. No one would ever say her mother was an easygoing woman, but after a massive stroke left Betty partially paralyzed, the bitterness cemented inside her mama was inoperable. Sunny didn't know how she was going to last much longer as a caretaker and prayed the résumés she'd dropped off around town would net her a reprieve from playing nurse… along with the much-needed money to complete the renovations to the house. How her sister Eden had dealt with their mother on her own for over a decade baffled Sunny.

"You're nothing like Eden. She never talked to me so disrespectfully," Betty complained before picking up her fork with her good hand and eating the potpie despite it being cold.

"I'm definitely not my baby sister, Mama," Sunny said, walking out of the room and through the small kitchen to the back porch.

"You got that right. Your sister's ten times the person you are." Betty's arrow found its mark even as Sunny escaped into the crisp winter day.

Her breath crystallized in the air as she tapped a cigarette from her emergency pack. Much more of dealing with her mother and she'd go from emergency cigs to a pack-a-day habit. She'd started smoking almost sixteen years ago—a week after she'd left Morning Glory. She'd picked up the habit from the Marine she'd met and married, but every time she got pregnant, she quit. And each time she lost the baby, she'd dry her eyes, go down to the gas station, and buy a carton. Last time she'd gone five months without lighting up. Five damn months.

Taking a drag, she contemplated her life at the moment. Thirty-four years old. Widow. Survivor of five miscarriages. Unemployed. Living with her ex-stripper, ex–drug addict handicapped mother.

Wasn't life just dandy?

Sunny blew out a cloud of smoke and tried to focus on the positive. She still had her looks and a degree in business administration. She had food. A roof over her head. And an offer from Rosalind to go out to California and work with her at the insurance agency in the fall.

She needed a new start, and the West Coast sounded good. Sunshine and beaches.

But first she had to do something about her mother.

"Sunny," her mother called, her strident voice easily heard through the back door that needed new weather stripping.

"Ma'am?" Sunny called, cracking the kitchen door, refusing to relinquish the first good thing about her day—the cigarette.

"Come here. Please."

"Yes, ma'am." Old habits die hard in the South. Move back to Mississippi and pick back up with what her aunt Ruby Jean had beaten into her when she was five. *Please, Thank you, Yes ma'am. No, sir.*

Sunny sucked in a long drag, stabbed out the cigarette in the chipped dish balanced on the wooden rail, and reentered the old house, skirting around the stacks of tile she'd left sitting in the path. She'd already spent nearly two thousand dollars of her widow's benefit in the kitchen, splurging on a big farm sink because that's what all the women oohed and aahed about on HGTV. She'd tiled the countertops because granite or quartz would have no return on investment in the neighborhood they lived in. She still wore the neutral gray paint color flecked in her red hair, and she loved the new light Jimmy Joe had installed for her for the price of a case Bud Light and some oatmeal cookies. Now if she could just talk Betty into letting her list the house for sale.

Her mother swiveled her head when Sunny came into the living room. Betty's face drooped on one side, making her look unbalanced. And pitiful. Which would work more in her favor if she weren't as deadly as a cobra. "I'm sorry for yelling at you about the potpie."

Sunny raised her eyebrows. "You are?"

"I am. You're not used to taking care of anyone. But yourself." Betty made the comment a backhanded compliment. Of course she would. That was the way the woman operated—sly comments, selfish tendencies, and plenty of blame.

At one time, Betty Belle Voorhees had been full of smiles and dreams. Sunny had seen the pictures of her mother in Aunt Ruby Jean's family albums. The innocent girl in the tinted photos grinned, posing impishly, looking so much like Sunny herself when she was young that they might have been mistaken for each other. Blond hair, violet eyes, and pink cheeks, shining in fluffy Easter dresses and kitty-cat Halloween costumes. Betty had been a girl unsmudged by the ugly smokestacks of reality. A girl far removed from the crackhead stripper she'd become. A girl who could never imagine she'd end up wheelchair-bound and hateful at age fifty-seven.

"I'm going out for more paint," Sunny said, picking up the remote control and setting it on the old TV tray her mother used as an end table. Staging. That was something she might have to consider if they put the house on the market, but how in all that was holy could she afford to pay for staging? Would anyone come to Grover's Park to stage a house for sale?

Probably not.

She needed to get a job. Her money was stretched tighter than Dick's hatband. Whoever he was.

"I ain't going to no damn nursing home," Betty said, trying to swivel her head. "So you might as well just save your money. This house ain't gonna sell no way."

"It's not a nursing home, Mama. It's a retirement community. They have fun activities like pizza night and trips to the movies. You'll make friends."

"I don't want friends. Or pizza. If I'm staying in Morning Glory, I'm staying here. In this house. The same one we've had in our family for three generations."

Sunny ignored her mother and grabbed the keys to her bike from the credenza. Her mother's secondhand van needed a new transmission and was in the shop, which made it very inconvenient to carry much from the hardware store. Besides, there was no sense arguing with her mother when she was in such a mood. Better to escape, though that was a stretch. Morning Glory was far from an escape. Instead, the small Mississippi town was an albatross of memories, dragging her further down.

Blue-collar folks populated Grover's Park, which meant all

was quiet as Sunny straddled her deceased husband's Harley-Davidson. She wedged the helmet on her head, imagining the scent of Alan lingering in the foam lining. But it wasn't there. Alan was gone. In fact, he'd been gone from her before he'd been killed in Afghanistan. The only thing holding them together had been the baby, a weak anchor at best. Even if their daughter had been born, she and Alan would have drifted further apart. The chasm had been too deep, the blame too immense.

Sunny pulled on her gloves, snapped the chinstrap, and fired the bike. The roar was satisfying, and she was glad she'd sold her Acura in favor of the bike even if she'd frozen her ass off on the way down to Mississippi. The black-and-silver beauty suited her now. Or at least who she wanted to be—a tough chick who didn't give a damn.

Pulling out of the neighborhood, she headed toward the town square, passing the elementary school she'd once attended, a rare smile forming as children tumbled out the double doors and onto the playground like frisky puppies. The frigid air on her face and neck made her wish she'd grabbed her wool scarf to tuck beneath her chin. Naked trees lined the streets leading to the town square and Mick Seaver's hardware store. She pulled into a parking space near the flowerbeds containing early-spring pansies and snapdragons.

"Hey, Sunny," Mick called from behind the counter when she pushed into the store.

"Hey, Mr. Seaver," she responded, shaking her head so she didn't have helmet hair. "How's it going?"

"Same old, same old," Mick said, tapping at his phone. His silver hair looked dull in the dim fluorescent light. Sunny had gone to school with his youngest son, Will. In school, Will had gotten into tons of trouble, so Sunny found it vastly ironic that Mick's son was now the associate pastor of Morning Glory Baptist Church. Weird how some people changed. People probably would say the same kind of thing about her. *That Sunny Voorhees used to be the homecoming queen and valedictorian. Can you believe what a loser she is now? Such a shame. Tsk, tsk, tsk.*

Screw 'em. She didn't care what anyone thought about her.

"I need a quart of the gray paint, just a pint of the white trim," she said, eyeing the trim brushes.

"I got the colors on your index card in my file. Won't take a minute to get 'em mixed."

"Thanks." She headed to the paint aisle, picking out the cheapest cutting brush. Then she grabbed a package of paint-pan liners and blue painter's tape. The door dinged as she walked toward the desk Mick stood behind, operating the paint shaker.

Sunny's stomach dropped when she saw the brown curls at the base of the new customer's neck.

In an instant she was sucked back to Morning Glory High School's cafeteria, standing in line with her then best friend Marcie, spying a clump of sophomore boys cracking jokes by the milk and juice fridge. His hair was shaggy, the color of aged pennies, and the way he smiled made her extend her neck to watch him, like a curious meerkat. She remembered thinking she'd never seen anyone like him before. The way he moved, the way everything about him was so natural, like he didn't care what anyone thought. He knew exactly who he was.

But that was nearly twenty years ago. Henry Todd Delmar wasn't a boy any longer. He was a full-grown man.

The boy turned, giving her his profile, and she could see he was maybe fifteen, close to the same age Henry had been standing in the lunch line, smiling as his friends goofed off.

"Can I help you, young man?" Mick asked, glancing over his shoulder at the boy. "Oh, Landry, I didn't recognize you. Grown a foot or more since I saw you last."

"Yes, sir," the boy said. The kid seemed so serious.

Henry and his wife had had a boy, so the kid could be Henry's. But just because a teenaged boy had hair the same color as Henry's didn't mean it was his son. She was being paranoid… and creepy standing there watching the kid scuff his sneaker against the aged tile of the store.

"My dad sent me to pick up that lawn mower filter he

ordered."

"The Tecumseh?"

"I guess," the kid responded.

Sunny turned and concentrated on her short list. Still needed some paint remover. One small bottle. The kid was not Henry's. Besides, Henry was out of town on a project. Or so she'd heard around town.

"Here you go, kiddo," Mick said, tapping at the cash register. "I can put this on your dad's account if you want."

"Okay," the kid said.

Wasn't much of a conversationalist. But most kids weren't these days. They walked around with their heads down, studying their cell phones.

The door dinged again.

"You got the filter, Lan?" the man entering the store asked.

Sunny ducked.

She'd know that voice anywhere. Henry Todd Delmar.

Her heart raced as she crouched beside a row of drop cloths, amazed that her first inclination was to hide. Good Lord, she was thirty-four years old and way past hiding from confrontation. Not that there would be confrontation. Maybe awkwardness. Definitely awkwardness.

She should stand up and stop acting like an idiot. She and Henry were water under the bridge.

A creaky old bridge.

One that groaned beneath the weight of emotion… of hurt… of pus-filled, festering betrayal.

Which was why she stayed exactly where she was.

"Hey, Delmar, good to see you back," Mick called out, hammering something. Probably her paint. *Please don't say anything, Mick. Please for the love of God, don't tell him I'm here.*

"Thanks, Mr. Seaver. Take this out to the truck, Landry. I'll be right out. Forgot I needed some—"

"You won't believe who's in here," Mick said. Sunny could

hear the excitement in his voice.

"No, no, no," Sunny whispered, steadying herself with her fingertips since her arms were full with the supplies she'd already picked up.

Dear Lord, she was hiding behind paintbrushes like a moron, but maybe that's what a gal did when she wasn't wearing makeup and her hair was ratty from a bike ride. Not to mention there was a pimple on her chin she chalked up to the stress of dealing with her mother. And she wore a jean jacket that had a mustard stain on the elbow. No woman in her right mind would want to see her ex with a zit on her chin and condiments on her jacket.

The hardware store's phone rang.

"Thank you, Jesus," Sunny mouthed, closing her eyes.

"I was going to say— Hold on a sec," Mick said. There was a rattle and the lifting of the receiver. "Seaver's Hardware. This is Mick."

Sunny slow-released the breath she held. Maybe whoever was calling had a complicated question that would keep Mick from blabbing about her being there. Either way, it bought her a reprieve.

"Excuse me," someone said to her right.

Oh crap. Henry.

"Sorry," Sunny said, grabbing a roll of plastic and standing, letting her hair swing forward to hide her face.

Henry slid by and walked to the end of the aisle. Sunny wanted so badly to look at him. It had been a long time since she'd laid eyes on him. He'd changed his cologne—no more Polo. It had been replaced by something more sophisticated. Something his ex-wife or a girlfriend probably picked out for him. Something that likely cost more than anything she owned except maybe the leather jacket Alan had bought her for Christmas one year.

She watched Henry from the corner of her eye as he picked up a can of spray paint. John Deere green. Then he put it back. Standing there for a few seconds, he reached for another and gave it a shake. She felt his perusal and turned her head away from him as she made a production of putting the plastic drop cloth back and picking up a different brand. The arm that held her other items ached.

If it had been a scene in a movie, she would have smiled. Awww. Two fairly attractive people checking each other out in the hardware store. Oh, the possibilities. Oh, the stories they'd tell their grandchildren. How romantic.

But this was the man who'd broken her heart.

Completely.

Nothing warm or fuzzy about that.

Finally Henry picked up a canister of paint, slid by her, and walked to the register. She took that moment to walk to the back of the store and turn her back to Henry. Mick was still talking to someone on the phone about an order that had been delivered to the wrong location. An older woman pushed through a door to Sunny's left, pulling on an apron, and walked to the front. She made casual conversation about the weather as she rang up Henry's purchase. Sunny pretended to peruse furniture polish and scratch cover-up, feeling relief pooling in her stomach.

Goodbyes were exchanged and the door opened and closed.

Safe. Whew.

Sunny cautiously made her way to the register just as Mick got off the phone.

"Hey, Sunny, you just missed Henry Delmar."

"Oh, well, that's okay," she said, setting down the items she'd juggled while hiding like a freak-a-zoid.

"Didn't you two date in high school?"

"Yeah, we did." For three years, seven months, and eighteen days. The best days of her life… even if she and Henry had ended badly. "Long time ago, right?"

"To you maybe," Mick said with a smile. "Seems like just yesterday you guys were small sprouts playing Wiffle ball in the parking lot."

She'd never played Wiffle ball, but she wasn't going to burst

Mick's memory of little boys doing little-boy things. "Time does fly."

Mick gave her the total and she swiped her card, praying it wouldn't get declined. She needed to call Eden and see if she could cover the medicines for their mother since the van's transmission would take away any extra money they'd had for the month. Eden had inherited some money from one of her friends who'd passed away almost a year ago. Her younger sister had used most of the money to go to college in New Orleans, something she'd failed to do as a senior almost thirteen years ago when Betty had her stroke. Sunny had promised her sister she'd get a chance to go to college. That Sunny would take her turn taking care of Betty, but between her husband deploying and the multiple dangerous pregnancies, it had taken longer than Sunny had planned.

Eden had never complained and damn sure deserved her break from Morning Glory and dealing with their mother.

"All right then, Sunny." Mick handed her the brown paper bags with the things she needed to finish up the painting in the kitchen.

"Thank you, Mr. Mick," Sunny said, hoping she could fit the items in the saddlebags on the sides of the bike. Might have to bend the plastic paint liners. "I'll see you later."

She walked to the glass door, trying to ascertain if Henry and his offspring were lurking around the square. Just as she put her hand on the door handle, her cell phone rang. She pulled it from her back pocket. She didn't recognize the number, but it was local.

"Hello," she said, electing to stay inside the warm store and put more distance between herself and Henry.

"Is this Sunny Voorhees?" the woman huffed and puffed, obviously out of breath.

"It's Sunny David."

"Yes, of course. That's right. I'm calling about the résumé you dropped by."

Sunny's heart leaped. Finally. "Yes?"

"I don't know if you remember me. This is Marilyn McConnell at Morning Glory High."

"Miss McConnell. Of course I remember you." Sunny summoned the memory of a small woman who wore her hair in Farrah Fawcett wings, complete with blue eye shadow, bubblegum lip gloss, and sweater-vests.

"Oh, good. Well, our attendance clerk fell and broke her hip last night and will be out for at least three months. Which is essentially through the end of the school year. Poor Melanie's got to have surgery, but before they can do that, they have to get her blood pressure stabilized. There's a steel rod and physical therapy. Good Lord, the poor thing has a long road ahead of her. At any rate, we're looking for someone to fill her place through the end of the year. Usually we go through the school board office. Protocol and stuff. And you'll have to go there for paperwork and such. But good thing your résumé was on my desk and Jim over in Human Resources owes me a favor. We love hiring former students if we can. Keep it in the family."

Finally the woman ran out of steam. An awkward silence sat a moment before Sunny snapped to attention. "Great. I mean, I'm sorry for Mrs. Geter, but I'm so happy you called me."

"Oh, good," Marilyn said, papers rustling in the background. "Why don't you head to the school board office in the morning? I'll call Jim and tell him you're coming around nine o'clock. They're going to need a background check, fingerprints, and lots and lots of paperwork. It'll take you a few hours at least. Then head over here in the afternoon. Sound good?"

Sounded perfect. How hard could working in the attendance office be? "Yes. It sounds very good. Thank you for calling me."

Marilyn laughed. "You may not be thanking me in a week. But it'll be an adventure."

Sunny made a face. What did that mean? "Yes. Of course. I'll see you tomorrow."

She hung up and pushed out the door. Having a job through May would be sweet. She could aim for getting the house on the market at the beginning of summer, an ideal time since many families were apt to move when kids were out of school. That would put Sunny in California for late summer. Perfect.

But only if she could talk her mother into the retirement community. And if she could talk Betty into listing the house. And if she could actually find someone who wanted to move into Grover's Park.

If… if… if.

As she stepped onto the sidewalk, she noticed several people gathered around a huge truck. A huge truck that was very near the spot where her bike had been parked.

Hurrying her steps, she crossed the street, dodging a lookie-loo who had slowed to see what all the fuss was about. Rosemary Genovese, one of her sister's BFFs, glanced over at Sunny, delivering an "I'm sorry" face.

"What?" Sunny asked.

Rosemary's eyes went to the back of the truck. To part of the motorcycle sticking out from under the colossal tire.

"What the fu—" Sunny started, her words dying when she saw the girl in pigtails standing beside the boy she'd seen earlier in the hardware store. Landry. The boy looked stricken… and scared.

Henry Todd Delmar stood staring down at the motorcycle beneath the tires of the truck. His face was a thundercloud, and for a fraction of a second, Sunny was struck at how good he looked pissed off… at how much a man he was now. No lopsided grin, teasing eyes, flirty hands. Henry had grown up.

His gaze rose to meet hers. "Ma'am, is this your bike?"

Sunny closed her mouth, her eyes sliding to the crushed Harley. "Yeah, it's mine."

Henry's arms had been crossed, but at that moment he dropped them like a release. She felt the exact moment he realized who she was. It was like a crackle of static, a record needle falling into the groove, a key turning in the lock. Connection made.

"Sunshine?" Henry's voice sounded far away.

"Hello, Henry."

chapter two

HENRY TODD DELMAR didn't shock easily. He'd known Sunny Voorhees or whatever she went by these days was back in Morning Glory. But he hadn't been prepared for the impact of seeing her again. Maybe nothing could have prepared him.

Because this woman looked nothing like the girl of his memories.

As a teenager, Sunny had been soft and pretty with golden hair the full spectrum of the sun. She'd worn funny T-shirts that clung to breasts he'd written silly poems about. "1,001 Odes to Sunshine's Girls" always made her giggle. She'd ridden beside him in the old Toyota truck he'd loved so much, and she'd worn lip gloss that tasted of strawberries and a locket he'd given her for the anniversary of their first date. She'd been everything he'd ever wanted—a soft place to land, the orb he'd spun around. His sunshine.

But the woman frowning at him was all hard angles, slashing mouth, and tough attitude that demanded a guy be uneasy. Too thin and hair the color of sin, this Sunny was so far removed from the girl he'd idealized that he couldn't grasp it was actually her.

He wanted to ask, "What happened to you?"

But he knew.

He'd broken her heart. She'd run away and made a life that included a recently deceased Marine husband. She'd only come back home because she'd promised Eden. He'd heard she was fixing up the old house in Grover Park, some said to sell. Small-town people talked. And when it came to the girl he'd once loved, he always listened.

"I heard you were back in town," Henry said, aware the crowd that had gathered around the crushed motorcycle was hanging on his every word. He and Sunny would be fodder for the dinner table that night.

"Yeah, but not for long," she said, her gaze going back to his truck crushing her bike. "Have trouble backing out or something?"

She was cool as shit, but he could tell she was upset. He could always tell when his Sunshine was out of sorts. Or maybe he wanted to think he still had that connection with her. Because at least it was something to hold on to.

"I did it," Landry said, his voice cracking.

Sunny turned toward the boy. "*You* did it?"

Landry's shoulders sagged. "I'm sorry. I… I… have my permit and Dad said I could drive home. Thought I would show him how good I could back into a spot. I didn't see your motorcycle."

Henry lasered his son with the pissed-off-dad look his father had used on him all too often. Nothing more effective on a boy than that look. At least until he got married and had to deal with pissed-off-wife look.

Landry swallowed and glanced away.

"But he decided to get behind the wheel before I was back in the truck. It's something we've discussed at length since he just got the permit a few months ago," Henry said.

"Should I call the police?" someone asked.

"No," Sunny said before he could. "No need to involve insurance companies or make things more complicated. I'm sure

Henry and I can work something out."

"Of course," Henry said, relieved she didn't want to call Morning Glory's finest. Landry was in hot water enough without involving the authorities and addressing the fact he'd driven without an adult in the car.

He wanted to clap his hands and declare the show over, but he knew some people in town had just pulled out pretend popcorn and were waiting to watch the showdown they'd missed all those years ago. Instead, he swept the crowd with a firm, perhaps accusing, stare. A couple of them shifted nervously, one or two wandered back toward the businesses ringing the square.

Rosemary touched Sunny's elbow. "You need me to do anything, Sunny?"

Sunny shook her head. "No, it's fine. We'll sort it out."

"You need a ride home?" Rosemary asked.

"I can take her," Henry said.

Sunny jerked her gaze to his, her blue eyes hard as sapphires. "I can—"

"It's the least we can do. We'll put the bike in the back and take it to a shop," Henry said.

Rosemary nodded as if she agreed, but then she looked at Sunny. "You sure?"

Sunny finally shrugged, though she looked reluctant as hell. "Sure, but thanks anyway."

When Rosemary left, the crowd followed her lead.

"I'll need to pull forward and then we can load the bike into my bed and take it to Deeter's." Henry pointed to his children. "Landry, take Katie Clare over to the benches and wait there."

Landry tugged his sister's elbow. "Come on."

The girl jerked away, her eyes on Sunny. "Who's she, Daddy? Why'd you call her Sunshine? Is that her name?"

"Katie," Henry said, unable to hold in the sigh. His daughter was like a terrier, ferociously cute and apt to not let go of anything she wanted. In this case it was information. "Do what I said, chicken."

"But Daddy, I just want—"

"Katie," he said, this time with a growly voice.

"Fine," she said, turning and flouncing off after her subdued brother. The girl was sheer drama and too much like her mother. Still, he'd lay down his life for her. As difficult as Katie Clare was, she brought him the joy he needed to make it each day. Whether it was yet another pet frog in the bathroom sink, "trying on" makeup at his mother's house, or putting kitten stickers on his briefcase, Katie made life worth living. Landry did too, though his serious boy never wanted to play tickle fight or watch movies that featured people who burst into song. Landry was steady, honest, and colored within the lines, which made this accident with Sunny's bike atypical of the boy.

Sunny's gaze stayed on his daughter as she sashayed away, a bemused expression on her face. It was the first glimpse of any softness in Sunny.

"Sorry about that. Katie Clare is… dramatic. And stubborn. And—"

"Wonderful?" Sunny finished, something tender slightly curving her delicious mouth.

"Yeah, most definitely," Henry said, flicking away the thought that Sunny's mouth was delicious. *Stop being an idiot.* He walked around to the open driver's door and climbed inside. He stuck his head back out the door. "Stay back, okay? Don't want to hurt you."

The look Sunny gave him tore his heart. But quick as spit, she shuttered her expression.

Henry pretended away the words he'd uttered. Not going there.

Instead of acknowledging the slip, he shut the door and shifted into Drive, looking carefully both ways as he gunned the engine. The truck rocked and then shot forward, releasing its predatory hold on the helpless Harley.

Luckily the parking spot next to the scene of the crime was empty. Only a few more feet and his son wouldn't have done any damage. And Henry never would have run into Sunny. At least not today. He had been out of town for three weeks, working in Mobile on a project demanding special handling. Or as his dad had called it, "ass kissing." Since Henry had missed his weekend with the kids, his ex-wife Jillian had let him take them back to Morning Glory for back-to-back weekends.

Henry maneuvered into the spot next to the ruined bike and shut off the engine.

Sunny stood staring at the bike, a sorrowful look on her face. "Wow, it crumpled like a toy. And it's a Harley, not a flimsy dirt bike."

"Well, my truck's pretty big."

"I noticed," she said dryly.

He waited for the requisite big truck, small penis implication, but it never came. "Think I'll need Landry to lift this into the truck."

"Or maybe we should call a tow truck?" Sunny suggested.

Henry bent and lifted the bike. It was heavy but not ridiculously so. "Think we can get it. Save the expense."

The look she gave him said it wouldn't be coming out of her pocket. And it wouldn't. Still, being a do-it-yourselfer was ingrained in him, so if he could load the bike and get it to the shop, why involve anyone else?

"Lan, get over here," Henry called.

The boy jogged over, looking like a whipped puppy—eager to please, afraid of getting swatted. Like he'd ever swatted the boy. "You gonna put it in the back of the truck?"

Henry put his hands on his hips and studied the back of his truck and the dimensions of the bike. "It'll fit and save us some time and money."

Landry shrugged and dropped the tailgate, maneuvering the boards he'd picked up earlier so that they could roll the bike up the makeshift ramp. Five minutes and one slipped curse word, he and his son had the bike loaded. Sunny stood there with Katie Clare, his daughter sliding interested glances at the stoic woman who looked so different than the girl he'd known.

So incredibly different.

"There," he said slamming the tailgate. "Let's get this over to Deeter's garage before he shuts down. Ever since Tracy had him a grandbaby, he closes earlier and earlier."

"Tracy had a baby? I used to babysit her," Sunny murmured.

"You used to live here?" Katie Clare asked. "That must be how you know my daddy. He grew up here too. But we live in Jackson. And kinda here. Dad's divorced."

"Motormouth," Henry said, shaking his head at his daughter. "Sunny and I went to Morning Glory High School together a long time ago."

And she was once my everything.

But he didn't say that of course.

Sunny issued a smile because it was expected. "A long time ago."

"Let's get moving, crew," Henry said to his children. They obediently slid into the back seat, shifting the day's packages onto the floorboard. Henry didn't open the passenger door for Sunny because that would have been weird. But he'd almost done it. Out of habit.

Sunny climbed into the cab, settling her own packages by her feet. She looked about as comfortable as a farmer's goose on Christmas Eve. "This *is* a big truck."

"I work construction."

"For your daddy?"

"Yep," he said, wanting to defend the fact he'd stepped into the family business. Wasn't like he'd had much choice. A nineteen-year-old with a baby on the way and a new wife had to have money coming in, and though his parents could have footed the entire bill while he finished at Ole Miss, Henry couldn't allow that. Wasn't the man he'd wanted to be. Of course, he'd never wanted to work for the family business either. But life had a way of kicking you in the teeth. A guy didn't always get what he wanted. "Since my father has sort of retired, I run the business now."

"Daddy, you said we could get ice cream. I wanna see Miss Sassy. I lost another tooth, and she said I could get an extra scoop from the frog prince." Katie Clare leaned forward and tugged on his sleeve.

"We'll go to the Lazy Frog tomorrow."

"Awww," Katie Clare whined. "Not fair. Landry's the one who ran over the motorcycle. I didn't do nothing."

"Anything, and this is life, sweetheart. Doesn't always go as planned," Henry said, his mind still on the fact his life hadn't exactly panned out. Well, it had in a lot of ways, but there was still a hole. A hole left from how things had ended with him and Sunny.

And here she sat next to him.

He had no way to fix the mistake he'd made long ago, but he sure wished he could. It was like an unfinished painting cropping up every time he examined his life. A section of the happy paint-by-number left a glaring, obvious white.

But in life some things were left undone, and a person couldn't go backward to repair the tears. He had to accept he'd messed up and move past it.

He glanced over at Sunny. She seemed so broken. So *not* Sunny. And there was nothing he could do about the hurt in her life… or the fact she likely hated him.

"So how old are you guys?" Sunny asked turning her head to his kids.

"I'm fifteen," Landry said.

"I'm eight and a half," Katie Clare said. "My birthday's in October. When's your birthday?"

"August eighteenth," Henry said before he could think about it.

"You *know* her birthday?" Katie Clare asked, her little voice squeaking as her pitch went up.

Henry glanced over at Sunny. "I have a good memory."

"No, you don't." Landry snorted. "You forget tons of things.

Like *my* birthday."

"I didn't forget your birthday," Henry said, not wanting to have this conversation again. "I mixed it up with my cousin's. You two are a day apart."

"Whatever." Landry sighed.

"Hey, if you want to talk mistakes, we can." Henry eyed his son in the rearview mirror.

Landry's eyes widened. "No, that's okay."

The kid slid back into the seat and popped in his earbuds, but Katie Clare wasn't going to check out as easily.

"How come you know her birthday?" Katie's eyes grew big. "Oh, was she like your girlfriend or something?"

Sunny turned around. "You ask lots of questions. Are you a reporter? Or a detective?"

Katie Clare made a face. "I'm just a kid."

Sunny chuffed a laugh. And his heart warmed at the sound. It had been so long since he'd heard that laugh, but even it had changed. Somehow her laugh was huskier. Sexier.

"Actually, Sunny was my girlfriend in high school, Katie," Henry said, flicking on the blinker and waiting for Fred Odom to tootle by in his mail truck before turning onto Spruce Street where Deeter had a busy garage.

"She *was*?" Katie Clare asked, sounding positively titillated.

Sunny shifted in her seat. "Back when we were young. Your brother's age."

"He doesn't have a girlfriend, but I saw a picture of him on Instagram with a girl at a party. They were hugging. Mom got mad at him and said he couldn't go to any more parties. He's a freshman in high school. She said that's too young for girls."

Katie Clare was a fount of information and Henry made a note to talk to his son about parties, drinking, and girls. He'd tried to pretend his little boy wasn't a teenager, but the kid had started sprouting body hair and the occasional pimple to remind him that it was beyond time to have a refresher talk regarding sex and other things that could get a young guy in trouble.

"Do you live here now?" Katie Clare asked Sunny.

"Sorta. I'm staying with my mom for a while."

"Oh," Katie Clare said, and Henry could hear the wheels turning in his daughter's head. Ever since Jillian had gotten remarried last year, the child had been playing matchmaker. Katie was determined to see him remarried too. So far she'd written her dance teacher's email and cell phone on a note card and left it on his kitchen island. Then she circulated him through back-to-school night like it was a dial-a-date function. He'd apologized to five women over his daughter's insistence they go out to coffee.

Of course, he'd made a half-hearted resolution this year to start dating more. He had finally reached a point in the business where he could take more time off. He'd been lonely for too long and wanted someone to share his life with.

So Katie wasn't too far off… just a bit too pushy.

"Here we go. Let me run in and talk to Deeter." Henry shifted into Park.

"I'll go with you," Sunny said, unclicking her seat belt.

"I can handle it."

Sunny's face darkened. "It's my bike, Henry."

Henry paused for a moment then shrugged. This Sunny took care of herself. And she wasn't going to give any power over herself to Henry.

Deeter was happy to see Sunny, and after regaling her with a dozen pictures of Cecily Anne, his new granddaughter, he had the bike unloaded and sent them on their way with a wave and a promise to get to the bike by Monday.

They climbed back in the truck, and Henry angled the tires toward Grover's Park. Sunny didn't seem to be interested in conversation, so he turned on the radio, hoping Miranda Lambert would ease the tension. Instead, the country singer crooned about baggage and done-you-wrongs. No help there. Luckily it took very little time to get anywhere in Morning Glory. As he bumped over the tracks and pulled into the rougher part of Morning Glory, Katie Clare pressed her nose to the window and said, "This is where a bunch of poor people live."

Sunny issued a paper-dry chuckle.

"Katie Clare, that's not polite," he said.

"But it is," his daughter insisted, pointing at a house with a collapsing patio and rusted truck in the yard.

"It's okay, Henry," Sunny said.

"It's not okay."

"It's the truth that only eight-and-a-half-year-olds are brave enough to say. A lot of poor people live in Grover's Park. That's a fact."

For a moment her words lay there, throbbing, naked and too real to touch.

"Do you have another way to get around?" he asked.

"Why? You have a car I can borrow?" Sunny asked as they wove through the cramped streets.

"No, but I can give you a ride if you need it."

"I'll figure out something," Sunny said before her body stiffened. "Ah, damn, I have to be somewhere tomorrow morning." Her shoulders slumped and she issued a heavy sigh.

"I can pick you up."

"No. That's ridiculous."

"It's no problem. Once Deeter locates the parts and has a time frame for repair, we can get you a rental or something. Just temporary."

"I can take care of myself, Henry."

"I know you can, but this is my fault. Or rather my son's. I owe you not being inconvenienced. Surely you can tolerate me long enough for me to get you to wherever you need to go."

Sunny shrugged. "Fine. I need to be at the school board office at nine tomorrow morning. Then I have to go to the high school." Her words didn't invite any questions. Sunny was a private person, a woman who didn't want anyone to meddle in her life.

"I'll be here at eight forty-five to take you. I'm actually working a job at the high school. New gym."

"Great." But she didn't say it like it was great. She said it like she dreaded climbing into the truck with him again.

Henry pulled into the driveway at 223 Park Street and let the truck idle. He wanted to apologize for so much. For his daughter being so blunt. For his son running over her bike. For what he'd done all those years ago. But the words were stuck inside him. If he said all he needed to say, they'd be here for days upon end. "Here we are."

"Hey, this is the yard you mow, Dad." Landry leaned up, peering through the windshield at a patch of yard enclosed in a chain-link fence.

"Yard you mow?" Sunny repeated, whipping her head toward him. "You mow the yard?"

Henry wanted to grab hold of the words his son had released, ball them up, and toss them out the window. He'd forgotten that he'd come by once with Landry to mow and edge the Voorheeses' yard. "Sometimes I helped Eden out. When it was really hot and I was in the area."

"*You* mow the yard? When are you ever in this area?" Her violet eyes crackled in anger.

Her questions were bullets he wanted to dodge. He helped Eden and Betty out with the yard and things that needed repair because they were a link to Sunny… and because he still carried around guilt. But he didn't want to say that aloud. So he said nothing.

His failure to respond seemed to piss Sunny off more. She grabbed the bags at her feet and hopped down to the uneven pavement. Not even bothering to issue a goodbye, she slammed the door and stomped toward the sagging front porch of the small house she'd grown up in. Her jeans were baggy, the heels of her boots scuffed, and in that moment, Henry's heart squeezed so hard in his chest dampness crept into his eyes.

"She sure is mad about her motorcycle, huh?" Katie Clare said.

"Yeah, she is," Henry said, shifting the truck into Reverse.

"I didn't even know girls rode motorcycles."

chapter three

SUNNY DIPPED THE brush into the pan, swishing the bristles against the edge before swiping a final coat of paint on the upper cabinets in her mother's kitchen. The semigloss gray was a perfect neutral, and with new hardware, the kitchen would look somewhat modernized. Amazing what a little paint could do.

Her blood pressure had finally normalized, though for a good hour after Henry pulled out of her driveway, she'd thought she'd blow a gasket.

Charity.

That's what people had always given the Voorhees. And Henry continued the practice by being the benevolent landowner. Okay, so the Delmars no longer owned the Voorheeses' house, but Delmars had at one point. The same way they'd owned most of the rental properties in Grover's Park. The Delmar family dabbled in real estate development, land management, and construction. In other words, they ate the whole enchilada.

It irked her that Henry had felt so sorry for Eden and her mama that he'd stooped to help the poor. Probably trying to win the citizen-of-the-year award or something. *Hey, I mow the yard for my old girlfriend's crack-whore mama and pitiful sister. Look at me. I'm*

Sandra effing Dee. Give me your shitty Man of the Year award so I can put it on the shelf beside my daddy's.

Bunch of effing hypocrites with their scholarships and declarations of community renewal. *We help people get on their feet, but don't think for one second you'll end up with our boy Henry. He's not marrying Grover's Park trash no matter how pretty or smart she is.*

Anger made her hands shake and she dropped the paintbrush.

"Motherfu—"

"You sound like me in there," her mother called out in a singsong voice. She almost sounded cheerful. Which was alarming for Betty. She'd never done cheerful very well. Usually if she was happy, she was coked up or something.

"Apple doesn't fall far, right?" Sunny called back.

"What's wrong with you anyway?"

"Nothing." Sunny clenched her jaw and tried to forget Henry had taken pity on them… once again.

"Was that Henry's truck I saw pull out of the drive?"

Sneaky woman. Sunny had thought her mother had been asleep in front of the TV when she returned. Obviously not.

"His kid ran over the Harley," Sunny said, picking up the brush and using the paint thinner she'd purchased to wipe up the swoop of paint on the new tile.

"What? I can't hear ya."

Sunny set the brush in the pan and went into the living room. "I said his kid backed over the bike. Crushed it. Henry took it to Deeter. Then gave me a ride home. When will the van be ready?"

"Dunno. You're the one who took it in to be serviced." Her mother slid her gaze over to Sunny. "That must have been an interesting trip home."

"It was a ride. That's it."

"Yeah, but that boy's been pining after you forever."

"Don't, Mother." Sunny issued a warning. Henry Todd Delmar had not been pining over her. He'd married the girl his parents had chosen for him despite what he'd professed to have wanted, and he'd stayed married to her for many years. Close to ten years. Henry had moved on and so had Sunny. They were a closed book and every other euphemism she could scrape up to indicate nothing could happen between her and Henry.

Ever again. Because she wouldn't let it.

"I'm just saying. He's got plenty of money and he ain't bad to look at," Betty said, her smile making her leer like a scary clown. Her mother persisted in wearing bright pink lipstick and coloring her hair platinum, a sad attempt to cling to what she'd once been—a fantasy pinup girl.

"You *do* remember what he did, right? He knocked a girl up while we were together." Saying those words ripped her heart like they always had. She was over Henry, but the betrayal, the loss of all she'd thought would be hers, still tore at her. Like an old injury flaring before an advancing storm.

"Technically you were broken up, remember? Besides, he's a guy. When a girl shoves it in his face, he does what a man does. He takes it."

"Are you serious?" Sunny said, feeling disbelief wash over her. Back when the news hit, her mother had been incensed at Henry. She'd stood by Sunny, shaking her fist, cursing men, bemoaning the loss of a rich son-in-law. And now it was just "boys will be boys"?

"I'm realistic. You broke up with him. He was a college frat boy at a party where there were drugs, booze, and conniving debutantes wagging their asses. You can't really blame Henry for picking up what bitches were dropping down."

"Yeah, I can. I absolutely can."

"See? That's the trouble with women like you." Her mother scoffed. "You don't understand men. You thought Henry would stay in his room studying, pining away for his sweet Sunny girl. No. Guys are hunters by nature. They're always looking for a place to put their peckers. You can take a priest, get him drunk, get him high, shove your tits in his face, and he'd have you facedown, going to town before you could say—"

"No, you're wrong. You can't take your strip-club philosophies about men and apply them to the real world. There are men who don't go to strip clubs, Mother. There are men who don't think with their penises. There are men who are loyal and true."

"Ha." Betty snorted, waving her good hand. "You can believe what you wish, but Henry was a nineteen-year-old boy gulping down bourbon and looking for tail. That's what they all do, so don't deceive yourself. You think Alan didn't step out on you while he was deployed? He was gone for six months at a time. Come on, Sunny. Don't be stupid."

"You are such a bad person," Sunny said, swallowing the acid that had crept up her throat. "I don't know if Alan slept with someone else while we were married. I can't ask him, can I?"

"Nope, but you can own the fact you split up with both of them men. You might as well have handwritten them a pass to get some ass."

"I don't want to have this conversation with you. Your track record for romance is nonexistent." For the second time that day, Sunny felt tears prick at her eyes. What was wrong with her? She hadn't cried the entire time Alan was missing in action. She hadn't cried when Alan's commanding officer came to her door to give her the news his body had been recovered, and she damn sure hadn't cried at his funeral in front of all those other military wives watching for the slightest crack so they could swoop in with tissues and casseroles.

"Who said anything about *romance*?" Betty said, picking up the controller and changing the channel. "Henry's got money and security. You could do much worse. In fact, you have. If you'd have gotten knocked up by Henry instead of that other gal doing it, we wouldn't be sitting here having this conversation."

"You are truly horrible," Sunny whispered.

"So you already said. But that don't make me wrong." Betty cranked up the volume and dismissed her eldest daughter with *Judge Judy*.

Sunny closed her eyes, said a small prayer to forgotten God, and then walked to her bedroom. Sinking onto the bed, she marveled at her mother. At the thoughts the woman had just unloosed. No wonder Sunny had grown so cynical. Outside of the sadness of her life, she now lived with the Queen of Mean. People just didn't get it. They saw Betty and felt pity for her. What they didn't understand was the abject misery the woman splashed on the people around her. Sunny knew she should feel bad for seeing her mother as such a burden, but being eternally in her presence wore on her. So the idea of taking the temporary job at the high school appealed to her on more than just a financial level. She wouldn't make much money, but the time away from her mother might save her sanity.

After she went to the school board office tomorrow, she needed to call home health services to make sure Vienna could cover the hours Sunny would miss while working. Someone had to deal with her mother. But not now.

Tomorrow.

The day she would see Henry again.

Henry Todd Delmar.

He'd changed, but not by much. He was still loose-limbed, his hair curling behind his ears. A man now, for sure. His shoulders had broadened and his body thickened. The little squinty lines around his eyes made him look wiser, and the scruff on his jaw was thicker. He still made her heart stop, not that she would ever admit it except when sprawled in her childhood room, a place where she'd dreamed of kissing him, of going all the way with him, of having his babies. Only here could she even begin to acknowledge that what she'd felt for Henry had been locked away and never dealt with. Once upon a time, she had loved him as desperately as a girl who had nothing much in her life could.

And she'd had not much good in her life growing up. Henry had appeared on the horizon, bright and shiny in his armor, with his soft smile, big heart, and gorgeous hands that held hers as he told her he'd change everything for her. Of course, she wasn't absolutely pathetic. Her mother might have been embarrassing as hell, but her little sister was a bit of a local talent—Eden could dance and croon like a '40s jazz singer. Her aunt Ruby Jean had made sure they had school clothes, a bit of churching, and good manners. Her brother had been a scoundrel but always willing to help a neighbor repair a fence. Of course, her brother had died in an accident on an oil rig in the Gulf, but he'd been a good thing in her life. And Sunny's life up until the day Henry had destroyed her had been better than most could imagine for a girl who'd grown up in Grover's Park. She'd been the valedictorian, prom queen, and head cheerleader. Ole Miss had pretty much given her a free ride for college. Not everything was good because of Henry… but much of it had been because of him. Because he'd loved her, found her worthy and vowed to spend his life making her happy.

But that's what a small-town guy did when he was eighteen and hadn't experienced anything else in life.

Henry couldn't have known he lied like a snake oil salesman when he told her she was the only woman he'd ever love.

Sunny wanted to hate him for that lie, but part of her had known all along that Henry could never belong to her. She was a Voorhees and he was a Delmar. They'd been young kids who'd built a house of cards that collapsed with a giant puff of wind.

Henry Todd Delmar watched his mama creep around the rose garden behind Magnolia Dawn, the early nineteenth-century convent that had been turned into a residence by William Clayton Jeems III, his mama's cousin and the former president of Newcomb College. Neither Uncle Billy nor Newcomb College was around any longer, but his mama worked diligently to keep the heirloom roses that had been collected over the years thriving.

That was the thing about his mama—she believed in preserving the past and traditions.

He stepped from the shadows, throwing his hand up to shade

his eyes from the blinding sun sinking lower in the Mississippi sky.

"Oh my, Henry Todd. You like to have scared me into an early grave," his mother said, her accent thick as honey on cathead biscuits. She placed a gloved hand over her bosom. The large sunglasses she wore made her look like a predatory bug.

"Hello, Mama," Henry said, shoving his hands into his pockets and strolling toward where she'd set her lawn bag containing spiny clippings. "Brought the kids for supper."

"Good. Your daddy's been complaining about missing them. How was Jackson and your lovely ex-wife?" Her voice held displeasure when she said "ex-wife," not because she disliked Jillian but because she'd been determined Henry would stay married to her. His failure in marriage was something his mother had taken quite personally.

"Doing well. She and Eddie are expecting a baby in the fall."

"Moved along quickly, didn't she? And with a mechanic at that."

"Eddie owns three garages in Jackson. He's not just a mechanic. Besides, Jillian and I have been divorced for two years now. Not exactly fast."

"Well, to me it is. Young people don't have much stickability these days. In my day people made a vow and stuck to it."

"Like Dad did," Henry said, wishing immediately he'd bitten his tongue. His father had kept a mistress in Pearl for five years. His mother had found out when she'd taken a wrong turn on the way home from a shopping trip and spied his distinctive Bentley in the driveway of the duplex. She'd called to ask where he was. He'd said a business meeting in Jackson. She'd parked on the curb and laid on the horn until he'd emerged half-dressed and very much busted. The mistress had moved away, and his father had handed his testicles to Annaleigh Jeems Delmar along with a vow to never stray again. Everyone knew his daddy had been a hound dog, but his mama didn't like to be reminded.

Thus she leveled a wintery glare his way, her mouth flat as a catfish's.

"Sorry," Henry said, kicking at the brown leaves clinging stubbornly to the concrete pavers. Wind chimes clinked in the distance, and the late-afternoon light fell through the naked branches, tossing flickering patterns on the dead lawn. The landscape surrounding him reflected what sat inside him at the moment. His life had changed over the past few years, and he'd been going through the motions. He longed for better days. For green grass and birds singing. For happiness and contentment.

His mother shuffled along, her sciatic nerve no doubt giving her issues again. "So why are you out here with me?"

"Ma'am?"

"You came outside for a reason. Roses aren't your cup of tea."

"No, they're not." He waited for a moment, not knowing exactly why he'd come out. After seeing Sunny today, he'd been swept back to the memories he mostly tried to forget. Inside, he was a jumble of emotions—sadness, anger, and regret. He'd not seen Sunny since the day her mama's muscle-head boyfriend dragged him out the front door. His last image of Sunny had been her eyes blazing with hate, her pretty mouth trembling, her soul absolutely crushed. That day he'd lost everything he'd ever wanted. The blame had rested on his shoulders. He'd made the mistake, but he wanted someone to share in it. His mama had played a part, and he wanted her to answer for that. Finally own up to the fact she'd snatched his dream from him long before he'd screwed up. "I saw Sunny today."

His mother's gaze seemed to narrow. "I had heard she was back in town."

He said nothing.

His mother turned away. "Heard she lost her husband. They did an article in the paper. Why, I'm not entirely sure. The girl hasn't lived here for some time and her husband wasn't from here."

"Their family has lived here for generations. Maybe it was for Eden or Ruby Jean."

His mother watched him for a moment. The unstated

question sat between them, a fat toad of ugliness they had stepped around for far too long.

"Why didn't you like her?" he asked. *Say it. Say she wasn't good enough. That she was trash. That your precious little boy deserved someone better than a Voorhees.*

His mother sniffed. "I never *disliked* the girl."

Henry made a noise of disbelief. "You've never been a liar, Mother."

Annaleigh drew in a measured breath before sinking onto the marbled bench engraved with the names of deceased family members. She crossed her blindingly white sneakers she wore when she exercised at the church. "Good Lord, Henry Todd, her mother was a stripper at a gentlemen's club outside Jackson, though I daresay calling them 'gentlemen' is a stretch. Not to mention, they spelled Legz with a *z*, for God's sake."

"Sunny couldn't help who her mama was."

"No, but that didn't change the fact Betty *was* her mama. That child couldn't pretend away living in a shack in Grover's Park or that she had a mother who smoked a crack pipe. I had nothing against the girl, but I had plenty against what she brought to you. A mama wants more for her boy than a girl like that."

"Brought to me?" he repeated those words, each syllable growing heavier on his tongue. His mother had seen only the negatives, things Sunny could do nothing about. She didn't know the good she'd covered him in. From the very beginning, that fifteen-year-old, gorgeous girl had reached inside him and made him believe in himself; she'd given him a purpose. With Sunny, life had been biting into a ripe pear and letting the juices dribble down his chin. "She never brought me anything bad."

"Her stepbrother was a hooligan, her stepfather a criminal, and her aunt a Pentecostal. So yes, I discouraged you from spending time with her. My job has always been to protect you, even from yourself. I know that sounds harsh and probably politically incorrect—"

"—or unchristian."

Annaleigh pursed her lips. "Some might think so, but I always thought it rather necessary. You were blind when it came to that girl. Not going to college. Wanting to run off to Vegas. You lost every lick of sense is what you did. So I did what I thought was necessary. That girl never belonged with you, Henry, and I know where this is going. She's back. You're single. But you can't get back what you had. You're two different people, and I imagine she's still grieving. Don't forget, it's not just you anymore. You have two children who deserve some thought."

"Sunny doesn't want me, Mother."

His mother gave him a bitter smile. "Yes, I imagine you think so, but whatever she was, Sunny wasn't stupid. I imagine she doesn't have much in her life, does she?"

Henry lifted his head and stared at the woods just beyond where the property dropped off, yielding to Sorrell Creek, which wound through his parents' land. "She's not her mother."

Annaleigh's back straightened. "I hope for her sake she's nothing like her."

Henry knew his father had dated Betty before he met his mother at Plantation Ball. Annaleigh had attended private school in New Orleans before her family moved back to the familial estate outside Morning Glory when she'd been a senior in high school. Henry's father had a wild streak a country mile long and embraced racing his Mustang on Saturday nights, sneaking white lightnin' from the pantry, and hound doggin' women from one side of Rankin County to the other. Betty Voorhees had been the "it" girl, bouncy, big-breasted, and not afraid of the back seat. She'd led Henry's father on a merry chase and then dumped him for a pool shark who took her to Memphis. Calm, poised Annaleigh had been there to offer her white-gloved hand for small comfort. His daddy had married her in June, and she'd given birth to Henry two years later. Her job had been to raise decent children, chair the Junior League benefit, and sit on the third pew of the Episcopal Church.

Yet, for all her shallowness, Annaleigh was his mother. She'd kissed his boo-boos, fed him chicken soup, and cheered at every baseball game he played in. She was horrible, wonderful, and complicated. He hated her as much as he loved her.

"She's nothing like Betty."

"Just let Sunny go, Henry. Things worked out the way they did for a reason. You're a businessman, a good father, a good citizen. Don't chase rainbows thinking you can find what you need. Rainbows are illusions."

Henry wanted to argue, but he remembered Sunny's words, the dislike, the fact she was leaving Morning Glory as soon as she was able.

"I'm heading inside. The kids are doing homework with Jocelyn. I need to go out to the barn. Don't wait dinner for me," he said, moving toward the back entrance where the solarium sat, fat with outdoor plants and shiny-leafed houseplants. He would win no battle with his mother today. He couldn't undo what had been done, by his mother or himself. This whole conversation had been an exercise in futility, and he wasn't even sure why he'd started it.

Because he was still angry. He knew that much. And there had never been closure. Sunny had kicked him out of her house and then left town. Their unfinished business had sat a long time. Or maybe it felt unfinished to him. Maybe Sunny didn't give a damn about closure.

"I'll keep a plate warm for you. Tell Jocelyn not to give those babies too many of her cookies. They won't eat their dinner," his mother said, turning back to her roses.

He didn't answer. Instead, he entered the house, smiling as he saw Katie Clare biting a nibbled-down pencil as she attacked her math homework. Minutes later he was in his truck, heading to the place he went when life got too hard to handle. He called it the Barn, but it wasn't merely a barn. It was the land he'd bought long ago, refusing to let it go to anyone else. It was a delightful woods, a rustic barn, and a small pond where he'd taught Landry to bait a hook. It was a half-finished house with a wide porch.

He'd rented the barn to Clem Aiken, who ran his

woodworking business from the cavernous depths, but Clem had moved his business to South Carolina at the first of the year and was in the process of clearing out the barn. The house he was building sat on the hill overlooking the pond, offering him quiet solace. Sitting on the porch steps, watching the wrens build their nests in the window ledges, studying the darkened lumber stacks, and listening to the sounds of the squirrels digging for treasures they'd hidden months before layered balm onto his soul.

What if echoed outside that half-finished house.

He'd bought the land with the money his grandfather had given him for high school graduation. The old man had approved of his investment, but Henry's reason had gone beyond making a good investment. That land was where he and Sunny had dreamed of building their dream house. They'd snuck out there to park by the pond and make out under the full moon. When he and Jillian had gotten a divorce, he'd moved into the garage apartment over the carriage house on his parents' estate. He traveled so often for work it didn't make much sense to buy a huge place. The kids came only every other weekend, and they mostly wanted to stay with their grandparents in the main house when they came.

But last summer he'd convinced himself it was time to have a place of his own. The temporary feel to his life wore on him. The land belonged to him, so he'd started building a house, keeping it on the down low from most the town. He'd hired an architect and then contracted Clem's business, Country Boy Construction, to build it. The resulting farmhouse wasn't exactly what Sunny had dreamed about, but it was close. Very close. Which made him wonder about himself. But whatever, he liked the floor plan and it fit the beautiful rustic property and barn. He was determined to one day fill the house with laughter, maybe get a dog or two. Try to make a home for his children. And maybe find a faceless woman who would give him a soft place to land at the end of a hard day.

He bumped down the gravel path, the trees arching to lace

together. The bare branches made it spooky, something out of a horror movie, but then when the road ended, it opened to a beautiful pasture sloping down to the pond. The red barn sat on the right, and just through the woods, not half a mile away, sat the large, nearly completed house on the left. The dying sun hit the mullioned transoms above the double french doors, sending a kaleidoscope of color onto the porch slats. A black cat shot under the porch.

He'd never seen a cat out here before.

Climbing out, he breathed in the fresh crisp air. The grass was still mostly dead, dotted with determined weeds, but the trees had just started greening up. Soon, nature would show out with pink dogwoods, brilliant purple redbud trees, and the row of forsythia lining the gingerbread shed holding the lawn equipment. He knew. He'd watched many other springs out here.

The half-built house looked sad though. Like it longed to do its job—provide shelter for a happy family. And since there was none, it had dipped into a depression. Or maybe it was the way winter had worn on it. Construction had stopped in the fall when Clem had decided to sell his business.

"Hell," he breathed before stomping up the steps and sinking onto the top step.

The cat peeked out from the bottom step, its green eyes almost glowing against the inky fur. Slowly it crept up the steps, sank onto its haunches, and stared at Henry as if he were the unwanted guest.

"Who are you?" Henry asked the cat.

The cat lifted its back leg and scratched beneath its chin.

"Right. Fleas, I bet." Henry clasped his hands between his knees, and the cat settled into a comma, content to watch Henry and seemingly not alarmed in the least.

Sunny had always wanted a cat, but her mother was allergic. She'd talked about pots of geraniums, a little herb garden, and a fat ginger cat. She'd reach over and squeeze his hand. *One day we'll have that. Our kids will love Marmalade. I bet Marmie will sun in our window seat. Lazy ol' cat.*

Sunny had plans for them, and he'd nodded like an idiot because whatever she wanted, he wanted too.

"Shit," he said again, closing his eyes on the memories. On the silly dreams of two kids who didn't have a clue about real life.

The cat licked its paws as the sharp north wind whipped through the trees. This time he could find no peace here in this place he'd built on memories. There was only hurt and anger and regret.

And the ghost of what could have been if Henry hadn't gotten Jillian pregnant at Kappa Alpha Old South.

chapter four

SUNNY RIFLED THROUGH her limited closet for something that said "professional" but wasn't ridiculously overdone. She had a great pencil skirt she could pair with a plain white blouse, but when she tugged that on, not only was the skirt too big on her but she looked like a hostess at an upscale restaurant. Not an attendance clerk. Finally she settled on a pair of leggings beneath a navy tunic. She wound a scarf one of her friends had given her around her neck. There. She looked like she could work in a high school office.

"Where you going all dressed up? Thought your bike was in the shop," her mother asked when Sunny emerged from the bathroom wafting Bath & Body Works pumpkin latte or some other maple-scented lotion Eden had left behind.

"I told you. I have a job interview." Sunny glanced around for her jacket. The house needed to have an energy audit. Had to be cracks as big as a moose somewhere.

"You ain't gonna make enough for it to be worth your time," Betty said, pushing her chair back awkwardly from where it sat parked in front of the television.

"That's my business." Sunny hoped her mother's words wouldn't be true. She might not make much, but every little bit would go toward completing the renovation on the house so she could get the hell out of Mississippi. California sunshine sounded like an answered prayer. "Do you need anything before I go? I can help you get into the recliner if that would be more comfortable."

Sunny had woken around six and helped her mother attend to bathroom stuff, get dressed, and eat breakfast, and then she'd disappeared to get herself ready. The sitter would be here in thirty minutes. Henry Todd should arrive in—she glanced at her watch—five minutes.

Just enough time for a cigarette.

"I'm good," her mother mumbled. "Can you bring me some candy or something? If I can't have a damn cigarette, the least I can have is a damn Butterfinger or something."

Strike the cigarette. The longer Sunny spent here with her mother, the more she feared turning into the same bitter husk who complained about everything from the hangnail on her pinky to the neighbor's dog who howled at every ambulance siren.

"I'll see what I can do," Sunny said, nixing another cup of coffee too. She didn't want to feel any more jittery than she already did. Last night she'd dreamed of Henry—jumbled dreams of kisses, a football game, and then losing her car keys. She'd awoken anxious and tired. The bags under her eyes were a testament to her disturbing lack of sleep.

She stepped onto the porch and sank into the plastic chair the sitter used when she needed to get away from Betty. Around her, the neighborhood moved. Mrs. Warner swept her driveway, a dog that seemed to have been abandoned nosed through a pile of leaves, and rhythmic clanks came from the neighborhood auto shop. Grover's Park was a tattered blue-collar hood with scraggly weed-choked cracks and dirt patches in the front yards, but it had been her home. She understood the people who lived here. They were hard, private, and fiercely loyal to one another. Sometimes honest, sometimes kind, but always ready to protect their own.

Henry's fancy truck glided down the street and pulled into her driveway.

She didn't move because she was afraid to climb into his truck, scared of herself and of what opening the door to Henry in any way might do to her. She couldn't handle too many more sleepless nights.

"Hey," Henry said, sliding down the window. She was almost certain he'd debated whether he should get out and come to the porch like the polite Southern gentleman he'd been raised to be or stay inside and treat this casually. "You ready?"

Sunny rose, opened the front door of the house, and grabbed her purse from the faded tweed chair. "I'm going, Mama. Vienna will be here soon."

Her mother grunted a response.

Sunny walked down the steps and rounded the truck. When she opened the door, she was hit by the warmth and the smell of Henry—cozy flannel with a hint of citrus and nutmeg.

"Good morning," he said, indicating the disposable cup in the holder. "I brought you some coffee."

"You didn't have to do that," she said, eyeing the seductive waft of steam rising from the small opening in the lid.

"I know, but I fixed myself some so it seemed the polite thing to do."

She shrugged a shoulder and lifted the coffee. Special brew, dark, rich roast with cream and sugar. Just the way she used liked it. "Thank you."

He backed out of the driveway. "So to the school board first?"

"Yes. You don't have to wait for me, you know. I can find a ride if I need to." She could probably call her aunt Ruby Jean, but her aunt worked for an accounting firm and didn't like to ask for time off. "Stickler" was her aunt's middle name.

"No problem. I have to make some calls anyway. I'll use my truck as my office. Well, hell, it *is* my office most days."

"So you're working for your dad, huh?" He'd always said he'd never work for his father. Henry had wanted to be an orthopedic surgeon.

"Yeah, that's what I'm doing," he said, his voice flat.

"You don't like it?"

"We've expanded our operations all over the state, so I travel a lot. We built a stadium down in Hattiesburg last year and several big projects in Jackson. That's where the kids live, but Morning Glory is where we have our main office."

"You didn't answer my question."

He glanced sharply at her. "I like it fine. What about you?"

"I don't have a job. That's why you're driving me to the school board," she said, taking another sip of the coffee. Good stuff, that coffee.

"I meant what did you do back in… North Carolina, was it?"

"Alan and I lived all over. Once I worked as a receptionist for a dermatologist, once as a waitress at another duty station. Then I got my degree in business administration from a two-year college and worked as an accounts manager for a large advertising and marketing firm. They were just jobs. That's it."

"But you were good at them," he said, a smile tilting the corner of his lips.

They'd not been together in the same space for over fifteen years, but nobody knew her like Henry Todd Delmar. What she did, she did well. If she took on a project, consider it successful because she would work sun up to sun down to make sure it was. "Pretty much."

Henry snorted. "You always were something else."

Sunny jerked her gaze away, refusing to be moved by his warmth. This man had betrayed her, hurt her, driven her from Morning Glory. Everything she'd believed to be true had shattered that afternoon in her bedroom. Melodramatic? Maybe. But that didn't make it any less true. He'd crushed her, and she needed to hold on to that hurt because it was her only protection against the power of what she'd once felt for him.

Her coldness must have worked because Henry turned up the

radio. Nirvana pulsed from the speakers, somehow suiting the mood. Sunny sipped her coffee and stared out as Morning Glory flashed by. Eventually they arrived at the cinder block building that looked, well, pretty depressing. So many gorgeous, historic buildings in Morning Glory, yet the place that should inspire learning and higher things looked like a prison.

Henry parked in the front. "I'll wait here."

"Thanks," she said, unclicking her seat belt, picking up her purse with the documents she needed, and sliding to the pavement. "Henry?"

His gaze met hers.

"Thanks for the ride." She walked toward the glass front entrance, her heart beating erratically. She wasn't certain if it was because she was nervous about the application or because she'd sat beside Henry in his truck, the same way she had too many times to count.

The receptionist wore a little headset and pressed buttons. She glanced up at Sunny and gave her brusque directions to Personnel. "Sorry. Had two buses break down this morning. Parents calling out the wazoo."

Sunny smiled and waved before moving down the gleaming hallway toward the office. She pushed through the glass door and nearly mowed down her former principal, Mr. Mel Marler.

"Hello, Mr. Marler," Sunny said to the bulldog man with square glasses, an underbite, and a heart as big as Texas.

"Well, I'll be danged. If it isn't Sunny Voorhees herself. What did you do to your hair?"

Sunny fingered the ends. "I went red."

"I don't care for it myself," he said.

"Well, don't hold back or anything," she said with a laugh.

He grinned. "Guess I forget my manners sometimes. My mama would have tanned my backside if she'd heard that. It's good to see you. You back for a visit?"

"Something like that. Eden's in New Orleans taking some classes, so I'm staying with Mama for a while."

"I heard about your husband. I'm sorry about that, Sunny."

Sunny swallowed a sudden lump in her throat. She longed to be past mourning, but every now and then, the loss struck her. Alan hadn't been the love of her life, but she'd cared about him when she wasn't pissed at him. "I am too. He was too young to die."

"He was," Mr. Marler said. "What are you doing here at the school board?"

"I'm applying for a substitute job at the high school. The attendance clerk was injured, and I guess Ms. McConnell over at the school heard I was looking for something."

"Yeah, I heard. Poor Melanie's got a tough road ahead." Mr. Marler closed the door and turned around. "Let me put in a word with Jim."

"You work here now?"

"Yes. Director of communications and curriculum. No kids to hassle or herd. Instead I get to work with the real morons. No offense, Sharon," he said to the woman behind the long counter.

"As if anyone would believe your old ass," the woman muttered, unfolding the readers hanging on a chain around her neck and plunking them down on her thin nose. "Baby, I'm going to need you to fill all this out. We're going to get your fingerprints right here. No ink, no hauling your cookies down to the sheriff's office. We're uptown around here now."

"She really loves me," Mr. Marler called out before disappearing into the inner sanctum of the offices. Sunny smiled at Sharon's eye-roll and sat down with the clipboard of copious paperwork.

Twenty minutes and two hand cramps later, she made it back to meet with the head of Personnel. Mr. Marler stood in his office, talking about coaching changes in the SEC. When Sunny came in, he winked at her and shot Jim a look. "Take care of this one. She's special."

Sunny hadn't felt special in a long time. Why the words warmed her, she didn't know. But it felt good remembering those days in high school when she'd been something more than average. "Thank you, Mr. Marler."

"You betcha," he said with a smile.

After twenty more minutes, Sunny emerged from the building, blinking at the bright sunlight. She found Henry still parked in the front, talking on the phone.

"How did it go?" he asked after clicking a button on his steering wheel.

"I have a job through May," she said climbing into the cab. "Doesn't pay as much as I would like, but it will help me finish remodeling the house so we can get it on the market."

"You're selling the house?"

"If I can talk Betty into it. I'm not staying in Morning Glory, and I would like to get Mama into an assisted living community. It would be better for her."

"You're leaving?" He sounded surprised. Did he think she would move in with her mother and live in Grover's Park for the rest of her life? A block of ice was warmer than that woman.

"Why would I stay?" she asked, trying not to sound incredulous. For some people Morning Glory was a great place to live and raise a family, but Sunny had no reason to stay. She didn't have a family outside of her mama and Aunt Ruby Jean, and the town was too full of memories. That was why she'd never visited before. Every corner hid a memory for her, and she'd always been determined to forget those memories. She slept better with them tucked away.

"Yeah, I guess so," he said putting the truck in Reverse.

"Why did you come back?" she asked.

"I don't know. It's home, I guess."

That had always been their plan—go off and figure out life, then come back to Morning Glory and live it. They'd agreed upon the number of children they'd have (three), what kind of bed they'd buy (a sleigh bed), and where they'd build their house (right off Frasier's Forty). They'd name their first son Andrew, their daughter Willow. They'd drink french vanilla coffee every morning and never go to bed mad.

They had been idiots.

"Yeah, you always wanted to live here," she said, clicking her belt into place.

"So did you."

"I was a dumb ass." She tried to make it sound light, but it came out bitter.

"I never thought so." He pulled out of the lot and headed south toward the high school.

Sunny could have argued with him, but she didn't. Why bother? They were two different people now who were on two different paths. What she did or didn't do wasn't his business.

Henry cut through a subdivision that looked to be new, and Sunny marveled at the cookie-cutter houses with the stacked stone and cedar posts. They looked expensive but common. Sort of sad in a way. Henry pulled out onto the county highway, and just as he went around Preacher's Bend, he stomped on his brakes, sending them careening toward the deep ditch.

"Christ Almighty," he said, skidding to a stop. One wheel of the truck dangled over the ditch. He shifted into Reverse and backed up, rocking to a stop.

Sunny tugged the seat belt nearly choking her. Her heart beat hard against her ribs. "What was it?"

"I don't know—a raccoon or something. I think I missed it."

Henry slammed the truck into Park and slung open his door. "Where did it go? I don't see anything."

Sunny carefully opened her door, scared to see if Henry had indeed dispatched some woodland creature into the Forest of the Great Beyond. She unbuckled and slid to the ground, looking around. Nothing horrible met her gaze, thank God.

"It went that way, I think," Henry said, pointing over to the right where brush clogged a tree line.

Sunny stepped through some faded weeds and peered at the area. From behind one of the brushes, a black nose appeared. "There."

Henry followed her as she climbed down into the thankfully dry ditch and up the rocky iron-ore slope. The two eyes accompanying the adorable nose held fear.

"It's a pup," she said, holding out her hand. "Here, little fella. I won't hurt you."

The dog didn't move. From what she could see, the poor thing was missing hair. Maybe mange? And it looked thin as a whippet with mottled fur that looked to be blue merle with leopard splotches. Two big bat ears twitched and then lay flat as she approached.

"Easy, fella."

The dog darted deeper into the woods, tail curled beneath it, ears down as if it were being hunted.

Sunny turned to Henry. "Do you happen to have any food in the truck? Something I can coax it out with so we can make sure it's okay?"

"Maybe we shouldn't try to do this. That dog might be dangerous, Sunny."

"It's not dangerous. It's scared." She eyed the dog. "Bring my purse too. The strap unhooks. We can use it as a leash of sorts."

"I'm not sure—"

"Well, I am, Henry. It could be someone's lost pet. We can't leave it here."

He studied her for a moment, nodded, and went back to the truck. Sunny turned back toward where the dog had disappeared. She was nearly certain it wasn't injured, but it needed help. Thin and diseased, the dog was in danger from passing cars and other predators that lived in the Mississippi woods.

"Here, baby boy. I won't hurt you," she cooed.

Henry came back, holding her cross-body purse strap, a protein bar, and half a sandwich. "Katie Clare must have left this sandwich in the back seat, and I had this in the glove box. Sometimes I don't have time for lunch."

Sunny plucked the sandwich from his hand and pulled open

the plastic bag. Tearing off half a piece, she tossed it toward where the dog had disappeared. Then she stepped back and waited, taking a moment to fashion a short lead from her purse strap.

Only seconds passed before the dog belly-crawled out of the brush toward the offering. Warily, it cast its sad eyes on them, then daintily took the bit of sandwich and swallowed it whole. On closer inspection, she saw the dog had burnt-sienna legs, a thin muzzle but broad head along with a bushy tail. Sunny knelt down and extended the rest of the sandwich. The dog watched her, eyeing the sandwich with a hungry gleam in the marbled brown depths of its eyes, but was still too wary to approach.

"Move back, Henry."

Henry chuffed irritation but moved toward the truck.

Sunny lowered herself to a sitting position, ripping open the protein bar as she did. No chocolate, thankfully. That was a definite no-no for dogs. She laid the bar on her thigh and waggled the remainder of the sandwich. "Come on, fella. I won't hurt you."

The dog inched forward, tail still curled beneath its haunches.

"I don't want you to get bitten, Sunny," Henry called.

The dog stopped its progression, ears twitching.

"Shh!" she hissed over her shoulder before turning to the dog with a smile. "It's okay. Come get this sandwich. You're a hungry fella."

The dog inched forward. Finally it got about three feet away from Sunny and stopped.

She wagged the sandwich. "Here it is. Come get it."

The dog sat and watched her. Clever thing. Probably smelled a trap.

"I won't hurt you," Sunny said in a conversational way. Then she set the sandwich down in front of her. The dog looked at the offering and then back up at Sunny.

"Go ahead," she whispered.

The dog carefully approached and took the sandwich,

whipping around quickly and edging back into the brush. No time to try to pet it, much less get the strap around its neck. What if Henry was right? What if it bit her? It could have rabies. Humans died from rabies too. She should toss the rest of the bar and call someone from the county about a dog running loose off Dogwood Ridge. That would be the smart call.

But something inside her told her she needed to gain this dog's trust.

"I have more," Sunny said, lifting the peanut protein bar. "Yummy."

The dog stilled and twisted its head in the most adorable way. Sunny broke off a tiny piece and popped it into her mouth. "Mm. Very good."

The dog lay down, crossing its paws. Sunny ripped off another piece. "You can have some too." She tossed a piece close to her.

The dog trotted over and scooped it up. Sunny reached out a hand and ran it over the pup. It scampered away like a scalded cat. But it didn't disappear into the brush. Sunny tried with another piece. Same result. Soon she had only one piece left. Last shot to catch the pup and get it to a vet. She'd spied the ticks covering its body. The poor thing needed help. She held the piece in her left hand and waited. A few seconds passed. How hungry was the little beast? Hungry enough to take the last of the bar from her hand?

The dog approached, ears twitching as a passing car roared by. But its eyes never left the piece of food in Sunny's hand. Carefully it moved closer, dainty paws moving one slow step at a time. Soon the dog was near enough to touch, but very, very wary. Sunny extended a hand to it. It sniffed and pulled its head back. Still, it eyed the last of the bar in her left hand.

Carefully the dog extended its neck, eyes rolling toward Sunny and then back at its goal. Slowly the dog opened its mouth and tried to take the last bite. Sunny held on to it tight while grabbing the leather strap at her side. Quick as spit, she looped it over the dog's head. The dog reared back and Sunny caught hold of it. It wriggled like the very devil, scratching her legs through the leggings.

Sunny gave the dog the last of the bar but held the animal tight against her body. "Shh, shh, it's okay." She stroked the dog that now trembled against her.

"Poor baby, you're covered in ticks. Oh, and fleas. Yuck."

Henry appeared over the rise of the small hill. "You got it?"

"Yes, poor thing is skin and bones and is"—she glanced down—"a girl."

The dog had gone dead still against her, but Sunny still stroked its mangy fur. "Can you help me up?"

Henry came behind her and lifted her beneath her arms so she could find her feet. She brushed against his big body, and even in the midst of a stray-dog crisis, she registered the solid warmth, the way he smelled so manly and good. She longed to lean against him for a moment. Just a second or two of pretense. But she didn't. She couldn't allow herself any such fancy.

The dog squirmed, wriggling as if its life were on the line.

"That's enough, doggy. We're going to get you some help. You can't stay out here by yourself. You nearly met your maker a few minutes ago." Sunny squeezed the dog tight, petting its ears, using her sweetest voice.

"What are we going to do with it?" Henry asked.

"Take it to a vet. Do you know one?"

"But you have to go to the high school," he said, eyeing the dog with an odd expression. "That's a pitiful excuse for a dog."

"I think she's pretty. Or will be once she gets cleaned up and something better to eat than leftover sandwiches. Let's help her. It's the least you could do since you almost killed her." Sunny started walking back toward the truck.

"You're going to put that thing in my truck? It's covered in Lord knows what," Henry said, following her.

"Do you have a towel by chance?" Sunny asked, conceding that Henry had a point. She would likely have dirt and… no, not fleas… please no fleas… along with dog hair all over her. Not the best way to show up at the high school. Plus Henry had work. Still, they had to do something to help the poor creature.

"Maybe," Henry muttered, sounding less than enthused at putting a stray pup in his immaculate, leather-soaked cab.

"Are there rescues around here?" she asked, wondering if there was someone they could call to help the pup. She'd done the books, at one in North Carolina and knew the good work the people there had done to get strays and shelter dogs into homes. Maybe the rescue for Rankin County could help them out.

"What do you mean? We can call animal control or take it by the pound."

"Is it a no-kill shelter?"

"I don't know."

"Well, it will have a stray hold regardless. Maybe we should take her by there?" Sunny wasn't capable of paying a huge vet bill or taking the dog home. Betty would shit a brick. She'd always had a no-pets policy for their home, professing to be allergic. But Sunny knew the woman wasn't allergic. She'd never wanted to care for anything more than herself. She and Eden were lucky they'd been fed each day when they were kids. Well, most days.

"I guess." Henry stood looking at her. "But maybe we should take it to Bennett Robertson first. I hit it. Maybe not anything beyond a glancing blow."

"Okay," Sunny said, still stroking the trembling dog.

Henry rifled in the back of his truck, which housed a toolbox, and withdrew an old blanket before helping her climb into the cab and wrap the dog in the blanket. The warmth of the blanket, which smelled like motor oil, combined with her tight grasp seemed to quell the dog's shaking. Ten minutes later they pulled into Long Oak Veterinary Clinic.

Dr. Bennett Robertson was new to town. He was also young, enthusiastic, and… expensive. He gave the dog some oral medication designed to get rid of the ticks and fleas, a round of shots, some special dog food to help her put on weight, and an appointment for the following week. She needed to be spayed and unfortunately had heartworms. Sunny tried to explain it was a stray and it wasn't her dog, but Dr. Robertson chuckled at the notion.

"She looks pretty attached to you."

The poor thing kept hiding behind Sunny's legs, trembling like a leaf clinging to an autumn tree.

"But she's not mine. She's a stray. Is there a rescue around this area?" Sunny asked him.

Henry stood silent, hands shoved into his jean pockets.

"Unfortunately, not any longer. Mrs. Eppie Henderson ran the Humane Society, but when she passed last year, it sort of fell apart. There are several rescues in Jackson. I can get you a number. Meanwhile, keep Miss Fancy warm and well-fed. Bathe her once the ticks fall off."

"Fancy?" Henry echoed.

Bennett pointed to the name at the top of the folder. "That's what it says."

Henry looked at Sunny. "You named it?"

"I had to tell them something. So I went with Fancy."

Henry snorted.

"Like the Reba McEntire song. She might have been born plain white trash…"

"But Fancy was her name," Bennett finished with a laugh. "I like it."

"But she's not white trash," Henry said, his meaning somehow deeper than intended. Sunny felt warmth travel up her spine. When they'd been in high school, she'd once told him she felt a lot like the subject of that country song… except her mama hadn't exactly told her to sell her body to a man. Though come to think of it, if Betty had thought she could reap something by whoring her daughter out, she might have been more apt to buy her a red, velvet-trimmed dancing dress that fit her good.

"Nope. She's a down-on-her-luck doggy, but we're going to

help her," Sunny said, stroking the trembling dog's head. The mutt leaned hard against her, as if she could melt into Sunny. Sunny felt her heart expand in her chest. She didn't have much, but she could save this one little dog. Surely she could find someone to help the dog get into rescue or a home in which to get fat and lazy.

Henry rolled his eyes and followed Dr. Robertson out to the front desk. Sunny noted him withdrawing a credit card and started to protest. But then she remembered how little she had in her checking account. Henry had almost killed the little dog with his big truck… and she knew very well he had the cash to shell out.

She carried Fancy to the truck, settling her in her lap, murmuring endearments to the quaking pup. "It's okay, Fancy girl. I'll make sure you find a good home. It's the least I can do for you."

Henry opened the door, tossing the bag of food into the back. "What now?"

Sunny tapped on her phone, calling Aunt Ruby Jean. "Hey, Auntie dearest. I need a favor. Don't you have a dog crate left over from when you had Ranger?"

chapter five

HENRY WALKED AROUND the perimeter of the freshly poured concrete pad that was the start of the new gym for the high school. "Looks good, Ted."

Ted Newsom, his site manager, nodded. "We're on schedule. Got some rain coming in over the next few days, but we should be able to catch up if we hire a few extra welders."

"Talk to Carol. I have to stay on budget on this one. The Jackson Bank and Trust project went too far over the projected costs. No leeway with this one." He headed toward the small trailer sitting behind the existing gymnasium. The old gym would be converted into a study center and student-run coffee shop once the new gym was operational. He liked the direction the new principal, Sarah Whitmore, was taking. She wanted to teach real-world skills to the students, so she'd initiated a lot of business classes to pair with the academic classes.

He glanced at the main entrance to the high school. After taking the stray dog to Sunny's aunt's house, he'd dropped her by the main office and then come here to check on things. He really didn't need to be on-site today, but he wanted to be on hand if he needed to take Sunny back home.

God, why was he bending over backward to help Sunny?

But he knew.

Already he'd allowed hope to creep inside, which was extra stupid of him. Hadn't she just said she was working to get the hell out of Morning Glory? But still his stubborn heart persisted with the slight, slim, marginal prayer's chance that he might… No… No, that was stupid. He and Sunny could be nothing more than… whatever they were now. She wouldn't forgive him. Hadn't she told him that long ago? His actions at that frat party had set off a domino effect that blew him apart and left nothing between them but… nothing.

He should leave her the hell alone. Get her a rental car and stop doing what he was doing—trying to be near her. She wasn't the same Sunny. And he wasn't the same Henry.

And wasn't that the problem?

He hadn't felt like himself in many, many years. Once, he'd been cocksure and full of dreams… and then he'd changed everything when he'd taken Jillian to a room in the fraternity house that night. Jim Beam and lust had spun his life on a dime, and he'd lost the one thing he'd been so sure of.

"Suck it up, buttercup," he muttered to himself, shuffling toward his desk. Papers covered every square inch. Work had become the balm to his soul since the divorce. He'd thrown himself into wheeling and dealing new clients, scoring new projects for Delmar Construction. His father had balked at Henry's ambition, but still Henry pushed the company to stretch itself. His efforts had paid off with innovative projects spread across Mississippi. They'd hired more employees and opened a permanent office in Jackson along with a small satellite in Hattiesburg. So even though he wasn't saving lives, he was making his community better with quality structures that housed the arts, businesses, and, now children.

So he'd failed at all things romantic, but kicking ass in the career department balanced the scales… even if it was doing a job he'd sworn he'd never have. He'd always said he'd never work for his father, but oddly enough, Henry excelled at putting together deals, building innovative spaces, and making lots of money. He clicked on his email, noting all the requests for meetings. Eh, maybe too good at it.

"Hey, boss man," Carson Thomas said, opening the door and taking off his hard hat. Carson was the head engineer on the gym project. Thirty-three years old and so good at what he did that Henry kept having to raise his salary to keep the buzzards from circling, Carson was Henry's go-to guy when it came to difficult projects. The gym wasn't the hardest build they'd done, but the intricacies along with dealing with the Department of Education's codes meant he'd pulled Carson from a multistory build in Jackson to oversee the Morning Glory High School project.

"I told you not to call me that."

"I know, but I was never good at following directions. Besides, if it gets your goat, I'm always up for that." Carson tossed his iPad onto the second desk and pulled out his phone. "Did you talk to Ted? He needs welders."

"Yeah. I told him to talk to Carol."

"So who was that fine thing you dropped off at the school office? I'm up to my eyeballs in ass cracks and beer guts twenty-four seven, so you know I didn't miss what climbed out of your truck."

"Says the married man. You know Tomeka would skin you alive if she saw you checking out anyone but her," Henry said, not wanting to talk about Sunny with Carson. Carson didn't know his history with Sunny. He wasn't from Morning Glory.

"Meka'd have to catch me first, and since she's seven months pregnant, my chances are good," Carson said with a grin. His head engineer was head over heels for his wife, who would deliver their first child that spring, so Henry had no competition from Carson. Not that there was a competition. 'Cause there wasn't. Henry wasn't even on the damn field.

"Wasn't Tomeka all-SEC in track?" At Carson's nod, he continued. "Yeah, she could be nine months pregnant with triplets and still catch your slow ass."

"True, but you're avoiding the question. The redhead… who

is she?"

"Sunny Voorhees."

"Any relation to Eden?"

"Yep, her older sister."

"Huh, didn't know Eden had a sister," Carson said, his mouth curving downward as his eyebrows lifted. "Well, Sunny's a looker."

"Always was." Henry tried to focus on his computer screen but failed. He was as tightly strung as a man awaiting a sentencing, and he wasn't sure if it was because Sunny was a hop, skip, and jump away or the aftereffects of nearly hitting and killing the stray dog. More than likely, it was because he'd realized exactly how screwed up the situation between him and Sunny was. The woman treated him like he was anyone else… like he hadn't meant beans to her.

And he hated to feel like he'd never mattered to her.

"Damn it," he said, accidently clicking out of the browser. He leaned back and closed his eyes. It was obvious he wasn't going to get any work done that afternoon.

For years he'd allowed his mind to wonder where Sunny was, what she was doing, how she'd changed, and then he hadn't even recognized her at first sight. The woman had been standing in the hardware store, stooping to get something from the shelf, letting her hair fall over her face. *Wait… Sunny hadn't wanted him to notice her.* Something squirmed in his stomach.

But what had he expected?

He'd destroyed something pretty damned special. Lots of people thought young love was ridiculous. Teenagers couldn't make commitments. They were too immature. But from the very beginning he'd known he and Sunny were different. They complemented each other, could understand what the other felt with a single glance, and had chemistry off the charts. They were supposed to be together forever—Sunny had even made a binder of all their plans—their dream book.

His first glance of Sunny had been in the A wing of Morning

Glory High School on the first day of his sophomore year. It had been a weird day for him because he'd never been to "real" school before. His mother had sent him to Saint Pius Catholic School for elementary school and then insisted he attend McCullough Prep in Tennessee. She'd packed him up at the conclusion of fifth grade and moved him north to spend the next four years playing lacrosse and learning Latin with other well-to-do young gentlemen. He often said such with his tongue in cheek because a couple of those "gentlemen" had gone on to slap their wives around, embezzle money, and overdose on heroin. And a few were congressmen. At any rate, he'd finally convinced his father to let him come back home to Morning Glory to finish out high school. He had his eye on attending Ole Miss, his father's alma mater, and his mother finally conceded that Henry Todd Delmar wasn't going to attend Yale or Dartmouth. So home he came.

His mother had petitioned for him to attend a small private school in Jackson, but thankfully his father had quashed the idea of so much time spent on a commute. Henry had never attended public school before that day.

But he'd loved Morning Glory High School on first sight.

That day had been hectic and raucous, with a jumble of people of different colors, different beliefs, and different mindsets tearing down his lily-white walls of privilege. He'd loved it all, but the absolute best thing about attending public high school was the girls.

He'd tried not to study the curve of their cheeks, the peek of thigh beneath miniskirts, the way they applied lip gloss at their desks with small compacts and the tempting scent of their perfume when they passed his desk. Hair ribbons, ponytails, and occasionally showing bra straps, they were all so tempting. But nothing had prepared him for the luscious gorgeousness that was Sunny Voorhees.

He'd just shut his locker, stressed because he didn't want to be late for the lacrosse meeting after school. The one thing he knew for certain was he could play the hell out of lacrosse.

Morning Glory High had just started their first team, and dreams of team captain, scholarships, and owning the field knocked around his head. His first day had been good—he'd liked his teachers and somehow had collected a few of the cooler guys to hang with. All he needed for the cherry on top was a stellar day of ripping the rock.

He'd closed his locker and turned toward the exit for the field.

And there was Sunny Voorhees.

She'd been wearing a pink shirt and a pair of jeans that hugged her body and flared at the bottom. Her blond hair tumbled about her shoulders, framing her baby-blue eyes, plump lips, and pert nose. Her arms wrapped around her books, and though she looked like a bombshell, whatever that was, intelligence shone in her eyes, sensibility reflected in her expression, and stubbornness rooted the determined set of her jaw.

He walked toward her. "Hey."

"Hi," she said, averting her eyes as pink stained her cheeks. Immediately his heart expanded. She'd blushed. Over him.

He turned around. "I'm Henry."

She looked over her shoulder. "I'm a freshman."

Like that was a reason not to talk to him.

"What's that got to do with anything?" He donned his best flirty smile.

She turned toward him, forehead furrowed. "I don't know. I mean… I don't know why I said that."

Her confusion was damned cute. "Well, freshman, you're the prettiest thing I've ever seen."

She turned the color of the crimson streamers lining the wall, her blue eyes widening. And then she did something that made his heart grow even bigger. She started laughing.

Which made him laugh too.

He took several steps backward, the clock in his head reminding him that he was going to be late. "I'd love to stay and flirt with you, Freshman, but I gotta run."

He made it down the hall, smiling like someone in a loony bin.

Just as he made to push out the door, she called down the empty hallway, "I'm Sunshine Voorhees."

Turning, he called back, "You damn sure are."

And then he ran toward the practice field, knowing his life had changed that day. He had found a place in Morning Glory High School, and he'd found the girl who belonged with him.

His phone vibrated, jarring him from the past and into his reality. A desk. A failed marriage. A shitload of paperwork.

I can get a ride if you need me to.

Sunny, once again, trying to wriggle out of being near him.

His fingers flew over the phone keyboard.

No problem. I can drive you whenever you're ready. You done?

He wasn't getting any work done anyway. Besides, it was his fault Sunny had to rely on the kindness of… well, ex-boyfriends to get around town. Or rather it was his kid's fault. The slight irony that Landry was the reason he'd lost Sunny in the first place didn't escape him. Of course, it wasn't Landry's fault. He hadn't asked to be conceived from bad drunken sex in a fraternity room in the KA house. That was Henry's eff up and his burden to shoulder. Still, Landry had torn them apart and then reunited them sixteen years later. Sort of full circle.

I'm ready.

But not to forgive him. Not to smile at him the way she once had. No, Sunny Voorhees David wasn't ready for anything other than forgetting what had been between them.

Question was—did Henry have a chance at convincing her any different? And did he want to? Sunny coming home wasn't about a second chance on a meant-to-be, but he now had a chance to get closure. He could finally apologize and get over the past.

He texted that he was on his way, picked up his keys, and pushed back his chair. "I'm off."

Carson looked up, his forehead crinkling. "To do what?"

"To take the redhead home."

Carson laughed. "Damn, you work fast, bro."

"Not like that," Henry clarified, giving a wry smile. "Landry ran over her Harley and that's why I'm giving her a lift. And paying a, no doubt, huge repair bill to have the bike repaired."

"She rides a bike?" Carson asked, lifting his eyebrows.

"Did."

"You're telling me that hot redhead straddles a hog? Dude, did you raise Landry's allowance?"

Henry shook his head. "Just wait. One day you'll be cleaning up your teenager's mistakes."

Then he pushed out the door of the office and into the cold sunshine. In the distance he saw Sunny standing in front of the main office of the school, her shoulders hunched against the wind. She looked lost and not at all like the sweet blonde who'd charmed him in the hallway of the same school all those years ago. As he climbed into his truck, he watched her light a cigarette and take a few drags, blowing the smoke high into the air. It was as if pain vibrated around her, and she looked so tired and hard.

This Sunny made his heart hurt.

He looped around the drive and pressed unlock. She dropped the cigarette, put it out with her high-heeled boot, and picked the butt up, flicking it into a nearby trash can. She looked hard but cool as shit. Like the girl in high school with the dark eyeliner, Bon Jovi shirt, and bad attitude. Like the girl she should have been long ago—tough, hard, ready to battle—but hadn't been. Because she'd been so heartbreakingly innocent, pure, and… his.

"Hey," he said as she climbed into the warmth of his cab. He'd put the seat heaters on because the wind outside was a knife between the shoulder blades. "Everything go okay?"

"Yeah, though I never knew how much work being an attendance clerk is. Tracking down excuses, reporting truants, dealing with actual kids. Jeez."

He chuckled. "Well, I suppose most of us never realize how hard everyone at a school works until we have to do their job. I once volunteered to sub for a teacher who had to go to a conference. Good Lord, it was like trying to train a herd of cats to sit still for a photo. Impossible."

"You're not making me excited about this," she said.

"You'll be fine. You've always been good at organization and getting people to do what you want them to do."

She clicked her seat belt. "What does that mean?"

"Relax, it's a compliment. You're good with people. Or you used to be. Of course, I haven't been around you in a while." He turned out on the highway.

"No, you haven't." Sunny turned to look out the window. "Thanks for putting on the seat warmer."

"You're welcome."

Nothing but politeness or matter-of-factness sat between them. Sunny wasn't going to open up to him, wasn't going to let him in any more than she had to. He might as well be an Uber driver. "You left the dog at your aunt's. Are we going there?"

"No, just take me to my mother's house."

He lifted his eyebrows. "Is Ruby Jean going to take care of the dog?"

"No, but I can walk to her house. No need for you to run me all over town."

"Let me take you. I can wait while you get the dog."

She shrugged. "Fine. My aunt has a kennel I can use… as long as I can get Betty on board with keeping the pup until I can find a better situation for it. No way I can keep the thing."

"Yeah, well, I'll try to help find a place for it. Maybe a Facebook post? Surely we can find someone who wants a cute dog. Or what will be a cute dog once she grows some hair back."

"I've learned the hard way that most people don't want to

take on someone else's problems. It will be harder than you think. Rescues are usually at full capacity. Too many homeless animals out there and not enough resources. It's a shame Morning Glory doesn't have an organization to help strays."

"Maybe you can do something about that," he said.

Sunny shook her head. "Not me. I'll help this one pup because you nearly made her roadkill, but I'm not the person to do something like that. I'm not hanging around any longer than I have to. By summer's end, I'll be gone."

"Sure, but you're here now," he said, for some reason hating the idea Sunny would disappear once again, even though he shouldn't have any reason to feel that way.

"Don't remind me."

chapter six

BATHING THE STRAY dog was almost as traumatic for Sunny as it was for the mutt. The thing was covered in fleas and ticks. Who knew fleas actually jumped? And when she'd picked the horrible things from the fine little hairs on her forearms, the damn dog had jumped from the old tub, soaking her and shaking dirty droplets all over the bathroom.

"What the..." Sunny clamped down on her anger. At her ire, Fancy had slunk down between the toilet and wall, looking as if she wanted to blend into the 1950s pink tile. Her tail was tucked so tight against her belly it looked painful.

"I'm sorry, girl. I've never bathed a dog before. I did the admin stuff for the rescue. So let's try again, shall we?"

She carefully approached the pup, muttering sweet nothings to the frightened thing. Lifting her stiff body, she set her back into the tub filled with warm, now-dirty water. Squirting the medicated wash into her hand, she scrubbed the dog's sides, noting that a lot of fleas had died as a result of the shampoo. Thank God.

"That's a good girl. We'll get you all clean and then dry you in a big fluffy towel."

She eyed the folded towels on the toilet lid. "Okay, they're not fluffy, but they are dry and somewhat warm."

Her mother had a handheld shower attachment that was perfect for rinsing the dog. She pulled the plug and let the tub drain while she blasted warm water to rinse the flea carcasses from the permanent ring around the old tub. Five minutes later, she had Fancy, still stiff with fear, sitting on the periwinkle bath mat, flea spray coating her fur. She couldn't let Betty glimpse one single flea or tick. Her mother had already coldly informed her that if she could get to a gun, she'd put the mutt out of its misery.

Thankfully, there were no guns in the house.

Betty had given her two days to find the dog a home. Sunny wasn't exactly sure what Betty could do about it if Sunny couldn't rehome the dog, but she respected her mother enough to agree to her dictates. That was pretty much the limit of her respect for Betty.

"You do smell better, girl." Sunny rubbed the dog's head, earning a cautionary wag of the bushy tail. The dog's feet were tipped in white, the clumpy gray fur speckled in black, and her coat held enough tan to mark her Australian cattle dog. Sunny only knew that because her neighbor when she'd lived in California had raised the nippy breed. "And your hair will grow back once the medicine starts to work."

Another tail thump.

"Wonder where you came from? Poor girl. Maybe I should give you a more fitting name than Fancy. 'Cause honestly, you ain't that. Well, it can't be Fluffy," she said, studying the rashy-looking bumps on the mangy patches. "Hmm, Cookie? No, maybe something Australian. Mathilda? Alice? Sydney? Crocodile Dundee?"

That made her laugh.

The dog's tail thumped again, even as her eyes watched Sunny warily.

"I get it. You're set on being Fancy." Sunny dropped the dog shampoo, and Fancy jumped and tried to hide in the bathroom corner. Sunny plopped onto her bottom and reached out a hand.

"I'm sorry. Come on, girl, come to me."

The dog trembled, and Sunny's heart nearly broke apart.

"You're a sweet little girl. Come on, Fancy Pants. Come see me."

The dog turned one ear toward Sunny but didn't move.

"Here, little girl," Sunny singsonged softly.

The dog turned around and sank onto her belly. Sunny wiggled her fingers. "Come on, Fancy."

Fancy belly-crawled toward Sunny, stopping just inches from her outstretched hand.

"Good girl. I know how you feel. Banged up and missing a little hair. I know what it's like to have fleas. Not real fleas, but things that drain the life from you. I know, Fancy girl."

The dog lowered her head between her paws and sighed.

Sunny set her hand atop the dog's head, slowly stroking so as not to scare her. Fancy's sweet brown eyes, still suspicious but also hopeful, lifted to watch Sunny.

Sunny had once heard that petting a dog increases serotonin levels, flooding a person with satisfaction and contentment. A bunch of baloney was what she'd told Alan when she'd read as much to him from a Facebook post over breakfast one morning, but now she understood the inclination. Something about the easy glide of her hand over the damp, trembling dog soothed her. It was as if the simple act of kindness eased over her like a cozy quilt. Or maybe she wanted to believe the nonsense because it was something she needed.

Sunny gave the mutt one last pet and slipped the old collar her aunt had found under her bathroom sink over Fancy's head, cinching it tight enough to keep her from pulling loose. Then she clipped the leash to the collar and opened the bathroom door.

"About damned time," Betty grumbled from her wheelchair in the hallway. Her mother's chair was electric, and the woman got around pretty well considering she had the use of only one side of her body. Not that anyone would know just how capable

Betty was. Her mother liked being waited on hand and foot. "I'm hungry."

"Your physical therapist said you were to work on simple skills, so tonight let's give that a go. The milk can be opened with one hand, and there's prepackaged oatmeal or macaroni and cheese. The microwave is now on a stand you can reach."

"I can't do that."

Sunny gently tugged on the leash. The dog wasn't budging from the bathroom. "Yes, you can. Eden spoiled you and kept you from practicing autonomy. The therapist has asked you to use your body so you strengthen it. Go do that."

"That woman is crazy if she thinks I can fix my own meals, and that dog is going outside. I told you I don't want no fleabag in my house." Betty's eyes gleamed in the bad hallway lighting, reminding Sunny of Cruella de Vil.

Sunny looked back at the dog, which refused to move. Fancy's tail was tucked tight, and she regarded Betty with fear. "Stop being ugly, Mama. The dog's clean. No fleas. She's staying inside because it's too cold outside. I have a kennel in my room, and I'll find someone to take her soon."

"I don't like dogs," Betty said, the good side of her mouth curving downward, making her frown overly exaggerated.

"Why not?" Sunny asked the question before she could think better of it. Betty didn't like much in life. At least not since the stroke. Probably had no good reason to dislike a dog.

"They're dirty. And they have sharp teeth."

"Well, so do you and we still keep you," Sunny said, trying for lightness.

"Ha ha." Betty snorted, expertly whipping her chair toward the kitchen.

"Hey, make me some mac and cheese while you're at it," Sunny called.

Betty flipped her off.

Sunny looked down at the dog. "See what I have to deal with? Bathing you is a piece of cake compared to dealing with her,"

Quick as rabbit, Sunny stooped and scooped the damp pup into her arms. The dog struggled briefly but then stilled. The dog's wetness soaked Sunny's sweatshirt, but she didn't put the pup down. Instead, she hummed a song by Dolly Parton and nuzzled her chin against the still dog, hoping to ease its fear.

Minutes later, Sunny had Fancy resting on a fluffy old pillow inside the kennel her aunt had loaned her. When she'd showed up earlier with the dog, Aunt Ruby Jean had looked at the mutt Henry held in his lap in the running truck and said, "Don't get too attached."

"I'm not."

"They're easy to get attached to when they need you. If you're not sticking around, you better not open up your heart. They'll wriggle inside, and before you know it, they're sleeping in your bed," Aunt Ruby said, running a thin hand over Sunny's shoulders, giving her a quick hug.

"You *are* talking about the dog, right?" Sunny asked.

Aunt Ruby Jean merely smiled. "I think you know what I'm talking about."

"Well, I'm not keeping either one. I have no need to have something to take care of." Sunny said it but knew even at that moment she told a half truth, because at one time she'd wanted to keep one of the things her aunt spoke of.

Sunny studied the sad dog Henry struggled to contain behind the wheel of his truck. Taking care of something other than the crotchety woman who'd given birth to her years ago would be a temporary distraction that she likely needed at the moment. Odd how the need to nurture something seemed embedded in a woman's DNA. When she'd been younger, she'd not thought too much about having something so vulnerable in her care, but as she'd gotten older, as the insanity of marrying a man she'd barely known had waned, she'd started longing for something to tend. Having a baby had become a near obsession. It was as if Sunny thought having a child could give her purpose.

Five times she'd held the promise inside her. She'd cherished the tenderness in her breasts, the way tears sprang to her eyes at the oddest moments, and browsed websites filled with nursery paint colors and tiny pinafores. Five times that promise had disappeared, slipping bright red and horrible from her womb, dropping her to her knees, teeth clenched against the sobs, pieces of herself flying to dark places never to be seen again. A dog wasn't a milk-drunk, sweet-smelling baby, but this dog needed someone.

Her aunt brushed a hand against her hair and nodded toward the man and dog in the truck. "Baby girl, you need something. Not sure it's either one of those things." Through the windshield, they could see Henry murmuring to the frightened animal. Sunny felt something inside her plink like a taut cello string surrendering to the inevitable.

Fight it.

Now, standing in her room, her mother in the kitchen grumbling loud enough to be heard and a beaten-down little dog eyeing her with suspicion, life seemed even harder than any other time before. Because she had nothing good on the road before her. She had a temporary job, no future, and she currently slept in a bed she'd left long ago. And now she had to find someone willing to take in a sad little dog.

Maybe Henry?

She'd not even thought to ask him. He had kids. Didn't they always want a dog? Yeah, kids always wanted pets. Maybe she could talk him into taking the dog home to wherever he lived.

Call him?

No. She didn't want that much intimacy with him. Still, this was something better asked face-to-face. He would pick her up Monday morning to take her to work. Bright and early. She had to be at the school office by seven thirty. Henry had never been much of a morning person, but then again, neither had she. How open would he be to her suggestion with the rising sun hitting him in the eyes?

A dog was a lot of work.

Fancy whimpered at that particular moment. In agreement or protest?

"What's wrong, girl?" Sunny asked.

Fancy looked up, brown eyes so sad. But she made no further noises.

"I'm going to make sure Betty didn't blow up the microwave. You rest." Sunny turned out the light, catching sight of her suitcase still sitting in the corner of her bedroom. A reminder that she wasn't staying.

Sunny closed the door and moved toward the kitchen where her mother grumbled words that would make a virgin blush. Hell, they'd make anyone blush.

Definitely not staying.

She needed to get the painting done and find cheap light fixtures. Fast.

Henry hated mornings.

"Dad, Landry took the pens you gave me," Katie Clare screamed though the Bluetooth in his car. "They were mine."

"I had a test, stupid," Landry said in the background.

"Do not call your sister stupid, Lan," Henry said, rubbing a hand over his face. He wasn't in the mood to deal with squabbling kids. He'd spent all of last night tossing and turning in the bed above his parent's garage. Dreams of past regrets and, oddly enough, a dog chasing him clogged his sleep, rendering him a virtual zombie. He'd nicked himself shaving and then spilled coffee on his shirt while driving out of the driveway. With a full day ahead, he didn't have time to pick up Sunny and take her to the school, but he couldn't seem to bring himself to rent her a car. The bike would be repaired as soon as Deeter got the part he'd ordered in. Who knew how long that could take?

Long, he hoped.

"But you bought those for me. He had no right to take them," Katie Clare insisted.

"You're right. He should have asked, but you need to be

more understanding. Sharing with your brother is something you should be willing to do."

Silence met what he considered to be sage advice. Surely he'd just scored a goal in the game of parenting.

"I don't have to share. Not when they're mine," Katie declared.

So his shot had been wide right. He sighed and turned onto Sunny's street. "That's enough, KC. You're being ugly, and it's too early to deal with this. Let me talk to your mother."

"Whatever. You always take up for Landry," his darling, precious daughter said.

His ex-wife sounded out of breath when she answered the phone. "Hey, what's up?"

"You tell me."

"What do you mean by that?" Jillian asked, sounding annoyed. She always sounded annoyed when she talked to him. Gone was all pretense of sweetness. That meant the kids were out of earshot.

"They call me, fighting over pens. Like I can do something from here. What's going on there?"

"Don't call me and accuse me of something, Henry. Things are crazy here. Mary Ellen's getting married, this kid is sitting on my bladder, and Eddie just had a manager quit. If you have a problem with how I'm doing, make the attempt to be more present in their lives rather than calling and criticizing me."

Henry shook his head, wishing he'd hung up instead of asking to talk to his ex-wife. "I'm not criticizing, Jill. I'm asking if everything is okay. Katie's giving me attitude, and—"

"When does she not give attitude?" Jillian interrupted, the slightest hint of humor in her voice. "That child was born giving us attitude. Oh, and we need to discuss Landry's punishment for getting behind the wheel and having an accident. He needs to share in paying for the repairs. We're lucky the owner of the motorcycle didn't file charges. That could have been disastrous. I think Landry understands he could have been in way bigger trouble."

"He's going to help Dad paint the barn, and I told him he'd be punished," Henry said, trying to relax his grip on the steering wheel as he turned into Sunny's driveway.

"Two weeks with no video games and no outings with friends sound good?"

"Perfect," he said, watching Sunny exit the old house. The shutters needed a new coat of paint, and the porch sagged in the middle. He could send some guys over to run support beams underneath. If Sunny would let him. Stubborn woman.

"Katie Clare said something about the motorcycle owner being an old girlfriend. She's not talking about Sunny, is she?" Jillian's tone hardened. Sunny had always been a point of contention between them. In fact, Sunny had unknowingly ended their marriage. No, that wasn't exactly true. More like the torch he carried for Sunny had ended his marriage.

He and Jillian had tried damned hard to make their relationship work. Jillian had been the perfect mother—warm, silly, and ever present. She had social connections, made their four-bedroom house feel more home than showplace, and took great care with her appearance. He should have adored her, wept at her feet to have such an extraordinary, saintly wife. But he hadn't… because he'd given his heart away to Sunny long ago and had not asked for it back.

And deep down, he supposed Jillian had always known that.

Which hadn't been fair to the girl he'd met at an Ole Miss mixer the fall of his freshman year. His mother had all but shoved him toward the willowy brunette, gushing over her grandfather who'd served as governor for eight years. Jillian had been easy to talk to, a nice stand-in for Sunny at the homecoming game and at winter formal. He'd held her hand when escorting her and draped his arm about her shoulders for party pics, but he'd never been into her the way she'd been into him. He'd been waiting for Sunny to get to Ole Miss so they could be what they'd always been—together. But a little something called Jim Beam had other plans.

Okay, not just Jim Beam.

He and Sunny had fought. Technically, they'd been broken up at the time, but they still talked every week and tried to see each other when they could. That day she'd called to tell him about her gown for the Miss Morning Glory High pageant. She'd been so excited about the dress her aunt had helped her sew and had mentioned that Chris Havens had told her how good she looked in it. Of course, he now knew Chris was gay, but back then he'd been seized by such jealousy he'd lashed out at Sunny and let it slip he was taking Jillian to Old South, Kappa Alpha's biggest social event, that night. Their conversation had ended in tears with Sunny refusing to answer any more calls from him and declaring she would accept the scholarship to Mississippi State instead of going to Ole Miss.

That night he'd gotten wasted, and so had Jillian. And when Jillian drank vodka, she got frisky, and Henry had used the condom he carried in his wallet… a condom he'd carried around for four years… a condom that had expired.

He couldn't undo what he'd done.

His first time was supposed to have been with the girl he loved, but Sunny had sworn she wouldn't have sex until she was out of high school. They'd gotten close to actually going all the way too many times to name, but Sunny always came to her senses. She'd been firm—she wasn't getting pregnant. She was going to college and making something of herself before she got married or had a baby. And Sunny was stubborn as hell.

The afternoon after the party, Sunny called him and apologized. She'd been nervous about the pageant. Henry had wanted to put the mistake he'd made the night before behind him. He told her he was sorry for being jealous and drove home to spend a few days of spring break with her. He'd tried to forget about Jillian and the condom… until Jillian cornered him in the library and told him the mistake he'd made would be one he'd pay for over a lifetime.

"Henry?" Jillian interrupted his thoughts of past mistakes. "Is she talking about Sunny?"

"Actually, she is."

"Well, I bet you're just loving that, aren't you?" Though Jillian was happily in love with Eddie, she still carried resentment against him. And Sunny, obviously.

"Not really, Jillian. Sunny hates my guts. Not much fun dealing with someone who hates you."

Silence met his response.

"I need to go," he said, watching as the subject of the conversation emerged from the house.

"Yeah. Right," Jillian said before hanging up.

"Shit," Henry breathed, clicking off his phone and shoving it into the holder.

Sunny opened the truck door and climbed inside. She smelled like fall. Like campfire marshmallows, vanilla, and pumpkin pie. Like the way home should smell. He longed to drop down on a pile of leaves with her, nuzzle her neck, explore the petal-soft skin beneath the cowl-neck sweater she wore.

She pulled the door closed. "Morning."

"Good morning. Coffee," he said, nodding at the cup awaiting her.

"You didn't have to."

"I know." He backed out of the drive once she clicked her belt into place. When they were on their way, he said, "You smell good."

Her shoulders stiffened. "Eden left some lotion behind. I'm not much on perfume, but this cold is drying my skin out. Think it's called pumpkin soufflé. Out of season, but beggars can't be choosy."

Why had he said anything? She probably thought he was a nut. "I might pick some up for my mom. She likes stuff like that."

"And how is Miss Annaleigh? Still chairing committees and designing the perfect life for her only child?" Sunny smiled, but her words held an edge.

"She's older and less involved in social things."

"Huh," Sunny said, turning her head and staring out into the gray morning. Even as a teen, Sunny had known the score with Henry's mother. She knew the woman was opposed to her son dating someone from the wrong side of the tracks. Not that Annaleigh was openly hostile or anything. His mother would never be so crass. She was a Southern lady, after all.

The phone rang. Jillian's number. He ignored it.

Sunny glanced over at him before returning her study to the trees flashing past. The mood was definitely uncomfortable.

He cleared his throat. "Uh, Deet said the part should be in by tomorrow afternoon at the latest."

"My mother's van might be ready by then. Or not. We had to send it to Jackson to get the transmission fixed. They don't seem too concerned about getting to it."

"No worries. I'm going to the school anyway, so…" He wondered what to say next. Maybe just *I'm sorry*.

He should rent her a car from Townplace Autoplex. Surely Bryce Barham had loaners he'd be willing to lease for a week or so. Then Henry wouldn't have to be trapped in a cab fifteen minutes each way with someone who hated him, who blamed him, who still made his heart squeeze into a tight fist of regret and desire.

"Yeah," she said, her attention seemingly outside the cab. "Like I said, I appreciate it."

A minute passed and he turned up the radio. The Eagles begged him to take it easy, and he rather thought that was good advice. Pick her up, take her to work and back home again. Take it easy because there was no need to do anything the hard way.

He pulled around to the parking lot because buses crowded the loop. Teens poured out, mingling in the cold morning, their breath making small puffs of air as they punched each other on the arm, high-fived, and clumped together like magnetic shavings. "What time will you be done?"

Sunny paused with a hand on the handle. "Uh, I'm not sure. Around four?"

"That should work for me. Hope your day is good."

"Yeah, me too," she said, her voice sounding a bit lighter. "I'm nervous, which is silly. I handled multiple high-level tasks for my last company, but somehow dealing with teenagers makes me feel like one all over again."

"You'll do great."

"Or die trying." She gave him a half smile. Just that little twitch of her lips did something to him. Damn, he was such a fool, and he hated himself for taking pleasure in something she tossed his way so easily.

Sunny slid out of the truck, taking her lunch bag with her. When she planted her feet, she glanced back at him. "Thanks again."

"Sure. The least I could do."

"No, you didn't have to be kind, but then again, you're Henry and always kind. Mostly." Then she closed the door with enough force to make him wonder about those last words.

Henry watched her walk toward the front office. She wore black boots that encased slim legs and a dress the color of wild plums. Her hair looked too bright against her creamy skin, but she still looked good, which was probably why a clump of boys wearing Morning Glory High letterman jackets turned to watch her enter the school. Something ugly reared inside him for an instant—that age-old, primitive need to smash faces in and toss Sunny over his shoulder and run off to his cave.

Mine.

But she wasn't.

Henry shifted into Drive and started down the hill to the construction area.

Not even close.

chapter seven

SUNNY STUDIED THE jumbled folders in the drawer. Each had odd initials and made no flipping sense at all. She shoved the drawer closed and watched as a sloe-eyed beauty wearing a short skirt and too-tight shirt made her way to the attendance desk.

"Oh hey," she said, looking uncertain. "Uh, is Miss Melanie here?"

"No. She's on medical leave. I'm Mrs. David, and I'll be taking her place. Can I help you?"

"Um, yeah, so, like, I need to check out for fourth hour. Here's my note." She placed a piece of paper on the counter.

"Place it in the basket by the door," Sunny said, gesturing to where Melanie Geter had the students deposit their excuses and notes for checking out. It was already quite full, and as soon as half the staff and faculty stopped coming in for coffee and welcoming her to MGHS, she'd get started on entering the information into the computer. "Come by between third and fourth hours to verify the checkout."

"But Miss Melanie never makes me—"

"Sorry, but I need time to verify," Sunny said, tapping at the computer because it made her look like she was doing something. "Once I get the hang of things, I'm sure we can go back to how Mrs. Geter was doing it."

"'Kay," the girl said, tossing her note into the basket and sashaying out.

Pushing in at her heels was a huge guy wearing a basketball jersey. "Yo, I need to get a temp ID."

Sunny lifted her eyebrows. "A what?"

"Temp ID. Like over there." He pointed toward a roll of stickers sitting on a table. On the table was a machine that made student IDs. Supposedly every student had to have an ID on a lanyard around their neck. The machine made the permanent IDs, but she didn't know how to run it yet. Mrs. Yancey, the school secretary, had said she'd show her how to run it later in the day.

"Sure," Sunny said, scooting her chair over to the table.

The giant slapped down three dollars and crossed his arms.

"What's your name?"

"Woozy."

She turned and looked at him. "Woozy?"

"Yeah, that's what they call me."

Sunny rolled back over to the computer. "What's your legal name?"

"Aww, I don't want Wayne written on my tag."

Sunny gave him *the look*. The one she used on handsy coworkers and dumb asses in general.

Woozy's shoulders sagged. "Fine. It's Wayne Curtis Jefferson."

Sunny carefully printed WAYNE "WOOZY" JEFFERSON on the temporary sticker. She peeled it off and handed it to him.

He glanced at it, gave a jerk of his head as approval, and then slapped it on his massive chest. "We cool."

"Great." Sunny spun back around toward the computer, trying to remember if there was a screen for making IDs. She'd only spoken to Melanie Geter briefly, jotting down indecipherable notes about the computer programs designed to make her life easier.

"Wait, who are you anyhow?" Woozy asked.

"Like that ID on your chest, I'm temporary."

"'Cause Miss Melanie broke her leg?"

"Actually, I think it was her hip, but yeah, pretty much."

"That's cool and all," he said, holding out his fist. Sunny stared at it before realizing he was giving her some kind of approval. "What they call you?"

She bumped her knuckles against his. "Mrs. David."

"Aww, I can't call you Mrs. David. That's like for old ladies."

She didn't know what to say. Was he flirting with her or just being nice? "You don't have to call me anything really. If you remember to bring your ID and stay out of trouble, you don't even have to see me again."

"Red."

"Beg your pardon?" she asked.

"Your hair's red. I'ma call you Red." With that declaration, he pushed out the door. A bell rang, and the hall filled with noise and bodies. Her door bumped a few times, and a few kids opened it and placed their notes into the basket.

Red? Did kids give staff nicknames that they actually used? She and her friend used to call Mr. Trayner "Crypt Keeper," but never to his face. Of course, she didn't know much about kids these days at all, outside of what she saw on TV and social media. But maybe she was about to find out.

The door opened before she could reach for her phone to call and check on her mother.

Two hours later, she felt like she'd been run over by a Mack truck and left to be scraped off the pavement. Twenty-four students had come and gone through her door, along with the security guard, two teachers, and Mrs. Sarah Whitmore, who looked more like a polished executive than a high school principal.

"You can take a break for lunch now," Marilyn McConnell said, appearing in Sunny's doorway. Marilyn was the vice principal and had been at the school since the beginning of time. In fact, the woman was as much a fixture at the school as the school mascot, Benny the Buccaneer. "I can get Tina to cover for you."

"I can eat in here unless you would rather I didn't."

"If you want to," Marilyn said with a shrug, her otter earrings brushing her sweater, which featured frolicking kittens and balls of yarn. Marilyn either wore vintage 1985 because she was stuck there… or she could foresee brightly patterned sweaters making a comeback. Lord, Sunny hoped that style didn't make a comeback. "How's your mama doing?"

"Still breathing."

Marilyn snorted. "Tough cookie, ain't she?"

"That's putting it kindly." Sunny allowed herself to smile. Betty had lived in Morning Glory most of her life, minus the couple of times she'd tried to get out with some guy or another. People in town knew her mother's history. Hell, they knew Sunny's history. To pretend anything else was like trying to fill a broken vase with water. "I'm trying to talk her into moving into the Arbor. She needs around-the-clock care and someone to make sure she doesn't resurrect her coven when the moon is full."

Marilyn laughed, leaning against the doorframe of her office. The woman wanted to talk. Sunny would rather not, but she knew how to get along in an office. She had several months ahead of her. Things were easier in a small Southern town when you at least pretended to be "one of them." "You know, she was in the same class as I was. Of course, I didn't know her well. I was a band nerd and she was… well, popular."

"So I hear," Sunny drawled but added a smile lest Marilyn think she was offended. She'd learned long ago to pretend away the shame of her mother's past. "She's digging in her heels about it, but I think some social stimulation would be good for her. Currently, she does nothing but watch police procedurals and try to sneak the cigarettes I'm trying to hide from myself."

"How do you hide things from yourself?"

"It ain't easy, but I'm good at it." In fact, she was a freaking pro at hiding things from herself. Wasn't bad at lying to herself either. That's how a girl got through life sometimes. She just didn't acknowledge the truth. No owning up to wishing she had someone to lean on, no more hoping for something good down the road. She also didn't admit that she still stooped to pick dandelions, scattering the seeds while sending up useless wishes. But she did, because hell, it might just work.

"If I need tips at hiding things from myself, I'll know who to go to." Marilyn grinned.

"I'm a pro," Sunny said, uncorking the thermos of coffee she'd packed and hadn't had time to sample. She knew things were about to get hairy since many of the kids she'd managed to log into the system would be checking out around noon. "Oh, I wanted to ask you something. I found a stray dog a few days ago, and I'm looking to rehome it without taking it to the shelter. You don't happen to know anyone looking for a family pet, do you? She's a sweet dog."

Marilyn made a face. "Well, I'm a cat person."

She wasn't surprised Marilyn was a cat person. The cat sweaters made that obvious. "Well, if you hear of anyone in the next day or two…"

"Oh, you know who you need to talk to? Grace Metcalf. She teaches biology. You'd love her. She's your age, I think." Marilyn didn't elaborate any further.

"And why would I talk to her? Is she looking for a pet?"

"No, but she's trying to put together a group to help strays. I think they're actually working on setting up an official rescue organization. She's really into it."

"That's exactly who I need. My mother wants this poor pup gone yesterday."

"I'll tell Grace to stop by if I see her. Now, I better get this evaluation to Mr. Paul. He's lighting my phone up every fifteen minutes. Enjoy your lunch."

Sunny looked down at the peanut butter and jelly sandwich

she'd pulled from her lunch bag and wanted to toss it into the trash can. But she forced herself to eat at least half of it. Wasn't like she could afford new clothes, so she needed to eat. Before the last miscarriage and Alan's death, she'd at least enjoyed food. People always said grieving made food taste like cardboard, but she'd not believed them until she'd been surrounded by casseroles and fried chicken after the funeral and wanted nothing more than to throw it all out.

The door opened and in tumbled three students.

Maybe she could talk to Grace Metcalf before the day was over, but until then…

"Hi, I'm Mrs. David. Can I help you?"

Henry was running late. It was already four thirty, but a series of emergencies at the site of the small credit union addition paired with a goose chase for an old account had him running out the door after Sunny had texted him for the third time.

Get her a rental, stupid.

But he knew he wouldn't. Because he wanted to be close to her, like some friggin' sadist who enjoyed the sting of the whip or the burn of the lighter. He'd rather feel pain with Sunny than not have her around at all.

God, he was pathetic.

He roared up the hill, his truck kicking up gravel when he stopped in the lot next to faculty parking. Sunny stood huddled in the shadows, talking to Grace Metcalf. Her gaze slid to where he idled, and then she shook hands with Grace and headed his way.

In she climbed as the cold snapped at them from outside the warmth of his cab. Sunny rubbed her hands together as soon as she slid into place. "Brr. It's cold out there. Where the heck is spring?"

"I know, and it's going to get colder this weekend. Front coming down."

"Yay," she deadpanned. "What happened to the groundhog not seeing his shadow?"

"It'll be warm before we know it. How was your day?"

"Crazy," she said as he pulled from the lot. She gave Grace a wave as they passed her going to her car. "But I survived."

"That's good. Hey, I see you met Grace."

"Yeah, she's going to help me find a home for Fancy. I hope. And she may have talked me into helping her with a 5K she and her group are doing next month."

"Easter egg hunt weekend? I think I heard something about a 5K, but I didn't know Grace was involved."

"Yeah, Easter Egg Hunt weekend. I couldn't say no to her after she said she'd help me find a place for the dog. Plus she said they needed someone with some rescue experience. Problem is, they've done very little toward organizing that race outside of applying for the permit to hold it and advertising it in the paper."

Henry warmed at the idea of Sunny doing something worthwhile rather than trying to get out of Morning Glory. Not that she wasn't going to leave. He knew she would, but he also knew that one of the best ways to get over hard times in one's life was finding distraction. He'd started carving duck calls after the divorce. Clem Aiken, who'd leased his barn, had taught him to use a lathe. Spending time with Clem had distracted him from the drama of dealing with lawyers, judges, and the guilt every time he looked at his kids. Henry had even formed a small business, selling his duck calls online. Whistling Dixie was a minor success and kept him busy on the weekends when his kids weren't with him or he wasn't working. "Grace is a great person."

"And a lesbian." Sunny's mouth twitched. "She, like, led with that, which was a bit weird."

"Well, she got hit on so much when she first moved here, I think it's become a habit," Henry said, smiling. Grace Metcalf had been the hottest thing to hit Morning Glory outside of Sal Genovese's spunky sister, who'd gotten a few guys all atwitter, including his bud Clem. Henry had even thought about asking Grace out until she gloriously kicked open the closet door by taking her girlfriend to dinner at the grand opening of Sal's New York Pizzeria. The willowy, perpetually cheerful biology teacher's preference for her own gender had deflated any hopes of local bachelors who were looking for true love.

"I understand," Sunny said, frowning at the beeping from his dashboard, grabbing the seat belt she'd obviously forgotten to click into place. "Rare to get new people in Morning Glory."

She said it like there wasn't much the small town offered, and maybe to some it didn't. It was, after all, a typical small Southern town full of the run-of-the-mill characters. People made it their business to know where their neighbors went to church, and if they didn't, they made sure to take them a pie and invite them the following Sunday. Morning Glory wasn't Mayberry—they had a few drug dealers and thieves—but it was relatively friendly and safe. They were proud that their town rarely made the Jackson six-o'clock news. In fact, the last time Morning Glory was mentioned in the *Clarion Ledger* was when their library received a grant to buy new computers. Seriously. That was the newsmaker for September.

"Not too many."

Just as he turned onto the highway, he remembered he'd forgotten to grab the files he needed to take home to his father. He muttered a curse word and jerked the steering wheel, making a sharp turn.

"What are you doing?" Sunny, who was in the process of buckling up, tilted toward him and her sharp shoulder hit his ribs.

"Sorry, I forgot something I need at the office," he said. He didn't want to enjoy the scent of her shampoo or the brush of her hair on his forearm. But like the nutcase he was, he did.

"Jeez, a warning would have been nice."

"Sorry."

"Which is something you say a lot." Her voice was flat. And annoyed.

"But it doesn't matter with you, does it?" he muttered, pulling into the graveled space where he normally parked. "I won't be a minute."

Sunny looked at him, her brow furrowed. She hadn't expected him to say something pissy, but honestly, her attitude had started to rankle him. Yeah, his kid had run over her bike, but he'd bent over backward to make sure she wasn't inconvenienced. And, yeah, he'd had an ulterior motive—he wanted to make things right between them—but she didn't know that. Her suck-ass attitude had gotten on his last damn nerve.

He stared back, his hand hovering on the door handle. "What?"

She looked away. "Can I use your restroom? I had a lot of coffee today."

"Sure." He climbed out, fishing his keys from his pocket. His team was still working at the site, but the office was empty since Carson had left early to meet Tomeka at an obstetrician appointment and Carol had gone home early with a headache.

He flipped on the lights and pointed toward the small bathroom in the temporary office. "Right in there."

"Thanks."

He found the files and wasted the next minute checking his Twitter feed, noting sports trades, and rolling his eyes at all the political commentary. Sunny came out, drying her hands on a paper towel.

"Ready?"

She nodded but then hesitated. "Why did you say what you said?"

"About my apologies meaning nothing to you?"

She nodded.

"Isn't that obvious? No matter what I say or do, I'm still the boy who screwed you over." He pocketed his phone, wishing he didn't give a damn about how she treated him.

"You didn't screw me, Henry. You screwed *her*, and that's the problem. That's always been the problem." Her words were like bullets slamming into him.

He deserved her anger, but that didn't change the fact that it was hard to hear those words come from her mouth.

"God, Sunny, I was nineteen, and we were broken up," Henry said, clenching his teeth against the sudden surge of his own anger. She acted as if he'd killed babies and burned villages. Okay, he'd made a mistake, and it had been big one. But Sunny had run away and given him no chance to fix it. Or try to fix it. She'd been the one to give up on them. Not him.

Her empty-eyed stare was a challenge. Time to wade in. To say everything he'd been wanting to say since he'd seen her last week.

"You know I didn't mean for it to happen. It's not like I went to the party intending to have sex with Jillian. We just both got wasted. And… and you said those words. You said we were over."

"Wait, you're blaming me?" Her expression went from remote to furious in less than a second. "Seriously?"

"I'm not blaming anyone. I'm just saying that I wasn't in a good frame of mind to begin with—"

"You *slept* with her. You gave away everything we ever were and everything we could have been because you got horny. Being drunk doesn't negate that you took yourself away from me."

"You didn't want me. You said those words." He couldn't forget that phone conversation. The way she'd sounded so resigned to them being done once and for all. No "pretending" to be broken up. She'd said she was done. Everything they'd planned was over. She'd screamed for him to go to the party and forget about her. That time he'd believed her.

"No. Because those words were the same we'd hurled at each other every time we got into a fight, Henry. You'd say that maybe we should just break up. And I would say that you were right. That we shouldn't stay together. We said the same things to each other six months after we first started dating. Then again your junior year. And again the day after you graduated. They were just scared words, Henry. You know I didn't mean them."

He stared at her. "Didn't mean them? Then why in the hell did you say them? Why did you tell me to go have fun and forget about you? That you were accepting the scholarship to State."

"Because I wanted you to come home. I wanted you to ditch that debutante bitch and show up at my doorstep like you had every other time." Sunny's face suffused with color, her blue eyes flashing with fury.

"Well, why in the hell didn't you *say* that?" He swiped a hand through his hair and tried to figure out what she was talking about. But he knew. Now. It had taken him many years of marriage and a year of therapy to figure out that many times what a woman says is not what she means. *I'm fine* means she's not fine. *Do whatever you want* means don't do whatever you want. *I don't care* means I DO care. But at nineteen, he'd had no clue that Sunny hadn't meant what she said, that she'd been following some unwritten relationship script meant to motivate him into doing the opposite of what she'd told him to do.

"I shouldn't have had to tell you. You knew the way I felt about you," she said, her voice sticking. She cleared the catch in her throat.

"I was a dumb kid, Sunny. I didn't know you were scared, that you wanted me to prove something to you."

Sunny shook her head. "You know what? I don't want to do this. I never wanted to do this. Let's just go."

"Well, you brought it up."

"No, I didn't. You're the one who said your apologies aren't good enough."

"They're not," he said.

"That's right. Being sorry isn't enough. You ruined…" Her words fell off, and she looked away, blinking. Were those tears? Or was she so furious at him she couldn't bear his sight?

"What do you want me to do, Sunny?"

She whipped her head around. Definitely tears. "Nothing.

You can't undo what was done. So drop it."

"So why are you treating me like I'm something you scraped off your shoe? If there's nothing I can do to fix what I did, why torture me?"

She dashed away the dampness with the back of her hand. "Torture you? That's what you think I'm doing?"

He didn't answer.

"I don't want to be around you, Henry. I don't want to remember everything that existed between us. Don't you understand? I don't want to sit beside you in that goddamned truck." Her voice, so filled with hurt, dropped to a near whisper.

And those words found their mark. "Then don't. I was just trying to be nice."

Closing her eyes, she shook her head. "No, you're trying to fix things. You like everything nice and neat, but that's not how life is. I learned that on the day you told me you'd knocked up Jillian. Suddenly all my plans, all that stuff we dreamed about, well, that was just wishful thinking. It was a kid's dream. Not real life. Real life sucks the marrow from your bones and leaves you hollow and empty."

Henry watched her, wondering if she truly believed her words. He didn't think life was easy, and he knew firsthand after a failed marriage and a cancer scare that life was messy as hell, but empty… or hopeless?

Sunny pressed her lips together. "You can't fix me, Henry. You can't repair what was done that day."

"So you think everything turned on that dime, Sunny? I mean, please, get over yourself and this idea that I'm to blame for everything bad in your life."

A wall of anger hit him as she advanced. "Don't give yourself that much credit, Henry Todd Delmar. You don't have that much power over me."

"Well, that's the way you make it sound," he said, lowering his voice and holding his ground as she stopped in front of him.

Sunny parked her fists on her lean hips, her blue eyes glacier chips.

"We were kids. And kids make mistakes. You're grown now and you can't possibly blame me for all the bad stuff in your life."

"I don't blame you for everything bad in my life. I made my own decisions. But you lit the match, Henry. You lit the fucking match."

Sunny stood in front of him, closer to him than she'd been since that day years ago. He stared down at her, at the lips that were still just as lush, at those eyes he'd loved once upon a time. His body, mind, and soul were in knots, and he couldn't untangle them.

He couldn't fix her.

He didn't owe her anything. Not really.

Then it happened. The air shifted, an undetectable scrape of one thing against another. A sudden spark. A flare. Ignition.

Henry felt his body sway toward hers. He was a moth, unable to resist the flicker of light that was Sunny.

"Say something," she demanded, her breath hitching.

But he couldn't.

"Henry," she whispered, her blue eyes not so hard anymore. They'd softened, ripened, giving him permission.

He lowered his head. She rose to meet him.

Their lips met.

The initial touch was gasoline tossed onto a flame—igniting, expanding, blowing up. Henry pulled her to him, fisting his hand in those fiery locks as Sunny grabbed his neck, pulling him down. She opened her mouth and he lost himself, hauling her up against his body, stumbling back into the desk. Papers fell, something thumped, but he didn't give a damn. All he cared about was the woman in his arms, a woman who was so familiar and yet such a mystery. A woman who bit his bottom lip, giving a groan of desire so guttural it tilted him into a frenzy.

One hand fitted to her ass, lifting her to his hardness.

He devoured her. She returned the favor. Hands grasped, mouths melded, tongues danced as Henry found not a homecoming but a new place to explore. This was a woman who gave as good as she got. Her hand twisting in his hair hurt, but he didn't care. He wanted to drown in her, dominate her, take all her sorrow and rip it from her. He wanted her goodness, the sweet honey he knew she hid beneath the hard veneer of a woman who didn't give two shits about anything.

Because she was in there somewhere. There was a ghosting in the sigh of surrender, an unspooling of memories in her scent, a page turned back to a time when they held something precious in their hands.

Sunny pulled his head back, making his scalp sting. "Stop."

"No." He dipped his head again, intent on capturing those lips and stopping the words.

"Henry, stop," she said, pushing against his chest. "Stop."

He released her and stepped back, his body unwilling. His mind reeled with what he'd done. No, what they'd done. Sunny hadn't been unwilling. But now she was.

"Don't ever do that again." She swiped a hand across her mouth. Her eyes blazed against her pale skin, and her hands trembled. "We don't have that anymore."

He begged to differ, but he wasn't going to argue with her over what was between them. They both could deny it until the end of time.

Sunny moved toward the door, and he wondered how she could move so easily. His own knees were weak and his hands shaky. Not to mention, his pants were a bit tight in the crotch. Sunny had taken him back to being a teenager with the first taste of her lips.

She stood with her back to him, waiting for him, refusing to look at him.

"Sorry."

"Yeah, I think we covered that already," Sunny said before opening the door and walking back into the cold, dying day.

Henry reached down and crumpled a flyer sitting on Carol's desk and tossed it into the trash can. "Shit."

chapter eight

"I'M BARELY MAKING it myself, Sunny. I just don't have much money to spare," Eden said.

Sunny bit down on her frustration. "I understand, but I'm trying to finish the house, maybe get some carpet put down in the bedrooms. I'm working during the day and doing this at night, so—"

"Do you really think this is a good idea, Sunny? I mean, Mom isn't the social type, and I'm pretty sure she's not going to let you sell the house. It's the only thing she's got."

Sunny tried not to be exasperated with her sister, but it was hard. Of course, if anyone knew how hard it was to live in a falling-down house, it was her younger sister. Somehow Eden had learned how to fix every major appliance, something Betty revealed every time something broke. *Eden could fix it if she were here.*

When Sunny had bolted for the East Coast and a new life at the ripe age of eighteen, she'd left behind a mother with a drug problem and a fifteen-year-old sister who wasn't ready to handle the life she'd been given. But at that time, Betty had been capable of paying the rent, as long as she didn't spend it all on booze or drugs, and Eden had Aunt Ruby Jean for stability. No one could have foreseen the overdose and resulting stroke that would debilitate their mother. Eden had been eighteen when Betty had her stroke, the same age Sunny had been when she'd left Morning Glory. Eden had put her plans on hold and taken the reins of holding everything together. Sunny had felt bad her sister got saddled with taking care of their mother, and she'd promised Eden she'd do her duty taking care of their mother one day. She just hadn't expected it to take so long.

"Look, Eden, I understand what you're saying, but this house is falling down, and I don't want to spend the rest of my life in Morning Glory. I mean, are you coming back here after you get your degree?"

Sunny could feel the hesitation, and she knew the answer.

"Well, I'm not sure, but…" Eden's voice fell away.

"No, you're not. I know you're not, and Betty can't live alone even though she can do more for herself than she lets on. If I can get her into a place like the Arbor, then we can have a life and she can too. She's lonely, though she would never admit it."

"You think Mom's lonely?"

"Yeah, I do."

Silence sat on the line.

"E?"

"I'm here. I never thought she was lonely, but I guess you could be right. But selling the house? That seems so permanent."

"Do you want the house?" Sunny asked, feeling like she was cajoling a toddler. Eden didn't let go of things easily. Eden never ran away. She stayed and handled the crap flung at her. Sunny's baby sister didn't deserve to have to come home and care for their mother again. She deserved her own life. "I don't think you do, and it's falling apart. I'm making the necessary repairs to get it marketable, but it's an old house."

"I guess," Eden said. In the background, Sunny could hear the chatter of many voices.

"Where are you?"

"My job. I'm doing some, uh, dancing in the evening hours.

I'm nannying during the day. I told you about Sophie and taking care of her."

Eden had moved down to New Orleans, and the job she'd originally procured had been nonexistent, leaving her younger sister to scramble to find employment. Ironically, Eden had found a job taking care of a special needs child. Sophie was school-aged, which allowed Eden to go to classes herself, but taking care of a child in a wheelchair was challenging.

"How are you going to do all that? And by dancing, you don't mean—"

"No, it's a speakeasy and more thematic. It's called Gatsby's, and actually, they just moved me up to headlining. Think the Haynes Sisters in *White Christmas* rather than Mama at Legz."

"Whew," Sunny breathed, relieved that her sister hadn't taken something that… well, would haunt her for the rest of her life. Because Sunny was fairly certain that when Betty had taken the job at the airport strip club to make enough money to pay for nursing school, she'd cemented what her life would be like. Legz had been a gateway to bad choices. And Betty had run to them with both arms out. "I worried for a moment."

"Don't worry about me, Sunny. I learned well. Just take care of Mama. I don't have much time off, but I'm hoping to come home for a visit soon. Maybe in a few weeks, I don't know. I'll send what money I can. I'm meeting with a talent agent tomorrow. He says he can get me more from the owners. We'll see."

Sunny got off the phone with her sister and looked around the kitchen. She was pretty much done in this room, and it looked enormously better. If she squinted her eyes, it almost looked like something flipped on HGTV. Wasn't perfect, but it was pretty cute. Now to get Betty out of the living area so Sunny could freshen the paint and put up new light fixtures. She'd love to sand and strip the old pine floors, but she wasn't up to that task. And the porch needed fixing and fresh paint. Hanging a few plants from the overhang would give some curb appeal. Nothing like putting lipstick on a pig.

"Sunny," Betty called from the living area. "When are we going to eat? I'm hungry."

"I'm heating dinner now, Mama," Sunny said, pressing the one-minute button on the microwave in order to reheat what she'd already reheated while talking to her sister. She poured her mother some sweet tea. Needed something good to soften the blow that she was moving the TV to the corner of the kitchen. Betty would have to set up base ops in the kitchen so Sunny could work in the living room.

Betty rolled into the kitchen. "About damn time. And that mutt of yours is whinin' and drivin' me batty."

Sunny moved toward the doorway and heard Fancy crying. The little dog stayed in her kennel during the day. Sunny hated cooping her up, but she wasn't certain the dog was house-trained and didn't trust Betty not to smack the poor dog if she got in her mother's way. "I'll get her. We already went for a walk, but she needs some playtime."

"When are you getting rid of her? You said two days. It's been almost four."

Sucking in a deep breath, Sunny closed her eyes and released the inhalation. "Mama, I'm trying. I called some rescues in Jackson, but no one can take her. I'm not putting Fancy out or taking her to the shelter. It's a kill shelter."

"So?"

"You mean-ass woman, your dinner is in the microwave. You get it," Sunny muttered, walking out. Seconds later, Fancy emerged from her kennel, head lowered, tail tucked. She thumped her tail when Sunny talked sweet to her, but otherwise she remained mistrusting.

"Come on, Fancy Pants. Let's take another walk. It's cold out but better than hanging in the kitchen with Mean Betty."

Fancy wagged her tail and looked at Sunny with eyes that could melt the Grinch's heart. Hadn't worked on Betty, of course. The Grinch had nothing on Sunny's mother. Sunny hooked the leash onto the collar that Fancy tolerated, then tugged on her coat. She added a scarf because the sun had gone to bed, leaving nothing but the cold dark.

Most people wouldn't be caught dead walking around Grover's Park after nightfall, but Sunny wasn't most people. Most everyone knew the Voorhees and didn't mess with them. They were small in number now, but their family name still carried weight. Her great-grandfather had run moonshine out of the area back during Prohibition. Her grandfather had been a loan shark and had run a handyman repair shop three streets over. Sunny had no clue who her father was. She and Eden hadn't shared the same one, which was fairly obvious when people looked at them. But Betty's brother, her uncle Kev, had been big, burly, and as likely to hit you as look at you. He was doing twenty years in Parchman Farm, the state pen, for killing a guy in a bar fight outside Mobile. He wasn't around to rough anyone up in the hood anymore, but people still steered clear of his people. And if they chose not to, Sunny knew how to handle herself.

Fancy squatted on a patch of weeds in the neighbor's yard. The weak light from the lampposts seemed almost ominous in the haze of Sunny's condensed breath. February's cold fingers slid down her back, chilling her. She longed for the warmth of someone to snuggle against.

Henry.

She squeezed her eyes shut and tried to stamp out the feel of his body against hers, the way he'd kissed her, like a man starving for air. For a moment she'd given in and taken a little piece of what she knew she shouldn't have. He'd tasted so good. Like he always had.

Henry had always had a crazy-fast metabolism, which meant he always felt like an oven. When they'd been together, they'd snuggle on the couch watching a movie, and after thirty minutes next to him, she'd have to move away and fan herself. And he'd always chase her, grinning naughtily, when he was sweaty from lacrosse or the heat of the day. Either way, she loved that about him. In his arms, she found what she needed. And today she'd remembered.

God, had she remembered.

But she couldn't let her mind or body travel down that path. Henry had hurt her, had set her on the road she now walked. She wasn't ready to open herself up to something so intimate yet, especially not with Henry. Her life was in shambles, and the only way she could put it back together was to get her mother in a facility, sell the old house, and start a new life in sunny, warm, wonderful California. There on the beaches, she could find peace and maybe the stirrings of something more than being lonely. She and Alan'd had good times, but they'd not had what was necessary to truly build a life together. They fought too much, mistrusted too often, and never took comfort from each other. Oh, they tried. Alan hadn't been a bad guy. He had his moments, times when they laughed, loved, and thought they could push past the knots of hurt they'd yanked into the cord that bound them. But Sunny had known, and somehow that made grieving for Alan even worse. Because she wasn't just grieving his death, she was grieving what they'd never had.

Placing her hand on her abdomen, she blinked back sudden tears.

Grief for her unborn babies had fastened itself to her and sometimes caused such ripping pain she could hardly catch her breath.

Fancy barked, startling Sunny from her grim thoughts.

A small gray cat darted beneath the porch of a nearby house. Mrs. Shaffer fed feral cats, and it was likely one of hers.

"Oh no, Fancy girl. That cat would mess you up. Don't tangle with Grover Park kitties. They are street tough. But then again, maybe you are too," Sunny said, dropping to a crouch and rubbing Fancy behind her little bat ears. Fancy shied away at the touch of her hand but didn't pull the leash. Eventually she sat and let Sunny pet her.

Progress.

"Back we go. It's too cold out here to contemplate cats and the mistakes we've made." Sunny stood and lightly tugged the leash, drawing the speckled dog back toward the house where

Sunny had learned to walk, talk, and run from the things that were hard.

Betty met them at the front door, giving Fancy a scathing look. Well, as scathing as one can give with half an expression. "The microwave ain't workin'."

"What?"

Her mother shrugged one shoulder. "It just stopped. Smells like it's burnin'."

"Well, hell."

"Ain't my fault. You're the one who plugged it into that outlet. I told you it was bad, but you don't ever listen to me. If you did, you wouldn't have a dead husband, no real job, and no life."

"Well, thank you, Miss Merry Sunshine. I had forgotten that you're the epitome of making good decisions and listening to common sense."

Betty tried to twist her lips. "I ain't said I was good everything. But I know one damn thing I wouldn't have done—I wouldn't have let the Delmar boy go. You should have sucked it up and stuck with him. But no, you had to be prideful and run off. Look what that got you."

Sunny stopped midstride. Fancy cowered behind her, anticipating the strike of the snake. "Pride? You're talking pride, Mama? That's something you wouldn't recognize if it slapped you in the face. You have none."

Betty snorted. "Well, maybe so. I made lots of mistakes, so I damn sure know what that looks like. I'm an effing expert on mistakes."

"Yeah, that you know," Sunny said, tugging on Fancy's leash. "Come on, girl. Let's put you in your kennel. You wanna treat?"

Fancy's ears pricked. Funny how a dog learned that word before all else.

"Let me see that dog," Betty said.

Sunny frowned. "No way. I don't trust you not to go all Cruella on her."

"She does have a nice spotted coat," her mother said, trying to smile. Sunny almost laughed because Betty had made a joke, but didn't because she wasn't so sure the woman wouldn't try something with the pup. "Just hand me the leash. I ain't going to hurt the dog. Lord, Sunny."

Sunny eyed Fancy and then slowly extended the leash to Betty. Betty took it with her good hand. "Now go make sure the house ain't going to burn down."

Sunny reluctantly walked into the kitchen. The acrid smell of burned-up electronics met her nose. The microwave was toast. Another damn expense because a microwave was a necessity these days, at least for someone who now worked a day job. Even though she knew the thing was fried, she unplugged it and then replugged it. Nothing. She punched some buttons. Nothing.

"It's done for," she called to her mother.

Her mother didn't answer.

"Mama?" For a moment her heart leaped in her chest. She scurried back to the doorway, expecting to see her mother either transfixed by an old episode of *Bones* or quite possibly dead. But neither sight met Sunny when she paused in the threshold. Betty sat in her wheelchair, a look of intense concentration on her face as she stroked the fur between the ears of the dog sitting at her feet. Fancy sat as still as a puddle, eyes closed in rapture.

"Well, I'll be damned," Sunny whispered.

Henry didn't want to pick Sunny up the next day. What had happened between them at his office the night before had made for an uncomfortable ride home. But today would be the last day he had to endure the awkward silence and polite speech that had become their habit. Deeter had left him a message on his cell, telling him the part he needed to repair the bike would be in that morning and he should have the bike out the door by the end of the day.

Even so, the thought of Sunny riding a motorcycle in such frigid weather bothered him. Hell, the idea of her riding a motorcycle in any kind of weather bothered him. A Harley-Davidson might make the rider look like a badass and deliver a feeling of freedom on the open road, but they were also dangerous, especially in a town with too many jacked-up pickup trucks with horrible blind spots ready to send Sunny to an early grave.

But maybe that was the point.

The Sunny who had kissed him yesterday wasn't the same Sunny he'd fallen in love with in high school. The Sunny he'd once known had been overly cautious. He used to tease her when she obsessively washed her hands during flu season or refused to take off her life jacket when they went boating. He remembered her looking both ways one time before crossing a dirt path they'd taken to a fishing pond. He'd gotten such a kick out of joking about a stampeding herd of deer, but Sunny had just laughed and spouted off facts about how dangerous wildlife could be. This new Sunny didn't seem to give much of a damn about anything other than getting out of Morning Glory, and if it took flirting with death to do it, so be it.

The promised cold front had swept through overnight, blanketing the tiny yards in Grover's Park in crystalline lace. It should have made the late-February morning prettier, but instead it seemed to only emphasize the dingy surroundings, steeping the patched houses in tired gray. Perhaps March would finally deliver spring and cover the ugly with tender green and happy flowers.

When he pulled into the driveway, Sunny dropped her cigarette and ground it out with the toe of her boot. She wore all black today. Maybe it was a message.

"Good morning," he managed as she slid into the truck. He hadn't brought her coffee. Probably petty, but she'd not been very nice to him. He didn't owe her anything anyway.

But as her eyes darted to the empty cupholder, a twinge of guilt hit him. Pouring a cup of coffee was such a simple thing.

"Morning," she said, clicking herself into the seat.

He smelled the remains of her cigarette and tried not to grimace. He hated that she smoked. Just another reminder that he didn't really know her any longer. A good reason to stop trying to recreate what they once had. A good reason for not kissing her again.

Backing out of the drive, he spent the next few minutes about as comfortable as he'd be having a root canal without anesthesia. More than silence sat between them. The pain, the mistrust, the anger had built a wall, and neither of them seemed to know how to scale it or knock it down. And he wasn't sure if either of them wanted to.

He should have gotten her a damned rental car. None of this would have happened in the first place. They could have danced around the things that needed saying and pretended that they were grownups who had gotten past, well, the past.

"Are you going to say anything?" she asked, looking again at the empty cupholder. "Am I being punished for what happened last night?"

"No."

"Okay then."

Another few seconds of silence.

"I should have brought you coffee. I, uh, didn't have time to make a new pot before I left though."

"You don't owe me coffee. That's not what I was talking about."

"But it probably looked like I was being childish." And he had been. Not that he was going to admit to it.

"Deeter called me last night and said the part came in. I should have my bike back today, so you don't have to worry about coming to pick me up anymore. In fact, you don't have to worry about me at all." Her words sounded flat, but there was something in them. And that something he couldn't put a name to made him hurt.

He couldn't figure out why. It wasn't as if he loved her

anymore. Not really. Perhaps he still loved the concept of who she'd been—or rather who they'd been together—but this was a woman he didn't know any longer. A faint trace of who she was remained, and that wasn't enough to hold his heart hostage.

"I'm not worried about you," he said, more to himself than to her.

"Good."

He pulled into the school faculty parking lot. "Since we've cleared the air on not caring about one another, let's move on to what we do have between us. I'll pick you up about four to take you to Deeter's. I may be a little late because I have to run to Jackson today and don't know if I'll get held up."

"I can get a ride if I need to. Don't worry about me."

Her gorgeous blue eyes met his. The words he's said before sat between them—*I'm not worried about you.* But Henry knew he'd lied. He did worry about her, not because he loved her, but because it was who he was. So what? He was sucker for helping people, for trying to fix things, for going the extra mile. No one had ever said Henry Todd Delmar was a hard-ass.

"I'll text you."

"Bye," she said, shutting the door, shouldering the bag she carried. Then she walked away from him.

Henry sighed, wishing he could go back to how it was between them yesterday. At least they could talk to one another about the weather or the new development Wilson Caruthers was building on the edge of town. Something other than this discomfort.

Still, what they'd said the previous evening to one another was like lifting the edge of a scab to drain away infection beneath. The wound between them had been festering for a long time. Neither of them could pretend it had healed and faded. So maybe it had been a good thing that they'd said what each had been afraid to say. They exposed the ugly to the light. They released the infection, and now maybe, finally, the wound could heal. The words they'd spoken, as hard as they'd been to hear, were their only chance to find some sort of peace.

Or maybe he was hoping for something that would never happen.

Last night he'd lain awake thinking about her words… about the hurt in her voice. Maybe deep down in a place he didn't want to explore too much, he'd known she'd not meant what she said that long-ago afternoon when she'd declared they were over. Or maybe he had believed she was serious. Either way, it didn't change the fact he'd gone to the party with Jillian, drank half a bottle of bourbon, and given his virginity to a girl who hadn't mattered to him.

What he could remember was a knot of anger and hurt pulling tight inside him after he'd hung up the phone. At first he'd been so upset he'd told his roommate James that he wasn't going to attend Old South at all. James had flat-out refused to let Henry miss the party of the year. He'd liquored him up with Beam and 7 Up, light on the latter, and dragged him out the door. By that time, the anger and hurt had made Henry reckless. He picked up Jillian—who insisted on driving after seeing his condition—and spent the first thirty minutes of the party on the dance floor. After that, everything became a blur of loud music, booze, and Jillian unbuttoning his shirt.

He woke up naked the next morning in a frat brother's room. He'd rolled over and found a discarded condom package, the one he'd been carrying since junior high, and everything he'd drank the night before had come rushing back up.

After he'd brushed his teeth, he'd stared at himself in the mirror and uttered, "Well, shit."

Then crushing guilt had descended. His first time was supposed to have been with Sunny. They'd essentially promised that to each other. But hell, she'd broken up with him. Told him they were done and she wasn't even going to come to school at Ole Miss. She was the one who'd betrayed their promise to one another. Wasn't like he could do anything about it now. Besides, she'd never have to know.

Or was that cheating?

No, not cheating if they weren't together. Or at least he didn't think so. Were there guidelines for giving up your virginity to another girl the same day that your girlfriend told you she would never, never, NEVER get back together with you? Had to be, and he was pretty sure he wasn't in the wrong. And if Sunny gave her virginity up to someone the night before… Well, he'd kill the son of a bitch she'd slept with.

End of story.

Henry hadn't said anything to Sunny when she called that afternoon to apologize and tell him she'd won the school pageant. Miss Morning Glory High and he were back on track, maybe not officially but as legitimately as they could be. He told Jillian he wasn't ready to be in a relationship and he'd settle for being friends, and he called Sunny every day and snuck home to see her whenever he could duck out of class early.

It was all good.

Until Jillian had shown up with a giant wrecking ball that had plowed through the defense he'd erected between himself and the truth that he'd screwed up.

Henry had driven home, sobbing, punching his steering wheel, cursing the god who'd done this to him. Telling his parents hadn't been as bad as he'd expected. His father had never been particularly impressed with his only son and seemed to have been waiting for Henry to screw the pooch in a colossal way. His mother saw the opportunity to attach their name to one of the most prominent families in the state. The idea of her son marrying the granddaughter of a former governor and the child of a wealthy banker, even at such an early age, was preferable to Henry marrying white trash. But breaking the news to Sunny had been the worst experience of his life.

That afternoon had been breathtakingly pretty, with daffodils flaunting their cheerfulness and songbirds providing irritating accompaniment. The sky had been cloudless and blue as Sunny's eyes, mocking him as he pulled onto Park Street in Grover's Park.

Dread twisting his gut, he shut off his truck, knocked on the door, and found temporary reprieve in the form of Betty answering the door.

"Well, Henry Todd Delmar," she said, grabbing his arm and pulling him into a hug. Betty wore a shirt cut so low he could see all the way to China. Hooker heels made her tall enough that she was almost eye level, and she smelled of Virginia Slims, Poison perfume, and beer. "Here to see our girl, are you?"

Her words were slurred, but she wasn't out of her mind like she sometimes was.

"Uh, yeah. Is Sunny home yet?"

"Not yet, but come on in," Betty said, drawing him into her lair… um, living room.

A guy with motorcycle boots, paint-stained pants, and a sleeveless T-shirt weighed down the recliner. He glared at Henry and then went back to watching a weight lifting competition on the television.

"That's Claude." Betty jabbed a scarlet-tipped finger at the moody, muscular man who did not fit his name.

"Hello," Henry said to the sullen mountain.

The mountain grunted.

"You want something to drink? The beer's cold." Betty gestured to a Styrofoam ice chest sitting on the couch.

"You ain't giving that shithead my beer." Claude eyeballed Henry.

"No, I'm good," Henry said, shifting from one foot to the other. He didn't want to deliver this news to Sunny while Claude was here. A sobbing Sunny and a pissed-off Betty might set Claude off. They'd probably never find Henry's body. "Uh, maybe I better come back later."

"Why? She'll be here in a little bit. I made some brownies. The good kind." Betty laughed. Even Claude managed a smile at that.

"No, thanks." Henry tried to remember all the ways out of the house. The back screen door stuck sometimes. He'd have to remember that if it came to running for his life. Mount Claude was big, but Henry was likely much quicker.

"Come 'ere." Claude pulled Betty into his lap. He squeezed her ass and nuzzled his head between her breasts.

Henry looked away, studying the print Sunny had told him belonged to her grandmother. There was a windmill and wildflowers. And a tiny field mouse in the corner. When he heard the slap on Betty's butt, he knew Claude was finished mauling her.

Just as Betty clacked toward the kitchen, Sunny pushed into the house.

"Henry," she crowed, running to him and throwing her arms around him. "Oh my gosh, I can't believe you surprised me like this."

He hugged her, savoring the feel of her in his arms. Her hair smelled clean, and she squeezed him so tight he thought he might like to go ahead and die right there. "Yeah, I had to come home to do a few things."

She peeled herself off him and sparkled like only Sunny could. "I'm so happy."

And then he decided it might be good for Claude to rip his arms off and beat him to death with them. Because he was lower than dog crap. "Yeah, uh, good."

Her gaze narrowed. "What's wrong?"

"Can we go somewhere, um, more private?"

Betty cackled. "I bet you want to."

Claude snorted, and Sunny turned the color of Betty's fingernails.

"We can go outside." He motioned to the porch. "It's pretty today."

"You can go to her room, boy," Betty said, perching on the arm of the recliner and dragging her nails through Claude's receding hairline. "Y'all are old enough."

Sunny's color didn't fade, and Henry found heat rushing to his face too. Jesus, Betty needed a filter.

"Come on," Sunny said, obviously wanting to escape her mother and new paramour more than Henry did. "I have some homework, and you can keep me company."

"Is that what they're calling it these days?" Claude called before he and Betty dissolved into laughter.

"I need to do some homework too," Betty cooed.

"God," Sunny said, turning on her light, pulling him inside her room, and shutting the door. "Sorry."

Henry tried to smile. "That's okay. I know how your mother is. At least she's entertaining. All mine does is drink tea and host committee meetings."

Sunny rolled her eyes but then turned to him, pulling him into an embrace. She rested her head against his chest. Tears sprang into Henry's eyes.

"Hey, Sunny. Um, I gotta talk to you."

"What's wrong, babe?" She peered up at him. She was so pretty, and at that moment, totally untouched by the pain he was about to bring her. He took a mental picture because he knew he was about to erase her innocence.

"It's something not easy to say."

Her gaze clouded. "What's wrong? Is it your grades? Your parents? I know things have been hard for you. For us. Not being together. But—"

"I messed up. Not on grades. On us."

Her arms dropped from his waist. "I don't understand."

"Remember the day of the pageant? When you broke up with me and said you were going to Mississippi State?"

"Yeah. Of course I remember. But that's in the past..." Understanding dawned on her face. Her beautiful face. "You had Old South that night. That's why you didn't come to the pageant."

A curtain of silence whooshed down.

Sunny swallowed, her gaze searching him. "What did you do?"

"I, uh... Jesus."

"Henry?" Her voice nearly squeaked, and he saw the panic in

her eyes. Her hands fisted and unfisted. "Tell me."

"I got her pregnant." His words were like the crack of a felled tree crashing through the underbrush and landing so hard he nearly lost his balance.

Lightning flashed, thunder shook the house, the floors opened, and Satan reached up to grab him by the throat. Or at least that's what it felt like to watch Sunny's eyes widen, her pretty mouth gape, her face crumple into hopelessness.

Sunny's knees buckled and she landed on the bed. "What? Who… I don't understand how you got… You got someone pregnant?"

She sat there. He stood there. One second ticked by. Another. And another.

"You slept with that girl? Jillian? The one your mother pushed on you?"

Henry couldn't swallow. His mouth was as dry as Mississippi baked clay on an August afternoon. A nod was all he could manage.

Sunny's eyes filled with tears. "I don't understand. You… you were *with* her?"

Henry couldn't talk. Couldn't confirm. He stood there, worthless, while Sunny sat on the bed, her eyes blinking, her hands latching, unlatching, latching again.

Effing bluebirds chirped at the windowsill. Betty laughed in the living room. The thunk of weights hitting the floor came from the too-loud TV. Time should have stood still, but it didn't.

Eventually her gaze found his, and he could see she finally understood exactly what he'd done. Because her eyes hardened and her mouth flattened.

"Get out," she whispered.

"Sunny, I know this seems bad, but I can fix it." He had no clue how, but he'd figure out something. Jillian was insistent that she was going to have the baby, but maybe they could put it up for adoption or something.

"How?" Her blue eyes crackled. "Make her get an abortion?

What the hell would that matter? You *slept* with her, Henry. You… It was supposed to be me. Me for you. You for me. That's what you said. You promised that we were meant to be and—"

"I know what I promised." He went to her, caught her hands.

Sunny ripped them away, standing and pushing him back. "Don't touch me. Don't you dare touch me."

"Sunny, please." He tried to reach out to her. He had to make her understand that he loved her. That he'd been drunk and Jillian had been drunk too. That nothing could change how much he loved Sunny. It was a stupid mistake. A mess-up. "I'm sorry. I'm so sorry. I didn't mean for it to happen."

"Get out of my house. Now. And don't ever call me, touch me, or even look at me ever again."

"Please, Sunshine, you're my life."

"Get out. Or I'll call that piece of shit my mother's screwing and tell him to kick your ass. I mean it. Out." She turned her face away from him, tears streaming down her cheeks. Sunny closed her eyes.

"Sun—"

"Claude!" Sunny screamed. "Claude!"

"Okay, okay," Henry said, patting the air. "I'll go, but just know I love you, Sunny. I love you. I'll always love you."

She turned to him right as the door opened. "You're dead to me."

"No," Henry said as Claude filled the doorway.

"What you need, Sunny?" Mount Claude asked.

"Get rid of him," Sunny said, her tearful eyes cold as ice.

Henry went backward as Claude grabbed his shirt and pulled him from the room. His feet scrabbled on the worn hardwood floor but couldn't find traction. Everything became a blur after that. Betty screaming at him, Claude shaking him so hard his teeth rattled, and the cut from slamming into the porch rail when the big guy tossed him out the front door. Henry slunk to his truck, climbed inside, and let his head fall onto the steering wheel. Tears mingled with the blood from the cut on his cheek.

Two weeks later, after avoiding his calls, dodging his attempt to show up after school, and refusing the letters, flowers, and desperate pleas he sent her, Sunny Voorhees left Morning Glory.

And she never came back.

Until over a month ago.

Henry ran his hand over the center of his steering wheel. He wished he could rub out the memory of that terrible day. It had happened long ago, yet felt so fresh in his memories. The life he'd had… the love for that girl… wouldn't fade.

His phone rang.

Work.

"Yeah?" he barked into his cell phone.

"Hey, bud, we got a problem here at the site. This cold's messing with the pour, so we may need to get Ronnie Primm out here. Or Mother Nature on the line," Carson said.

"I'm there in two minutes. Put in the call and I'll meet you at the site."

"Which one? Ronnie or that cold-ass bitch Mother Nature?" Carson laughed.

"Both." Henry hung up and pulled away from the school and the woman whose heart he'd broken all those years ago.

chapter nine

SUNNY TAPPED HER pen on the white space of the agenda and sipped her coffee as Grace Metcalf outlined the plan for the 5K race to raise money for a local animal rescue. The small committee had decided to meet at the local coffee/ice cream shop—the Lazy Frog—to discuss how to raise seed money for the organization. Henry had dropped her off, and she'd asked her aunt to pick her up afterward. Her bike wasn't ready because they'd sent the wrong part to Deeter.

Because, of course.

Deeter had apologized profusely and promised to have it done by the beginning of next week. Next Wednesday at the latest. Sunny just had to get through one more week of depending on the kindness of strangers… and her ex-boyfriend.

Dammit.

"What's the actual name of the rescue?" Sunny asked when Grace took a breath.

"Uh, we haven't really come up with one yet. Right now we're calling it Rankin County Animal Rescue Organization. I mean, we'll figure it out before the race. This is just preliminary."

"You *have* applied for nonprofit status, right? Businesses will be receptive to donating money and services if they can write it off as a donation."

"Um, not yet," Grace said, looking around at the small group as if questioning whether one of them might have thought of that.

Sunny took in a deep breath. She didn't want to overstep since she was low man on the totem pole so to speak, but Grace's organizational skills were nil. "We can't ask people to support something that isn't actually in existence. I would say putting on a 5K is a great idea, but if you want people to buy in, you need to have a mission statement, a vision, and a catchy name that says we love animals and are here to help them. I volunteered doing paperwork at Happy Hounds Dog Rescue in North Carolina. Happy Hounds. Sounds like something people want to support, right? Rankin County Animal Rescue is fine but it's also very utilitarian. Maybe we could host a contest to name the animal rescue? Is there a Facebook page?"

Grace stared at her for a few long seconds.

Sunny wondered if she should have turned down the invitation to help. Who wanted a bossy volunteer who wasn't going to be sticking around anyway? She had no skin in the game. Other than finding Fancy a home, of course.

Grace sighed. "No. We've just been doing work on the ground—building doghouses, delivering hay, picking up strays, and trying to find them homes. I guess maybe we shouldn't have put in to do the race until we had our ducks in a row. It's just we're so overwhelmed with doing the actual work, you know? And we need some money. We can't keep using our own funds."

"I understand," Sunny said, giving a smile to Ed Hermann, Nancy Odom, and Peggy Lattier, who were part of the committee… and likely the only members of the soon-to-be rescue group. "And that's the most important part. You're helping animals, and that's the main goal, so a mission statement should be easy to compose. I can build a Facebook page and file the paperwork with the state. Do we have any seed money to pay for applying for our status?"

"I got it," Ed said. He was a gruff man who ran a lawn-care

service. Sunny had known him all her life. "Just tell me who to write the check to. We gotta do something. Too many people letting their dogs and cats have litters. It's become a problem."

"Which could become part of our action statement. Education for owners about spaying and neutering. There's a lot we can do, but we need to do some administrative work first."

"I'm so glad you're helping us," Nancy said, reaching over to pat Sunny's hand. Nancy had been Sunny's Sunday school teacher once. She was as quiet as her husband Fred was talkative. "God sent you to us."

God had nothing to do with it. Sunny needed to find a home for Fancy… even though her mother had relented and let the dog stay longer than the initial two days she'd been given. Besides, helping this group of animal activists gave her something more to dwell on than Henry, the kiss, and the memories she'd tried to bury. And she was tired of spending all her free time with a paintbrush and her mother. A person can only watch so much crime television. And painting was lonely business. "I'm happy to help. This is something I believe in. I like dogs."

"You don't like cats?" Peggy asked, sounding offended.

"Uh, sure. I like cats." Sorta. The ones she'd grown up with had hissed and spit at her. And though there had been some scary dogs, her aunt's sweet Maltese-poodle mix had endeared her to puppies.

"I have five cats," Peggy said.

"Oh wow," Sunny said as she watched Peggy pull her phone out.

"This is Mr. McFluff, here's Rosie, and this is Stitch. These two rascals are Han Solo and Chewie." Peggy flipped through, like, a bazillion pictures of cats. Cats on top of laundry baskets. Cats rolling on the floor with ribbons. Cats licking themselves. "Oops, those are private ones."

Peggy stifled a giggle.

Oh jeez.

"Well, my point is we need a name, a logo, a website, a nonprofit status, a board, and maybe some brochures. Who's working with county animal services? We need a good contact who wants to help us and serve as a liaison. We can use our Facebook page to post animals and perhaps get some home owners' associations on board to help us network lost pups and recruit fosters. Oh, and we need to contact the paper. Do a press release about the run. That needs to be done yesterday." Sunny made notes on her legal pad. If she was going to do this, it needed to be done right.

No one said anything, and when she looked up, everyone was staring at her.

"What?"

"That's a lot of stuff," Grace said, looking worried. "We already sent something to the paper, didn't we?"

Nancy nodded. "I learned how to do a press release online and sent them one."

"Good, and it's not really that much work. There are four of us and we can divide up some of the tasks. We need some more volunteers. I'll call my sister's friend Rosemary Reynolds and see if she might help out. She knows everyone, and if you want something done in this town, she's a sure bet."

Grace nodded. "Yeah, if we can get her on board, that would be awesome. But she's Rosemary Genovese now."

Sunny shook her head. "I always forget, but I'll call her. Now, we need to get the race applications printed and put up online. I'll create the form."

An hour later, Sunny waved goodbye to the committee members. They each had a list of things to do by the next meeting.

Grace lingered. "Thank you, Sunny. I mean truly. I am a big-picture kind of person, and I'm all in when it comes to trapping cats or picking up hurt puppies, but websites and Facebook pages make me feel nauseated."

Sunny shrugged. "I'm happy to help y'all get started. I loved volunteering at Happy Hounds. I'm going to put in a call to Sherrie Woods who started the rescue group and run everything past her to make sure we're not forgetting something."

"That would be awesome." Grace picked up her coffee cup. "By the way, Henry Delmar said he'd sponsor and assist with the race. He's helped with several other races around here. One for St. Jude's and another for the American Heart Association. I know you and he have a past. That won't be a problem, will it?"

Sunny shook her head. "I guess people still talk, huh?"

Grace looked a bit embarrassed. "Well, it's a small town."

"Yeah, it is, but Henry would be a good person to help. He cares about this community."

"I wasn't being nosy. I mentioned your name to one of the other teachers. She told me about how you were, like, the valedictorian, beauty queen, cat's meow… and what happened with him."

"Yeah, well, that's all in the past." Sunny believed her words. Or tried to. The accusations they'd hurled at each other the night before had loosened something inside her. For too many years she'd bottled up the pain, ignored it, nailed the entrance to her heart shut. Which was probably why her marriage had floundered so badly. She'd let Alan only get so far with her before warning bells went off. If she'd been braver with her heart, perhaps she and Alan would have been much happier and she could have erased the damage Henry had done.

She wished she could go back in time and berate herself for being so protective of her heart. Lots of people lost in love. Plenty of women had their guys cheat on them. She'd gotten her heart broken when she was a teenager. Big deal. Alan didn't deserve to suffer the repercussions of her broken heart. But he had because she'd not been able to let it go. So much of who she was had hinged on Henry, Ole Miss, and their dreams.

When Henry burned her down, he'd destroyed more than her heart. He'd broken her spirit.

If she could talk some sense into the girl she'd been, she would. That stupid child had thrown away a full-ride scholarship, her title of valedictorian, and a shot at being the first Voorhees to get a college degree. She now realized she'd been ill-equipped to deal with her world falling apart. She'd had little support—her emotional gene pool was barely deep enough to get her feet wet when wading in.

And after enduring two weeks of the town talking about Henry Todd knocking up the governor's granddaughter along with suffering pitying glances, she'd reached a tipping point. Which pretty much happened at the end-of-the-year PTA meeting. She'd attended because as the outgoing student council president, she had to make a final report on student activities and receive her PTA gift. Right after the meeting concluded, she'd overheard Patsy Reynolds tell Lydia Mason that the Delmar boy was marrying the girl he'd gotten pregnant that May.

Henry Todd was getting married.

No fixing that.

After Sunny had finished sobbing in the girls' bathroom of MGHS, she caught a ride to Henry's house, hoping he'd come home from college by now. Her friend waited while she knocked on the front door of his colossal home. Annaleigh had answered. Sunny had tried to smile, but she knew she wore her grief.

"Is Henry home yet, Mrs. Delmar?"

"He is, but he's out with his father. Buying wedding rings." Annaleigh's expression was almost sly. As if she thrilled at delivering that news.

Sunny felt as if she'd been punched in the face. Henry was going to marry the debutante. Or almost debutante. Maybe they didn't let girls who were preggers be presented at their fancy shindigs. Sunny wouldn't know.

"Will you tell him I came by?" Sunny managed, swallowing the raw ache in her throat.

Annaleigh had cocked her head, her eyes finally softening. "Sunny, I think it would be best if I didn't tell him you were here. Darling, you're gonna have to let Henry Todd go. His situation has changed, and he doesn't need you distracting him from what he's honor bound to do. Besides, Jillian will make him an appropriate partner in life."

Sunny had stared at Henry's mother. Appropriate partner? "But—"

Annaleigh stepped outside onto the porch and took her elbow, turning her around. "Now, sugar, I know it's hard, but sometimes you have to let go of the thing you wanted because it's not meant to be. I know you and my son had fun in high school, but high school is over. That time is over. Now go on home and don't make trouble. Do that because it's the right thing to do."

Sunny didn't respond as she walked down the steps toward her friend's car. She felt like a zombie on the outside, but inside something had broken. Her heart had fallen and shattered into a million pieces. Sunny knew she could never in a hundred years put herself back together again. As her friend backed out of the drive, Sunny watched Annaleigh Delmar raise her hand in farewell and knew that Henry's mother was right.

Sometimes a meant-to-be could never be.

When Sunny got home, she packed her suitcase, pulled out the graduation money she'd hidden in the floorboards beneath her closet, and bought a bus ticket to Charlotte, North Carolina. A friend she'd met at Close Up in DC lived there and said she could come stay until she could figure out what to do with her life.

Sunny didn't tell anyone she was leaving. She put a letter to Eden underneath her pillow that her sister didn't find for a week. By then Sunny had met Alan David in a bus station, lost her virginity, and was living in a one-bedroom apartment outside a Marine base.

She married Alan one month later.

Game over.

Grace snapped her fingers in front of Sunny's face. "Hey, Sunny."

"Oh, sorry. Too much on my mind. What were we talking about?"

"Henry Delmar. I saw him giving you rides. Heard about his kid running over your motorcycle too." Grace didn't seem to be nosy, just matter of fact.

"Yeah, heck of a way to run into your old boyfriend." Sunny shrugged into her jacket and glanced at her phone. Her aunt still had a half hour before she could pick Sunny up.

"You need a ride?" Grace asked, glancing out the glass door toward the parking area.

"My aunt is coming. I'll hang out here with Sassy. Been a while since I visited with her."

"You sure? I mean, it will give people something else to talk about. A lesbian with a Harley-riding former beauty queen. We could make headlines."

"Won't that upset your girlfriend?"

"Nah." Grace laughed. "I know where my bread is buttered. I don't look for any other… other…"

"Buns?" Sunny winked.

Grace burst out laughing. "Oh Lord."

"Thanks for the offer, but I'm set. Have a good night, Grace. I'll be in touch about all the things I'm doing."

Grace waved to Sassy and slipped out the door.

"It's a good thing you're doing, helping them get set up," Sassy Grigsby said from behind the counter. "We've been needing something like this for a while. Got a whole passel of feral cats out by my house. I hate to call animal control. They'll just put 'em down."

Sunny nodded at the older woman. The Lazy Frog had been in business longer than most small businesses in Morning Glory, namely because of Sassy. The coffee and ice cream were always good, but the company was better. Sassy had a warmness that extended beyond the counter and permeated the cheerful eatery. People came for the treats but stayed for the atmosphere. The café had been Eden and her group of friends' go-to place for years. In fact, Sunny knew exactly what table they always sat at and what chairs they occupied.

"Well, it's something I can do," Sunny said.

"To give back?"

"If you want to call it that. I might as well be useful before I leave."

"You're getting out of town that quick, huh?" Sassy smiled.

"By the end of summer. I'm trying to get Mama in the Arbor. I think it would be good for her to have some stimulation. Do some activities and not be alone."

Sassy sniffed. "She ain't alone if you're there, is she?"

"I'm not staying here." No sense beating around the bush.

"Yeah, that's what I thought once too," Sassy said, tapping at the register. "I moved to Chicago, but I came back. Too damn cold up there."

"That's why I'm moving to California. I have a friend there who married a guy who owns an insurance agency. He's going to give me a job."

"Well, that sounds nice. A new start, huh?"

"If I can get my mama to sell the house."

"Mmm," Sassy said, looking out into the inky night, her brown eyes searching for something likely not there. "So what's with you and Henry?"

"Nothing. He's giving me rides since his kid destroyed my bike. That's it."

"But it's unfinished business, ain't it?" Sassy looked back at Sunny.

"Not really. All that happened long ago, and it's not like it's that big of a deal. We were two dumb kids who found out life ain't so easy. Two kids who built a dream world, pretty pages with pretty pictures, and thought love was enough. But when you're eighteen, love is like an empty box wrapped in fancy paper finished with a bow. It looks good, but when you pull the ends of the ribbons and tear off the paper, you're left with an empty box. So there's nothing unfinished between me and Henry. We're two people tolerating each other until we can move on and forget again."

Sassy studied her for a few seconds. "Well, hell, if that ain't the saddest thing I ever heard."

Sunny lifted a shoulder. "But it's the truth."

"Is it? Or what you want to believe?"

"So is this the part where you give me sage, mystical advice? Like you're Morgan Freeman playing at God? You gonna reveal to me how stupid or blind I am?" Sunny tried to keep her words light because she'd always liked Sassy Grigsby. The woman had a gentle spirit, a weakness for weird shoes, and a soft spot for Sunny's sister, but she didn't need anyone trying to make something from nothing.

Even if it hadn't felt like nothing last night when Henry had kissed her.

"No, I guess I'm asking the questions everyone's too afraid to ask you. I know your aunt Ruby Jean's a good woman, but she's running that office and it's tax season. Trusting your mama for good advice is like trusting a timber rattler."

"I don't need advice, Miss Sassy. I need to finish my mama's house and find a new life in California. There's nothing left for me here, and maybe there never was." Sunny believed those words. She couldn't imagine staying in Morning Glory. Or maybe she couldn't imagine herself being happy in Morning Glory. It had been so long since she'd been content, and even then those moments had been fleeting. The only time she'd felt like she belonged, like she fit somewhere, was when she'd been with Henry. The rest of the time she'd been pretending.

"I understand, Sunny. I do," Sassy said, pushing the change drawer shut and walking to the glass door to flip the CLOSED sign over.

Her words made Sunny's heart ache, but aching was her normal. She felt much like a wounded bird flapping around, merely existing.

Lights swept the front of the coffee shop. "Aunt Ruby Jean is here. Enjoy the rest of your evening."

Sassy walked over and pulled Sunny into a hug. For a moment

Sunny stiffened, but then she relaxed, inhaling the scent of lavender mixed with coffee in Sassy's cornrows.

"Don't be too set on always leaving, Sunny. I spent a lifetime running from who I am, and I wasted a lot of time. I ain't saying you're wrong, but when you only keep your eyes on the road in front of you, you miss the life passing you by."

Sunny pulled away. "Dang it. You had to go Morgan Freeman on me, didn't you?"

Sassy just smiled and turned to wave at Aunt Ruby Jean, who'd tooted her horn during the hug. "Can't help who I am, and I still think Morgan Freeman is a fine-ass man."

"I wouldn't change you for the world, Sassy Grigsby," Sunny said, grabbing her bag and slipping out the door. The cold wind met her, but the warmth of Sassy's hug stayed with her, along with words she didn't want to hear.

Nothing wrong with fixing one's eyes on the prize.

Her prize would be California.

Not Morning Glory. Not Mississippi.

And damn sure not Henry Todd Delmar.

Fancy wasn't in her kennel when Sunny pushed into her bedroom and dropped her bag on the bed. Alarm coiled through her gut. When she'd gotten home, her mother was parked in front of the television, as usual, an empty paper plate scattered with toast crumbs indicating she'd fended for herself. Another step in the right direction. After years of giving up, maybe Betty was showing a little fight.

"Mama, where's the dog?" Sunny called, hurrying back into the living area. Her aunt had let Fancy out when she'd come home for lunch and to check on Sunny's mama. And Vienna, the aide who came to help Betty each day, had assured Sunny she would let the dog out occasionally to stretch its legs. "Did Vienna leave her out?"

"She's in my bedroom," Betty said, her eyes not leaving the

sight of a detective roughing up a suspect on the television.

"Who?"

"The damn dog. I told Vi to leave her out. The mutt was whining."

Sunny stared at her mother. "You told her to leave the dog out?"

"Are you effin' deaf? I couldn't take all that caterwaulin' it was doin'."

Sunny arched an eyebrow.

Betty ripped her gaze from the television. "That stupid dog was driving me batshit crazy. Easier to let her out. I don't care as long as she don't come bothering me, begging for food and stuff."

Sunny opened her mother's bedroom door to find Fancy curled up on the afghan her great-grandmother had made. The makeshift pallet was messy, as if the dog had dug around on it, or perhaps her mother had pulled it down from the bench underneath the window. Either way, Fancy's tail thumped before she rose and stretched. A yippy little yawn followed, and then the dog sat, tongue lolling out, looking like she was smiling at Sunny.

"Well, didn't take long for you to settle in, did it, girl?" Sunny waggled the leash. "Let's go out and potty."

The dog didn't move because she didn't particularly like the leash.

Sunny sank down on the floor and patted her knees. "Come here, Fancy Pants. I'm not going to hurt you. I won't let anyone hurt you ever again. I won't let you be cold or hungry. I won't let a truck mow you down. Come here, girl."

Fancy inched toward her, ever wary, but she came to Sunny. Sunny took a moment to fuss over the dog, liking the way it felt to rub her bat-like ears and clench a fist in the ruff of her neck. The sarcoptic mange had made her hair thin beneath her neck and on her chest, but Sunny could tell the dog would have thick, gorgeous hair once she healed. She clipped the leash onto

Fancy's secondhand collar. "That's a girl. Let's go out and see what's what in the hood."

Fancy pulled her head back, but with Sunny's cooing, she finally took a few steps.

"Mama, I'm taking Fancy out. Be right back."

"Stupid name for a stray mutt. Fancy, my ass." Betty tucked something away with her good hand.

"Are those my cigarettes?" Sunny said, dropping the leash and stalking over to her mother.

"No." Betty shoved whatever it was underneath her thigh.

Sunny reached down and found her pack of cigarettes. Betty had had a stroke and was on enough medication to kill a moose. She wasn't supposed to be sneaking cigarettes. "So these are yours?"

"God, Sunny. I don't have shit in life. The least you could do is let me have a smoke."

"You could have more in your life if you'd stop feeling sorry for yourself and stop stewing in your own poisonous juices. You can change, you know. You can do something more than sit here and watch television. You can do a lot of things, but the one thing you can't do is smoke. Unless you want to have another stroke?"

"Only if it will kill me this time," Betty said, sounding defeated.

"Good. Then I wouldn't need your permission to sell the house." Even as Sunny said the words, she knew they were the wrong ones. And she was sinking to Betty's level. If she went down there, she might stay there.

"You'd like that, wouldn't you?" Betty said, lifting up eyes the same color as Sunny's. Sunny thought she might have seen some hurt radiating within the depths, but then again, it could have been the flicker from the TV. "You're nothing like your sister. Eden didn't like me much, but she was respectful and kind. You're as empty as I am."

Betty's words slammed into her. Empty. Was that what she

was? "Maybe so, but I'm not taking your crap, Mama. You manipulate people the way you always have, except now instead of using sex, you use pity. The only way you're going to get better is if people stop catering to you and expect you to be better than what you are."

"You're a bitch."

"I learned from the best." Sunny walked back over to the dog, who sat looking wary. She picked up the leash, telling herself to calm down. Dealing with Betty wasn't easy. Especially after a long day of working at the school and attending the rescue meeting. "Come on, Fancy."

The dog obeyed, and they pushed out into the inky evening. Stars winked at them and cars whooshed past as they walked along the cracked sidewalk. Fancy sniffed every clump of weeds, every fence post.

Sunny jumped as a truck pulled to the side of the road.

Henry.

Great. Just what she needed. Someone else to argue with.

The engine shut off and the door opened. Sunny stopped, though she thought about ignoring him.

"Hey, Sunny, can I talk to you for a minute?"

"You're here, and I'm sort of unable to shut the door on you."

Henry stopped, frowned, and then shook his head. "Okay, yeah, I get you're mad at me, and so I guess that's why I'm here."

She didn't say anything because she wasn't going to admit to being upset, even though inside she was knotted up. No, not knotted, more like pressure building up. Grace's words, Sassy's remarks, and the whole kissing thing with Henry had compressed inside her until she felt like she might blow.

"I know you say I can't fix things, but we can't go on acting like this to one another."

"Why not?" she asked, turning away from him and back in the direction she'd been heading. Fancy sniffed along the sidewalk.

"Because it's petty and we're adults." Henry fell into step beside her, his big body somehow comforting beside her even though she didn't want it to be.

She knew his words were true. They *were* adults. And maybe she'd been attaching things she shouldn't attach to the stupid kiss last night and to the stupid residual feelings she obviously still had for him. She'd carried around the pain Henry had inflicted for so long now that it was hard to surrender it. Not like she was in the best place in life. Being rational probably wasn't even an option at this point. "I guess that much is true."

His arm brushed hers, and she moved to put more distance between them. Her mind tumbled over and over itself, and all she could conclude was that she had tired of so much in life. What Henry had done to her once had been shitty, but how much longer could she hold on to the resentment, to the pain, to the… oh God… emptiness? She could go on being a bitch to him, acting like her mother, but what was that worth? Her pride?

Maybe what it boiled down to was that she was just plain tired of being a victim.

"Grace asked me to help with the 5K. I hesitated because of you, but I like helping my community. I'm good at organizing races, and the animal rescue is a good cause, so I told her yes. But that means over the next month, you and I will occasionally have to deal with one another. I know you don't like me much anymore, but I'm hoping we can put all of this stuff behind us, including what happened last night."

She glanced at him. "You're talking about the kiss?"

Henry shrugged. "Not just that. Obviously, that was… something crazy and unintended. But I'm talking about the words we said. Some of them needed to be said, and it's not like we can take them back."

"I don't want to. I want you to know what you did to me." She crossed her arms over her chest before realizing she looked pathetic. She dropped them and lifted her chin, looking him in the eye. "But I'm tired of being angry."

Her words were the only peace offering she had. She had to

move beyond the past if she wanted to claim a better future.

His shoulders lowered. "That's good."

"Look," she said, jerking Fancy's leash when the dog moved toward a soggy mass of garbage that had been spilled from a trash can. "You're right. We were kids. You screwed up. Hell, I screwed up. We both got hurt. And we've lived our lives. I'm not saying I forgive you, but then again, maybe I should. I don't know. It's all such a mess."

"You don't have to forgive me, Sunny. I own what I did. I screwed up. But I can't change it. I wish I could. But it's done. I would rather we try to see who we are now. We don't have to be friends, but we can set aside our past in order to help put on this race. So we can help animals like Fancy." He bent down and rubbed Fancy's ears. She ducked away and went over to smell a clump of new clover.

"She's still a little afraid." And maybe Sunny was too. Trust was a hard thing to give when you'd been knocked down time and again for wanting to believe.

"It's okay, Fancy. You've probably got good reason."

The dog's ears pricked, and she looked at Henry.

"Hey, she knows her name," Sunny said, glancing over at Henry, feeling herself soften. "I guess that's what this rescue is about—do-overs."

"I'd like to think so."

Sunny looked up at the night sky.

The concept of a do-over was ludicrous. She and Henry couldn't start over. She knew too much about him. Like he loved strawberry shortcake and could fly-fish. She knew he had a scar on the back of his thigh. She had once counted the freckles across his nose, freckles that had disappeared with age. Yet there was much she didn't know about him, and she wasn't certain she needed to try to know him better.

Sunny ripped her eyes from the horizon and looked at the man next to her. "I think we can manage a friendship of sorts."

They walked a few yards before Henry dangled something in

front of her eyes. Keys.

"I'm going out of town for a week. Katie Clare has to have a small procedure on her eyes. I'll be in Jackson until next Wednesday. This is a loaner from the Chevy dealership. Deeter says your Harley will be ready next week, and I hope you won't be upset, but I called about your mother's van and got a little ugly with the guy there. They're going to pull her van up in the repair schedule so it will be fixed by the end of next week too. Riding a Harley in forty- or fifty-degree weather is tough. I get you're an independent woman, but I doubt you want to lose your nose to frostbite. It's parked over there."

He gestured to a small Chevy compact car sitting beneath the lamppost. She hadn't even noticed it earlier.

"Always fixing things for people," she commented, taking the keys. She wanted to ask about his daughter. She wanted to thank him for being kind. And deep down in places she didn't want to acknowledge, she wanted to kiss him again. But she did none of those things. "I guess this is a part of the old Henry that the new Henry never forgot. You're a true Southern gentleman."

He gave her a shrug. "Can't help who I am."

The same words Sassy had said earlier.

Maybe people couldn't help who they were. Maybe Sunny couldn't help who she was either. Life had made her hard, but it hadn't defeated her. She wasn't going to let it.

"I'll see you when you get back. Grace mentioned another meeting on Wednesday. Until then, let me know what sponsorships you get for the race. We need those finalized by Monday if possible, so use that Delmar charm to get us some money. I'll work on the logo. Peggy's nephew is doing the race shirts and posters, but I have to have the logo to him by Monday. Lots to do, but we can do it. Sometimes a shorter deadline is better than having months. It's going to work."

"Yeah, it's going to work," he said, his words sounding as if they were about more than the race. Henry seemed a bit lighter, and Sunny could swear she felt a bit lighter herself. Henry blew on his hands and then rubbed them together to thwart the chill of the night. "Better get back home. I have too much to do before moving headquarters to Jackson for a week."

"See ya, Henry."

"Yeah, have a good week, Sunny." Henry jogged toward his truck and opened the door. The cab light spilled out, so she could see his features. He lifted a hand and then climbed inside, shutting the door.

Sunny watched his taillights fade before heading back home. Her body felt frozen, but she wondered if her heart had started to thaw. Something inside her had shifted. Maybe she wasn't as empty as her mother had declared. Maybe she still had something inside worth nurturing.

"Let's go home, Fancy."

Home.

She'd said the words, but she knew the house on Park Street wasn't her home. Not really. Or maybe it was a little. After all, she couldn't point to any other place that could be called home. So, yeah, maybe it truly was home… at least until she could make a new one on the West Coast.

Fancy barked and pulled toward the tiny house with the sagging porch as if she agreed.

Temporary was better than nothing.

chapter ten

MARCH HAD COME in like a lion. Or at least a really pissed-off kitty cat.

Struggling to keep his jacket from flying up over his head, Henry walked toward the Lazy Frog and the meeting with the committee putting on the 5K race. He'd spent the past week doting on his daughter and running his son back and forth from soccer games and baseball practice. Katie Clare's surgery to correct her slightly lazy eye had gone well, and his little diva had milked all she could out of being a patient. Ice cream, a new American Girl Doll book, and fuzzy owl slippers had been bestowed, along with the watching of Disney Channel every afternoon. He knew all the lingo and cute new boy bands. Go, daddy.

He passed Sal's New York Pizzeria, stopping to wave at Sal who stood at the register. Sal gave him a salute and mimed Henry giving him a call. Sal had a natural love of history and had joined the Rankin County Historical Society, even carpooling with Fred Odom—bless him—to the meetings. He'd been after Henry to join them. They were thinking about turning Greg Batten's museum into the Morning Glory Historical Museum. Henry wasn't that into history, but he liked Sal and the man's enthusiasm for all things small town.

Rosemary pushed out the door and fell in step with him. "Jeez, this wind is terrible. Okay if I walk with you? Sunny asked me to join the committee."

"Sure. Glad you're joining up. We're a bit behind on some things, and no one knows how to get people on track better than you." He smiled down at the strawberry blonde who wore saddle oxfords. A pearl choker peeked out from beneath her oxford shirt. Rosemary indulged her fetish for all things vintage by dressing like a '50s Barbie doll. He rather loved that about Sal's wife.

Rosemary made a snorting noise. "No kidding. Grace isn't very good at details. I mean, one month to pull together a 5K? She better be glad she got Sunny Voorhees on board because— "

"David," he interrupted.

"Oh, yeah. Whatever. Anyway, we can do it. Just not on a big scale. Won't have as many participants as we'd have if we'd started months ago, but it can still make us money since so many people are donating services. I have a folder," she said, holding up a red-and-white polka-dotted file folder. The wind battered it. She tucked it under her arm.

"So you do."

"Hey, you're a good-looking guy. You enter the bachelor auction this year?"

Alarms clanged in his head. "Lord, no."

"Why not? You're single, and it's for a good cause. I talked Clem into doing it, and he's moving away soon." Rosemary slid a sly smile his way. "But maybe you have your eye on someone else? Someone who strikes up old feelings?"

Henry gave her a deadpan look. "Really, Rosemary? Sunny and I negotiated a truce, and I'm hoping I can keep her from carving me up and dining on my liver."

Rosemary laughed. "No one eats liver anymore."

"Tell that to Sunny," he said, trying for humor. Since he'd

gone to Sunny's house last week and waved the peace flag, he and his ex-girlfriend had been able correspond amicably about the 5K. Sunny had designed a cheerful website with frolicking puppies and cuddly kittens and started a contest to name the Rankin County Rescue. Peggy Lattier had taken care of filing for the nonprofit status, and Grace had set up a meeting with the director of animal control in order to facilitate a partnership so they could tag animals for foster. Once they had a physical location with regulation pens and facilities to take care of the animals, they could start taking animals from the shelter. Everyone had been working hard to get all the pieces in place. With the Easter egg hunt weekend approaching in less than three weeks, everyone had a long list of to-dos.

"Come to think of it, she asked Sal for a recipe for liver and onions. I thought nothing of it at the time, but…" Rosemary laughed.

"Very funny."

Rosemary paused outside the door of the Lazy Frog and turned her gaze to him. Her gray eyes seemed sad. "Sunny's changed so much. That surprised me. I mean, I knew through Eden things hadn't gone well for her. Alan and the miscarriages, but I didn't know how… well, how different she'd truly be."

"Miscarriages?" His stomach sank. "Wait, more than one?"

Rosemary's eyes widened. "Oh no. Look, that wasn't mine to tell. It just slipped out." She reached for the handle to the door as if looking for escape.

Henry set his hand against the door. "You can't just say something like that and then shut me down."

"I shouldn't have said anything. I'm embarrassed to have done so, Henry. It was a verbal slip, a confidence Eden shared with me. Please don't say anything."

"How many did she have?" he asked, his mind reeling at the thought she'd suffered through several miscarriages. She'd lost her husband last year, but the thought that she'd lost babies too made his heart ache. Rosemary pressed her lips together. He knew the woman was upset at herself, but he wasn't going to just let it go. This felt like something he needed to know. "Rosemary, how many?"

"Five."

"Oh my God," he breathed. "Five?"

"Yeah, the last one was a week or two after they reported Alan missing. She was four months along."

"Holy shit." He felt like he needed to sit down. To punch a wall. He'd thought Sunny's utter sadness had been because of the death of her husband. He'd hated himself for being jealous of a man he'd never met, a man who'd died for his country, but her sadness hadn't been only for her husband. She'd lost a baby too. The fifth baby.

Unshed tears gathered in his throat.

Jesus.

"Please don't tell anyone I told you, especially Sunny. She doesn't talk about it." Rosemary literally wrung her hands together and squeezed her eyes closed. "I'm so appalled at myself for letting it slip. I guess it's because I know you care about her. Or used to, and I just wasn't thinking." Rosemary looked pitiful.

"I won't say anything, but I'm glad you told me." Why? So he could feel even worse than he already did for Sunny? She didn't want his pity. She didn't want his apology. She wanted to do what needed to be done here in Morning Glory and then get the hell out of town. Now he understood even better her need to move on, to wipe the slate clean and start over.

"I'm so upset at myself," Rosemary said, shaking her head and entering the ice cream shop.

The committee to create the nonprofit animal rescue sat gathered around two pulled-together tables in the back of the eatery. Grace had an agenda in front of her, and the rest had various folders. Sunny's stack was color coded, and she had three pens lined up to the side.

"Good evening, everyone," Rosemary said, actually sliding an apologetic look toward Sunny. Sunny narrowed her eyes and looked puzzled but said nothing.

Henry took a seat next to Ed Hermann, leaving the empty chair next to Sunny for Rosemary. Sunny noted his action and looked down at her open folder.

"I'm going to call this meeting to order," Grace said, smiling at those gathered.

Sassy moved silently around them, filling cups with fragrant coffee.

"First, I feel like finally we're making things happen. I'm so appreciative to each of you for caring enough to be here, so let's get started," Grace said before covering her report about the meeting with the director of animal control.

"I thought we could announce the rescue name at the block party dance on Friday night. We can go ahead and reveal our official logo at that point too. You know, with the name," Peggy said, looking at Sunny.

"Has everyone seen the new logo?" Sunny asked, shuffling through her papers. She withdrew a single sheet. On it was a rendering of a dog that looked like the pup they'd nearly run over two weeks ago. Beneath the dog's head, a ginger cat peeked out. The bright greenish-blue background was a nice contrast to the colors of the dog along with the red bandana tied around its neck. "I have a friend who does this sort of work. I sent him a photo of Fancy, the homeless dog I'm trying to place, and I asked him to add a little kitten that looks like Peggy's Han Solo."

Peggy glowed.

Everyone oohed and aahed over the logo, which was very deserving of the praise. As usual, Sunny had knocked it out of the park.

"That's perfect, Sunny," Grace said.

Thirty minutes later, they pushed back their chairs, satisfied that things were progressing better than expected. Grace gathered up her papers, looking incredibly happy. Henry liked that so many of these people were passionate about helping animals. He'd never given much thought to what happened to stray animals before. His kids had clamored for a puppy, but he'd been able to put that off. Maybe he could adopt a dog once he completed the house.

Grace paused before standing. "Oh, Sunny. Do we need to pay your graphic artist friend?"

"Nope. He owed me a favor, so there's no charge for the logo design," Sunny said as everyone cleaned up their spaces, leaving generous tips to cover the cost of the coffee. Henry refused to allow the jealousy flooding him to continue. Sunny had a past he didn't know about. Guys who owed her favors. Guys she might have looked at with eyes void of hate. Wasn't his business.

Sunny touched his sleeve. "Hey, Henry. Wanted to let you know Deeter called about my bike. I'm picking it up tomorrow. I called the dealership and they said to bring the car back and they'd drop me at the garage. Is that okay?"

"Of course. I'm taking care of the bill." He pushed his chair in, noting a few of the committee casting curious glances at them. "Oh, and what about your mama's van? Any word?"

"Yeah, they're delivering it to us on Friday. I don't know what you said to them, but thank you."

"You're very welcome. They should be ashamed at taking so long to fix a van that someone like your mother needs."

"Well, it's being fixed now," she said with a small smile. "How's your daughter?"

"She's fine. She had surgery to correct a lazy eye. Wasn't too noticeable, but it was worsening faster than they liked. You know kids—they heal so fast." It struck him at the moment that she didn't know kids. She'd had five miscarriages. He was an insensitive ass.

"They do. I'm glad she's okay."

"Yeah, we spent several days listening to audiobooks and playing Barbie dolls. She's back in school already."

"That's good." Sunny picked up her things and slid them into the bag she carried.

It was an old canvas bag, army green. He was almost certain

it had belonged to her husband. He had the sudden inclination to buy her another one. Something pretty—leather and perfect for her. But he wouldn't. She had every right to carry her dead husband's bag. Every right to want to keep a connection with the man she'd been married to for many years.

"Guess I'll be seeing you. I'll send you the logo to use on the tax ID forms for the businesses. You did a great job at getting sponsors," Sunny said.

"He only twisted my arm a little bit," Sassy said from behind them.

They turned to find the owner of the Lazy Frog wiping down tables. The ice cream shop normally closed at six, but Sassy had stayed open late just for them. That was a thing about small towns that he loved. Couldn't get that in a big city. Or California.

Okay, yeah, they probably did things like that in California, but not with Sassy's panache.

Sunny smiled at Sassy. "I better run. Gotta take Fancy Pants for a walk."

"Be careful," Henry called as she pressed open the glass door.

Sunny turned. "It's my neighborhood. No one messes with a Voorhees there. Just rich boys like you." She winked at Sassy and disappeared into the darkness, her hair whipping around as the wind caught it.

"Well, at least she's smiling more these days," Sassy said when the door closed. "You responsible for that?"

"I don't think so," Henry said, picking up the bin of dirty dishes sitting atop the trash can and taking it to the back for Sassy. "I'm pretty sure she's in survival mode. Taking care of Betty, working a day job, remodeling a house, and helping start this rescue is a lot to take on."

"But it's keeping her busy, letting her heal a little. Losing a husband ain't no easy thing."

Henry set the bin down. "I guess not."

"But I think she seems a bit lighter than before. Having a purpose does that for a person. She may not care for dealing with her mother. Betty's a desert and ain't nobody poured water on her in a while. But like a desert, she still has potential. Sunny might be the absolute right person to help Betty see that and, in the process, find a bit of rain for herself."

Henry wasn't exactly sure what Sassy was talking about, but he thought he grasped it. Both Sunny and Betty had gone a long time without much good in their lives. Sometimes a person couldn't wait for the good to come. She had to find the good around her. Maybe it was a glass-half-full philosophy or, as Sassy said, just having purpose. Sometimes having someone rely on you was enough to get you to put your feet on the floor every morning. "That dog is a lot like Sunny. Someone tossed it away, and its life has been hard. I think Sunny sees herself in Fancy. I'm sure a psychiatrist would have a field day with all this, but I'm not smart enough to fully understand."

Sassy lifted a shoulder. "You're plenty smart enough. I don't know all of what happened between you two back then. I mean, I know you knocked a girl up and tried to do right by her. Jillian's not a bad sort, but I got eyes in my head."

"What does that mean?"

"I know you're still carrying a flame for the one that got away. The timing might have been the thing that was wrong. The feelings weren't."

"I care about Sunny, of course. I want the best for her. But timing or not, Sunny and I will never have what we once had."

"Of course not. You were kids. You can't go back to that, but that doesn't mean you can't find something worth saving. Sunny needs time. Just give her a little time."

"You know, you're a nosy old woman."

Sassy laughed. "Well, I don't have much to do anymore. My kids have grown up and gone off. My husband is content working in his garden and playing cards once a week. Life is boring at the Grigsby place. So I sit up here and watch the world go by. I put a well-placed word in when I need to because we all got talents, and mine is seeing what is right before me."

"That's your talent? Telling people what they should be

doing?"

"We all have one," Sassy said with a choking laugh, dumping the dishes into soapy water.

"And you think I should be… Wait, what do you think?" Henry found some amusement in the thought Sassy felt she was the great counselor of the lovelorn. Or just screwed-up people.

"Give Sunshine some time. Her world is very gray. But clouds don't stay forever."

"I'm not interested in Sunny David."

"And I'm the Queen of Sheba," Sassy said, shooing him out. "Go on and get home. Give some thought to what I'm saying."

Henry shook his head. "I don't have to. You're barking up the wrong tree."

"I got a good nose, Henry Todd." Sassy tapped her nose, her dark eyes sparkling. "Like I said, time has a way of taking care of these things. You'll see everything clear pretty soon. And then you can come back and tell me what you know. Things are at work. I feel them."

Henry had no clue what Sassy was talking about, but he wasn't going to wade any further into Sassy's deep pool. "Thank you for staying open and letting us meet here."

Sassy turned a knowing grin on him. "Okay then. I see. And you're welcome. Like I told Grace and Sunny, we need something like this. The Humane Society used to do some good around here, but when Eppie died, it did too. The good Lord told us to tend the land and its beasts. We don't do too good a job of that. Happy to help."

Henry gave her a wave, pulled on the jacket he'd left on the back of his chair, and pushed out into the night. The wind had died down some, but the old oaks in the square swished and the newly emerged daffodils bobbed their heads, the blooms almost neon against the darkness. The town had rolled up for the day, and only a few cars sat around the square. Bright lights spilled from Sal's New York Pizzeria, and Henry could see technicians still working in the nail salon, but otherwise the small town was still.

He stood for a moment and soaked it in. He rarely thought about this town and what it meant to him. His family had been here for generations, and when he'd lived in Jackson, he'd missed the comfort it gave him. Morning Glory wasn't for everyone, but it was for him.

A movement near the center of the square caught his eye, but before he could investigate, Sal stuck his head out of the restaurant. "Come grab a beer. It's on the house."

Henry caught the scent of fresh-baked crust and spicy marinara. "That I can do." He gave another glance at the square and at the redhead sitting on the bench near the fountain before walking toward the open door.

Mother Nature decided to be kind to the residents of Morning Glory on Easter weekend. The sun broke through the clouds, painting the morning with soft streaks, and a gentle breeze ruffled the tender green leaves arching over the town square. The committee to raise money for a new animal rescue couldn't have asked for a better day for the first annual Sunshine Fun Run.

For the past few weeks, Sunny had worked like the dog she was trying to find a home for to get the 5K race and the nonprofit up and running. As she pinned numbers on the runners, she felt satisfaction creep inside her. It was going to work. Everything had come together.

"Do we have any more safety pins?" Peggy Lattier asked, rooting around the box Sunny had set beneath the registration table.

"In the mint tin." Sunny handed race bags to the cluster of runners gathered around the table. She gave them a smile. "We're a new group, and we'll have permanent facilities soon. Until then, we're committed to finding fosters for the hundreds of animals in Rankin County shelters. We appreciate y'all helping us."

"We're always up for a race," one of the men said.

"And we love puppies," the woman with him said, pulling out her phone. "Here are our pugs, Suzy and Bud."

Sunny glanced at the two fat rascals in the photos. "Cute."

"They're so spoiled. We rescued Bud from a shelter in Tennessee. Isn't he adorable?"

"He is," Sunny said as the group wandered off to stretch or whatever runners did before a race. Sunny wasn't sure because she avoided most forms of exercise. She'd done a little Jazzercise a few years ago and one hot yoga class. One.

"Hey, how are things going?" Henry asked, appearing at her elbow. He smelled like Irish Spring soap and cheerfulness. Damn him.

Katie Clare rounded the table, took two peppermints from the bowl sitting on the table, and grinned at Sunny.

"Good. We have surpassed breaking even, and people are still signing up. Paired with the sponsors, we're looking at a couple of thousand dollars to put toward buying a place to house the rescue." Sunny smiled at Katie Clare. "You going to do some running, Miss Delmar?"

"Yep," Katie Clare said, pirouetting. "See my new running outfit? Daddy bought it for me at Target. It's got a unicorn on it. They aren't real, you know."

"Of course they aren't, but they're sparkling fun even if they're pretend." Sunny nodded at the glittery unicorn. IMAGINE THE FINISH LINE in fancy script accompanied the mythical beast.

"And look at my shoes," Katie Clare said, rounding the table and sticking out her leg. Pink shoes with more sparkles.

"Very nice."

"She likes pink. And glitter," Henry said, a wry smile twitching his lips.

"So I see." Sunny added a little laugh.

For the past three weeks, she and Henry had shelved the hurt and anger and instead focused on the work they were doing to get the rescue off the ground. And things had been fine.

She'd spent her days working at the high school, quickly learning the ropes. She'd cleaned out folders, reorganized the desk, streamlined the ID-making process, and learned the names of the entire office and janitorial staff. Meeting old teachers in the hallway had led to coffee in her office, and she found she enjoyed being part of the community of her former high school. She'd even gone to a basketball game last week and watched Woozy score twelve points. He'd thanked her by shouting, "Red" and then jogging over to give her a fist bump. For a few seconds, she'd felt like she belonged somewhere.

The evenings were spent taking Fancy for a walk, painting the wainscoting in the living room, or working on the brochure she'd designed for the rescue. Last night at the street dance, they'd unveiled the new name of the rescue—Sunshine Animal Rescue. The slogan was "No more rain in their lives." It wasn't something she would have chosen since it was her name, but of the ten suggestions turned in to the group, it was the one that had won the Facebook poll. It wasn't the worst of the bunch, and adding a sun behind the dog and cat on the logo actually looked better.

"Guess we're just checking in," Henry said, motioning his son over. "Landry, come say hello to Sunny and Mrs. Lattier."

The teenaged boy looked horrified his father had even talked to him, much less forced him to speak. "Hey."

"Hi, Landry," Sunny said, noting he looked a great deal like his father at that age. Of course, Henry had not only been athletic, good-looking, and well-spoken, he'd been able to charm the socks off any female within a two-mile radius. Or for that matter, any other article of clothing. Landry, however, seemed to suffer from a huge case of shyness. "Been knocking off any Harleys lately?"

Landry actually paled. "Uh, no. I mean, I haven't..."

"I'm kidding. My bike is all fixed. Just like new again."

Immediate relief flooded the kid's face. "Good. I'm so sorry about that. I guess I'm still learning how to back up."

"It's not easy to learn to drive. You should have seen me trying to maneuver that motorcycle. It's like wrestling an elephant," she said, trying to engage the kid. She shouldn't have joked about the accident. Landry was a serious guy.

"I could do it," Katie Clare declared, tugging on the end of her braid and lifting her little chin up cockily. "I learned how to ride my bike in a week. I'm good at lots of stuff."

Sunny laughed. That girl did not suffer from shyness or lack of confidence. "I bet you are."

"You couldn't ride a motorcycle, idiot," Landry said, shaking his head.

"Oooh, Landry called me an ugly name, Daddy. He can't do that. You told him he couldn't."

"Lan," Henry called, giving him the side-eye, his voice holding warning. "What did I tell you?"

"Sorry, KC," Landry said. "I meant to call you dum-dum." The kid grinned, tugging his sister's braid and dodging her when she tried to swat at him. His smile was so much like his father's that Sunny's heart clenched.

"Daaaaddy," Katie Clare whined as only an eight-year-old could do.

"He's teasing you. And he said he was sorry. Don't take everything to heart, Katie bug. Your brother likes to irritate you. So do us all a favor and ignore him."

"Okay, I'm going to see those dogs," she said, pointing to the kennels holding a few of the rescues they'd tagged.

Three dogs, not including Fancy, had approved fosters. Grace had put together a checklist for fostering and was sitting with the animals, trying to stir up interest in potential fosters and adopters. Sunny had put Fancy in one of the kennels, but the thought of someone wanting to adopt her made her stomach hurt. Which was not the reaction she wanted to have. Fancy deserved a good home. She deserved kids who would play with her, a bed in front of a fireplace, and most importantly, she deserved to not be yelled at by a demon in a wheelchair.

Though Sunny *had* caught her mother loving on the pup when Betty thought no one was looking. Her mother talked a big game about the smelly mutt who probably had diseases, but she was quick to pull Fancy to her when she could. Sunny knew that if someone wanted to adopt the rescue, her mother would miss the dog. Well, at least a little bit.

And Sunny could admit that she would miss the pup too. Having Fancy's warm little body next to hers when she slept each night provided a comfort she couldn't name. Maybe it just felt good to have something with a heartbeat next to her in bed.

"She's going to want one," Henry said. His gaze roamed over her. Sunny wore a pair of yoga pants, a warm fleece jacket, and tennis shoes that had seen better days a year ago. She'd applied makeup and put curlers in her hair since she wanted to make a good impression as an organizer.

"A dog? Or a cat?" She'd been meaning to ask Henry about adopting Fancy, but something inside her still held back. She wasn't sure why. So each time she bit her tongue.

"Probably both," Henry said, casting a glance toward where his daughter had sunk to her knees to pet the animals through their crates. Grace was already doing a hard sell. "How are you this morning? Not going to run?"

"Not a runner." She eyed his no doubt expensive running gear and running shoes. "You run?"

"I did a marathon three years ago, but nothing more since then. Bucket list."

"Ah," she said, trying not to stare at his flat stomach and toned thighs. Why couldn't Henry be balding and fat like everyone else's former high school boyfriend? That would have been so much easier to deal with. But, no, Henry had to be even better looking now, with gorgeous hands, golden-brown eyes, and a body to drool over. And he smelled like morning rain and sex.

Not sex.

Do not think about sex and Henry.

"Well, I suppose we should mosey over to the start line," he said.

"Yeah, before you end up with all the rescue animals." She nodded toward Katie Clare.

"Right." He paused and then went to fetch his daughter. "Do you want to come sit with us for the bachelor auction and picnic? We have plenty of food and plenty of room on our blanket."

Her first inclination was to say yes, but her sister had arrived with the family she worked for, and Sunny hadn't been able to spend much time with Eden. Besides, spending time outside of the rescue work with Henry seemed… dangerous. She didn't want to like him any more than she already did. Because, like it or not, her heart didn't always communicate well with her head. And she already knew the sexual energy was there. One simple strike of the match and she'd be on him the same way she'd been that evening in his construction trailer. "That's really nice of you and your children, but Eden came in with the family she's been nannying for, and I need to spend some time with her."

"Oh yeah. Of course," he said, managing a smile. But she could read Henry Todd Delmar like a book. He was disappointed. He wanted her to sit with him and his family. And why? That would only cause more talk than there already was. But deep down she knew why he wanted her there with him. She just didn't want to acknowledge it. Because that was the most dangerous thing of all.

"See you around." She sank back into her chair, determined to not give in to the desire to sit beside the first man she'd ever loved.

"Yeah, have fun today," he said, walking toward his daughter.

Sunny distracted herself by picking up her phone and double-checking her messages. She had none. Her mother had been sidelined for the day after having shown her butt yesterday at Sal's pizzeria. Somehow Betty had gotten wind that Eden was in town and had talked Vienna into taking the van into town. Betty had essentially tattled on Sunny to Eden and then proceeded to say ugly things to the wheelchair-bound child whom Eden took care of each day.

Sunny had never seen her younger sister so angry or disappointed in their mother. Sunny had told Betty she couldn't go to the egg hunt and picnic. Betty hadn't spoken to Sunny since. It had been very awkward assisting her mother with the restroom and bathing while not speaking, but both she and Eden had things preventing them from mommy-sitting. Plus, after being such a pill, Betty deserved to eat mac and cheese and watch reruns.

For the next hour, Sunny handed out brochures, took the pups on walks designed to attract potential adopters, and chatted with those interested in volunteering. All the while, families around her laughed, compared Easter egg finds, and ate homemade potato salad and barbeque. Across the blanketed square, she spied her sister laughing with her two best friends from high school, Rosemary and Jess. They looked about as happy as three thirty-year-old women could. And then the talk of the town, hunky Clem Aiken and Sal's sister, strolled past her, essentially wrapped in each other's arms. Jealously wriggled around inside her, a feeling almost as bad as she'd had on Valentine's Day.

The great alone. She was totally living it.

After her shift ended, she texted Eden that she had a headache and went back to her mother's house. She didn't have a headache, but she couldn't stomach any more of the happy spring weather and the reminder of what she didn't have in her life. Her mother was asleep in her recliner and didn't move an eyelash when Eden slipped inside. Scooping up Fancy, Sunny tiptoed back to her room, stripped out of her jeans, and snuggled under the covers with her dog.

No, not *her* dog.

But as Fancy rubbed her head against Sunny's chin and curled against her shoulder, Sunny decided to pretend the fuzzy canine did indeed belong to her. For now.

With a soft sigh, Sunny closed her eyes and fell into hard sleep.

And then woke to someone banging on her door.

chapter eleven

AT THE SOUND of the knock on Sunny's bedroom door, Fancy leaped up, hackles raised, issuing a low growl in her throat. Sunny struggled to sit up, blinked to clear her bleary eyes, and stroked the dog.

"It's okay, girl. Shh."

"Sunny?" her sister Eden called from the other side of the door.

"What?"

"Can I come in please?"

Sunny reached for the lamp on the bedside table and clicked it on, illuminating the almost dark room with weak light. "Sure."

Eden opened the door. Standing behind her were Rosemary Genovese and Jess Culpepper.

Sunny pulled the covers she'd kicked off over her bare legs. "What's going on?"

Her sister edged into the room. "Uh, well, it's kinda weird— "

"No, it's not," Rosemary said, slipping into the room and plopping onto the bed much like she'd done when they had been teenagers intent on bugging the crap out of Sunny.

Fancy shot off the bed and slid underneath, her claws scrabbling against the floor.

"What's wrong with your dog?" Jess moved into the space and leaned back against the wall holding the posters of 311 and NSYNC. Jess was taller with loose limbs and curly brown hair. She looked like she could whip a gal's ass on the basketball court, but she'd never been much of an athlete. She'd recently started dating the once-upon-a-time geekiest guy in Morning Glory. Ryan Reyes had grown into a stud-muffin with a doctorate and a six-pack.

"It's not my dog. I'm just fostering it. You lookin' for one?"

"Nope." Jess shook her head, making her curls dance.

"So what's the deal, gals?" Sunny asked, pushing her tangled hair back and patting the spot beside her. "Come on, Fancy. It's okay."

Fancy peeked out, checked out the surroundings, and then hopped onto the bed. The dog curled into a circle and studied the intruders warily.

"Sure looks like she's your dog," Jess said with a quirk of her lips.

Eden sank onto the bed, elbowing Rosemary over. Sunny's sister was small, dark with haunting blue eyes that made Sunny a little nervous at the expression in them. "So, I don't know if you remember me telling you about the bracelet Lacy left us?"

"Vaguely. It was part of the money she left y'all? Doing something courageous or something you've never done?" Sunny narrowed her eyes at her sister. Eden was acting weird. Like she was about to get dental work done or something.

"Yeah, she had this charm bracelet she loved." Eden held up a Vera Bradley ditty bag. Or Sunny assumed it was Vera Bradley since it was brightly colored and swirled with paisleys.

"And once we did what we'd chosen to do with her money, we were supposed to put a charm on the bracelet and pass it on to the next person. See? I put on the Empire State Building," Rosemary said, grabbing the bag and jerking open the strings.

The bracelet slid into her hand.

Jess took it from Rosemary. "I added this flip-flop." She tossed it to Eden.

"And I added this dancing shoe earlier today. I got an audition in New York City, and I'm leaving in a few days." Eden's blue eyes flashed with something more than excitement. Regret? Pain? Sunny assumed it had something to do with the dynamic New Orleans businessman who couldn't seem to keep his eyes or hands off her sister.

"That's great, E. You're doing what you've always wanted to do. Broadway's all yours now."

"I don't know about that, but I'm going to give it a go. It's my one shot."

"Yeah, but I don't understand why y'all are showing me this bracelet," Sunny said.

The three friends looked at each other.

"So, well, the last thing Lacy wanted us to do was, uh, give the bracelet to someone." Rosemary glanced at the bracelet Eden still held in her hand.

"Okaaaay," Sunny said, tiring of the game they played.

"We're giving it to you," Jess said.

"Why?"

Both Jess and Rosemary looked at Eden.

Eden swallowed. "Well, she wanted us to give it to someone who needed it."

"I don't need a bracelet."

"Well, it's not about the bracelet, per se." Eden looked at Rosemary and then at Jess. She wasn't getting any help from them. Rosemary picked at some nonexistent fuzz, and Jess seemed to find Sunny's old bulletin board with high school pictures of sudden interest. "It's more about the sort of person we have to give it to."

Sunny lifted an eyebrow.

Eden held out the bracelet. It dangled, charms making a soft clink. "You see, Lacy believed in destiny or something like that. Or maybe it was more like she believed in the power of love. Her bracelet and the money she gave us was about giving us something we didn't have."

"Okay, but I'm still confused why I'm involved," Sunny said.

"The last thing she said in the letter was after we completed her bracelet we had to give it to someone who had... no hope." Eden said the last bit softly, an apology.

No hope.

The words sat there, fat and ugly like an old bullfrog in the mud.

Sunny stared at the bracelet and then lifted her eyes to her sister. Eden looked quickly away. "And you think I have no hope? Is that what you're saying?"

Rosemary ran a hand over the worn coverlet. "Look, we thought of you because I had this dream. I mean, I saw you in my dream and you were all alone by a pond, and well, there was some other stuff too." She glanced at Eden, her eyes begging for help.

"We just think you're the person who's supposed to get the bracelet," her sister said.

"Are y'all batshit crazy?" Sunny ignored the bracelet her sister had extended toward her. "Dreams and hocus-pocus and... Shit, coming in here and saying I'm hopeless? What the hell?"

"Don't get mad, Sunny. It's a good thing. It might bring you some luck," Rosemary said, reaching toward Sunny as if she wanted to deliver an encouraging pat.

Sunny knocked her hand away. She *was* mad. How dare these three little twits barge into her room, wake her from a good nap, and insist she take a stupid bracelet because she was hopeless? God, is that what everyone thought about her?

Her mother's words about her being empty wafted back to her. *You're empty like me.*

Maybe that *was* how everyone saw her. Poor Sunny. First Henry screwed her. Then life screwed her with a dead husband

and broken womb. And now she has a temporary job and is taking care of her bitch mother. Oh, not to mention she's trying to renovate a crappy house that likely wouldn't sell for over seventy-five thousand dollars. Hell, yeah, she was freaking hopeless.

Sunny batted the bracelet and it flew into the corner, smacking into the wall behind the suitcase that stood waiting for her escape to something better. "I don't want your damn charity. Or that stupid bracelet. I'm not without hope, you assholes."

"Sunny, that's not what we meant—" Eden began, moving toward her.

"Oh, it's not? You said Lacy wanted you to give the bracelet to someone with no hope. You just gave it to me."

"Or tried to," Jess piped up unhelpfully.

"What? Is Lacy's ghost going to magically make me happy? Is there, like, a secret wish attached? What's the deal here?" Sunny asked.

Jess shrugged. "We're just trying to do this for Lacy."

"News flash. Lacy's dead. Why would you do something like that to a very much alive *me*?" Sunny heard her voice catch and wanted to kick her own ass for showing any weakness.

All three women looked traumatized but said nothing.

"We weren't trying to hurt your feelings, Sunny," Rosemary finally said, rising from the bed. "Sorry if that's how you took it."

Sunny wondered how in the hell she was supposed to take it. How did one react to being told they were the most pathetic person someone could think of?

"Maybe we should go," Jess said.

"You think?" Sunny drawled, heavy on the sarcasm. She wished their stupid words hadn't hurt her. But they had. Their action was like poking a pin into an overinflated balloon, releasing anger and pain that Sunny had tried to ignore. "Go. Out. You've completed your great commission to find the most hopeless."

"Sunny," Eden said, her voice and eyes pleading.

"Get the hell out, E." Sunny threw back the covers and stood, not caring that she wore only a T-shirt and red lace thong. She gave her sister a hard look and pointed toward the door.

Eden left, taking Rosemary with her.

Jess lingered. "Don't be so hard on your sister. Wasn't her idea."

"But she did it," Sunny said, pushing the tall brunette out the door and closing it.

Sunny stood for a moment, looking at Fancy who lay with her chin between her paws. The dog thumped her tail and watched her with sherry eyes filled with adoration. Fancy seemed to offer an apology.

Walking over to the pup, Sunny ran her hand over the dog's coat but couldn't find the calm the act normally brought her. She glanced at the suitcase. The bracelet had fallen somewhere behind it, and the stupid thing could stay there for all Sunny cared.

Screw them and their idea she was hopeless. Screw her mother too. Sunny wasn't empty.

Grabbing her jeans, she headed to the bathroom. Eden and her friends were in the living room talking to Betty. Good. Sunny needed some space. She pulled her hair into a ponytail, washed her face, and stalked back out. Then she put Fancy in the dog crate, tugged on her boots, and grabbed the keys to her motorcycle.

Eden looked slightly alarmed when Sunny stomped into the living room.

"Stay with Mom a while. I need a ride."

"But I have to—"

Sunny silenced her sister with a go-to-hell look.

"Fine." Eden didn't look happy, but tough stuff. At this point, her sister owed her a little reflection time. Or time to deal with the anger threatening to spill out of her and break her apart.

Sunny pulled on her helmet, fired up the hog, and backed out of the driveway. She wanted to punch someone… or just drive until she hit the Mississippi state line. And never look back. Her body burned, her throat ached with unshed tears, and the old recklessness that had landed her in the arms of a good-looking Marine in a Memphis bus station years ago raised its head inside her. Sunny tore out of Grover's Park like the devil himself was after her.

Heading out to the old country roads where Henry had taught her to drive, she increased her speed and leaned into the curves. The power thrumming beneath her thighs and butt seeped into her, and she became one with the machine. All the hurt and anger tied itself into knots again. She had to control her emotions. Take it out on the ribbons of road before her.

"Fuck them," she whispered into the graying day, ignoring the tears trickling toward her ears.

The full moon snuck into the horizon, hovering as the dying sun turned the opposing sky brilliant shades of melon and rose. Newly green fields sped past, dark forests casting gloomy shadows onto her path. Eventually her heartbeat slowed, but the anger and hurt refused to be crammed back into the abyss inside her.

So Sunny kept riding, trying to lose herself in the Mississippi twilight.

Eventually she came to Henry's parents' place, a big old stone house that looked right out of a Gothic romance. The iron gates were parted in invitation, and her bike seemed to turn in on its own accord.

Sunny slowed as she came to the carriage house sitting to the side.

Henry had told her he had yet to build a house on some property he'd purchased, and instead stayed in the carriage house that his parents had converted to an apartment years ago. She'd been there with him once. They'd snuck up to make out on an old tweed couch a caretaker had abandoned long ago.

Why was she here?

She shook her head. She should turn her bike around and go

back home.

But she didn't.

Because Sunny hurt and she needed something. Someone. She killed the engine and parked the bike to the side of Henry's big truck. This was probably a dumb idea. After all, his kids were with him, but he'd always been so good at talking her through things. They were friends, weren't they?

She squeezed her eyes closed.

Lie to herself all she wanted. She knew why she was there. She needed Henry even though she didn't want to need him.

She rang the bell, thankful the entrance was on the side hidden from the main house. For some reason, it felt safer. Like she needed to hide her vulnerability.

The door opened and there was Henry, barefoot with his button-down shirt opened to reveal a trim stomach and lightly furred chest. He had a pencil tucked behind his ear and a pair of readers perched on his nose. He looked about as sexy as a man could look.

The confusion in his eyes cleared when he saw her. "Sunny, hey."

"Hey. Are your kids here?" she asked, tucking her helmet beneath her arm.

"No, they're staying the night with my parents at the big house," he said, motioning to the house sitting far off to their right.

"Good," she said, sliding past him.

She caught a whiff of his cologne and felt his warmth as she brushed against him. A set of stairs she knew went up to the loft lay to the right. She set her helmet on the glass table in the small entry. Henry turned, closing the door behind him.

Sunny reached over and twisted the lock. Then she started up the stairs, pulling her shirt over her head as she climbed.

Henry's first thought while watching Sunny Voorhees David climb his stairs as she removed her T-shirt was that this was a test.

His second thought was hot damn. Finally.

And because he hadn't had sex in over a year and the woman climbing his steps, presenting him with a delicious back and red lace bra, was the woman he'd been in love with for longer than he could remember, he went with his second thought.

But even so, as he followed her up the steps, he wondered if he should use his head… and not his penis to figure out what in the hell was going on. Obviously, something was wrong with her, and he didn't want to make things any worse between them by doing something stupid like stripping off the rest of her clothes with his teeth and then doing stuff to her he'd only seen done in dirty movies.

When he reached the top step, he found her next to his neatly made bed, shucking out of her jeans. He stood for a moment, shocked that she was actually undressing. In his room. By his bed.

Sunny pulled her hair loose and it fell in a scarlet, seductive mass around her shoulders. Her pale belly was flat, her breasts still amazingly plump and her hips, though lean, rounded the way a woman's hips should be. She looked like his best teenaged wet dream as she came toward him.

He needed to say something. To figure out what the game was. "Sunny, baby, what's—"

She silenced him with her finger, pressing it so firmly against his lips he could do nothing more than close them and drop his eyes to her mouth. To those lips he'd dreamed about far too often. Then he lowered his gaze to the breasts filling the push-up bra. Then to the curve of her womanhood in the matching red thong. At that point, he lost his will to do anything other than whatever she wanted him to do.

"Don't," she said, taking his hand and placing it on her waist. Then she wound her arm around his neck and lifted onto her tiptoes. Her mouth brushed against his and she whispered,

"Give me what I want, Henry. What we've both wanted for too long."

That he could do.

He lowered his head and captured her mouth as he hauled her against him. He'd unbuttoned his too-tight shirt earlier as he worked on figures for a project, and her flesh meeting his felt like falling into heaven. She opened her mouth, twisted her fingers in his hair, and surrendered herself to him.

For several seconds, the world stood still. There was only him and this woman he'd once loved, their breath mingling, their bodies pressed so close there could be nothing between them.

Sunny broke the kiss and looked up at him, her lips glistening and her eyes dilated with desire. She plucked the pencil from behind his ear and tossed it toward his bedside table, then slid his readers from his nose, folded them, and set them beside it. Then she sank back on his bed, a pinup girl striking a pose.

And she waited.

Henry shrugged out of his shirt and went to her, stopping when his denim-clad knees bumped her bare ones. "I want you more than you will ever know, Sunshine, but are you certain?"

Her blue eyes flashed with brief annoyance. "You sure are trying hard to stop this."

"I don't want to screw up any more than I already have."

"I want this. I need this."

So he put his knee on the bed and laid her back, the same way he'd imagined it in his dreams for so many years. His Sunshine, her gorgeous body his playground. He covered her with his body, capturing her lips with his, bringing himself down so that all the good parts lined up.

Coming home.

Sunny's breath caught as his body settled against hers, and he ground his pelvis to remind her he was a man and she was his, at least for the next little while. Her body felt so good he thought he might actually cry. Instead, he buried his face in her hair, inhaling the scent of warm vanilla and honey.

Then his body took over. His fingers found her bra clasp, and her breasts spilled from the lace. They were as perfect as he remembered with dusky pink nipples and a porcelain plumpness that made him hard as a steel post.

"You're so damn pretty," he murmured against her neck as he filled a hand with her flesh. Sunny groaned and wriggled her hips. "Slow down, Sunshine."

She opened passion-dazed eyes. "I can't. It's been so long, Henry."

Henry nibbled his way to her mouth, dropping a soft kiss upon it. "I know. Me too."

Sunny caught his mouth with hers and kissed him hard. Her hand came up to caress his shoulders, and her touch on his bare skin stoked the lust spiraling out of control inside him. He kissed her back, their tongues tangling, their hands gliding over each other's bodies.

He pulled his mouth from hers and made his way down her neck to her breasts, and with each millimeter, his body amped higher and higher. He'd gone too long without release, and her scent, the feel of her body, her magnificent, gorgeous softness tipped him over the edge.

And Sunny must have felt the same. She tugged at his waistband, no longer content to remain passive. He caught one of her nipples between his teeth and nipped her before pulling back and shucking his jeans, kicking them free. His belt gave a satisfying clunk on the floor.

Lifting her butt, Sunny slid the scrap of lace from her hips and tossed them onto the floor. She lay back, totally nude and so gorgeous he felt his body actually tremble at the thought that she would be his… finally.

Making short work of his own boxers, he joined her.

"Babe, I want to savor every moment of this, but I'm not sure how much longer I can wait," he said, unable to stop himself from running his hands over the hills and valleys before him. She was too thin, but still so soft in all the right places. He wanted to feed her, protect her, kiss every inch of her body. She was the woman he'd waited too long for.

"I don't want to go slow," she said, rising onto her elbow and pushing him on his back. Her greedy hands covered him, and her lips followed over his collarbone, down between his pecs, brushing his sensitive belly. Then she rose and straddled his hips, her hair falling forward and covering her face.

He reached for her waist, holding her still. "We need protection."

She shook her head. "It's okay. I don't need it."

"But…"

Her hand encircled his erection, and he gasped at the pleasure, rational thought fleeing. Sunny lifted herself and sank down on him.

"Oh shit, Sunny."

She threw back her head, pleasure evident on her face as she rocked her body. Her eyes closed, but he couldn't close his own at the image of her above him, her beautiful face almost reverent as she moved, her breasts heaving with her quickened breaths, her thighs clasping his hips. He'd be content to watch her forever, but the heat of her body clenching around him drove him to action.

Henry clasped her waist and turned her over.

"Oh." She sighed as he caught her mouth with his and began to slowly drive into her. She was warm, wet, and perfect. Absolutely perfect.

"You don't know how much I've dreamed of this," he whispered into her ear, nipping her lobe and dropping hot kisses against the warmth of her skin. She smelled so good, felt like satin against him, and the little pants she issued only heightened the lust starting to spin out of control.

Sunny lifted her legs to clasp him, moving with him, her eyes still closed. And then she opened them, her blue eyes entirely engulfed in passion.

"Henry," she said, her hand cupping his cheek, which was raspy with five-o'clock shadow. "Henry."

He smiled at her, then closed his eyes and lost himself. She surrounded him so completely, the warm scent that was hers alone, the little moans in the back of her throat. She was everything he'd ever wanted, everything he'd ever need.

Sunny quickened her pace, and he felt her tighten around him, her back arching, and he couldn't slow down. He wanted this moment to last forever, but his body refused to listen. As Sunny shattered, he felt himself coming apart, millions of pleasure fragments vibrating in every recess of his body.

Eventually the orgasm faded, leaving him spent and heavy atop her. He rolled off with a huge sigh and stared up at the ceiling, his ragged breath echoing hers.

Sunny lay silently beside him, seemingly lost in a moment neither of them had expected or thought would ever happen.

Henry felt her body start to shake.

"Hey," he said, lifting onto an elbow. "You okay?"

But she wasn't. Sunny was crying.

Tears slid from the corners of her eyes to disappear into her hairline. For a second or so she lay there, staring at the fan. Then she rolled toward him and buried her face in his shoulder. Her body shook harder as she dissolved into sobs.

Henry couldn't say he was the best lover in the world, but he had never envisioned a woman sobbing after having sex with him. But this was Sunny. And something inside her was broken. He'd known that from the moment he first saw her again.

And if Sunny needed to cry in his arms, well, he was the absolute best person to hold her.

So he did.

chapter twelve

SUNNY COULDN'T STOP the sobs that wracked her body. One moment she was shattering into a breathtaking orgasm; the next she was engulfed in a sea of emotion that demanded she release everything she'd crammed deep into her soul. The wave was uncontrollable, the same way it had been when she'd been taking progesterone shots and dissolved into tears at every Christmas commercial or when she dropped jar of jam.

Henry held her, his embrace so familiar and yet so foreign. As he comforted her, he murmured endearments against her hair, his hands caressing her, letting her empty herself of all the heartbreak she'd carried around for too long. Like lancing an ulcerated blister, the bad stuff poured out. No way to stop it this time.

"Shh," Henry whispered, his body rocking her slightly.

"I'm… I'm sor-sorry," she managed through her tears. "I shouldn't do this. I'm—"

"Just let it out. Let it all go, Sunshine."

After a few more seconds of shuddering sobs, Sunny stilled. Her hands clutched Henry's waist as she buried her head against his now-damp chest. Her head hurt even as her body felt oddly loose. She felt as if she'd run a marathon.

"Hey, you okay?" he asked, lifting her slightly so that he could see her eyes.

"I think so."

"Good. I've never had that reaction after sex. My ego has taken a hit." He was teasing her, trying to take away her sadness.

She managed a chuckle. "You weren't that bad."

Settling back against him, she lay in the dimness, soothed by his teasing. Henry always wanted to make things right. After a minute or so, she pushed back the hair that stuck to her face and ran her fingers beneath eyes that were no doubt swollen. "I don't know what happened. The sex was amazing. I mean, if you couldn't tell."

"I could. I mean yeah, it was good. And it's okay to feel overwhelmed. You've had a rough year, Sunny, and coming home to all these memories isn't easy," he said, shimmying toward the edge of the bed. "Let me grab a towel and get you a tissue. Stay here."

He padded to the bathroom and must have done a quick cleanup before returning with a fingertip towel and a box of tissues. While he'd been gone, Sunny had slid beneath a soft quilt folded at the end of the bed. She combed her fingers through her hair and tried to regain some of her dignity, as if what had just happened hadn't affected her. She was embarrassed that she'd come here, pretty much forced him into sex, and then fallen apart afterward.

God, what had possessed her to do what she'd done?

But she knew. She'd been close to the edge of a breakdown for a while, and Eden and the bracelet had tipped her over the edge.

Wordlessly, Henry handed her the towel and then slid beneath the quilt. Once she did a manageable job of cleanup, he pulled her into his arms.

"Uh, Sunny, I'm… Well, I always use a condom." He sounded worried.

"I can't get pregnant, Henry." She tried to keep the emotion from her voice, but any talk of her inability to carry a child to term was too raw to dismiss.

"What do you mean by *can't*?"

"My progesterone's so low that I can't get pregnant without taking shots, and then if I do manage to get pregnant, my uterus is inhospitable. I think that's the term the doctor used." Sunny swallowed the pain. She didn't want to cry again, and those damn tears were so near the surface. *Talk about something else.* "I guess I should have asked for protection for other things though. STDs?"

His expression faltered. Nothing for ruining postcoital glow like a breakdown and then an ensuing discussion of miscarriage and the herpes virus.

"Shouldn't be an issue. I've never had unprotected sex except when I was married." He resettled her against him, and that soothed her. His hand cupped her hip, occasionally offering a little rub of comfort.

"I didn't figure you'd be one for giving me the clap, but you never know, I guess." She curled into him, her legs twining with his.

"So let's see, you lost your husband, lost your child, lost your ability to have children, moved in with your mother, and you're wondering why you had to cry? Hell, I would have cried over just moving in with my mother. I think you needed to release all that as much as you needed what came before. Which was very, very good, by the way."

"Yeah," she said, running her fingers through his chest hair. "It *was* very good."

"And you're still okay that we went there? I mean, we'd decided on a sort of friendship. That's not usually something friends do. If so, I'd probably have more lady friends." He grinned, giving her a little pinch.

She wriggled, just as she'd always done when he teased her.

Then he pressed his lips against her hair. "God, you feel so good here beside me."

"I think we *had* to do this," she said against his neck, catching the faint scent of his cologne with an underlying saltiness. "Or maybe I just needed to be with someone who… I don't know. Maybe it was about what we lost, the never-meant-to-be, or maybe I just needed to get laid and you were here."

"So you were using me? That's what this was?" Hurt shaded his voice.

"No." She paused, trying to figure out why she'd done what she'd done. "I don't know, Henry. My sister and her friends came to Mom's house and some of the things they said made me angry and… hurt."

"What did they say?"

"It's not important. Or maybe it was. Maybe I needed to know what others see when they look at me. Maybe I needed to face the truth about myself. If I accept that I lost everything, maybe I can get something back for myself." She wasn't sure if that was true, but she had to do something to move herself to a better place. Of course, being home in Morning Glory had done some of that—she had a job, she was doing something worthwhile in helping create an animal rescue, and she'd at the very least tried to put the hurt between her and Henry aside. She wasn't totally hopeless.

He lay silent as if examining her words.

She waited for him to say something to her admission, but his next words were totally unexpected.

"Tell me about Alan. About the life you had."

She lifted her head and peered at him. "Why?"

"Because you said a while back that I didn't know you anymore. Maybe I need to know who you were."

"You want to know about *Alan*? 'Cause I can tell you I don't give a rat's ass about Jillian." She'd hated Henry's ex for a long time. Jillian had gone after Henry, making no bones about the fact she wanted him. Sunny had even wondered if the pregnancy had been intentional, and every time she'd pictured Henry lying in bed with his wife, their cute-as-a-button children romping around them as the morning sunlight slanted inside the imaginary room, she'd felt sick to her stomach. She'd lied and told herself Henry and his perfect little family didn't matter to her. She was over him, after all. But still, she couldn't stop the jealousy every time she thought about him with Jillian. So how could he want to know about Alan?

Henry gave a shrug. "He was part of who you were."

"I guess that's true," she said, still feathering her finger through his chest hair. "I met Alan at the bus station."

"When?"

"When I left Morning Glory."

"Yeah, about that. Why did you leave in the first place?" he whispered, his voice anguished.

"You know why. Because you were *marrying* her," Sunny said. She wasn't going to mention Annaleigh and her directive to forget about Henry all those years ago. She knew he had a love-hate relationship with his mother. No need to tip the scales toward the hate side.

"I didn't want to. I was going to fix things between us, but my parents insisted. They used guilt to manipulate me. And Jillian did the same thing. She wanted to keep the baby, and she didn't expect to be a single mom. I was backed into a corner by familial obligation and cries of moral duty."

"Sounds like exactly what you would do." She didn't want to talk about the past. They should leave it behind and not turn over that particular stone. Too many icky things she didn't want to examine.

"Yeah, my mother essentially asked if I wanted a bastard in the family. My dad was quick to offer the old adage about dancing and paying the fiddler. They weren't going to give up until I did the 'right' thing." He crooked the fingers of his free hand.

"So you did."

"Yeah, but at the time I figured I would marry Jillian and provide the baby with the protection of my name, and then I would divorce her. I didn't want to spend my life with someone I wasn't in love with."

He'd wanted to marry Jillian and then divorce her? Was that because Sunny'd still been in the picture, or was it because he couldn't bear to be in a loveless marriage? Surely he didn't think she'd just wait around for him? Like some weird, pathetic loser waiting for her turn?

"But you didn't divorce her. I mean, not until much later."

"You left and made it very clear you wanted nothing more to do with me. I tried everything to find you. I begged your mother and sister to help me, but they didn't know where you'd gone. I left messages on your cell phone until it was disconnected. I haunted the internet, hoping to find some search engine that could find you. After three months of marriage, I started to think that it would be better to try to make things work with Jillian, at least for the baby's sake."

She stiffened slightly before forcing herself to relax. What would it have mattered if Henry had divorced Jillian after the baby came? Six weeks to the day she left Morning Glory, Sunny married Alan. "I couldn't stay here and watch that, Henry. Surely you can understand. Every corner I turned put me face-to-face with people talking about Henry Delmar marrying the governor's granddaughter."

"But you left before graduation. You left everything behind."

"I didn't want it anymore." And as crazy and melodramatic as it sounded, that was the truth. Once she'd found out that everything she'd ever wanted was gone like a puff of smoke, she didn't care if she lived or died. Now she realized she'd likely been suffering depression, probably inherited from her mother, but at that time, knowing Henry would marry a wealthy girl from Laurel, Mississippi, leaving her out in the cold, pressing her nose against a window like a beggar, nothing mattered to her. "So I left town. I missed the connecting bus that would take me to Charlotte. I had planned to stay with a friend I'd met on a school trip. She lived outside the city, but I sat by this cute Marine who'd also missed his bus. At the end of three hours, he wasn't a stranger. He was someone like me, looking to make a new start. I… Well, I just went with him."

He shook his head. "God, that was so dangerous. So incredibly dangerous."

"I know, but like I said, I didn't care. Alan made his life in the military sound pretty good. He said I could bunk on his couch and he'd help me find a job. He was attracted to me—I'm not stupid—and I guess I liked that this cute guy was into me. He wanted me."

Henry stilled and then said, "Sunny, I always wanted you."

"But you didn't pick me, Henry. I know all the details, the guilt, doing the right thing, all that stuff. But when it came down to it, you didn't choose me."

He didn't protest her words, and she wondered if he could understand how it felt to be thrown away. Whether the tossing over of her was easy or hard, the result was the same.

"For several years, Alan and I imagined we were happy. He wasn't a bad guy. A little rough around the edges, but decent. Maybe if I hadn't had such a hard time with the pregnancy stuff, it would have been better. I found out I was pregnant after his first deployment. He'd been back for only three months when I took that pregnancy test. He took me to the fanciest restaurant in town, and I thought things would work. We'd have a family and I would have a new purpose, but I lost the pregnancy at nine weeks. We were both pretty torn up."

"I'm sorry," he said, giving her a squeeze.

"Over the next few years, moving all over the country, going though deployments, we had our ups and downs like all marriages. There were times I thought we should cash it in, but then I would get pregnant again, and I would convince myself I could have a family. I wanted to have that, you know. I had grown up with such dysfunction. I never knew my father, or at least Betty would never tell me who my father was… if she even knew, and I wanted that perfect family."

"No family is perfect. Look at mine. My mother loved to present this Christmas-card image, but my father had multiple affairs in their early marriage. Perfect's overrated."

"Yeah, but I thought I could have that. And I guess you know the rest. Alan deployed for a third time, and I found out I was pregnant a week after he left. That time I was so careful. I took progesterone shots that hurt like hell, and the doctors put a stitch in my cervix to help prevent early labor. I stayed in bed so much I worried about bedsores. Then Alan went MIA. His copter went down."

"God, that's so hard to even comprehend."

"It was stressful. Alan had only a few more years until he could draw his full retirement, and we'd planned so much. I was going to move my mom up there with me and go back to school, and Alan had a buddy who owned a security company in Durham and had a job lined up. It was so sad, you know? I loved him as much as I could. It wasn't like this grand thing, but we were okay."

"I know how that feels." She could hear the understanding in his voice. He'd likely felt the same way in his own marriage, but had done as she had—tried his best to make it work.

"They found his body, and someone came to the house to deliver the news. I already knew he was dead, but hearing it was so awful. Four days after his funeral, I went into labor. The baby wasn't old enough to survive outside my womb, and the doctors couldn't stop the labor." Her voice sounded far away, almost indifferent. That was the way she had to be to get through a retelling of what had happened.

Henry didn't say anything. Perhaps he couldn't think of what to say to something like losing one's husband and child in one week. At any rate, his silence was better than a platitude. So many had offered her stupid excuses. *God knows what He's doing. This is part of His perfect plan. It will get better with time.*

"I had to decide whether I would dispose of the baby or have a funeral," she said, pulling away from him and sitting up. She didn't want to talk about it anymore but had to finish. "It was a girl. I named her Rose Elise. I buried her next to Alan even though the pastor suggested I bury her with the little angels in that section of the cemetery—you know the one—it has all the guardian angel statues. But they hadn't mowed it in a long time. It was like everyone had forgotten about them. Plus it felt better leaving her there with her daddy."

Henry's hand stroked her back. "I'm so sorry you had to go through that, Sunny. So sorry."

"Yeah," she said, wiping beneath her lashes at the moisture that had appeared yet again. "Me too." She turned to him then, noting the tears sheening his eyes. "I guess I told you more than you wanted to know, huh?" She tried to smile but found it impossible.

Henry sat up and placed his arms around her and held her. That was his answer. He held her. And there was no better answer than that one.

After a few minutes of sweet solace, she pulled away from him and slid from beneath the blanket. She picked up her underwear and walked into the bathroom. "I should be getting home."

"I wish you could stay."

The bathroom gave her a needed reprieve. In the low vanity light, she could see how puffy her eyes were and how blotchy her skin. She still wasn't sure how she'd gone from languid sex goddess to sobbing sad sack, but everything had pressed in on her until she could do nothing else. Maybe, oddly enough, the boy who'd once betrayed her had become the perfect man to support her as she fell apart. She'd held in her grief for months and finally it had found a path.

Sunny pulled on her underwear and splashed cold water on her face, using a fresh hand towel from the basket beside the sink. When she returned to the room, Henry had pulled his jeans on and turned on the bedside lamp, flooding the room with golden light. Wordlessly, she pulled on her clothes, not making eye contact because it was as if turning on the lamp had destroyed the sacred intimacy they'd cloaked themselves in.

"So… what are we doing here?" He crossed his arms over his chest. "Is this…?"

"What?" she asked, finally meeting his gaze. She pulled a ponytail holder out of her pocket and pulled her hair back so it wouldn't tangle on the ride back to her mother's house.

"We just had sex. I'm asking what your intentions are… about us."

She hadn't been thinking when she hopped on her bike and came to Henry for some sexual healing. Yeah. That was the problem—she hadn't thought at all. "Well, I'm not sure, Henry. I know this sounds really ridiculous, but I'm not ready for… us. I hadn't planned to come here, and I damn sure hadn't planned to, uh, take my clothes off. It just sort of happened."

"I understand why you came."

She gave a wry smile. "I'm glad you do, because I'm appalled at how easy it was to do that. One dumb instance of getting my feelings hurt and I did this." She waved her hand toward the rumpled bed and tissue-strewn bedside table.

"I'm glad though."

She stood for a moment and thought about how good he'd been to her. "There's been so much left unfinished between us, so much we never said. It's been good to say it."

"Thank you for telling me about your husband and the losses you suffered."

"I supposed I never grieved my husband or daughter. I closed myself up and refused to even think about what happened to me. It's crazy, but I finally feel like I have some closure."

His brow furrowed. "Closure?"

"Yeah," she said softly, hoping she could make him understand that what had happened hadn't been a beginning for them. More like something she needed so she could start to heal, start to forgive him, herself, and God. "I'm not ready for anything more at this point. I wasn't trying to mislead you into thinking anything other than—"

He uncrossed his arms and shoved a hand through his thick hair. "So you only needed me to make yourself feel better." It wasn't a question.

As much as Sunny had once wanted to hurt Henry, she found it pained her to hurt him now. "I wasn't trying to use you, Henry. I never intended for this to happen."

"I get that. I hadn't planned on it either." He quirked his lips. "So you said closure. Like this was an end. I had thought that was what I wanted. When you first showed up, I saw the opportunity to finally clear the air between us, but now… now I'm not so sure that's all I want."

His words were powerful, but she couldn't agree to what he wanted. She bit her lower lip and tried to find the words she needed. "Henry, I still need to heal from the grief. I know it sounds strange, but what just happened between us not only closed the door on the anger I nursed for years but it also opened the door to the possibility that I can find something more than darkness. You gave me that, and I know you want more. I'm not stupid. I know you, and deep down I know you want more than what I can give right now. But I'm just not ready to be in a relationship… despite what we just did."

He shook his head but said nothing more. She could feel his disappointment.

Guilt crept up on her, but she pushed it away. For the first time in a long time, her soul felt unfettered. "Can we get to know each other again? With the pain of the past pushed aside, I feel like we can do that. I feel like we can go slow and at the very least find some goodness."

After a few seconds, Henry's expression mellowed. "We already talked about a do-over. I'm not sure how the sex we just had fits in with that, but I already told you that I'm your friend."

"You are, but I think what I'm asking is for things to fall as they fall without defining anything. I've had two major relationships in my life—you and Alan—and before I can let my heart go there again, I need to get myself right. And that will take a little time. If it's okay, I would like to go back to where we were before I knocked on your door and threw myself at you. I can't deal with the expectation of anything else… for the time being."

"So you mean we're just friends?"

"For now."

"Well, I don't think there's really anything I can say at this point. Look, I get it. You've had a rough last six months. I'm not going to push you to do something you don't want to do. I've always cared about you. Nothing's changed that."

She searched his expression. Henry looked dissatisfied, but she knew that deep inside, he understood what she needed. He'd give her space. That was the kind of guy he was.

"You're a good guy, Henry. For a long time I wanted to believe different because you hurt me so badly, but I know you." She stuck out her hand. "Are we good? Friends?"

He walked over and took her hand. "For now."

"For now," she agreed.

chapter thirteen

HENRY WATCHED AS the cabinet guys used a level to check that the cabinets they'd installed were plumb. It had been over a week since Henry had put in a call to the new owner of Country Boy Construction and asked him to step up the timeline so he could have his house completed by the end of spring. There was a list a mile long, including repairs due to the house sitting unfinished so long, but things were finally happening. The Cararra marble counters he'd ordered a year ago would arrive the next day, and the custom-made light fixture would be hung.

The smell of fresh-cut timber and the hum of the sander being used in the dining nook were somehow comforting, signifying something he'd set aside for too long. Just as he gave an inward sigh of satisfaction, a flash of color drew Henry's gaze out the window.

Damn it. Katie Clare was climbing the magnolia tree again.

Henry made his way through the kitchen, out the half-finished mudroom, and pushed through the french doors. "Katie Clare, get out of that tree."

"Don't worry, Daddy. I'm a real good climber."

"I don't care. You're going to break something. Wait, are you barefoot?"

Katie was only about ten feet up in the tree. She stuck her foot out and wiggled her toes. "The bestest climbers go barefoot."

Lord. She was going to be the death of him. "It's too cold, chicken. I don't want you to get sick."

"It's not cold," she scoffed, like only a precocious, headstrong child could. "And you let me wear shorts."

She'd begged to wear shorts even though the morning had dawned overly cool for a normal April day. The sun had come out to play hide-and-seek with the spring clouds, and everything was covered in a delightful shade of pollen yellow. Thankfully, the house was painted a soft butterscotch and showed little of the springtime coating.

"Where's your jacket?"

Katie Clare pointed toward a lower branch. "I got hot. Climbing's hard work."

"Where's your brother? I told him to watch you."

"He's snapchatting a girl. Taylor Carey."

"I *am* not," Landry said from his perch on a pile of lumber over to the left. Henry hadn't seen his firstborn, likely because the kid had been so absorbed in his phone.

"I told you to watch your sister," he said, frowning because Landry had yet to look away from his phone. "You know, I think you've had enough screen time. Put the phone away and don't let me see it again."

"Oh my God, Dad. I've barely been on it." Landry looked up and gave him a withering glance.

"You heard me." He gave him the dad stare, which essentially communicated Henry was at his breaking point. A novice at stare-offs, Landry eventually pressed something on his phone and slipped it into his back pocket.

Henry stifled a victorious smile. "How about we walk over to the barn and see if Clem is there? He's getting the last of his stuff today. He'll be leaving next week."

"Clem said I can come see him and Frances in Charleston.

That's in South Carolina. There's beaches there and stuff. Remember when we went with Mommy to the beach? I was just a baby. I don't remember it good."

"I do. I'm down with going to see Clem. Let's shoot for summer, aka bikini season," Landry said.

Henry made a face at his smiling son as he waited for Katie to climb down, wincing when she nearly slipped. "Careful, bunny."

"Why do you call me bunny or chicken?" Katie Clare asked.

"'Cause you're fast as a bunny and squawky like a chicken." He grinned.

"More dumb like a bunny," Landry drawled.

Katie tried to kick her brother before she dropped to the ground with a minimal number of scratches and a bit of tree pollen on her denim shorts.

After insisting his daughter put on her jacket and shoes, Henry started down the trail that led to the other side of the pond where the red barn sat, doors open. Various crates and pieces of machinery sat out near the huge F-250 hooked to a trailer. Clem crafted beautiful furniture and sold it online. Henry had commissioned a few pieces for the new house, but since it was still being completed, he'd asked Clem to leave them in the barn. Clem had gotten an offer from a furniture maker and wanted to move closer to his hometown of Charleston so he could have better transportation options for his pieces. Henry was sad to see his friend go, but very happy that the man had found a new career and a woman who loved him.

Which was what he wanted for himself.

Well, not necessarily a new career, but it was beyond time for a new start. Which was why he'd called the man Clem had sold his construction business to and told him he wanted his house ready by the beginning of summer. He'd hired Clem to finish out the project after Henry's guys had done the concrete, framing, and drywall, but that was before Clem sold his Country Boy Construction to Larry Bricker. Luckily for Henry, Larry'd had a recent project fall through and had guys ready to complete the build. As for a woman, well, after what happened between him and Sunny last weekend, he wasn't sure where he stood on females in his life… outside of the one skipping in front of him.

Of course, hoping for something with Sunny wasn't smart. She'd said she wasn't staying and wasn't looking for a relationship. The sex had been amazing and they had a bond—no questioning that—but an orgasm and a shared past weren't enough to hold Sunny here.

Time.

Sassy had told him to give Sunny time, and he'd agreed to give her space last weekend. So he should stop thinking about how to keep her in Morning Glory. About how to draw her closer. About how incredible she'd looked rising above him, breasts jiggling as she rode him.

"Dad, what are you going to do with the barn when Clem leaves?" Landry asked, kicking a rotting log that lay across the path.

Nothing like your kid to pull you out of naked fantasies.

"I don't know. I have some of my duck call stuff in there. I could teach you how to make them. It's sort of relaxing," Henry said, smiling as his daughter took off ahead, chasing a yellow butterfly. This is what he loved about this land. He should have finished the house before now. The kids loved being out here.

"Maybe. Eddie told me he'd take me duck hunting in the fall. He has a lease on the Red River flyway, near a wildlife preserve. I probably need to practice my calls this summer." Landry walked with his hands in his pockets, his shoulder stretching the fabric of his T-shirt. He'd started looking more like a man and less like a little boy.

That thought paired with the news his ex-wife's new husband wanted to take Landry hunting made Henry feel itchy. Henry should be the one to take his son hunting, to teach him how to clean a rifle and dress a hen. "I can take you duck hunting. I didn't know you were interested. You used to cry when you saw anything dead."

Landry scoffed. "That's when I was a kid."

"You're still a kid."

His son cast a glance at him but didn't argue. So much communicated in one glance.

After a few minutes of tromping down the damp path, they emerged into a clearing. The pond sat to their left, the gentle breeze wrinkling its surface. A fish jumped, making a ring on the surface. Katie Clare scampered onto the pier, her bare feet slapping a rhythm. She stopped so fast at the end of the open pier she nearly tumbled into the lake.

"Careful," Henry called out.

"God, she's such a spaz," Landry said, shaking his head.

"She *is* an accident waiting to happen," Henry said with a laugh.

Clem and Frances must have heard them coming because the couple came out of the barn holding hands.

"Hey, guys," Clem hollered, lifting an arm. Frances was half a foot shorter than the big guy. Quiet with dark hair and gorgeous olive skin, she was a beautiful complement to the towheaded, blue-eyed big country boy she'd fallen for when visiting her brother Sal last fall.

"Clem," Katie Clare shrieked, reversing course and running back to greet Clem and Frances.

Clem caught her and spun her around. Katie's little legs flew up and she squealed like a stuck pig as he twirled her.

Frances smiled and then shook her head. "He's such a big kid."

"And I plan to stay that way," Clem said, lowering Katie, who was now so dizzy she staggered around giggling.

"How are things going with the packing?" Henry asked, eyeing the half-full trailer.

"We're getting there. Never knew I had so much stuff. I packed all the unsold pieces I had a few weeks ago. Now it's a matter of getting all my tools crated for transport. By the way, your furniture is covered and in the back corner for when you're ready to move in. Everything going okay with Larry?"

Henry knew Clem was nervous about turning over the successful remodeling and construction business he'd built to his former employee, even if Larry was well-known for his carpentry skills. Running a business was a helluva lot different than making sure ends met on crown molding or a floor was even. It was managing a crew, a schedule, and complaining customers.

"He's doing great. I really think you're leaving the business in the right hands. Plus, I'm here to advise him. I've been doing this for too many years."

Clem slapped Henry on the back. "Thanks, man."

Clem and Frances went back to work while Henry wandered up to the barn and peeked inside. The place smelled of sawdust and polyurethane. The place looked a bit sad without the machinery cluttering its space.

Henry walked through, heading toward the back of the barn. Noting the covered furniture in the corner, he yanked back the sliding door at the back of the barn. It creaked open slowly, a clear sign he needed to oil the wheels. Out back was a tangle of tall grass and vines. The land had stayed cleared because Clem would often bushhog to keep vermin away from the exterior. Henry had talked about putting in a garden but had never gotten around to it. Maybe this year he would. Of course, if he was going to do it, he was already late in getting it tilled and primed. April had snuck up on him.

Landry appeared at his side. "I kinda had an idea for the barn. I mean, I don't know if it would work, but it might."

Henry cocked his head. "Whatcha thinking?"

"Well, you know how the animal rescue is looking for a place?" Landry kicked an old coffee can that had been hidden in a clump of vine-covered boards. "Well, why couldn't they use the barn?"

Henry stared at the boy. Landry's gaze met his.

"I'm not sure there would be enough room."

"We could build kennels out here," Landry said, nodding at the large, mostly cleared plot.

"You want to build the rescue kennels out here?" Henry looked back at the area. His son was right—there was plenty of room to build several rows of kennels. They could build a huge metal roof to cover the entire spot. But that would be a big undertaking and would mean people and barking dogs intruding on his peace and tranquility.

"They need some land, and we have a bunch out here. There are two different entrances to the land, so it's not like people would be bothering us at our place. I mean, unless you didn't want to." Landry shook his head. "Never mind. It was a stupid idea."

"It's not a stupid idea."

"It would be a lot of hassle. It's just we have all this space, you know? They could use it until they found something more permanent."

"It's not a bad idea. I never thought about it, but you're right. We have the land and this would be a good place. It's a little far out of town, but until they find a bigger place, this could work."

Landry looked at him. "Really?"

"Yeah, and I'm proud you thought about helping the rescue organization. I need to do some checking about licenses and stuff, but I like the idea. Until I can do some research, let's keep this to ourselves."

Landry nodded. "Definitely don't tell Katie. She'll blab to everyone."

Henry smiled. "Your sister does like to talk, so, yeah, I think we should keep this to ourselves."

"It could be a cool surprise for Grace and Sunny."

"Well, I think Grace would have to know. She's the present director of the board. But we might be able to surprise the committee… and the whole community. That could be fun." But what would Sunny really think? She didn't even know that he'd bought the land they'd coveted as teens. Almost every time he watched the pond ripple under the moonlight, he recalled the way her shampoo smelled, the way she looked framed in the moonlight. They'd snuck out here at least half a dozen times to throw stones in the pond and lower the tailgate on his truck to make a place to lie back and study the stars… or each other.

"How long would it take to build?" Landry asked, interrupting his thoughts of strawberry lip gloss and working a bra clasp.

Henry was amazed at how much thought his son had given the rescue. Of course, Landry had a passion for helping animals, but to date, he'd not shown much interest in any big projects. Last weekend after the 5K and Easter egg hunt, Landry had talked a good bit about the rescue and how he might raise some money to help at his school. Seemed there was a community service club that chose a different charity each month. Pride in his son flooded him.

"My first priority is to finish the house, but I think we could pour some concrete and get some pens up without too much trouble. So maybe a month or so depending on the weather. But first I need to talk to Grace and see what she thinks."

"She's going to say yes. She told me last weekend that until they get a physical space, they can't take on many animals. They all have to be fostered, and finding enough people to foster animals is harder than she thought. I mean, maybe we could do that too. You said we could get a dog or something once we got the house done." Landry sent another hopeful glance his way.

"We're already feeding that cat," Henry said. As soon as Landry and Katie Clare had seen the black cat living beneath his porch, they'd given it a name. Casper the Ghost Cat. Because according to Landry, the name was ironic. And there was the fact Casper didn't like to be seen much. Of course, the food bowl on the porch was emptied with regularity, but during the day when construction was ongoing, the feline disappeared into the woods. Landry and Katie Clare were working on seducing the cat from hiding with treats and cat toys. It hadn't worked for them yet.

Some evenings, after the workers went home and all was quiet, Casper would join Henry on the porch while he nursed a beer or a cup of coffee, proving the cat wasn't totally antisocial. Just choosy about who he hung out with. Henry liked that he'd made the cut. A few days ago, he'd actually petted the cat, earning a soft purr before the cat realized the danger and darted back into the bushes beside the steps. When Henry could earn the cat's trust, he'd crate it and take the cat to the vet for a checkup and vaccinations. Probably needed to be spayed or neutered too.

"But that cat's feral, Dad. He won't even let us pet him."

"Sometimes it takes a while for an animal to trust you. You don't know what happened to Casper in the past. Give him some time to know you, to learn that you won't hurt him." Henry slapped his son's shoulder and stepped back into the barn.

Time.

Just like the ragged-eared cat, Sunny was too scared to trust, too afraid to allow herself any comfort. The moment after she lowered her guard and felt something, she ran off and hid. Sunny had been hurt in life, time and again, and like Casper and the animals she wanted to help, she needed time.

He'd once had a horrible infection after being hooked in the palm by fishing tackle. The jagged cut had closed and looked fine, but beneath the fatty thumb pad, infection set in. Within days, his hand had swollen and the healed cut had turned an angry red. The doctor had drained it, giving him sweet relief, but he had to take a strong antibiotic and wait over a week before he could grip a steering wheel. Just draining the infection away hadn't been enough. He'd needed salve and time to completely heal. That realization made it easier to give Sunny the breathing room she'd asked for.

Question was, after she healed, could he convince her that the fresh start she wanted wasn't necessarily in California?

As Henry pulled the barn door closed, Katie Clare appeared. "When the house gets built, can we get a dog? Mama says we can't have one at her house 'cause of the new baby and stuff. But we don't have to worry about a baby here. I wanna puppy like Fancy."

A dog again. "We'll see, KC."

"That's what you always say," she whined.

"Whining doesn't make me want to change my mind," he said, rubbing her on the head.

Katie brushed his hand away. "Daddies are supposed to say yes."

"Who told you that?"

"Everyone knows that," she said, skipping off to flirt some more with Clem, who unlike her daddy, gave her what she wanted. Last time they'd visited, he'd found a ten-dollar bill in her jeans pocket. *For ice cream.*

Clem was a sucker for a pretty face. The man would make a great dad someday.

Sunny waved at Woozy, who sat on the bench across the gym. The Morning Glory Bucs were up by twenty points, and Woozy was close to fouling out. The kid wiped the sweat from his face and gave his chin a jerk to acknowledge her.

"I don't know why you brought me to this game. I don't like basketball," Betty complained beside her.

Sunny looked over at her mother, who wore a bright tracksuit from the 1990s and had conceded to pinning her hair up into a platinum bun. "Because it's Saturday and I promised Woozy I would come to the game."

"Woozy. That's the dumbest name for a kid I ever heard."

"You named me Sunshine after a porn star, Mom."

Betty managed a snort. "I was on a lot of pain medication."

"That's what you call it?" Sunny turned her attention back to the game. Over the past week something had changed inside her. She wasn't quite sure what, but she felt calmer. More content. Which shouldn't have been the case because she'd slept with the man she swore she'd never even speak to again. Her life should feel heavier, but it felt quite the opposite.

"I used to come watch you cheer here." Betty inched her wheelchair forward and peered around Sunny's shoulder at the cheerleaders swishing pompons. "You were always the best one. You had straight arms and a perfect toe touch."

Sunny stared at her mother. "I don't remember you ever coming and watching me."

"Eh, every now and then I'd sneak in. Harry Melton let me in at halftime and didn't charge me."

"Really?" Sunny made a face, surprised her mother would even bother. When Sunny was growing up, Betty was either at a bar, working the pole at the club, or sleeping. Every now and then though, she'd go through a Betty Crocker stage where she went to a PTA meeting or baked cookies for Sunny and her siblings. Somehow those times were scarier—neither she nor Eden knew how to take Betty when she was wearing an apron. "I never knew."

"Probably because you were so wrapped up in Henry Todd." Her mother picked up the soda from the bench and took a sip. "How are things between you and him? You finally kiss and make up?"

"Why would I do that?"

"Because I know you," Betty said, carefully dabbing her lower lip so her lipstick didn't rub off.

"And that means what? You expect me to roll over?" Is that what she'd done? Just given in and let Henry have what he wanted? No. She'd gone to Henry. She'd set the rules. And she didn't regret that night. All those things she'd said had done some good for her.

When she'd gotten home, she'd showered and taken Fancy for a walk. A hot cup of tea and a good book tucked her into bed, and the next morning she'd awoken to warm sunshine. She'd put the television on the channel that showed church services, sat her mother in front of it in the hope that God would do some work on the woman, and plowed through the weeds and overgrowth in the backyard to the old shed her mother's ex-husband had built in the backyard. Dank earth and the smell of fertilizer met her, along with some suspicious movements near the back that she tried not to think about. Sunny pulled out an old machete, a pair of pruning shears, a saw, and shovel and then tackled the vines and bushes overtaking the backyard.

She'd worked until sundown, the warmth of the day soaking into her, the arduous task of bagging vines and digging up cherry laurels tiring her to the bone, but when she'd finished, the yard looked much like a tornado had ripped it apart. Hacked and bare, it was ready for a new beginning.

And so was Sunny.

She felt just like that backyard—finally free from the hurt that had invaded her life and hidden who she was. Making love to Henry, getting that closure, had ripped aside the pain and anger that had tangled her heart and burrowed into her soul, twisting her into something she'd never wanted to become—a hard, empty woman. Her sister and her friends hadn't been wrong. She didn't have much hope. But sometime between Jess dangling that bracelet toward her and Sunny tossing the tools back into the shed, Sunny decided she would fight for her life.

She was too determined to reclaim who she'd been to accept the title of Miss Hopeless 2018. Like the yard she'd cleared of weeds, she was ready to plant some good things, to allow the rain, the sunshine, and Mother Nature do some needed restoration.

So that week she'd started viewing her life through new lenses. She made an appointment to get her hair cut and colored and threw out her cigarettes. She'd baked a cake for Aunt Ruby Jean's birthday, even hanging up some streamers and buying some flowers for the table. Betty had complained about Sunny taking down the old dark drapes, but she'd finally admitted that the sunlight pouring into the house made her feel better. Sunny had even called Henry and asked if he could send some guys to fix their front porch. She'd pay the bill with the money she'd gotten selling the antique comic books her brother had collected and left in plastic sleeves in the hall closet. She'd sold the whole kit and caboodle to Jess's boyfriend Ryan. The hot nerd had actually teared up over some original Superman something or another. It had been surreal to see a guy that hot get so emotional over a comic book.

"No, not roll over. I'm not talking about taking shit from Henry. I'm talking about opportunity," her mother said, interrupting her thoughts just as a basketball sailed toward Sunny's head. She ducked right before a kid from the other team snatched it from the air.

"Oh jeez," she breathed, uncurling and looking around sheepishly. A few fans around her laughed.

"Well, thanks a hell of a lot for protecting me," Betty drawled, rolling her one good eye.

Sunny raised her eyebrows. "Eh, it might have knocked a little mean off you."

"That's what everyone thinks about me. That I'm mean. That's exactly what your sister said last weekend, but I'm not mean. I'm cranky, sure. You'd be cranky too if your life sucked as much as mine. Nope, I'm realistic. No need to mince words. I say what I'm thinking."

"Well, sometimes it's good not to say whatever pops into your head. You hurt people's feelings, Mama." Sunny shouldn't have to say that to her mother. The woman knew what she did and why she did it. This is exactly what Sunny wanted to protect herself against—being like her mother. She didn't want the bad things in life to sour her to the point that no one wanted to be with her. Her life was far from over. And Betty wasn't done yet either. "And I don't need the kind of opportunity you're talking about. I don't need Henry to rescue me."

"You need someone to."

"How about I do it myself? I'm capable. I sort of forgot that, but now I'm remembering how good I am when I put my mind to it." Her mother didn't respond. Which meant she either agreed or didn't care enough to answer. "Oh, and after the game, I thought we'd get some ice cream and then go by the Arbor. The director's going to take us on a tour."

"Hell to the no. I told you I ain't going to no old folks'

home." Half of Betty's mouth pressed into a line. The other half drooped.

"It's not an old folks' home. It's a retirement community. They have a pool and a game room. There's a walking trail."

"News flash. I can't walk."

"But you can steer and get outside to enjoy the day. In fact, if the sidewalks at the house were smoother, you could walk Fancy."

"I don't want to walk your stupid dog. When are you getting rid of it anyway? I've been sneezing from all that dog hair."

Sunny smiled because over the past three weeks, her mother had secretly fed Fancy bacon and she even caught the dog sleeping with Betty one afternoon. Betty had claimed the dog had gotten out of her kennel and she couldn't get Fancy off the bed, but Sunny knew there was no way the dog unlocked her own kennel. Either the aide or her mother had let Fancy out. "I'm trying. The rescue is looking for a place to buy where we can house the animals."

"We ain't keeping that mutt until they find a place. That could be forever. And I'm not going to the Arbor."

"We're just going on a tour. That's all," Sunny said, turning her attention back to the game as Woozy came off the bench. She clapped and cheered for him. He caught her eye, apparently pleased she'd come to watch him play in the Walt R. Grigsby Memorial Classic. The big kid came to visit her in the attendance office a few times a week. He still called her Red and had promised to come help her and Grace at the adopt-a-pet event they were holding in front of Seaver's Hardware next weekend.

After the game, she introduced her mother to Woozy—Betty thankfully didn't tell him his name was stupid—and then took the grump to the Lazy Frog for ice cream. Sassy gave them each an extra scoop on the house, and Betty was cordial if not friendly. It was a vast improvement over her last outing downtown.

"I hear Eden's heading to New York City," Sassy said, wiping down the table beside them.

"Who said?" Betty asked, smearing vanilla ice cream on her chin. Sunny reached over and swiped at it, and her mother gave her the evil eye, taking the napkin from her and mopping her own chin. "Eden hasn't said a thing to me."

"She told me. I can't believe I forgot to tell you," Sunny said.

"Well, why would you? I'm just her mother after all." Betty made an ugly face.

Sunny hadn't heard anything from her sister since she'd left. Sunny had been dirty and sweaty and still working in the backyard when Eden had come by to say goodbye. Her boyfriend slash boss had stayed in the van with his daughter as her sister slunk into the house and back out, tossing Sunny a wave and another look of apology. Sunny had gotten over her indignation at her sister and friends trying to give her the bracelet, but she wasn't going to make it that easy on Eden. Fact was, it had hurt her feelings, and if she had found the bracelet, she would have made sure her sister took it back. But the thing had disappeared.

"Sorry. I overheard Rosemary saying something to Sal and assumed you knew." Sassy disappeared as quick as chocolate cake in a teacher's lounge. Sunny knew how fast that was. She hadn't gotten a piece of Mrs. Turner's forty-fifth-birthday cake. Gone by nine thirty on a Monday morning.

"I thought she was doing good at that fancy speakeasy place on Bourbon," Betty said, shrugging a shoulder. "I always wanted to go to NYC. Made it to Philly once but ended up hitchhiking back to Mississippi. That was before I had you. Once I had a bunch of kids, those days were over. I'm glad Eden's doing something with her life. You ain't gotta go to college to make it."

"She deserves some success." And that was the truth. Spending almost three months caring for their mother was enough to drive Sunny to drink. Eden had done it for ten years. Ten… long… years.

Half an hour later, Sunny loaded her mother back into the van and set off for the retirement community that sat not far from the highway leading out of town. The Arbor had been modeled after an antebellum house with two distinct wings. One was for Alzheimer's patients and the elderly who were so sick they couldn't function without around-the-clock care. The other side was for retirees, including a string of small cottages that were more like patio homes. The attractive apartments offered autonomy for older adults who were still active.

"What the hell? No. I said I ain't going." Betty clenched the arm of her chair with her good hand and shook her head.

"The least you can do is look, Mama. That's all I'm asking. It's not a nursing home. It's a retirement community."

"I ain't retired."

"Well, you damn sure aren't working anymore, Miss Legz 2001. You kinda shot your wad when you OD'd and then nearly died. There are plenty of people living here who aren't even as old as you. Hilda Klingman's sister Jude lives here."

"She's retarded."

"That's politically incorrect and hurtful, Mama."

"I ain't interested in being politically anything, and I ain't going to a home. I got a home."

Sunny sighed. She needed her mama to at least consider moving to a place where she could be cared for if she was to have any hope of leaving Morning Glory and going to California by late summer. Glancing back, she prepared to do battle with Betty, but what she saw stopped her cold.

Tears streamed down her mother's face.

"Mama?" Sunny said, swallowing the fussing she was about to do.

"I don't want to go to some old person's place, Sunny. I'm not old."

"I know you're not old, but you have to have someone care for you." Guilt pooled in her, and for the first time she wondered if she might be wrong for coercing her mother to go somewhere she didn't want to go. Yes, she had selfish motivation—she didn't want to stay in Morning Glory—but she also wanted more for her mother than sitting in a falling-down house watching TV. Her mother was correct—she wasn't that old. Not even sixty.

"That's what *you're* doing, ain't ya?" Betty swiped the tears with her good hand, looking pissed that she hadn't been able to control the emotion. "What the hell you so ready to leave Morning Glory for? You just got here, and you ain't got nothing to go to anyway."

"I don't want to live here, Mama."

"Then take me with you, 'cause I don't want to live here either. I never did." Betty turned away and looked out at the snapdragons blooming in the bed around the Arbor's sign. "But we don't always get what we want, do we?"

Sunny cranked the van. "I guess we don't."

She texted the director and told her that something had come up and they'd have to reschedule their tour, then she pulled out of the parking lot and headed back toward Grover's Park.

After five minutes of silent driving, Betty said, "Thank you."

"You're welcome," Sunny said, something she hadn't felt for her mother in a long time stirring inside her. Compassion, understanding, and connection.

And that was as scary as anything she'd felt since she'd arrived in Mississippi.

chapter fourteen

HENRY WATCHED AS Grace shook the hands of the family who'd just adopted two sibling tabby kittens and posed for the official adoption picture that would go on the rescue website. All the volunteers clapped as the two little girls cradled their kittens and gave gap-toothed grins. It was almost like a commercial.

"Congrats on your new baby," he heard Sunny say before handing the father of the twins the plastic bag containing the adoption information.

Henry walked in circles with Rex, the oversized, fluffy dog that had just been neutered. The dog had given him a head duck when Henry first pulled Rex from the crate. It was as if the poor beast knew he'd been emasculated and was embarrassed. Henry had given him an extra treat because he sympathized with Rex. Couldn't be easy to lose the jewels.

Landry sat next to Sunny, putting together packets while Katie Clare walked up and down this side of the square with a stack of flyers, doing her best to drum up business. A very pregnant Jillian and her husband were celebrating their anniversary weekend in Memphis, so he'd gotten an extra weekend with the kids. They were pleased as punch that it was the same weekend as the first Sunshine Animal Rescue adoption event. So far two dogs and the kittens had been adopted, which was pretty good considering it was their first event.

Henry had talked to Grace about converting his barn into a temporary shelter for the animals, and Grace had been thrilled. They'd explored permits, filed them, and with the green light given by county officials, he'd started prepping for the facility. Grace had agreed to keep quiet for the time being. Once the kennels were built, they'd make next month's board meeting a field trip to the Sunshine Animal Rescue.

He knew Sunny would be thrilled.

He glanced over at her. Sunny had brought Fancy, but Henry could swear that she'd been hiding the dog from any interested adopters. The dog hadn't left her spot at Sunny's feet.

"Hello," someone said behind him.

Henry turned to find a young couple standing there.

"Oh hey," he said, trying to prevent himself from tripping over Rex's leash.

"That little girl gave us this flyer," the guy said, holding up a Sunshine Animal Rescue adoption event circular and motioning toward Katie Clare, who looked danged proud of herself. She gave Henry a thumbs-up and a cheesy grin.

"Did she force you to come over? I'm sorry. She's determined."

The man laughed. "That she is, but actually we've been talking about getting a rescue, so it felt providential." He extended his hand. "I'm Ben. This is my wife Marie. We moved to a place just outside Morning Glory a few months ago."

"Nice to meet y'all. I'm Henry Delmar. I'm a volunteer. Now Grace, right over there, is our fearless leader. She can tell you more about the organization and what dogs are available."

Ben rubbed Rex's head. "Hiya, boy. You're sure a big fella. Is this one available?"

Marie shook her head. "No, he's much too big, Ben. I'm thinking I want a female anyway."

Uh-oh.

"Yeah, well, we have one girl. Her name is Fancy. She's right underneath our other volunteer over there." He pointed toward Sunny and immediately felt guilty. Sunny loved that dog so much. He wasn't sure if she shouldn't just keep Fancy. It was pretty obvious to everyone that letting Fancy go would be harder than Sunny thought.

The couple turned to where Sunny sat, absentmindedly stroking Fancy.

"Oh, she's really cute," Marie said, walking over.

Sunny looked up and smiled. But her smile wavered when Marie sank to her knees and started petting Fancy.

Henry wrangled Rex and followed the couple over to the table.

"How old is she?" Marie asked, smiling at the dog and tugging her husband down so he could pet Fancy.

"Uh, the vet thinks she's maybe two years old." Sunny bit her lower lip before rising and taking Fancy's lead so she could round the table. The dog obediently followed and seemed to enjoy the couple's attention. "She's a mixed breed, but as you can see, mostly Australian cattle dog."

"Oh, like a blue heeler? Those are great dogs I hear," Ben said, rubbing Fancy's head.

"Yeah, that's another name for the breed. They're very loyal, like to herd, and need a lot of space." Sunny watched the couple carefully, her expression undecipherable.

"We have five acres and some chickens," Marie said, smiling as Fancy sank onto her haunches and lifted her head so they could scratch beneath her chin. "What do you think, Ben? Think this sweetie would be a good one? We have lots of room."

Henry glanced at Sunny. He could tell she was trying very hard to be positive and smile. But he knew she'd fallen in love with Fancy, whether she wanted to admit it or not.

"Well, she would probably like a big place. She has a lot of energy," Sunny said, trying on another smile.

Grace toddled over. "Hey, guys. Y'all looking for a new family pet? Sunny's been taking very good care of this one. She rescued Fancy herself."

"Fancy, huh? Well, what's wrong with the fur under her neck?" Marie asked, her eyes narrowing. She pulled back her hand and rubbed it on her shorts.

"She had sarcoptic mange, but it's nearly healed. Don't worry. It's not contagious. She sleeps with me, don't you, girl?" Sunny said. She looked down at Fancy with so much love in her eyes that Henry almost took Ben's elbow and steered the man and his wife away from the table. Yet it wasn't his call to make.

"Hmm," Marie said, looking at her husband. "I like her name. Fancy is cute."

"Have you owned a dog before?" Grace asked as the couple rose and faced her.

"My mom had a poodle," Ben said, looking at his wife. "And didn't you grow up with a cocker spaniel?"

"Yeah, Muffin. She was such a pretty girl. I had thought I wanted one of those again, but this one's nice too." Marie looked back at Fancy. The little traitor thumped her tail as she once again became the center of attention.

"Come on over and let's talk about the qualifications for adopting a dog," Grace said, moving toward the table where she'd placed all the adoption paperwork. The couple followed, but Sunny stayed put, looking down at Fancy.

Rex tugged on the leash, but Henry ignored him and moved closer to Sunny. "Are you sure you want to let her be adopted?"

Sunny shrugged. "Of course. That was the goal. They seem like nice people."

"Yeah, I guess, but—"

"She needs owners like them. She needs a family. Besides, they have a big place, room for her to run. She's cooped up with me."

"I think she likes being cooped up with you."

Sunny shot him a warning look. "Don't do that. You know I

can't keep her. I have a motorcycle and I'm going out west. I'll have to find a place, and if I had a dog it would just be harder." Sunny squared her shoulders and sighed. "Yeah, Fancy deserves a better life, one a family can give her."

Henry hated when she talked about moving. Made his gut ache, or something close to his gut. "You're right. She deserves a family, but aren't you her family?"

"We could do it, Dad," Landry said, rising and looking about as excited as a fifteen-year-old teenager could. Which was slightly more than mildly interested.

"A dog isn't a capricious decision, Landry. Your father said he didn't want a pet until he built his house," Sunny said.

"Well, Dad's working on our house now. It'll be done in a month or two," Landry said, leaning down and calling Fancy by slapping his thighs. The dog waggled over. Fancy had put on some weight, and her fur had grown thicker. Her tongue lolled out like she was laughing, and she looked about as happy as a dog could look. Being rescued by Sunny had agreed with Fancy.

He turned his attention to Sunny. She'd cut her hair so it fell softly against her shoulders, and praise Jesus, she was back to being the blonde he remembered. She was still thin, but she somehow looked softer and more at peace. Seemed being rescued by Fancy agreed with Sunny.

"You're building a house? I remember you said you'd bought some land, but I had no idea you'd started. I mean, it's none of my business though, so…" She looked embarrassed that she'd said anything. She glanced over at the couple with Grace and then back at Fancy and Landry.

"I actually started on the house a while back, but when Clem sold his business and had to wrap up some projects, I told him it was fine to take a break. Spring's making me feel like it's time to get it finished. I've been in my parents' apartment too long, and the kids need more space. I wanted to wait until we were all settled before adding another stressor, but if Fancy's not adopted before you, uh, leave"—he could hardly get those words out—"maybe that's a sign."

"It would be perfect for her. There's even a pond," Landry said, rubbing Fancy's ears and dropping a kiss on her head. The sight of his teen kissing that dog did something funny to Henry's gut.

"Let's see what happens," Henry said, not wanting to commit to adopting Fancy. He believed with all his heart the dog belonged with Sunny, that Fancy was one more tentacle intent on keeping Sunny in Morning Glory.

"A pond, huh?" Sunny managed another smile. "Your dad always liked to fish. You remember that time you caught that old boot?"

He was glad to get off the subject of the house. For some reason, he didn't want her to know he'd built a house on the land they'd always coveted. But then again, that was silly. He had every right to buy the land he wanted and build a house on it. It had been their dream, but now it was his reality. Still, he felt weird about it. "Yeah, I thought I had landed ol' Granddaddy, and instead it was an old cowboy boot."

Sunny laughed. "You were so certain you were going to mount that lunker on your bedroom wall."

"Yeah, and then you mounted that boot and gave it to me for my birthday," he said, grinning at the memory. Sunny had always had a good sense of humor. She'd been so amused at herself. He still had that silly mounted boot somewhere in his storage shed. Couldn't bring himself to throw it away.

Landry looked up at them and rolled his eyes. "Y'all are weird."

"No, we're not. It was funny," Henry said.

Grace walked over. "Hey, the Boltons are considering adopting Fancy girl. They want to talk it over first. But that's good news, huh?"

"Sure," Sunny said, growing sober.

"You sure you still want to do this, Sunny?" Grace waved at the Boltons as they walked across the square toward an SUV.

"Yeah, that's been the plan all along. She deserves a happy

family."

"They have a three-year-old, so I want to do a site visit and make sure it's the right fit. Sometimes cattle dogs are a bit nippy." Grace tucked the folder with the paperwork under her arm.

"She's never nipped at me. Well, sometimes she tugs on my pant leg when she wants me to feed her. She likes her kibble." Sunny leaned down to rub the dog's head. Rex sidled up next to Sunny and rubbed his head against her knee. Sunny indulged the big furry lump. "Hey, Landry, will you take Fancy for a stroll? She might need to potty. Here are the baggies in case you need one."

Landry looked at the plastic pet-waste bag with horror. "You mean I have to pick up her poop?"

"That's what dog owners do." Henry winked at Sunny, and she put her hand over her mouth to stop from laughing.

"Fine." Landry groaned, grabbing the bag and leash.

"And take your sister. She's assaulting people and making them take flyers. I don't want to have to chase these papers all over the square." Henry eyed his daughter, who was ambushing a woman coming out of Parsley and Sage. The older woman had what looked to be a bag of yarn and was hotfooting it toward her car.

Landry took Fancy and pulled her along behind him. The dog turned and looked plaintively at Sunny but eventually followed the boy.

"She really *is* assaulting people, isn't she?" Sunny said, her voice filled with humor and warmth.

At that moment, déjà vu hit him. How many times had he stood somewhere with Sunny laughing over something inane? Too many to name. And it felt good to see Sunny smile, to be involved in something that mattered to her. This was the Sunny he remembered. This was the Sunny he'd always loved. For the second time that afternoon, his heart clenched.

"I might want to discuss the art of subtlety with the kid."

Sunny tilted her head. "Wait a minute, *you* are going to talk to her? If I remember correctly, subtleness always escaped you. You went after what you wanted."

"I always knew a good thing when I saw it," he said, allowing his gaze to slide from her baby blues to her lush mouth to her delicate collarbones to her gorgeous breasts. And damned if his Sunshine didn't blush.

And it was cute. She actually looked a little tongue-tied, and right then and there, Henry decided this woman needed more in her life. More flirting, more laughter, more good stuff.

Backward. They were doing it all backward. Weeks ago, they'd had soul-stirring, healing sex, but that door had been shut. His task was clear—he had to seduce her. Not her body, but her heart. Sunny was right—he went after what he wanted. And Henry Todd Delmar had always wanted Sunshine No Middle Name Voorhees.

Always.

Grace fanned herself. "You two are making me blush with all that flirting."

Sunny's eyes widened. "We're *not* flirting."

Grace laughed. "Um, that's the very definition of flirting, and hey, go right ahead. I'm enjoying it."

Sunny turned to Henry and shook her head. "Stop flirting, Henry."

"Like I can help it when I'm around you. You just said yourself that when I want something, I go for it." Henry could have done a bit more of that flirting, but at that exact moment a squirrel decided to hop across the path in front of them. Rex jumped and pulled Henry off-center. He stumbled and went down on one knee like a complete klutz. Thankfully he managed to keep the dog from tugging the leash from his hand. "Damn it, Rex."

Both Sunny and Grace started laughing as the big dog woofed and lunged at the offensive rodent swishing its tail and darting indecisively between two oak trees.

"Smooth," Sunny said, walking over to take the leash from him. The dog's constant pulling kept him from struggling to his feet. "Come, Rex."

The dog glanced behind him but returned to his incessant barking as Henry managed to stand. "He's not so great at listening."

Sunny glanced up at him. "Neither are you."

"But we're both adorable, right? And you want to take us home?"

She shook her head. "You are incorrigible."

"That's just what Mrs. Peterson said about me in the third grade. I didn't know what that meant, but I embraced it. Mrs. Peterson had good legs and a pretty smile. I figure anything that made her come to my desk was a good thing." He gave her his best incorrigible smile. "Why don't you let me take you out tonight?"

"What?"

"Out to dinner."

"Like a date?"

He smiled. "Why not? We're friends, right? Going slow. Right?"

"Yeah, but your kids are with you."

"Technically, but my parents are taking them to see a movie in Jackson."

"I'm not sure we want to go there, Henry. I'm going to leave. Isn't it better to stay friends and not… you know." Her cheeks were still flushed, and she looked prettier than he'd seen her look since she left Morning Glory.

"I'm talking about eating together," he said, tucking a piece of blond hair behind her ear. How many times had he done that? Baby-soft hair, sweet curve of her cheek.

Her eyes lifted to his. "I'm not sure this is a good idea, Henry."

"It's food and conversation, Sunshine."

"Everyone will talk," she said with a heavy sigh.

"Do you really care?"

Something in her eyes hardened. "No."

"So I'll pick you up at seven?"

"You really don't take no for an answer, but I guess going on a date might be nice. I like food and conversation."

"Perfect." He took the leash from her hand. "I've got Rex. Go ahead and help Grace with the cats. Looks like she's struggling to get Honey Boo into the crate. I'll take Rex for another romp and check on Fancy and the kids. Tonight we'll adult with some wine and hopefully enjoy reminiscing about catching boots and that time you tried the Sun In in your hair."

"Oh Lord. I don't want to remember that," she said, relinquishing the dog. "Some things are better left forgotten."

"True." He turned back around, his heart oddly light and full of hope. Maybe, just maybe, he could nurture the remnants of their love and create something new… something strong enough to keep her in Morning Glory. It was a long shot, but still a shot. "But there are some things worth remembering."

Her gaze searched his. "Maybe you're right."

Sunny hadn't bought a new dress in forever, but as she left the pet-adoption event, she spied a pretty sundress in the window of a recently opened boutique. Normally she'd admire and then move on, but today she stopped and went inside.

Because she had a date.

She hadn't had a date since high school. Not really. She and Alan had hooked up, but there had been no wine and moonlight. More like a pool hall and beers if she was lucky. Most of the time she elected to stay home and watch TV rather than endure drunk guys hitting on her and causing Alan to get into fights. Jealousy had been Alan's middle name.

The dress in the window came in her size and looked about

as perfect as a dress could look on her. A stretchy bodice hugged her curves, and because she'd lost weight, there were no odd bumps or lumps showing. The skirt fell with a soft swoosh midthigh, and it was the perfect shade of summer pink. She felt a little guilty spending money she needed to complete the remodel, but it was so pretty, so feminine, and harked back to a time when she enjoyed being a girl, that she stuffed the guilt and embraced the feeling of being pretty.

Besides, the way things were going with Betty, she had little hope she could convince her mother to sell the house. Seemed the thought of going to the Arbor had motivated Betty to be more active. Instead of begrudgingly doing her therapy exercises or working on managing everyday tasks, Betty had tackled them with a gusto Sunny'd never seen before. Betty now fixed her own breakfast and had been working on strengthening the limbs on the working side of her body so that she could perform simple tasks like sliding onto the toilet and moving to the bed on her own. When Sunny had told Eden the strides her mother was making, her sister had been shocked.

"Where are you going dressed like that?" Betty asked when she came out, fastening a pair of dangling earrings she'd found in Aunt Ruby Jean's jewelry box. They'd been her great-grandmother's, and the vintage shell-pink beads just matched the color of the dress.

"Out to dinner."

"Like on a date?" Betty used the chair to maneuver so she could better see Sunny. "With Henry?"

"If you must know, yes."

Betty gave a Cheshire smile.

"Don't," Sunny warned, looking for her purse. She needed a cute clutch but had sold all of hers when she'd had a moving sale last fall. Her wallet looked a bit like a clutch. Maybe she could make that work. There was even a slot for her phone.

"And you bought a new dress?" Betty's tone was knowing. She might as well blow on her fingers and buff them on her tracksuit lapel.

"Yes, but not for him. For me. I saw it, and I haven't had anything new in forever."

Betty stared at her.

"What?"

"You are the most stubborn girl I've ever known. You're even more stubborn than I was."

"I'm not stubborn." Sunny didn't have time to argue with her mother. She needed to find her lipstick and the mints she'd bought at the grocery store. Not that she needed fresh breath for Henry. She just… needed fresh breath for Henry.

"Or maybe it's not being stubborn. Maybe it's being stupid. I mean, you are the girl who chucked her entire life and ran when things didn't go her way." Betty smacked her lips like a courtroom attorney making the point that would win a case.

Sunny jerked around, abandoning her search for the mint tin. "I did not."

"You did. You run from everything. That's what going to wherever it is you're planning on going—California, is it?—is about. You don't fight for anything. You quit and run." Betty's expression had narrowed, her good eye fixing her to the wall like an entomologist pinning a moth. Made Sunny feel wriggly. Yeah, her mother had definitely missed her calling. She would have made a good attorney.

"That's not running away. That's running toward. My husband is dead and I need a new start."

"So why go there? Can't you start over here? With Henry? With me?"

"Henry is not an option, Mother," Sunny said, wanting to mean it. She couldn't even begin to hope that kind of happiness could be hers again. How many times had she thought she could create a future for herself, her fingers brushing against contentment, only to find herself grasping at cold, dank air? Henry was her past, and going out with him was… well, just going out on a much-needed date. Okay, so she'd bought a new dress. Whatever. This date was about two adults having a decent dinner, drinking wine that wasn't from a box, and having a conversation that wasn't about student IDs or drawer pulls.

Or at least that was the argument she'd given her heart… which seemed to beat faster when it thought about moonlight, wine, and kissing Henry.

Which she wasn't going to do.

Nuh-uh, no way, not a chance. Unless…

"Henry's always loved you, you know. I don't know of any man who would take care of a woman's mother and sister unless he felt something pretty damn strong."

"He did that out of guilt, not love. You should have told him to stop. It wasn't his place to take care of you and Eden."

"No, it wasn't his place, but he did it anyway. Look, I know men. Henry didn't know if he would ever see you again, but he came to the house and mowed the yard and trimmed the bushes just the same. He didn't do that because he had to. He did it because he's a good man who couldn't do anything else to make things right between y'all. It was his small way of trying to right the wrong he'd done."

Her mother's words sent a huge spider crack across her soul.

Henry loved her.

Deep in her heart, she knew he'd always loved her, but that didn't erase all that had happened between them. No, she couldn't blame him for her stormy marriage or the painful loss of her babies, but neither could she just let it all go.

Or maybe she could. Maybe to an extent she already had. Maybe that's why she'd carefully lined her lips for a pouty effect and pulled on her best lacy panties.

Best not to think about that.

"I'm going to be gone a few hours. I'll have my phone in case you need me. Would you like to move into the bedroom? Or stay out here until I get home?"

Betty looked like she wanted to continue their conversation, but Sunny was done. When it came to Henry, she was no longer sure where she stood.

"I'll stay out here. Where's the dog?"

"In the kennel."

"That kennel is tiny. Why don't you just let her out?"

"Because I'm leaving you here alone. If Fancy gets into trouble, you can't corral her."

"She ain't gonna do nothing but lay on that couch and look at me with her tongue hanging out. Probably planning all the dishes she could make out of my sad ass," Betty said, her voice sounding oddly fond of a dog she claimed would just as soon as eat her as lick her.

"Are you sure?"

Betty shrugged. "Whatever."

Sunny hadn't told her mother that Fancy was close to being adopted. The thought of the little dog vacating their lives made her heart ache, but she'd determined on the day she brought Fancy home that the scared little pup deserved a happy family. She and Betty were paper thin on happiness at the moment. "I'll let her stay with you. If she gets to be too much, just tell her to kennel. She's learned what that means and usually goes without having to be secured."

Sunny walked back to her room and released the hound. Fancy trotted into the living room, jumped onto the blanket Sunny had placed on the couch, circled twice, and lay down. She grinned at Betty and then turned her head toward Sunny, tongue lolling out, eyes happy.

God, she was going to miss that dog.

And judging by the way her mother looked positioning her chair near the couch, Betty would too.

The doorbell rang just as Betty turned on the television.

"I'll be home soon," Sunny said.

"Aw, don't come home too soon. That would be a waste of that dress… and those pretty panties I know you're probably wearing." Betty turned up the volume.

Sunny shook her head and went to the door.

Henry was not going to see her lacy thong.

But when she opened the door and saw Henry standing there with a clutch of buttercups, she wondered just how fast those panties would hit the floor.

The man really took her breath away.

chapter fifteen

HENRY STARED AT Sunny framed in the doorway, looking like Grace Kelly in her fancy dress and kitten heels. Gone was the tough girl wearing a biker jacket and motorcycle boots. Sunny's former cold indifference had softened into something that seemed almost content.

"For you," he said, thrusting the flowers her way.

Sunny took the buttercups and lifted them to her nose, inhaling deeply. "Oh, they smell like spring."

"And you look like sunshine."

"I am Sunshine," she said, playing along with the joke he used to make back when they were in school.

"So you are." Henry grinned like the fool he was for her. Damn it.

"Let me put these in water and then we'll go." She turned and walked toward the kitchen, and he decided the view from behind was almost as good as the front. The dress molded to her body and swished round her killer legs when she walked.

"Hello, Henry Todd," Betty said from her place in front of the television. A pair of ninjas were facing off on the screen. He rather envied them. Clean fighting. With Betty, there was no such mercy. "I hope you've got protection. I hear you knock up your dates."

"That's right. Thank you for reminding me, Betty."

Her laugh was a creaky pipe. "Always had a good sense of humor. That was never your problem."

"Wait, you know my problem?" he asked, playing along.

"Yeah, you have a dick." She kept her eyes on the fight scene.

He held up his hands. "I'm afraid I'm guilty of that."

Sunny walked back into the room. "Okay, we can go. Wait, what's going on? What did she say?" She leveled a glare at her mother.

"An anatomy lesson," Henry said, motioning Sunny toward the door.

"You kids have fun," Betty called out, her tone almost gleeful. Henry knew the woman didn't get her jollies from much besides eviscerating unsuspecting people. He wasn't unsuspecting. He knew Betty's game. It was to always draw blood, and he rather respected that about her.

They stepped onto the porch, and Sunny turned and locked the door. "Whatever she said, I'm sorry about. She can't bite her tongue. Ever."

"It's cool. Is she staying alone?"

"She is. Over the past few months, she's been working on developing independence. I asked that they change her physical therapist to someone she couldn't bully. Ever since Caron took over, Mom's been making progress in gaining strength and mobility. Plus Aunt Ruby Jean promised to stop by and drink some iced tea with her later. And I have my phone."

They moved toward the truck, and he made sure to beat her to the passenger side in order to open her door for her.

"Same old Henry," she murmured as he took her elbow and assisted her up the running board. Her hair brushed his cheek. Lilacs or lilies or some other flower that bloomed in the springtime assaulted him.

He'd love to get lost in her garden, drink in the honeyed

sweetness, but he couldn't stand there huffing the air like some weirdo, so he jogged around and climbed inside. "Music?"

"Sure."

Cueing up a pop station, he backed out. "I thought we might go into Jackson and eat somewhere fancy, but then I had a better idea."

"A better idea?"

"Yeah," he said, heading out of Grover's Park and toward his land. They'd driven this route too many times as teenagers, each buzzing with the anticipation of being alone. Of what might come. He'd banked on using those wisps of memories to create an intimacy he wanted to explore with her.

That afternoon he'd mowed the grass around the pond and then rented a piece of dance floor from Little Bird Productions, which belonged to a nearby event planner. He'd commandeered a bistro table from his parents' storage unit and bought an iron trellis he could use outside his house when the garden was completed. A battery and some lights woven throughout made the perfect backdrop. He'd added a few mosquito-repellent candles on each corner. A white tablecloth, a Yeti cooler filled with cheeses, shrimp salad, and petit fours would complement the chilled prosecco nicely. The weather had played nice, giving them a clear night, a full moon, and a gentle breeze.

"Wait, is this the place we used to go?" Sunny looked around as he approached the gated entrance. "Oh my goodness, Henry. You're trying to get lucky." She jabbed a finger at him and gave him an affected frown before laughing.

"Well, I'm not opposed, but this isn't me trying to fling up your skirt, sugar. I just remembered how much you loved sneaking out here to fish or skip stones."

"And one time it was our dream," she murmured. "Oh, there's a gate. Someone bought it."

"Don't worry. I made sure it was okay with the owner."

Yep. It was okay with him.

He turned into the graveled drive and headed down the dirt

road where the trees arched before bowing like liveried footmen lining up to greet their master. Stars peeked through the branches, making the darkening twilight somehow magical. Eventually he passed the drive to the barn and pulled up to the pond.

Sunny hadn't spoken. The only sound was Fergie singing about her lumps. Her lovely lady lumps. But Fergie had nothing on Sunny even if the woman next to him wasn't quite as curvy as she used to be.

"Wait here," he said, killing the engine and climbing out. He hurried over to the setting for the date and turned on the lights, then lit the candles. Then he synced his phone to the Bluetooth speaker. Soft jazz set the mood. Everything looked perfect.

When he returned to the truck, Sunny had already climbed out. She stood in the light of the cab, the door chime dinging like mad, looking stunned.

"How did you do this?" she asked, her gaze on the table sitting beside the pond where they'd once had a rock-skipping contest. "Henry, this is incredible."

"Come on," he said, taking her hand and closing the door.

She followed him, stepping gingerly around the uneven pieces of land. Once they reached the parquet flooring, she slipped her shoes off and rubbed her arms.

"I figured it was warm enough to have a nighttime picnic. If you feel chilly, I brought a few throws."

"No, I'm fine." She turned toward him, her blue eyes sparkling. "I can't believe you did all this. It's… No one has ever done anything like this for me."

"Well, he should have." He drew her to him and dropped a soft kiss onto her forehead. He wanted to do more but didn't want to move fast. Instead, he stepped away and started pulling the cheese board from the cooler he'd stowed beneath the table. The bubbly had been chilling in the wine bucket. When he'd popped the cork and filled their glasses, he turned back toward her. "Here."

She took the glass. "Champagne?"

"Prosecco," he said, clinking their glasses. "To first dates."

"You're funny," she said with a smile before lifting the glass to her perfect lips and sipping.

"Well, it's the first date in a way. We're adults and it's sort of a fresh start. I think."

"Maybe you're right." She stared at the bubbles rising to the top of her glass. "I'm not even sure what we're doing or if we should do it. Feels scary."

"Nothing wrong with being scared. What's that saying? If you're not scared, you're not alive. Or something. I'm sure it's revolutionary in thought."

"I've always heard that if you're scared, run." As she said the words, her brow furrowed. "But maybe I'm done with running. I don't know. Things are about as clear as mud."

He sat for a moment, staring out into the darkness falling around them. "Remember when we were in high school and we had that book?"

"The dream book?" she asked, taking another sip of the prosecco.

"Yeah. The dream book. We planned everything—college dorm room bedding, wedding dress, our house, our kids' names, all the things we loved and wanted. You would cut out pictures and paste them inside, and we'd talk about every aspect of our future lives."

Sunny shook her head. "We were just stupid kids."

"Yeah, but we were planners. Maybe we shouldn't do that this time around."

"What? Plan?"

"Yeah, like you said before. Let's just let things happen. We don't have to decide anything. No parameters, no rules, no expectations. Let's just enjoy"—he lifted his glass—"the wine, the moonlight, and the fact these mosquito-repellant candles are actually working."

Sunny smiled. "That sounds like a plan… or maybe I should

say not a plan?"

He snorted.

She held out her glass. "To no plans, rules, or expectations even though it totally goes against every fiber of my being."

"To challenging your need to plan." He clinked his glass to hers, sensing that his words had given her relief. He could feel her relaxing as she sipped the bubbly.

For the next thirty minutes, they ate and talked about old friends and memories. Henry couldn't deny how lovely she looked in the flickering candlelight and the glow of the large-bulb string lights. The night felt soft around them, only a faint hint of the cool front that had come in unexpectedly. Katydids chirruped a chorus that begged the frogs to join in as accompaniment to the saxophone and piano coming from the Bluetooth speaker.

Eventually Henry stood and opened the plastic container he'd stowed behind the large oak tree sprawling beside them. He withdrew a quilt and a few floor pillows he'd swiped from his house. The kids liked to use them to watch TV on, so he'd spot-cleaned them and used deodorizing spray to make them smell like a meadow rather than Cheetos, and oddly enough, pancake syrup. "How about we relax on this and have our dessert?"

"That looks like seduction," Sunny said as he slid his chair aside and spread out the thick quilt.

"Well, it's more comfortable than this tiny chair," he said, rocking the wooden chair so that it squeaked and threatened to come apart. "I won't touch you… unless you want me to."

She lifted a shoulder. "Okay."

They moved to the quilt and he handed her a throw. He'd bought new ones because the ones on his sofa had some funky fruit-punch stain thanks to Katie Clare not following the no eating or drinking in the living area rule. Sunny wrapped the fuzzy blanket around her shoulders, effectively covering the creamy expanse of skin he'd been staring at when he wasn't admiring her lips. Or her eyes. Or her pretty toes.

He handed her a strawberry and nearly died a thousand deaths as she bit into it, a little bead of juice clinging errantly to her lip. In order to keep his hands off her, he leaned back onto one of the cushions and folded his hands beneath his head, studying a sky that had lost its stars. Or rather was covered by a sudden cloud.

"These are delicious. I haven't had chocolate-covered strawberries in forever. Aren't you going to eat some?" she asked, nudging him with her toes.

"Of course. You know I love them. Hand me one." He held out a hand.

"Uh-oh, I just felt a raindrop."

Right as she finished that declaration, a drop plinked onto his forehead. "Aw, hell. Are you kidding me? The forecast said only a ten percent chance of rain." Henry scrambled to sit up just as a few more drops plopped onto his shoulders.

"Guess we're in the ten percent range," Sunny said, hopping to her feet. She started gathering up the remnants of their dinner, shoving everything into the cooler.

He set the opened strawberries and unopened petit fours inside beside the wine and grabbed the speaker. Scooping up the blankets, he ran to the truck as the rain intensified. He shoved everything into the truck bed, thankful for the cover he'd put on a few months ago, and went back to help Sunny, who had shouldered the cooler strap and grabbed the shoes she'd abandoned. Henry shut off the battery and took her elbow. The heavens opened as they dashed back to his truck, shoving the things they carried on the back seat floorboard.

When they climbed inside, he cranked the engine and switched on the seat heaters, handing her the clean hand towel he kept in the door pocket. Sunny wiped her arms and face, shaking her hair out. He took the towel and mopped off his head, then shoved the towel back into the pocket. Rain beat a concert on the windshield, and he saw the citronella candles fall victim to the raindrops one by one. "Well, so much for a romantic night. Sorry you got wet."

"I'm fine," she said, rubbing her shoulders with her hands. "What about the table and chairs and that floor?"

He switched on the dashboard heater in order to chase away the gooseflesh prickling her arms. "Guess we won't be dancing on it tonight. Surely the floor won't get ruined."

"We can wait it out and try to dry it with the quilt. Then you could load it into the back of your truck."

The rain beat steadily against the truck, creating a nice intimacy. "I hate this stupid rain ruined everything. I had some junior-senior prom music cued up for a little slow dancing."

"You really thought this date out." She dropped her hands from her arms as heat flowed from the vents. "I don't know whether to be flattered or concerned. This took a lot of effort."

"You should be flattered. I wouldn't do this for just anybody." He gave her his best crooked, flirty grin. Maybe his eyes even twinkled, but he wasn't sure. How did one make one's eyes twinkle anyway?

"Then I'll be flattered. And I'm not good at dancing if you remember that time at the Jackson Country Club. I stepped on your feet so much you had sore feet. Besides, making out in a truck with the rain pitter-pattering against the windows sounds like a good way to end a date. I mean, that's probably better than dancing."

He glanced over at her. "Oh, that's way better than dancing."

"But what about this?" she asked patting the huge center console. "You didn't have this in your old truck."

He glanced toward the back seat. "We could climb back there."

She gave a shrug and then hiked up her dress, turned, and clambered over the console. "Ouch."

"What?" he said, watching as she gracelessly plonked onto the bench seat and then promptly banged her elbow on the back seat passenger door.

"I hit my head." She rubbed the top of her head and then her elbow. "And my elbow."

He glanced outside where it was still pouring and then back at the narrow space he'd have to squeeze through. "Okay, make room for me."

It was an awkward fit, and his belt buckle got hung on the inset change container. His boots slipped on the front mats, making him lose his balance and bang his ribs on the console. Still he persisted, sliding toward her, his face bumping her midsection. She grabbed his shoulders and pulled. Like the cork from the prosecco, he popped loose and tumbled her backward, knocking her head on the window.

"Ouch again," she said, her hand flying up, making one breast pop out of her stretchy top. "Oh Lord, have mercy!"

She covered her breast with her hand, her eyes wide. Then she started laughing.

Which made him laugh. "Sure seemed easier when we were teenagers."

"Right?" she said, tugging her bodice up, her laughter trickling away as he grabbed her hips, tugging her down so she was sprawled on the bench seat. Then he lifted himself so he could cover her body with his. He kept one hand on the floorboard so she wouldn't have to support his whole weight.

Henry looked down at her. "I'm sorry I made you hit your head. I could kiss it better."

Sunny caught her bottom lip between her teeth, her gaze deepening. The old electrical buzz between them was back, and all he could think about was feeling her body against his, capturing her sweet lips, and losing himself for a few minutes.

"You could," she breathed, lifting a hand to smooth his hair into place. "Or you could just kiss my lips. I think that would make it better."

"I think you're right, but I have to ask—are you good with this?"

"You said the ball was in my court, right? That we wouldn't think or plan so much, right?"

"Right."

"So shut up and kiss me already," she said, pulling him down to her.

Henry wasn't going to ask twice—he'd already showed admirable restraint when it came to Sunny. He wanted to put his hands on her all the time, kiss the daylights out of her, strip her clothes away and do things to her that would make a whore blush.

But he could settle for making out with her in the back seat of his truck.

She tasted as sweet as the strawberry she'd bitten into earlier. Kissing her was like falling into heaven, and he became hyperaware of everything about her—the way she smelled, the throaty purring, the deliciousness of her soft curves against all his hard parts. Some parts harder than others.

For a beautiful few minutes, he reveled in just kissing this woman.

One of Sunny's hands twined in his hair, her fingernails scraping enough to bring chill bumps. She used her other hand to stroke his back, then slid it down to his ass and back up again. His body seemed to have one mission—invade, conquer, force a surrender.

Henry shifted to take some of his weight off her and nearly fell off the bench seat.

"Whoops," he muttered, trying to right himself but overshooting and instead drawing a woof of air from Sunny when he slipped and fell hard on her. His foot landed on the cooler and got tangled in the blanket.

Having enough of trying to fit on the back seat, he pulled her up and sat beside her, adjusting his jeans against the erection that demanded he figure something out. "This isn't working. I have a nice soft bed at my house that, if I remember correctly, fits both of us easily."

Sunny pushed her hair behind her ears. "I thought making out in your truck would be fun, but I just wanted to make out. Not, um, you know. What happened in your bed last time was about our past. This is a new beginning, and I'm not ready to…

I mean, I know this is confusing for you."

"A bit," he admitted.

"I don't mean it to be, Henry. I'm not being a tease or anything. It's just that I liked the idea of going slow and starting over."

Damn it. He needed to—

"You've been so cool about giving me space to heal and find my footing. I know it's frustrating for you, but I appreciate your patience with me. I've needed someone to care about me in that way. You have no idea how uncared about I've felt over the past months."

Damn it. How could he press anything more when she said things like that? Yeah, he was a man and he wanted to take her back to his place and make love to her until the sun came up, but he wouldn't. Because she wasn't ready. Because she'd lost her husband and her babies. Because she didn't know where she was headed or how she'd get there. "Well, I told you that you were in control."

"You did."

"So… you want to go back to my place for a drink or coffee? And I mean that in a literal sense."

She smiled. "Too much temptation with that bed upstairs, so how about we go into town and get a drink? Instead of the Lazy Frog, we can go to Sal's. More adult."

The sigh he'd held in slipped out.

Her brow crinkled. "Or not?"

"Nope. I think that sounds perfect. The rain has let up. Let me grab the stuff out there and then we'll roll."

"I'm sorry, Henry."

Her blue eyes were soft, and he could see she truly meant it. He didn't quite understand what they were doing, but he'd told her he would let her decide how far they went. He could control his body, but he damned well couldn't control his feelings.

"It's okay, Sunny. I'm not pressuring you into going where you're not ready to go." With that, he climbed from the truck and walked back to the place where they'd picnicked. Everything was soaked. He'd have to let some of it stay and dry out. He tilted the floor up against the oak tree and pulled the soaked tablecloth from the table, balling it up. He caught a glimpse of Sunny watching him from the cab, regret plainly etched on her features.

Why was she holding herself back? Because she thought he would hurt her again? Didn't she know how much he regretted their past and the mistake he'd made? Didn't she know he'd do anything to make her happy? That he'd always loved her and probably always would?

No, she didn't know all those things.

She wasn't ready to hear them.

And in all honesty, he wasn't ready to tell her.

chapter sixteen

SUNNY HAD WANTED to go to Henry's place and have crazy, wild sex, but she wouldn't let herself. She'd meant what she said after they'd had the healing closure sex weeks ago—she needed time before she climbed back into an intimate relationship. And so even though her body ached to have Henry inside her, she wasn't going to rush into anything.

The time you have in Morning Glory is slipping away.

She volleyed the thought away as they stepped onto the sidewalk in front of Sal's New York Pizzeria. The striped awning lent authenticity to the bank-turned-Italian-eatery, and the old-fashioned script on the large plate-glass windows set the tone for the experience diners would get upon entering. "Looks crowded."

"It's been like this since he opened. The food is just so good. People come from surrounding towns. The Jackson paper did a feature on it, so we even get people from the city."

"Good for him and Rosemary. It's odd how much he seems to like Morning Glory," she said, stepping inside when he opened the door for her.

"Weird, huh? Sal grew up in Manhattan but swears he always yearned for crickets chirping and big front porches. He's enamored of small-town life… even when neighbors broadcast his business from one side of town to the other. Last week it was a rumored pregnancy test."

Sunny snapped her head around. "Was it positive?"

Henry chuckled. "Didn't take you long to fall back into small-town gossip."

Sunny frowned. "I'm not gossiping. So was it?"

He laughed and then stopped abruptly. "Oh damn."

"What?" she asked, following his gaze across the restaurant. "Oh."

Henry's parents sat at a table with his two children. They hadn't spotted them yet, but knowing Annaleigh Delmar the way Sunny did, it wouldn't be long. The woman was always looking for something and never content to just be.

"Daddy!" Katie Clare shrieked, drawing everyone's attention. Sunny felt the question in everyone's eyes. Were Henry Todd Delmar and that Grover's Park trash back together again?

Henry threw up a hand in acknowledgment before giving Sunny a pained look. "Hey, you're the one who chose this place."

"Obviously I suck at making choices," she whispered as his shoulders slumped and he started toward his parents and children.

She followed him as he made his way through the crowded place, waving at people who said hello. Fred and Nancy Odom sat at one booth with their daughter Victoria. Little Tory had definitely turned from a chubby girl into a slim, capable-looking woman. Sunny waved to Nancy, who waved back. Fred tried to get up, but his daughter caught his elbow and gave him a look of warning. Thank God for small favors. The chatty mailman on top of Henry's parents might have done her in.

Sunny fought against the apprehension gathering in her stomach. She'd not seen either of Henry's parents since she'd returned to Morning Glory. They shouldn't have any power over her, but old insecurities were sometimes hard to hide. She was good at hide-and-seek, but not that dang good.

"Daddy! We didn't know you were coming here. We went to see the movie with the dinosaurs. What's it called again, Lan?" Katie clambered out of her chair and ran around to clasp her father around his thighs. "And Sunny's here too. Is she your girlfriend now?"

"Uh, no. We were… uh… Hi, Mom and Dad. Y'all remember Sunny, right?" Henry looked about as comfortable as a seal surrounded by sharks. Coming to Sal's had absolutely been a bad idea. She should have risked going back to Henry's even if it meant she ended up in bed with him. Screw her good intentions. She could be having toe-curling sex, but instead was on display in front of all of Morning Glory… with Henry's parents.

Mr. Delmar was an older version of Henry with fading brown hair that was silver at the temples and dusted with salt and pepper. His craggy face dissolved into a familiar smile as he rose and held out a hand. "Of course. Hello, Sunny. So nice to see you again. It's been a while."

Sunny slid her hand into his and shook it. He seemed to decide he should be more familiar, so he pulled her into a hug.

"Hello, Mr. Delmar. I've been out of town for pretty much fifteen years so, yeah, a long time." She drew back and tried to smile.

"Good to have you home. I know your mama's happy to have you with her."

"I wouldn't say *happy*. Betty's rarely happy, but it's nice to be back for a visit."

"Oh, just a visit?" Annaleigh asked, lifting an overly groomed brow. She didn't rise. Instead, she extended her hand like the freaking queen of Sheba. *Charmed, I'm sure.*

Sunny, uncertain whether she was supposed to bow or kiss the woman's honking diamond ring, settled for giving Annaleigh's hand a quick wag. She noticed the older woman had sun spots dotting her white hands, and for some reason she took pleasure in that. The woman had always been nuts about maintaining her lily-white complexion, slathering on anti-wrinkle creams and sunscreen like a fiend. Hey, Sunny had to take pleasure in the small things because the rest of Annaleigh Delmar looked amazing. She was still trim, poised, and dressed in only the most tasteful and expensive clothing.

"I'm not staying," Sunny said, answering the woman's question rather than giving her any greeting.

"Why not?" Katie Clare asked, looking traumatized. "Don't you like us?"

Sunny looked down at the child, not sure how to answer that. "Of course, I do, but I don't live here."

"Where do you live?" Katie challenged.

Sunny turned to Henry for help. He merely lifted his eyebrows like he, too, was interested in her response.

"I used to live in North Carolina, and I'll be moving to California."

"That's where Disney World is," Katie Clare breathed in awe. "Can we come see you and go?"

"It's Disneyland, moron," Landry drawled, tapping at something in his lap.

"Don't call your sister a moron, Landry. We've talked about that," Henry said, snagging a chair from a recently vacated table and dragging it over. He parked it between Landry and his father and gestured to Sunny.

They were staying? *Please. No.*

Dread parked itself in Sunny's gut. She didn't want to have coffee anymore. The total discomfort of Henry's parents paired with the too-familiar questions of his daughter had her wanting to run for the door. But she sat because it would be rude to actually run. But she thought hard about it. Maybe she could fake an upset stomach. Or pretend her mother had called and needed her to come home. That last one had merit.

Henry sat in Katie's chair, pulling her into his lap. "Tell me about the movie, chicken."

"But I saw a picture of the castle and everything, and that was in California. I want to go there and meet Cinderella… and Elsa… and Moana… and all the princesses. Plus Goofy." Katie Clare had fastened a most intent gaze upon her father. "Don't you?"

Annaleigh lifted her cup and looked at her granddaughter. "Darling, Disneyland, which was the original park, is in California. I went there when I was a girl. I rode the Matterhorn eight times."

"What's a Matterhorn?" Katie Clare asked, her attention now focused on her grandmother.

"It's a roller coaster," Annaleigh said, sipping what looked to be straight up espresso. Sunny was certain that's what all wicked witches drank. "Disney World is in Florida. Different ends of the country, dear."

Landry tucked his phone away and turned to Sunny. "So what did y'all do tonight? Dad actually put on cologne, so…"

Sunny smiled at the thought Henry's son had noticed his father actually trying to impress her. "Well, we tried to go on a picnic. Your father took me to this place we used to go, but the rain chased us away."

Annaleigh's attention shifted away from her granddaughter. "You went on a date?"

Sunny lifted her chin. "That's what they call it when two people put on cologne and go to dinner."

Henry's mother didn't blink. "It's always nice when old friends can catch up with one another."

Sunny started to say they weren't old friends. That they'd had hot sex in the woman's carriage house not so long ago, but there were children present. "Yeah, it's nice to pick up right where we left off."

Wasn't exactly a lie, but Sunny wasn't going to let this ass of a woman get her goat. Annaleigh had never thought Sunny was good enough for a Mississippi Delmar and took every opportunity to downplay all that Sunny and Henry had been. When Sunny had been younger, she'd mistakenly thought the older woman had taken her under her wing when she offered fashion advice or booked Sunny with her hairdresser for highlights. At seventeen, Sunny hadn't realized the woman was trying to prevent herself from being embarrassed by her son's girlfriend. She'd never allowed Sunny to dine with them at the country club or attend church with them at Morning Glory First Baptist Church.

Henry's eyes sparked. "We're definitely catching up, but I would categorize it as a date. I even had Jocelyn make chocolate-covered strawberries and petit fours. Sunny always loved strawberries as much as I do."

"So is she your new girlfriend, Dad? Will you get married? 'Cause I want to be the flower girl. Can I?" Katie Clare's eyes danced as she practically drooled over the opportunity to strew petals down a merry path of matrimony.

"We're not getting married, sweetie," Sunny said, smiling at the girl. "Your father and I are friends. We're taking things slowly."

"Define *things*." Annaleigh pursed her lips and lasered Sunny with amber eyes of dislike.

Sunny narrowed her eyes at the older woman. "Something that's none of y—"

"Well now, Henry asked about the movie. I thought it was pretty darn good myself," Henry's dad said, his gaze settling on his wife and sending a clear message. *Back off.*

"Yeah, Katie Clare, tell me about the movie." Henry jiggled his daughter on his lap.

Sunny arched an eyebrow at Henry's mother before looking away. She wasn't giving that woman the satisfaction. Hell, if Sunny wanted Henry, all she'd have to do was crook her finger.

Or maybe that wasn't true. Yeah, Henry wanted her, but she didn't know to what degree. In his bed? Yes. To stay in Morning Glory? Probably. But was he truly serious about her? Or was he wrapped up in the memory of what they'd had? Because if Henry wanted her forever, he could give her what she'd always wanted on a silver platter—a home, a place to belong, a family—and that was very, very tempting.

No. I can't let my thoughts go there. Just can't.

Her doubts were interrupted by Landry. "So there was a dumb girl dinosaur that lost a magic stone she was supposed to keep safe. I mean, of course she did. And there were bad dinosaurs and a caveman who helped her. The plot was stupid and predictable. I give it two thumbs-down because halfway through, I thought about killing myself." He mimicked stabbing himself with his spoon.

"It wasn't stupid." Katie Clare shot her brother a disdainful look, finally chasing the rabbit of thought Henry had first plopped in front of her. "Rosie the dino was really cool, and she had a cool bow. I want to get one just like it. It had flowers on it."

"Daisies," Annaleigh remarked.

Sunny glanced back at the door.

Please God. Get me out of here.

"That's right. White flowers. If I get to be a flower girl, I can throw those guys on the floor." Katie Clare slid a glance at Sunny and then smiled—a big gap-toothed, adorable smile that made Sunny wriggle in her seat.

"Give it a rest, kid," Henry said, tickling her and making her shriek.

Sunny glanced away and saw Grace making her way toward them. Here was the escape she had been searching for. *Thank God.*

"Hey, Sunny," Grace said, stopping at their table. Her eyes widened when she noticed Henry and his family were at the table with her. "And Henry."

Henry smiled but also looked alarmed. Which was weird.

Grace said hello to everyone before zeroing back in on Sunny. "I tried to call you earlier."

"I'm sorry I didn't answer. I, uh, was busy and thought I'd call you back later. Everything okay? I sent the graphic for the volunteer T-shirts."

"Yeah, I got that, but I have some good news. We have someone who is leasing us some land for a temporary shelter. It's going to be perfect." Grace slid a glance toward Henry before returning her gaze to Sunny. "And the Boltons called. They want to adopt Fancy."

Sunny felt her heart drop into her stomach. "Oh."

"You're sure you're good with this? I mean, you said you wanted to foster, not adopt."

Sunny's heart felt like it was breaking, but a place with a lot of land and a loving family was what she wanted for Fancy. She didn't need a dog, not when she would be leaving Morning Glory. But even as she had that thought, she wondered if she *should* leave. Maybe the West Coast wasn't such a great idea. Who needed sunshine, palm trees, and mild temperatures? Because Californians also endured mudslides, fires, and earthquakes. Surely smothering humidity and mosquitoes the size of small birds was preferable to dying. Besides, if she stayed in Mississippi, she could keep Fancy. And—she glanced at the man bouncing his daughter on his lap—Henry.

But staying was insane. She couldn't. Sunny had a plan for her life.

Nothing about Morning Glory was a fresh start. Too much history here. Bad history that one date with Henry couldn't erase. Yeah, it had been a good date—wildly romantic and almost orgasmic—but letting those old feelings carry her away wasn't a good enough reason to change everything she'd planned. She and Henry were flirting with disaster. She could feel that in her bones. *You can't go back…*

"I'm sure." She blinked away the threat of tears. "Actually, I'm positive."

"Okay, then. I'll come get her tomorrow. I think it would be easier if I transported her out there."

"No. I want to do it," Sunny said, hoping like hell she could surrender the dog she'd grown to love to the "happy" family. Surely if she could endure sitting in Sal's Pizzeria with Henry's family, she could survive giving Fancy her own new start.

Grace looked unconvinced, and Henry looked concerned.

"Wait… you're giving Fancy away?" Katie Clare said, her big eyes filling with tears. "You can't do that. I'll never see her again."

And then Katie Clare started crying.

Sunny swallowed the unshed tears in her own eyes and caught Henry's glance. His eyes mirrored her own thoughts. *What a shitty ending to a date.*

Henry watched as Sunny helped his daughter buckle into the back seat of her mother's handicapped van. Fancy sat on the front seat, a special treat since she was going with Sunny to the Bolton's place. He'd encouraged Sunny to take his daughter with her so she would have some distraction from the heartbreaking task in front of her.

The Boltons had asked for Sunshine Animal Rescue to wait a week while they prepared to receive the dog, and that had turned out to be a nice reprieve for Sunny, who had admitted she'd spent the time doting on the Australian cattle dog mix and soaking up as much doggy kisses and cuddly snuggles as she could get. He knew Sunny was sad, but she was also determined that Fancy deserved a loving home. He admired her for that.

Of course, over that week he'd also spent rewarding time with her. They'd gone on another date—this time a restaurant in Jackson. No rain. Which meant no making out in the truck. But they'd ended on a sweet note—a hot kiss on her newly constructed front porch. She'd also taught him how to drive her motorcycle, and they'd spent an evening thankful for daylight savings and spectacular Mississippi sunsets as they twisted through country back roads, the wind whipping their hair and loud rock music blaring over the headsets in their helmets. They'd stopped at a roadside café in Charming, Mississippi, and had apple pie while reminiscing about *JAG* episodes, which had been their favorite TV show when they were in high school.

Sunny had also spent some time with Landry and Katie Clare when they'd gone fishing yesterday on a nearby oxbow lake that had good fishing. They'd taken his dad's old bass boat, the one they'd had for too many years. Though the engine wouldn't start, they'd used the trolling motor and caught an ice chest of fish they'd proceeded to fry and eat last night.

Henry had been pleased that Sunny seemed loose and open to hanging with his kids, something many women didn't like. But Sunny seemed to genuinely like his children. And they liked her. Even Landry, though it had gotten awkward when Landry had asked about their dating in high school. They'd just finished cleaning up the mess created when they'd filleted the large white perch and hand-sized bream they'd caught when Landry brought up the "old" days.

"So, like, when did you and my dad date?" Landry asked.

Sunny was sitting in a lawn chair on the small deck just off the carriage house, thumbing through a huge sticker book with Katie Clare.

"Pretty much all through high school," she said absentmindedly as she helped Katie Clare find the appropriate spot for the ballerina sticker she'd peeled off.

"Like, even when my dad went to college?" Landry asked.

Sunny looked up then. "No. We broke up."

"We were on a break," Henry said as a follow-up.

"Like on that show Mom used to watch? *Friends*? I remember the one where Ross slept with another woman when he and Rachel were on a break. Didn't seem like a break on that show." Landry watched them intently.

Sunny's eyes widened, and Henry didn't know how to respond to his son. He knew where the boy was going but didn't know why he wanted to poke a stick in that ant hill. He and Jillian had been honest with their son several years ago when they'd divorced. Landry knew his parents had gotten pregnant with him when they were freshmen in college. He knew he was an oopsie, but they'd shown him nothing but love and gratitude that he was in their lives. They'd told him God didn't make mistakes and that had been the path they were meant to take… just as they'd discovered they needed new separate paths that had nothing to do with not loving him or Katie Clare. But now his son was digging around, suspecting that he was the thing that had kept Henry and Sunny apart, which bothered Henry.

Mostly because the truth was that Landry probably had kept them apart… but that didn't mean Henry wanted his child to know he was the main cause of their split.

"Our break wasn't a break like that," Sunny said, sliding the sticker book over to Katie Clare and tapping the page they were on. "Your father and I broke up before he left for college because that was the sensible thing to do. I was a senior at Morning Glory High and had a lot of responsibilities. I needed to concentrate on my studies the same way your dad needed to concentrate on his. He deserved the opportunity to be a college freshman without feeling guilty or beholden to a girl back home, and I deserved to enjoy my last year of high school. We stayed friends, of course, but we thought it was best to break up."

Henry caught her glance and held it. Her words weren't entirely truthful because they'd always been more than friends. Thing was that even when they were broken up, he'd never believed it would be forever… and neither had she. Yeah, after that one fight, he'd thought that they were truly done. But not really. He'd landed himself in a drunken pickle and screwed up… but he'd always wanted Sunny. Always.

"Oh, 'cause y'all were in different grades and stuff?" Landry looked up from scrubbing the folding table they'd used to clean their catch.

"I guess," Sunny said, looking off into the distance.

"Being in two different grades is hard, huh?" Landry continued.

"It can be," Henry said, cautiously sensing this was now more about Landry and the girl he was "talking" to. The kid snapchatted with this unknown girl more than he did anything else. Henry had to confiscate his phone before bedtime each night to ensure he didn't spend all night on the phone with this new interest.

"Yeah, the girl I'm talking to is a junior, and I figure that it might be too hard to, like, be in a relationship with her." Landry's mouth went flat with disappointment.

"A junior? You're only a freshman." Henry didn't want to sound accusatory but probably did.

"Yeah, but she's only sixteen and I'll be turning sixteen before she turns seventeen. We're in different grades but only, like, ten months apart," Landry said, making a face. "Lord, you act like I'm a kid or something."

Henry bit down on the "you are" retort and gave Sunny a look. She smiled.

"Okay." Henry went to the large fryer he'd borrowed from his father and hooked up the butane so they could start the oil. "I guess that's not robbing the cradle. Any relationship can be difficult. I suppose you have to decide if it's worthwhile."

Landry folded up the table and paused. "Do you think if you hadn't met Mom you would have gotten back together with Sunny?"

Henry jerked his head up and felt Sunny staring at him. He didn't know what to say. He could tell the truth, but that might make his son feel as if he had truly been a barrier for him and Sunny, or he could lie and say that he and Sunny wouldn't have gotten back together.

"You know, Landry…" Sunny's voice carried over the whoosh of the burner igniting. "There are lots of wouldas and shouldas in relationships. People can wonder about what might have been, but what good does that do? Not much. Fact is, your dad and I weren't meant to be back then."

"But what about now? Are y'all going to get married? Or at least be boyfriend and girlfriend?" Katie Clare looked up from her sticker book. The child was a terrier with a bone.

"Well, bunny, Sunny and I are trying to enjoy the present—like catching fish with y'all and making cornmeal batter. Speaking of which, I need to go grab the tub of meal and get this fish coated so we can eat before Landry dies."

"I didn't say I was dying. I said I might die if I don't eat soon. It's not a given," Landry said, giving a crooked smile that Henry knew looked almost exactly like his own. "And way to avoid the question, Dad."

Henry walked toward the carriage house back door. "I'm not avoiding anything, son. I'm telling the truth. I don't know why you and your sister are so interested all of a sudden."

"I'm not being nosy," Landry called. "Just trying to make the conversation you complain I never engage in."

"Well, my mama got a new husband. His name is Eddie and he's pretty nice. He lets me stay up past my bedtime sometimes. He and my mama are having a baby. If it's a girl, they're naming her Lenora, and if it's a boy Leo. I don't like those names. Maybe you and my daddy can have a baby. That would be good, huh?" Katie Clare asked.

Henry stopped and looked over his shoulder at Sunny. She'd grown very still and a small, sad smile flickered at her lips. "I don't think that will happen, Katie bug."

"You don't like babies? You said you liked kids and dogs."

"I do. But I'm not staying here in Morning Glory. Remember?" Her words sounded sorrowful. Henry wanted to turn around and ask her why she couldn't just stay. But he really didn't have the right. He hadn't lied when he said he and Sunny were enjoying each day rather than worrying about the future. But still, that great unknown hung over them, just as it had all those years ago during their last summer together. Change was coming, and he didn't want it now any more than he'd wanted it then.

"You should stay here with us," Katie Clare said, sliding off her chair and wriggling between Sunny's knees. The crafty eight-year-old climbed onto Sunny's lap and gave her a hug. "We like you, and Daddy does too."

When he couldn't stand any more, he went inside the postage-stamp-sized kitchen and grabbed the meal and poured a glass of bourbon. Part of him wanted to toast the work his kids were doing on his behalf, the other half wanted to start drowning the pain that would probably come the day Sunny rode off into the sunset. Instead, he went back out and started frying the fish.

The night ended with a killer game of Uno in which so many teasing insults were bandied about that Landry hurt Katie Clare's feelings, which sent Sunny upstairs to the pullout futon to read a teary Katie Clare a story while Landry did the dishes… begrudgingly and with earbuds back in place. When Katie Clare finally drifted off, Sunny came down and joined him on the couch to watch *Late Night with Rhett Bryan.* Landry had gone up to bed, and they held hands and snuck a kiss or two. Before Sunny left, he suggested letting Katie Clare go with her to the Boltons' farm after she shot down his offer to ride with her.

"Katie wants to see the chickens. You know the kid. She always wants to see something," he said.

Sunny stared out at the darkness. "I don't want to stay long. I want to drop Fancy off and then go."

"Of course. But take Katie Clare. She'll be good company."

"You mean she'll be a distraction," Sunny said, finally meeting his gaze. In those violet blue eyes, there was sadness, and that wounded him. He'd grown accustomed to seeing a happier Sunny.

"Yeah, she will be. And besides, y'all can talk about flower girl dresses and wedding cakes. I think she mentioned a unicorn for a topper. Seems they're awesome."

"So I hear," Sunny said with a quirk of her lips.

He framed her face between his hands and softly kissed her lips. "If you won't let me come with you, at least take Katie with you, sweetheart."

Sunny had let him kiss her again and wipe the single tear from her cheek before she climbed back onto her bike and disappeared into the night.

So that morning as he waved at her through the windshield of her mother's van, he knew how much she would hurt after she dropped that dog off. Maybe he was wrong in wanting her to be too busy with Katie Clare to feel the loss, but he was almost certain that in order for Sunny to drive away from the Bolton farm, she needed a little help. He'd told her he would come over to her house that afternoon and help her paint the porch. She'd protested, but he'd insisted that he could be her handyman. Then he sang a James Taylor song and promised to bring fried chicken from Mrs. Ida Mae Robinson, who was Clem's next door neighbor and the best Southern cook Henry knew. The woman was an institution in the small town, and if someone was nice enough to bring her a mess of butter beans and held his mouth just right, he might talk her into frying some chicken. Henry had brought butter beans, two pounds of sausage from the Riggs farm, and fixed the clothesline that kept sagging in order to get the aforementioned chicken. He bet even ol' Betty would smile after having herself a piece.

Sunny backed the van up in the gravel beside the stone fence and headed down the long drive toward the highway. Henry raised his hand in farewell and hoped like hell a few bad jokes and some good fried chicken could put a temporary Band-Aid on Sunny's newly broken heart.

chapter seventeen

SUNNY PASSED MARTHA and Crazy Ted's place and turned into the dirt drive of the Bolton's farm. If she remembered correctly, one of her mother's old elementary school teachers used to live on the place, but she couldn't recall the family's name. The grass needed mowing around the mailbox, but she wouldn't fault Fancy's new owners for not getting to it. It had rained off and on over the past week, so the ground was too wet to mow.

The old farmhouse had been freshly painted and the flowerbeds had been tended. A swing hung on the porch with a cheerful red cushion and two turquoise pillows. It screamed for someone to grab a cup of coffee and enjoy the country serenity.

"This is it. What do you think?" Sunny asked Fancy, who had perked up as they bumped down the drive. Fancy just looked at her, tail thumping, tongue lolling out.

Betty had cried that morning when she'd taken Fancy out to the living room to say goodbye. Oh, Sunny's mother had tried to hide her tears, but Sunny had caught sight of the sadness and moisture on her mother's cheeks, and that had made her want to burst into sobs and call Grace and tell her Fancy wasn't available for adoption. The only thing that stopped her was she'd made a plan and needed to stick to it.

Besides, a farm was a great place for a dog. Australian cattle dogs loved space to run, and Grover's Park wasn't geared for a herding dog to shepherd people together. Too much togetherness in her neighborhood often led to someone getting shot or pregnant. However, the bucolic setting splayed before her would be paradise for the rescue dog.

"This is where she's gonna live now?" Katie Clare unbuckled the seat belt and leaned between the two seats.

"Yep," Sunny said, rubbing Fancy's head and sighing.

"That's a good climbing tree." Katie stared at the sprawling magnolia tree sitting to the left backside of the house.

"If only dogs climbed trees. Hand me Fancy's leash, and let's go meet her new family."

"Okay." Katie Clare gave Sunny the leash and clambered out of the van.

Briefly Sunny closed her eyes and sent up a prayer for strength. She had to do this for Fancy. She gave the dog one last quick snuggle, clipped on her leash, and then opened the door.

As they walked up the concrete path to the front porch, Fancy sniffed around the yard. Sunny tugged on her leash, pulling the dog to her side as both the Boltons came out the front door.

"Oh, here she is," Marie cooed, trotting down the steps and bending toward Fancy.

The dog tried to run back to the van.

"She's still a little timid of sudden movement," Sunny explained when she saw Marie frown.

"Well, that makes sense. She probably doesn't remember me." Marie squatted and held her hand out to Fancy. The dog sat down and looked at Sunny like she didn't understand why Sunny wasn't following her back to the van.

Ben Bolton carried a small boy, who kicked to get down. "This is our son Hugh."

"That's my doggy," the boy said, running toward Fancy.

Marie caught him and held him back.

"Now, Hugh, darling, you're going to have to let the puppy come to you. She's scared and not used to small boys."

"I'm not small. I'm big," The towheaded child said, pulling away from his mother. Fortunately, Marie persisted in keeping him from mauling Fancy, who had curled her tail and cowered at the strange presence of a child.

"She won't bite, will she?" Marie asked, casting a worried glance at Sunny.

"No, as Grace told you on her site visit, our dogs are vetted, but they are still animals. She's pretty gentle and very loving once she gets to know you. Maybe we could go in the backyard and play for a little bit? Fancy loves to chase the ball."

"That sounds like a plan," Ben said, eyeing Katie Clare. "And is this the young lady who gave us the flyer?"

"That's me. I'm Katie Clare. I'm here to help give Fancy to you guys." Katie Clare looked solemn like she'd accepted the job and was going to see it to completion. The way she crossed her arms over her chest made Sunny smile.

"Yep. And she's great at throwing the ball for Fancy." Sunny looked at Hugh. "Do you like to play ball, Hugh? Cause Fancy loves to chase a ball. She'll even bring it back to you."

The boy stopped trying to get away from his mother and looked at Sunny. "I have a ball."

Sunny smiled. "She'd love to play with it. Or I can get a tennis ball. It fits perfectly in her mouth and won't get your ball all slobbery."

"I'll get one," Katie Clare said, jogging back to the van and emerging with the small bag of toys Sunny had packed for Fancy. Inside was the much-beloved fluffy bunny slipper the dog had found abandoned in Eden's closet, a rope toy, a bone for chewing, and three tennis balls. Katie Clare pulled out a ball. Fancy sat up, her ears twitching in anticipation, her wary brown eyes growing alert.

"Let's play ball, Fancy Pants," Sunny said to the dog, who'd uncurled her tail and was now shifting back and forth on her paws, ready to attack the offensive bright yellow tennis ball. Sunny took the leash and followed the Bolton family around back. "You coming, Katie Clare?"

"I'll be there in a minute," the girl said, tossing her the ball and heading back to likely close the van's sliding door she'd left ajar.

Sunny led the dog around the side of the house and unhooked her. The dog didn't even try to sniff around. Her brown eyes were fastened on the ball in Sunny's hand. Sunny hurled the ball across the wide expanse of lawn sitting beneath a sprawling oak tree, and Fancy sped after it. This seemed to delight little Hugh, who clapped his hands.

After throwing the ball a few more times, Sunny knelt down and forced Fancy to sit. "Want to pet her, Hugh? Just be gentle and let her get to know you." Sunny took Hugh's hand and showed him how to pet Fancy between her ears. "See? She likes to be petted."

Fancy sat still, glancing inquisitively at the little boy biting his tongue and petting her. Eventually Hugh squatted down and looked Fancy in the eye. "Hi, doggy. I'm Hugh."

Fancy cautiously wagged her tail and licked the little hand the boy waved toward her in an attempt to pet her. Hugh picked up the ball and tried to throw it. It hit the grass and bounced. Fancy caught it on the second hop and trotted back.

Sunny rose and watched as the little boy took the ball Fancy dropped and threw it again. "She can do that all day. You might have found the perfect nanny for your little boy."

Marie smiled. "That could really work out. That boy's like the Energizer Bunny. I'm wiped out at the end of the day."

"I have some things for y'all. I know Grace gave you the paperwork, but I need you to sign a paper showing delivery. Jeez, sounds like I'm delivering a television or something." Sunny gave a wry laugh before realizing she'd left the bag with the papers in the car. "Oh darn. I left it in the van. Here's her leash. Let me grab the papers."

The Boltons clapped as Hugh threw the ball and romped with the dog as Sunny made her way back to the front of the house, her heart still heavy with the loss of Fancy but proud at how well Fancy was behaving. Katie Clare still hadn't made an appearance, which was odd. The child was all about being up in everyone's business, so she should have been right in the thick of things, instructing the three-year-old on proper ball-tossing technique and doing the job Henry had given her. Sunny scanned the front yard but didn't see the child when she emerged onto the gravel driveway. The van's door was still open. Where had that child gotten off to?

"Katie Clare?" Sunny called, walking toward the van.

"Up here."

Sunny looked toward the porch, expecting the child to be ensconced in the front porch swing, but she wasn't there. "Where are you?"

"Up here."

Sunny looked up and caught sight of Katie Clare halfway up the huge magnolia tree sitting near the side of the house. Her heart leaped into her throat. "What are you doing up there? Get down."

Katie Clare's denim shorts and skinned knees were just visible through the glossy green leaves. Sunny couldn't see the child's face.

"Don't worry. I'm an excellent climber," Katie Clare called back.

"I don't care. You need to come down. You're too high."

"Don't worry, Sunny. I told you. I'm good at this." The child continued her voyage to the top of the magnolia as if she hadn't heard Sunny.

Sunny thought she might hyperventilate as the child stretched her legs and pulled herself even higher in the tree. Katie Clare's grinning face appeared about three-fourths of the way up. "See? I'm fine."

Abandoning all thoughts of papers, dogs, and tennis balls,

Sunny jogged over to the tree. "Please come down, sweetheart. This is dangerous."

"Just a minute. I'm almost to the top. I can do it."

"I'm not asking you, Katie Clare," Sunny said, growing angry that the child wouldn't listen to her. "I'm telling you to come down. Right. Now."

"Aw, man. I'm almost to the top. This is the highest I've ever been." Katie Clare had inserted her infamous whine into her voice. But she'd at least stopped her ascent to the top of the tree.

"Too bad. Down. Now," Sunny called up, shading her eyes and holding her breath as Katie Clare started shimmying toward a lower branch.

Sunny felt Fancy at her feet and the Boltons at her back.

"Oh my God, is she in the tree?" Marie asked.

"Yes, but she's coming down, thank the Lord," Sunny said, breathing an audible sigh of relief. How in the world had the child gotten so high in the brief moment she'd been around back? Henry would kill her if she knew she'd let this happen. But just as Sunny had that thought, she heard a loud crack above her.

And then Katie Clare plummeted through the branches toward the ground.

Someone screamed and Sunny realized it was her own voice as she ran toward the trunk of the tree. Katie Clare bounced like a pinball, striking one branch hard, then flailing against another, crying out through the entire drop. Sunny couldn't reach her before she hit the ground, but by the time her body collapsed to the ground with a thud, Katie wasn't moving.

"Call 911," Sunny yelled, kneeling next to the girl.

Katie Clare had landed on her face, her arm apparently broken beneath her, a huge gash on her thigh pouring blood into the loamy soil. Sunny couldn't breathe for a moment and thought she might pass out.

"Katie Clare," she whispered, afraid to move the child but more afraid not to roll her over. Carefully, she turned the girl over and the slow movement jarred the child's broken arm.

Katie Clare awoke screaming.

"Oh God, Oh God," Marie said, dropping next to Sunny. Fancy tried to jump on Sunny and Katie Clare, but she pushed the dog back. "Ben's calling 911. What do we do?"

"Sunny!" Katie Clare screamed, her brown eyes wide with panic. "Help me. Sunny!"

"Shhh, shhh, baby," Sunny said, smoothing back her hair and trying to recall her first aid training. Katie's leg was wrenched beneath her but didn't look broken. A huge purply-red lump sat in the middle of the child's forehead. "Don't move."

"My arm!" Katie Clare shrieked, trying to do exactly what Sunny warned her not to do—move. Then her eyes rolled back into her head and she passed out again.

Henry couldn't find a parking place near the ER.

"Of all the damn times to not be able to find…" He grumbled under his breath, trying like hell not to panic at the thought of his daughter lying unconscious in the ER. He steered crazily down one row and then slung his truck around the end and roared down the next. Finally, finding no spot, he pulled through the ambulance bay and parked.

An orderly stood smoking a cigarette and yelled, "Hey, you can't park there."

"So tow me." What the hell did he care if they towed his truck? His daughter was injured, perhaps gravely. He wasn't sure exactly the extent of his daughter's injuries other than she'd broken her arm and hit her head, because Sunny had been nearly hysterical when she'd gotten through to him. He'd left her mother's house with an open can of paint on the porch and not much information on the child they were transporting to Jackson.

He plunged through the emergency room doors and nearly mowed down a nurse carrying a cup of coffee. "Sorry."

"Slow down, honey, and tell me who you're lookin' for."

Skidding to a halt, he turned to the older nurse and managed to huff. "Katie Clare Delmar. Brought her in an ambulance from Morning Glory. She's eight."

The nurse set her coffee down and stuck her head in the swinging double doors. "Mandy, you got an eight-year-old little girl back there? Someone just came in."

"I'm her father."

With his heart beating in his ears, he heard the nurse say, "Thank you, sugar" to whomever she spoke to in the back.

She turned to him. "Okay, they just brought her in and they're getting her stabilized. I'm sure Rhonda will want to get some paperwork started, so if you'll follow me, I'll show you to her office."

"Wait. Stabilized? I need to know what's going on with my daughter," Henry said, feeling panic grab him by the throat and slam him to the floor. "What does *stabilized* mean exactly?"

"Calm down," the nurse said.

At that moment Jillian ran in through the same door he'd just blown open. She wore sweatpants and a blousy shirt that barely covered her protruding stomach. Her wild gaze landed on him. "Oh my God, Henry, where is she? Someone called and said she fell out of a tree. How did this happen?"

"I don't know," Henry said, shaking his head, trying to beat down the fear and anger twisting into a tornadic column of guilt. He'd let her go with Sunny and had no clue what had gone wrong.

Jillian's face went feral. "What do you mean you don't know? She was with you."

"She went with Sunny to take a rescue dog to a farm." As he said the words, he knew what the reaction would be. Sunny had been the responsible party, and now their daughter was in the ER. When it came to his ex-wife, she didn't have even one warm fuzzy inside her for his ex-girlfriend, so this would not be good.

"What? Sunny? You let her go with your *girlfriend*? Good God, Henry, how irresponsible can you be? That's our daughter." Jillian hissed the words.

"Ma'am, are you two the girl's parents?" someone asked from the open doorway.

They both snapped their mouths closed and turned to the woman standing in blue scrubs with a stethoscope slung about her neck. Nodding, they moved toward her.

"How's Katie?" Jillian asked, her hand reaching for his arm. Her nails were talons, but he barely registered them.

"Why don't you both come on back, and we'll talk about what's going on." The woman, who seemed to be a doctor, pressed the silver square that opened the doors to the back.

Jillian, fear in her green eyes, looked over at him. He saw the tears sheening them, felt her apprehension.

Oh God, please don't let there be anything wrong with his little girl. She was only eight years old. So full of life, with so much left to do.

When they reached the last room at the end of the hall, he saw Sunny. She stood slumped against the wall, arms crossed and hands tucked beneath her armpits. She'd been crying, and when she saw them, she straightened and lifted her chin, guilt pooling in her expressive blue eyes.

"I'm Dr. Hargrove." The doctor stopped and gestured to Sunny. "Mrs. David brought your daughter in and told us what happened. It seems your daughter climbed a tree on the property of some people who were"—the doctor turned toward Sunny—"getting a dog? She said Katie Clare, unbeknownst to her, climbed a tree. On the way down, a limb broke and your daughter fell."

"Oh my God." Jillian covered her mouth with her hand and closed her eyes. "Those damn trees. She's always trying to climb them."

"I didn't know she would do something like that," Sunny said, reaching out a hand.

Jillian turned on her. "Don't you dare touch me."

Sunny snatched back her hand, and Henry shook his head in warning against commenting any further. The look on Sunny's face ripped his heart open, and he almost glanced down to see if his blood pooled on the floor. Her hurt was a throbbing, raw thing, but at that moment he could do nothing about the fact that Jillian was overreacting. He couldn't fault his ex-wife. Fear for his daughter had turned his spit to sand and made his gut roll.

"Mrs. Delmar, perhaps we need some privacy to discuss your daughter's condition?" Dr. Hargrove motioned toward a consult room.

"But my Katie might need me," Jillian said, her gaze searching frantically up and down the hall. "I need to see her. Please."

"Mrs. Delmar, your daughter is stable for now. Let's talk about her injuries and the tests we need to run." Dr. Hargrove's tone brooked no argument.

"Oh my God, I can't believe this," Jillian said, swiping her hand over her face and starting toward the small room.

Henry walked over to Sunny. "Let me talk to the doctor. I'll be right back, okay?"

Jillian turned to Sunny and narrowed her eyes. "She needs to go. Hasn't she already done enough? She let this happen."

Sunny sucked in a breath. "Jillian, I'm so sorry. I tried—"

"You shouldn't have been with her in the first place. I never gave my permission for her to go anywhere with you." Jillian jabbed her finger repeatedly at Sunny. Sunny flinched with each punctuating jab. "So why are you still here? You don't belong here. You don't belong anywhere near my kids."

His ex-wife moved toward Sunny like she might attack her. Henry grabbed Jillian around the waist, a very expanded waist, and pulled her back. Jillian turned and collapsed into his arms, sobbing. "Make her leave, Henry. She doesn't belong here."

Lifting his eyes, he tried to communicate how horrible he felt for the dramatic scene Jillian had put on display. Yeah, he felt sick to his stomach with worry, but they didn't even know the severity of Katie Clare's injuries. He patted Jillian's back. "It's going to be okay, Jillian. Let's just talk to the doctor now, okay?"

Jillian snuffled against his T-shirt but nodded. He handed her toward the doctor, who looked concerned and possibly shocked at how quickly things had escalated into a full-out scene.

Sunny stood frozen, her blue eyes filling with tears. "Henry, I… I didn't know… I don't understand. She just disappeared while I was with the Boltons. I didn't know she would climb a tree… Oh God, I'm so sorry."

"I know you didn't mean to do anything wrong, Sunny, but I need to talk to the doctor now. I need to deal with this before we can talk, understand?"

She nodded and looked away, wiping her eyes with the back of her hand.

"Mr. Delmar?" the doctor called. "We're waiting."

He walked into the consult room and closed the door. The last thing he saw before the door clicked shut was a look of utter dejection on Sunny's face. He wanted to hold her and tell her it would be okay, but he didn't know that it would be. His daughter had fallen from a tree and had arrived at the hospital unconscious. Before he could do anything further, he needed to know how his daughter was and he needed to make sure Jillian didn't fall completely apart.

Sunny would have to wait.

chapter eighteen

SUNNY SANK AGAINST the cold tile wall of the emergency room and tried like hell not to cry. She'd only been there ten minutes before Henry and Jillian had arrived. The entire ten minutes had been the longest of her entire life.

They wouldn't let her ride in the ambulance with Katie Clare, so she'd driven behind it, her hazard lights flashing to let other drivers know she followed. She'd sobbed the entire way, deathly cold on the inside, certain that she'd let Henry's daughter die on her watch.

While she and the Boltons had waited on the ambulance, they'd tried to keep Katie Clare still and had used the first aid kit Eden had put in the back of the van, trying to stanch the flow of blood from the jagged tear on her knee. Ben had fetched a cold pack, and the three adults had ignored the toddler twirling around them and the dog sitting with paws crossed, looking as anxious as a dog could look. Finally the ambulance arrived, sirens screaming, EMTs in blurred action. They'd loaded Katie Clare onto the stretcher while trying to revive her. They'd put a blow-up cast on both her arm and leg and taken all her vitals as they placed her in the back of the vehicle.

They hadn't been able to be revive the child even with the

smelling salts.

And now the doctor was having a consult, and Henry had disappeared with his ex-wife after consoling her and looking at Sunny with an accusing gaze.

"Oh God," Sunny breathed, closing her eyes.

"Ma'am?" someone said beside her.

"Yes?" Fear leaped against her ribs, knocking hard.

"Since you're not family, we're going to have to ask you to leave this area."

Not family. No, she wasn't. Jillian's words came back to her. *You don't belong here.*

"Of course. Um, you know, I'm just going to go. If Henry—Mr. Delmar—asks, will you just tell him that I had to go?" Sunny said those words and realized that the nurse or whoever she was didn't know her and shouldn't have to relay messages. "Um, never mind."

Sunny walked down the hallway, passing the quiet consult room, her legs leaden and her head throbbing from the crying she'd done earlier. As she pushed through the door, she encountered Henry's parents.

"Sunny, where's Henry? Is Katie Clare okay?" Annaleigh Delmar asked, grabbing her arm.

"He's in with the doctor. I'm not sure about her condition. I think that's what the doctor is talking to them about."

"What happened?" Henry's father asked, peering over her shoulder, trying to see into the inner sanctum.

"She fell from a tree."

"Oh my stars," Annaleigh said with a dramatic gasp. "How did that happen?"

"She was with me. We took Fancy to be adopted, and while I was acclimating the dog, Katie climbed the tree. I didn't know she was up there," Sunny said. She felt so terrible recounting the events that had led Katie Clare to the ER.

Annaleigh's eyes hardened. "Where was Henry in all this?"

"He was at my mother's house, I think."

"Well, that figures." Annaleigh rolled her eyes, sniffed, and released Sunny's arm. "This is what happens when he leaves his children to people who have no experience or business being with them."

"Anna," her husband warned, cutting his eyes at his wife before patting Sunny's shoulder. "Don't listen to her, dear. She's just upset."

"No, she's right. I never should have let Katie Clare come with me," Sunny said, stunned by the woman's words but knowing Annaleigh was right. Sunny wasn't a mother. She didn't know how to care for a child. It had never crossed her mind that Katie Clare could have been in danger. She knew the child was precocious and needed to have an eye on her, but she'd been so preoccupied with her own feelings and the hurt at losing Fancy that she'd not given a second thought to Katie being unaccounted for.

She walked away from the Delmars, not even caring she was being rude. She needed to get out of the hospital before she suffocated. The world felt like it was closing in, pushing down on her. If she didn't get some fresh air, she'd lose her mind. Sunny walked through doors that parted for her. Sunshine and cigarette smoke met her.

She'd kill for a cigarette.

Eying a man who wore cowboy boots, a huge buckle centering his Wranglers, and a Fu Manchu mustache, she walked toward him. "Would you mind giving me one of those? I could really, really use one." She nodded toward the pack of Marlboros peeking out of his plaid shirt.

The man lifted his eyebrows in surprise. "Not like I'm going to deny a pretty lady a cig." He took the pack, shook her one loose, and then quirked his eyebrow as he lifted his lighter.

Sunny nodded and he gave her a light.

The smoke she sucked into her lungs was an old friend and immediately stopped the trembling in her fingers. "Thank you."

He jerked his head in acknowledgment.

Zombie Sunny walked to her mother's van, drawing on the cigarette and trying not to let the tears glazing her eyes fall.

Damn.

She leaned against the van and took several drags on the cigarette, begging the nicotine to smooth her frayed nerves and give her the energy to get the hell home. After a minute or so, she dropped the cigarette, ground it out beneath her heel, and didn't even bother to pick it up before climbing into the van and firing the engine.

Litterbug.

But who cared? She'd already killed, crippled, or maimed Henry's daughter, so it wasn't like a simple act of littering would be her undoing. But she opened her door, slid down, and grabbed the butt anyway. No sense in losing all her morals… or leaving more work to whoever cleaned the parking lot.

She put the van in Reverse and pulled out, pointing her wheels toward Morning Glory.

Numb. That's what she felt. Like what had just happened couldn't possibly have happened. The image of Katie Clare falling kept replaying in her mind. Pair that with the accusation in Henry's eyes and the horrible words that had come from his ex-wife's mouth and she felt like dog crap on the bottom of a shoe. Totally worthless.

And those words—*you don't belong here*—were the worst.

Because she didn't.

For the past month, she'd been fooling herself. Going on dates with Henry, helping chair the pet rescue initiative, drinking coffee in the high school office like she actually belonged in Morning Glory—all that had distorted her vision for her future. Hell, even Betty had started in on her about staying, about belonging here. Sunny had let that little termite of a thought inside, and it had eaten away her determination to leave. Time to exterminate that niggle.

Her phone buzzed.

Henry.

She ignored it but then thought better of it. She needed to know about Katie Clare. "Hey."

"Where'd you go?"

Sunny switched on her blinker and headed toward the on ramp. "I'm heading back to Morning Glory."

"Why? Don't you care about Katie?"

"Of course I care about her." Maybe that was the problem too. Sunny had actually grown to have strong feelings about Henry's kids. She didn't know why she'd let her heart lean toward them. Hadn't the good Lord made it abundantly clear that she wasn't meant to be a parent? Case in fact—Katie Clare could have been killed on her watch. "How's she doing?"

"She's starting to wake up. Seems her body shut down to protect her from the enormous pain. They've given her pain meds and set her arm. She broke the humerus bone, sustained a likely concussion, and might have torn a ligament in her knee. They've still got to check her for internal injuries. Overall, she's very lucky it wasn't more serious."

With every word, Sunny felt worse and worse. "I'm glad it's not, but I'm so sad it happened. I should have made her stay with me. It never… You know, I think you know this wasn't intentional. She shouldn't have gone with me in the first place. I was distracted, and I own that she got injured because of me."

"Sunny, it's not your fault. I've talked until I'm blue in the face about her climbing trees. She knows she's not supposed to go high and has to have permission before she climbs. The fault lies with her."

"If that's what you want to believe," Sunny muttered, wiping away the lone tear that inched down her cheek. "Tell her I'm sorry and I hope she feels better soon. I gotta go."

"Sunny, don't shut down. This was an accident and no reason for you to run away."

"I'm not running. Didn't you hear your ex-wife? I didn't belong there. I'm not family and my presence wasn't good for anyone at that moment." She clicked the phone off before Henry could say anything else. She knew Henry. He was already in Mr. Fix It mode. He hated anyone being upset or feeling bad. His mission in life had always been to smooth things over and make things right. Some things couldn't be made whole again.

Like her.

The phone rang again and she glanced over at it, thinking it was Henry. It wasn't. It was her aunt Ruby Jean.

"Hello."

"Hey, Sunshine. I'm over here with your mama. She fell off the toilet, but she's okay. The stubborn heifer finally called me after not being able to get back in her chair."

"Oh God. I shouldn't have left her alone." Sunny shook her head, feeling even more guilt settling in on her. How could she screw so much up? Her decision-making was total crap. She needed to get it together and stop playing at being something she wasn't.

"Wrong. You should. Betty's been like night and day since you came home. Eden babied her too much and let her get away with being utterly useless. Your mama's still got some living to do. She made some bad decisions that delivered some really tough consequences, and then she spent years wallowing in self-pity and ugliness as if the world were to blame and not her own self. But you lit a fire under her, and you helped her see that she can do some things herself."

"But she just fell off the toilet."

"Three months ago she would have just gone in a diaper, and now she doesn't have to wear those anymore. In fact, she asked me for some Victoria's Secret underwear for her birthday, and if I would take her over to the VFW to play bingo. That's huge progress, Sunny."

"I guess. Maybe that will make it easier to talk her into moving into a community where she can do more than watch crime drama. She can take up painting, go to the movies, and make some friends. I think she's lonely, though she would never admit it." Focusing on her mama made it easier to forget about what had just happened that afternoon.

Aunt Ruby Jean paused for several seconds, making Sunny wonder if the woman had even heard her. Then her aunt cleared her throat. "Betty asked if I would move in and be her roommate."

"What?"

"She doesn't want to sell the house that's been in our family for generations… and she doesn't want to go to an old folk's home."

"It's not an old folk's home," Sunny said.

"Sunny." Aunt Ruby Jean always saw through Sunny's intentions. "You're manipulating the situation to benefit yourself."

"Well, I learned from the best. Now Betty's manipulating you." No surprise there. Sunny should have known her mother would be looking for a way out of selling the house. Of course, Betty didn't have to sell it at all, but Sunny had been hoping to convince her that she would be more comfortable at the Arbor. "I wasn't trying to force Mama. I truly thought it would be better for her to be somewhere she could make friends and socialize."

"And it would be better for you," her aunt said.

"Yeah. That too."

"Are you still planning on leaving Morning Glory? You've been seeing a lot of Henry, and I heard that Melanie's retiring. You could have a full-time position working at the high school."

"Henry and I are… we were just hanging out." Even as she said those words, her heart seized up. She couldn't continue to lie to herself. The hope that they could be something more than friends had interfered with her resolve to leave at the end of summer. She'd let her emotions override her reason. Being involved with Henry was too complicated. Henry should have stayed a part of her past. Why had she had let things go as far as they had?

Because deep down inside her heart bloomed the belief that she and Henry were soul mates and that they were meant to be together. Because deep down, sitting right beside that belief, was the knowledge that she would always love Henry Todd Delmar. Even when she and Alan were happiest, she'd always known that the love still existed. It had never been torn away and disposed of. She wouldn't allow it because what she and Henry had had was precious.

But she'd lived with loving Henry and not having him for many years. It was a role she was accustomed to.

"I don't have a future here, Aunt Ruby Jean. I just don't."

"Is that the truth or what you want to believe?"

"I don't know, but I have a job waiting for me in California. I can start over there."

"I guess I can help you with that. Can't believe I'm saying this, but I'll move in with your mama this summer. I'll sell my place and put the money from the sale into my savings account. That means I can retire in five years instead of ten. And since Betty's able to look out for herself for the most part, I wouldn't be assuming a caretaker's role. You can make a new life and know Betty will have family with her. Maybe I should have done that long ago for Eden, but I wasn't ready to surrender my total independence. And your mama, well, I think she's finally turned a corner."

Sunny scraped a hand through her hair, the blond evidence she'd tried to get her old life back mocking her. Even as her aunt dropped what she'd most wanted in her lap, she wanted to contrive an excuse to not leave.

Because of Henry. And Landry. And Katie Clare. And Woozy. And Grace. And, God help her, her mama. Morning Glory held people who meant something to her. She'd almost had the community she'd always wanted. She'd almost had the man she'd always desired.

But that was the part of herself she didn't need to listen to. That was the part that actually thought she could fall in love, have a family, and plant pansies on the doorstep each fall. That was the stupid part of herself that believed life would hand her love.

"That's terrific news, Aunt Ruby Jean. Mama will be happy to not leave her house, and the upside is I fixed up the house so it feels almost like new."

"I can reimburse you for some of that, Sunny. You'll need some extra money to get that new start you want out west."

"We'll talk about it later. I'm on my way home now."

"I heard Katie Clare fell out of a tree at the Bolton place," Aunt Ruby Jean said, her voice softening with concern. "Crazy Ted said he saw the ambulance and went to check out what happened. The Boltons said it wasn't your fault. I mean, I know you're probably trying to blame yourself, but that child is a hardheaded little jackrabbit. She tried to climb a tree in the town square during the Easter hunt picnic. Officer Webb brought her back to her daddy, who didn't know she was even missing."

"It happened on my watch," Sunny whispered, remembering Jillian and her accusations. The hate in the woman's eyes. God.

"It could have happened on anyone's watch. You're not to blame, sweetie. So don't go there." Aunt Ruby Jean was a woman who meant business. Her word was law. *Listen. Obey. Don't cross me.* "Now, I'll see you in church tomorrow and lunch afterward. I put a pot of peas on and told your mama to make cornbread. Let her do it. She can. And I'll see y'all tomorrow. Oh, and make sure your mama doesn't wear that whore lipstick."

"But—" Sunny bit down on her protest because her aunt had already hung up.

How in all of creation was she going to get her mama to go to church? And should they all wear hard hats in case the church fell in? Because that was a real possibility.

Finally Sunny could leave Morning Glory.

The timing couldn't have been more perfect. After the events of that afternoon, nothing sounded better to her. Time to move on down the line.

Even if she'd be leaving her heart in Morning Glory… again.

Henry stood on Sunny's front porch, feeling much the same way he'd felt that spring day over sixteen years ago. Though the birds were chirping, the sun was shining, and wind chimes tinkled nearby, change stirred in the air as he knocked on the door for the second time.

The door opened and Sunny stood there, clad in a Led Zeppelin T-shirt, old gym shorts, and a ponytail that was falling down on one side. She didn't smile.

A week had passed since he'd seen her. He'd texted her a few times but found her terse replies disconcerting. She'd inquired about Katie Clare who now wore a bright pink cast and still had a decent-sized lump on her forehead. The child had not had a torn ligament after all and was reveling in the attention from her classmates with typical Katie Clare zeal. So far she'd collected three "really cool" pencils, a friendship bracelet, and a package of Skittles. The teacher had let her stay in and help grade papers until the doctor gave the okay that she could go out for recess. Overall, his daughter had used her accident as an opportunity to regale her classmates with the increasingly embellished tale of her fall and to score some goodies.

"Hey," he said, smiling at Sunny. "Thought if Muhammed wouldn't come to the mountain, the mountain would come to her."

"Who said you get to be the mountain?" Her expression was guarded and she looked like the woman he'd first encountered months ago—a fortress prepared to repel anyone who might breach her defenses.

"Touché," he said, trying for lightness.

"So, what are you doing here?" She shaded her eyes.

"What do you mean, what am I doing here? I'm here to see Betty of course."

She twisted her lips. "She's napping, but if you want to wake her, you might take a gun. Or a baseball bat."

"You know I'm here to see you, but I'm gathering you're not going to ask me inside. Should we try out… are those new rockers?"

She nodded. "Found those at Lowe's. Got ten percent off using my military ID. Of course, technically I'm no longer a military spouse, but since my husband died last year defending our country, I figured the government wouldn't get their panties in a wad over my saving ten percent on some rocking chairs." She gestured to the two shiny black rockers.

"Your porch looks nice," he said, walking toward the chairs.

She looked around. "Yeah. It turned out good."

He eased into one. "Nice rockers."

She sat in the other, crossing her tanned legs. When had she had time to get so sun-kissed? Sunny turned and arched an eyebrow. "So… how are things?"

"Good. And how have you been?" He wanted to tell her to cut the shit and tell him what was up her butt, but he didn't want to spook her.

"Good. I've been cleaning up outside. Planted a few tomato plants out back and put in some shrubs over there." She pointed toward several Indian hawthorns lining the front of the house on each side.

He could give a squat less about landscaping. He needed to know why she'd pulled so hard and so fast away from him after Katie Clare's accident. Surely she knew he didn't blame her for what had happened. His daughter had eventually admitted to both him and Jillian that she'd purposely not told Sunny she was going to climb the tree because she knew Sunny wouldn't have let her. The kid also owned up to the fact she'd initially ignored Sunny's pleas for her to come down and had instead climbed higher. They hadn't had to punish her for being disobedient. Missing soccer practice for three weeks had proved more than enough punishment.

"What's wrong, Sunny?"

"Nothing. I've been busy getting this house wrapped up. It's May and school is winding down, so… I've been busier than normal."

"You know I'm not talking about that. I'm talking about why

you won't talk to me anymore."

She sucked in a deep breath. "Because it's easier that way. Things weren't going to work anyway."

"What wasn't working?"

Giving him a flat look, she turned her gaze to the house across the street. "All of it. I knew I couldn't get involved with you. I told you that, but I let you talk me into this friendship… and kissing… and it's just not what I need right now. It's not working."

"Bullshit. I talked you into kissing me? To sleeping with me? That was all you, sweetheart."

Her gaze snapped to his. "That may be, but that doesn't change the fact that I can't do this with you. Look, we have all these leftover feelings from our past. We were once good together, and we'll always have those memories, but we can't build a future on something so flawed. We had our chance and we blew it."

"Bullshit."

"It's not bullshit. It's the truth."

"You think because we messed up years ago—because I messed up—that we can never have something strong between us again? Because that sounds like an absolute. Like we could only possibly have one shot at something. If that were true, no one in the world would ever succeed at anything." It was a good argument. Maybe some things were one-shot dreams, but not most things. Thomas Edison once said he'd found hundreds of ways to not make a light bulb. Thomas hadn't given up and neither would Henry.

Sunny set her jaw and refused to look at him. "It's just how I feel. Katie Clare's accident woke me up to what I was trying to do."

He inhaled and exhaled. "Which was?"

"Trying to fit into a shoe I wasn't meant to wear. You're not my husband, and your kids aren't and never will be mine. I had started to lull myself into a false sense of belonging here… with you. And that life is one I wasn't meant to have."

"Again, bullshit." Anger rose inside him, and he had the inclination to shake her until she abandoned the idiotic thoughts that flitted through her pretty head. What? She thought she didn't deserve to love and be loved? Because she'd had her one shot at love and missed the mark? Or maybe this was because she couldn't have children. Either way, it was a messed-up view of life in general. "Sunny, you're throwing up walls when there's no need for them. Of course Landry and Katie Clare are not your kids, but they could be something more than just 'Henry's kids.' They like you. A lot."

"I know, and that's part of the problem. I don't need to get that close because I'm leaving, Henry."

"Why, Sunny? I mean, Christ, you have people here who love you. And if Melanie retires, they'll offer you a job with good benefits. You're already part of this community. It's where you were born, raised, and where you belong."

"No. it's where *you* belong. There are things I am not meant for. I know that. It's pretty evident that I couldn't have children for a good reason."

"Are you even listening to yourself?" he asked, rising from the chair and walking across the no longer sagging porch. "You think God is punishing you by not giving you children? What kind of god do you think we serve, Sunny? And do you know how ludicrous it is that you're using what happened to Katie Clare to justify this?"

"Don't tell me what I feel." She jabbed her pointer finger down on the arm of the rocker.

"I will when it's wrong."

She glared at him, and in her blue eyes he could see the stubbornness that had often been her downfall. She'd made up her mind and didn't want to be moved.

Try a different tactic. "So what about me? Don't I matter? I thought things were going good between us."

"Because we went on a few dates?" She spread her hands and

looked up at him. "Yeah, the sex was good and we've had some laughs, but I can't go back in time, Henry. I'm not some pathetic woman who needs you to rescue her."

"Who said I was trying to rescue you? I was *dating* you with the hope you'd see that we are good together… with the hope you could grow to trust me again. And I was giving you the space you had asked for. Shit, Sunny, give me some credit for trying to do the right thing."

"You always do the right thing, Henry. That was the problem from the beginning, and it's still the problem. You're trying to rectify what happened in the past. You still feel guilty and you want to fix things. That's what all this has been about—the past."

He couldn't believe the conclusions she'd drawn. How messed up was this woman? And how hard was she trying to run from anything remotely good in her life? "Are you effing crazy? You think I'm trying to make something up to you? You think that was a pity fuck? Or maybe because I'm a guy, it would mean nothing to me? And I suppose those dates were supposed to be about getting back in your pants, or maybe you thought they were some sort of payment? Hell, I have no idea what sort of intent you subscribe to my actions. You might think I'm a serial killer trying to lure you to my lair, because obviously nothing about me is honest or pure."

"Don't treat me like I'm crazy," she said, leaping to her feet. "I'm not."

"Then don't say insane things just so you can justify running away from me."

"I'm not running. I had a plan from the beginning—get my mama settled and go to California. That's not running away. It's running to something. I deserve a new life and a new start. I don't want to stay here where people know everything about me. Being a Voorhees in this town sucks, Henry. It sucks."

"You sure have a shitty opinion of people." He stood because he had to do something other than sit and listen to her bull. He stared at the neighbor's wind chimes clinking.

"All I'm saying is that my plan was a good one, and you"—she stood up and poked a finger in his chest—"are muddying my waters by trying to convince me I'm somebody I'm not. I'm not the old Sunny, and I don't want to belong to you or anyone. And I damn sure don't want to stay in this town."

"Then go."

"I will."

For a few seconds they both stood across from one another. Emotion stretched between them, and it hurt to feel the widening gulf she was intentionally creating. Sunny was afraid that someone loving her was too good to be true.

"You know what this is about, Sunny? It's about being afraid. You're afraid to love me. Afraid to love my kids. Afraid to want something good for yourself. You'd rather wallow in the sorrow, in despair, just like your mother does, because that's safer than actually taking a leap of faith. Essentially you're saying you'll be content to sit and watch life go by because you're too scared to get out there and actually live it. And that's really sad. In fact, that's pathetic."

She looked like he'd hit her with a shovel. "Get the hell off my porch."

Henry shook his head. "I thought I could change your mind. I thought you would be able to see that love is powerful enough to sew us back together again. But you just want to run from all you are and all you could be."

Sunny stilled, her anger leaving as suddenly as it had come. Instead, she looked defeated. "Maybe you're right. Maybe I want to escape who I am. Sometimes that's how people deal. They avoid what hurts, and you hurt me. Alan hurt me. Life hurt me. So maybe being afraid is the only way I can survive."

"Surviving's not living."

She inhaled and exhaled with a measured breath. "God, Henry, don't you understand? I don't want to love you."

"Don't or can't?"

She paused, looked away from him. "Can't. I can't be what

you want me to be. And I can't love you. I'm sorry. But I can't do it."

She might as well have throat punched him and then reached down and ripped his heart from his chest. *I don't want to love you. I can't love you.*

Turning, he walked down the steps his guys had rebuilt a few weeks ago. They were sturdy now. Fixed. But the woman living in the house wasn't. And might never be.

Leaving Sunny was something he'd done before. Last time a three-hundred-pound gorilla had tossed him out like a sack of rotten potatoes. This time all it had taken was her words.

When he got to the bottom, he turned back. "I won't bother you anymore."

"That would be best." She crossed her arms, refusing to look at him. "I'm leaving as soon as I can manage it."

The anger and hurt inside him leaked out like a deflated balloon. Being furious with her did as much good as being furious with Casper the Ghost Cat, who had bitten him when he'd tried to put him in a crate to take to the vet. When a creature was so hurt, so scared, so desperate for escape, there was no rationalizing with it. Sunny was convinced she didn't love him, didn't belong in Morning Glory, couldn't hope for a life beyond the golden one she'd visualized for herself in California. He felt sorry that she wouldn't allow herself to feel love.

"I hope life gives you what you want." He walked back to his truck, trying to ignore the heaviness pressing on his chest. Tears raw in his throat, he climbed inside the cab and started the engine. Sunny stood barefoot on her porch and watched him. Her mouth was pressed into an angry line, but her eyes, even from such a distance, looked sad.

And just like he'd done on a spring day sixteen years ago, he drove away with a broken heart.

chapter nineteen

THREE MONTHS.

Sunny had gone three months without seeing Henry, and truth be told, she'd cried herself to sleep more nights than not. Not wanting to deal with the emotion slamming into her at regular intervals, she'd done what she'd always done. She took her grief, folded it into an itty-bitty square and stuffed it into the empty box of her soul. And then she'd lain low.

With Fancy gone and her heart too tender to subject herself to caring for any more fosters, she'd bowed out of being on the Sunshine Animal Rescue board. Rosemary had taken her place. Sunny felt bad about it, but couldn't handle being such an integral part of something she'd leave behind. With no job to encumber her, she'd spent the summer trying to occupy her empty hours around the house. She'd grown the plumpest tomatoes in the hood, built a flower bed that rivaled any in town, and helped show potential buyers the redbrick house that her aunt had put up for sale. Luckily her aunt had sold the house a week ago and was poised to move into the old Voorhees homeplace with Betty. Sunny was free to leave Morning Glory.

Problem was—she no longer wanted to leave.

Last week, Marilyn McConnell had talked her into coming

back into the office and subbing for them for the first week of school. Seemed Melanie had decided to retire after all, and they needed someone to get the office ready for the new hire. Sunny secretly thought Marilyn was trying to lure her back into working as the attendance clerk… and she was secretly tempted.

And wasn't that just a kick in the pants?

Sunny had not only fallen back in love with Henry Delmar, she'd fallen back in love with Morning Glory too.

Damn it.

"I'm a senior this year. And I'm starting defensive back. Not to mention, we got a shot at state hoopin' this year. How you gonna go out to California when all this is going on? You gotta stay and watch greatness." Woozy crossed his arms and lifted his chin, but his brown eyes twinkled.

Sunny shoved the can of peanuts she'd left in the bottom drawer into the trashcan. "I can watch you on the computer. Don't they film the games?"

"Yeah, but that's not the same thing. You're going to miss your opportunity to be on ESPN and stuff. They going to tell my story one day, and you could have been my person."

"Your person?"

"You know, the person that gives all the insight into a star's early life. Like how they didn't have any shoes and were shoved into lockers and stuff."

"You have several pairs of shoes and wouldn't fit into a locker." She laughed.

"I'm just saying you going to be wishing you'd stayed to watch the great Woozy Jefferson." He flashed her a red-carpet grin, folding his arms in a cocky pose.

"You don't suffer from lack of confidence, do you?" she said, finally finding her smile. Today was the first day for students and her last day to sub for the county. She had to finish out the day, and then she could push out the doors of Morning Glory High and head for sunnier climes. She had reservations at several stops on her ride to California. She tried to bolster excitement for it but kept thinking about Fancy and how she'd love the coast. Or maybe the dog wouldn't. And then she'd think of Katie Clare and Landry and how they'd love California. Or not. She wasn't sure. And then she thought of Henry and how she really just wanted to stay here and make things right between them.

Because she'd overreacted. She knew that. But she didn't know how to fix the words she'd said. She'd told him she'd never love him.

Hard words to step around.

"Doubt builds mountains you can't climb, and I don't need no mountains in my way." Woozy smiled at her like a guru.

"You could probably market that and give seminars. Destroy your mountains." Sunny shimmied her hands. It was advice she needed to take. If she wanted to make things right, she could stay and climb the mountain she'd tossed in her own path. Instead, she was running. She knew she was running… but she couldn't figure out how to stop herself from carrying out the plan she'd adamantly clung to for so long.

"You think people would pay me?" Woozy asked, opportunity glistening in his dark eyes.

"Mr. Jefferson, class started three minutes ago. You better find where you're supposed to be," Marilyn said from the doorway, leveling Woozy with her patented administrator's scowl.

"Aw, Miss M, it's the first week. Be chill."

Marilyn narrowed her eyes. "You want to chill in detention this afternoon?"

Woozy's eyebrows shot to his hairline. "No, ma'am. I'm gone. Later, Red."

"Bye, Woozy." A ping of sadness hit her. She really liked the kid and would miss seeing him most days.

"That guy's gonna miss you." Marilyn's mouth curved up in affection. Everyone loved Woozy. He was just one of those kids who made you love him.

"I'll miss him. And the school. I've enjoyed working here,

and I'm glad you asked me to come back. I think I've got everything labeled and ready for whoever y'all hire."

"California, huh?" Marilyn said, ignoring the words Sunny had spoken. The woman crossed her arms over her blouse, which featured little cat noses and whiskers. Her denim skirt had buttons down the front, and she was pretty much a fashion disaster. But Sunny couldn't imagine Marilyn dressed in anything other than retro/feline/matron wear. It was her vibe. "Don't they have constant fires… and mudslides?"

"Don't forget earthquakes," Sunny added with a smile.

"Yeah, those too. I mean, are you sure you want to go out there? I hear the people out there can be weird."

"Weirder than the people here?" Sunny laughed, thinking about all the characters they had living in Morning Glory. "And don't forget, California has beaches, mountains, and low humidity. The weather's perfect where my friend lives. I'll never have to use hairspray again."

"Well, that's a selling point, I guess. I still wish you'd stay and work here. You've done an amazing job. Even Melanie said so."

"Yeah, I liked the job."

"We probably won't fill this position for a few weeks, so if you change your mind, call."

Sunny nodded. "Thanks."

Twenty minutes later, she pulled her Harley into the driveway of her mother's house. Every time she pulled in, she felt a glow of pride in the house and yard. The weed and feed had finally done its job, and the resulting thick grass grew where there'd once been weeds. The Indian hawthorns lining the front under her bedroom window had filled in, and the fresh-painted porch looked almost cheerful thanks to the large geranium squatting between the glossy black rockers. She'd spray-painted the porch light a shiny brass and bought a matching kickplate. Simple, inexpensive touches that created an almost hominess to a house that had sat sullen for far too long.

Greeting her on the doormat was a box.

Sunny opened the door and propped it open with her hip. “Mama, did you order something?”

“No,” Betty called.

Sunny stuck her head inside, trying to balance her things from her desk and pick up the delivered package at the same time. Betty wasn’t in the living room. The television wasn’t on, but she could hear music. Carly Simon. “Where are you?”

“I’m in my room.”

Sunny walked inside, set her things down, and peeked inside her mother’s room. Betty sat on the made bed, eating popcorn and typing with one hand on the old laptop Sunny had brought with her. “What are you doing?”

“Playing Words with Friends. It’s a game.”

“I know what it is. I’m just surprised you aren’t watching *Bones.*”

“Seen ’em all. I can’t talk now. This one is timed and Bob is really good, so I have to stay on my toes. In a manner of speaking, you know.”

Sunny blinked a few times. “I do.” Then she backed out of the room that was clean, bright, and smelled like Gain fabric softener. Her mother had brushed her hair and wore a bra. It was like a Christmas miracle at the end of summer.

There was no doubt about it, her mother had turned a corner. Oh, Betty wasn’t warm and fuzzy—more tepid and a heavy wool-blend—but she was definitely on a better path.

Sunny grabbed a small can of Coca-Cola from the fridge and tried not to think about cigarettes. She’d had a few after Henry left but then reminded herself that not smoking wasn’t about being a new Sunny or an old Sunny. It was about starting a new life, which included being healthier. So she’d tossed the supersecret hidden pack and bought a case of colas. Surely a Coke was healthier than a cigarette? And now she had a Coke addiction.

Kicking off her sandals, she went back onto the porch.

It was August hot, but the sun slanting in on the porch felt like a hug, so Sunny ignored the sweat gathering on her upper lip. She grabbed the package, which was heavier than it looked, and sank into a rocker. Her name was written with a flourish. Setting the can on the porch floor, she pulled at the clear tape.

No return label.

Weird. But not impossible.

She ripped half the box apart but finally pulled the contents out.

Then she gasped.

"What the hell?" she whispered to herself, running her fingers over the girlish bubble letters on the front.

Lying in her lap was the dream book.

Sunny and Henry's Book of Dreams.

Beneath the title she'd drawn a yellow house, a big oak tree, and a rainbow. Henry had made fun of the rainbow. *Rainbows aren't permanent.*

"But we are, baby," she used to say. And then Henry would laugh and tickle her, kissing her nose, trying to slide his hands under her shirt like the pervert he was at age sixteen. No, not a pervert. Just a sixteen-year-old guy with raging hormones and a dozen poems written to her breasts.

Who had sent her this?

The last she remembered, the dream book had been under her bed, wedged under a slat. When she'd packed her things and left before graduation, she'd forgotten it. Which seemed crazy as important as Henry was to her, but she'd not been in the right frame of mind, and what would she have done with a silly binder full of wedding accessories and cute dog pictures anyway? That wasn't going to be her life, so she stopped thinking about her dreams and the girl she'd once been.

She opened the book and the first page was pink with little heart stickers all over the page. In the center were the initials, HD + SV.

Lord.

Sunny flipped through the pages, pausing on the baby-name

list, the decorating ones with the pictures she'd painstakingly cut from the pages of *Better Homes and Gardens* and *Southern Living*, and the ones with the gazillion wedding dresses. She and Alan had gotten married wearing blue jeans. No white lace and gauzy veil. No tiered wedding cake. No wedding shower gifts or honeymoon on the beach. And she'd damned sure had no cause to use the names she and Henry had picked out for their nonexistent children.

A teardrop plinked on the last page.

She hadn't even realized she'd been crying.

The front door flew open, and her mother rolled out onto the porch. "What's that?"

Sunny looked down on her lap. "It's nothing."

Half of Betty's mouth tilted downward. "Then why are you crying?"

"I'm not," Sunny said, swiping at her cheek.

Betty made a face. "Cutting onions, huh?"

Sunny managed a choked laugh but nodded. "Something like that."

Betty rolled closer, eying the closed book. She extended something toward her. "I found this in your room. Was sitting right out in the middle of the floor."

Lacy's charm bracelet dangled from her mother's hand. Betty had wanted her fingernails painted, and Sunny had indulged her Sunday evening. The lilac nails were squared off and looked like an exact replica of Sunny's own hand. Sunny took the bracelet and cupped it in her hand. "I don't know how it got out in the middle of the floor. It's been missing for months."

"Dunno. The light caught it and I picked it up. Isn't that Lacy's bracelet? I remember she went to Paris and Eden raved over the pictures. Then she told me about Lacy's dream bracelet."

Sunny jerked her gaze to her mother's. "What did you say?"

Betty nodded toward her clasped hand. "Lacy's bracelet. It was like all the places she'd dreamed of going. When she went, she bought a charm."

The whole dream thing threw her off. She and Lacy had that in common—dreams that would never happen. "It was Lacy's, but Eden gave it to me."

"Why'd she do that? You weren't friends with Lacy."

"Seems she and her friends believed Lacy wanted them to give it to someone with no hope."

"So they gave it to you?" Betty sounded perturbed. "Well, that's a little rude and presumptuous. Damn it. *Rude*. That's the word I should have used."

"What?"

"Bob skunked me on WWF. If I had used *rude*, I would have blocked him." Betty slammed her good hand on the wheelchair arm. "But anyway, they should have given me the damn bracelet long ago. If people were looking for hope, I could turn out empty pockets. Though I don't know, you're pretty pathetic."

"Why, thank you, Mother," Sunny drawled.

"Eh, you're better now, but you were rough there for a while." Betty reached over and tapped the book lying in her lap. "Is this that book you had back in high school? The one you and Henry were always scribbling in like morons?"

"Yeah."

"Who sent it to you?" Betty lifted her good eyebrow.

"I don't know. It was just here. I don't see postage, so I think someone must have brought it by. Maybe Henry?" Sunny rubbed a hand over the book, her heart vibrating with… hope. But Henry had walked away just like he had all those years ago.

No. He hadn't walked away. She'd driven him away. Forced him to go.

"If he brought it, does that mean something?" Betty asked.

"No. I don't know. Maybe."

Her mother sighed. "I ain't never seen a woman as stubborn as you. Not even I was as pig-headed. That man loves you. You know that, right?"

"Yes. I know."

"So why are you sitting here crying over a book when you have a good man who loves you… and who you love back? I'm not blind. I know you've always carried Henry in your heart. And now we've spent months with you moping around here. You think I don't see what you're doing to yourself? Not letting yourself have any sunshine? You act like you want to live under a thundercloud for the rest of your life. Shit, Sunny. Don't be me, baby."

"I can't go backward, Mama. I'm not the woman who should be in his life. He needs a woman who bakes chocolate chip cookies, wears cute seersucker dresses, and chairs things."

"I think he had that already, didn't he? Didn't seem to stick, and why are you shortchanging yourself? You ain't never been any of that, but that man would burn the town down if you told him to. I've never seen a man so in love with a woman."

"God, Mama. Stop saying that." She groaned, her heart aching at the words her mother threw at her. She'd thrown his love back at him. She didn't deserve him. "I can't. I mean, I thought maybe, but then I let his kid fall out of a tree and his wife nearly attacked me. It was all so… so… horrible. I just think I couldn't have kids for a reason. I'm not made to—"

Her mother slapped the back of her head.

"Ow," Sunny said, shrinking away from Betty. "What's wrong with you?"

"What's wrong with *you*? I'm just trying to knock some sense into your fool head. If what you're saying is true, why did I end up with three kids? I was about as unfit as a mother could get, and my womb was practically a sperm magnet. I could sneeze and get pregnant. The good Lord has nothing to do with you not being able to have kids, and you damn well know it. So stop using myths and superstitions as a reason to run away from love. For once in your life, Sunny, fight for what you want."

Sunny smoothed her hair and stared at the book. Another tear slid down her cheek, and she wanted to sob, to punch something, to rip off her clothes and rail at fate.

A small piece of paper stuck out of the top of the book. Sunny fingered it and then opened to that page.

A picture of a big yellow farmhouse dominated the space. She'd cut out pictures of stained glass windows. And a picture of a wide-railed porch with a swing on one end. On the opposing page was a photo she'd taken of the pond on the land she and Henry had always wanted.

Betty took her hand and gave it a squeeze, making Sunny choke up.

"Mama."

"I know, baby. Love ain't easy. I had a man I loved once and, well, I screwed it up because I didn't think I was good enough for him. I took off with some asshole, thinking I could just run from my problems. But I got pregnant, and he left me in some flea-trap in Tennessee. I came skulking back, but by that time, it was too late. I let my insecurities keep me from a life I was too afraid to have. You going to let that happen? You going to just give Henry up?"

"It was Henry's dad, wasn't it? The man you didn't think you were good enough for?"

Betty laughed. "Well, I've always been a sucker for a Delmar."

"Oh Mama, why didn't you ever tell me?" Sunny wiped the tears on her cheeks and then reached over and wiped the ones on her mother's.

"Wasn't a need to. That ship had sailed, and it wasn't coming back. But you have a chance to get back what you lost." Betty reached over and tapped on the picture of the pond. "He bought that land, you know."

"Wait, who? Henry?" Something inside Sunny cracked open.

"Yeah, he bought it a long time ago. Rosemary told me he built a house on it when she came over to find a sweater she let Eden borrow. And Vienna's grandmother lives nearby and she said it was"—Betty's finger slid over to the picture of the yellow farmhouse—"a big yellow house."

Sunny swallowed hard and raised her eyes to the street out in front of their house. A small boy on a bicycle tootled by, singing a silly nursery rhyme. Normal things. Life happening. But inside Sunny every roadblock, every intention, every misconception she had about love, Morning Glory and Henry had imploded, scattering ashes.

He'd built their house.

"Oh my God," she breathed, leaning her head back and closing her eyes. "He built it."

Betty just squeezed her hand and stayed silent.

Sunny sat there, tears coursing down her cheeks, on the porch of the house she'd hated for most her life. She sat there holding the hand of the mother she'd hated just about as much. She sat there, a woman who'd experienced so much loss and had been prepared to walk away from potential happiness because she didn't think she deserved it.

Someone really should have kicked her ass.

Months ago.

After a few seconds, minutes, or half an hour—she wasn't sure—she opened her eyes and pulled her hand from her mother's. "I think I need to step out for a few minutes. Will you be okay?"

Betty smiled, and this time her half smile didn't seem so clown-like or deranged. "I bet you do. I'll be fine, honey."

It was the first time she could remember that her mother had called her an endearment.

chapter twenty

HENRY HAD JUST finished installing the last gate on the kennels behind the barn when the Ring security feature he'd put on his phone dinged. Normally he'd ignore it. Over the past month, he'd had so many deliveries to the new house that he'd not worried about monitoring the camera that recorded what was left on his doormat. He doubted anyone would steal the bedding and furnishings delivered at an alarming rate from Amazon in preparation for move-in next week, but he'd been waiting for the sign he'd ordered from Clem that would designate his barn and the kennels behind it as the home of Sunshine Animal Rescue.

Maybe today it would come. He wanted to get it up before Grace came out for the first time since he'd gotten the green light to work on Landry's suggestion. They were planning a grand opening and reveal in two weeks.

The results of building the animal rescue were pretty phenomenal. Henry had installed slides that allowed water and food bowls to be filled and slid back into the kennels for easier care, commissioned some local Boy Scouts to build raised platforms from leftover shipping pallets for the dogs to sleep on, and installed fans and heaters to keep the kennels temperate all year long. There were big dog runs, and he and Landry had even cleared an adjacent field to serve as a play yard. Sal and his historical society guys had put together some play structures—tunnels and bungee pulls—and a few ladies' Bible study groups from different churches united to do a bake sale that paid for the fence around the yard. Sassy Grigsby had donated her old washer and dryer so volunteers could wash the bedding, and Henry had paid to outfit a doggy spa where they could bathe and groom the animals. They still had a few things to add, but overall it was ready to accept some four-legged guests.

So when he heard the app on his phone ding, he grabbed it.

Standing on the front porch mat Carson, Tomeka, and their new daughter Kelsi had brought to him as a housewarming gift when they came out to see the house, was Sunny.

His heart dropped into his stomach, but he pulled it right back up again and pressed the button that would project his voice. "Yes?"

"Oh, you're here," she said, sounding surprised. "I mean, I didn't see your truck."

"I'm at the barn."

She blinked, her hands twisting in front of her. "Oh. Uh, it's Sunny."

"I can see that. There's a camera. You need something?"

She opened her mouth and then shut it. He wished the video feed was better. He couldn't read her well enough to figure out why she was there. He'd never told her about the house, but since they were housing the kennel now at the barn, he supposed word had gotten around town.

"Uh, where's the barn?" She turned and looked around her.

"Just hold on a sec and I'll be up there." He clicked off the app and headed toward the mud-spattered mule he used to navigate the property. He'd bought it when he'd started the build last year but hadn't much cause to use it; however, he'd gotten his money's worth over the past few weeks.

He navigated the path through the woods, noting the slight

breeze and cool darkness of the pines. Apprehension, anger, and ever-present pesky hope tangled inside him as he broke through the encompassing woods into a clearing that announced his house on the hill. He could see Sunny standing on the porch, watching his approach, and after not seeing her for months, he was surprised she was here. Someone had told him she was leaving next week.

He parked the mule and climbed out.

For a brief moment, it struck him that this was what he'd always wanted—Sunny waiting for him on their front porch.

But this wasn't that Sunny.

And that porch wasn't theirs.

And she'd said she would never love him.

Her expression didn't betray much as she crossed her arms and kept her gaze on him. He stopped on the top step and set his hands on his hips. "Thought you were leaving town."

"I am. I mean, I… was." She jerked her chin up, and he could see that she'd been crying recently. He wasn't sure what was going on and didn't want to hope that the winds of fate had shifted.

"So…?" He arched his brow.

"What's all this?" Her voice was soft, full of wonder.

"It's my house. I haven't moved in yet, but I'm planning on it next week. Waiting on some furniture and the fridge. They messed up the order and brought the wrong one." He knew he was hedging and not answering the question she was really asking, but she didn't deserve an answer. She'd pushed him out and shut the door, so she didn't get to stick her head back in and make him answer her questions.

"You know that's not what I mean," she said, her voice almost a whisper as she tore her gaze from him and looked around at the crisp gray paint on the floorboards, the swing with the black and white stripes, the shiny black shutters. Ferns swayed on chains extended from the porch ceiling and the stained glass in the front door threw patterns on the boards.

"You built our house."

"I built *my* house."

She walked over and picked up the dream book from the porch rail. He'd not noticed it before now. Something wriggly squirmed in his gut.

"Where'd you get that old relic?" he asked.

"You didn't send it to me?"

"No. I haven't seen it since high school." He eyed the book and wondered at the sudden emotion surging inside him. His throat felt scratchy. Something weird floated on the breeze. He wiped the sweat from his forehead and waited on Sunny.

"Someone left it on my doorstep with this page marked." She opened the book and the house he'd just built popped out from the depths. Not literally, of course, but it had just as much impact. The house on the page looked like the house he'd built down to the black shutters. He'd known they'd once talked about a farmhouse, and he'd always liked the idea of a cheerful yellow, but he'd damn near copied the exact house.

"Huh," he managed.

"You built this exact house," she said, her gaze so searching. "Why did you do that, Henry?"

Because deep down somewhere in his soul, he thought he could make the life they'd once dreamed about. Because he'd watched *Field of Dreams* too many times and was convinced that if he built it, she would come. Because he loved her and wanted her waiting on that porch for him every day of their lives.

Or maybe he was just a moron.

"I guess it imprinted itself so much in my memory that it just happened. I didn't plan it that way." He actually hadn't, but he knew it had been close enough. He'd started building the house way before Sunny had returned to Morning Glory. He'd built it similar to the one she'd wanted and took some measure of comfort that he'd have some tiny piece of something of her. But now he felt exposed in a way he'd not been ready for. "Don't read something into it that's not there."

She turned and looked at the stained glass transoms. "You used stained glass."

Well, she sorta had him there. "Yeah. Katie Clare asked for it."

Liar.

Well, he wasn't going to admit that he'd built her a house. Because he hadn't. He'd built it for himself. Pretty much.

Sunny walked over to the swing and sat down. "I'm overwhelmed."

Henry didn't move. Instead, he watched her, wary. He wasn't sure if she was upset, flattered, pissed, or embarrassed.

The hot breeze sent the wind chimes he'd hung into a tinkling fit, and the ferns swayed. Casper the Ghost Cat leaped onto the railing and blinked at both of them.

"You have a cat?" she asked.

"Sort of."

"It's not ginger."

"No," he said.

She kicked the swing into motion. "This is surreal."

It was at that moment that Fancy started barking. Henry sucked in a deep breath because that was another thing that had changed in the past week.

The Boltons had called Grace and told her they couldn't keep Fancy. Seems she really liked chicken. So much so that she'd killed two. They were afraid to let her loose and didn't feel it was fair to keep her chained up or confined to a pen. Marie had also mentioned that they hadn't been adequately prepared for being the owners of such a high-energy pup. They had tried to make it work but eventually accepted they hadn't chosen the right dog. Grace had driven out and picked up Fancy. He'd happened to call her when she was on her way back into town. Hearing the tears in her voice, paired with the horrible thought that Fancy might have to go to animal control if Grace couldn't find a foster, had sealed the deal for him.

He was now fostering Fancy.

Or rather, he was her new owner. Landry and Katie Clare had been ecstatic over the news, and Henry had to admit he'd enjoyed having her around the past month. He'd kept her up at the barn with him most days, but today he'd shut her in the laundry room because she'd eaten a lizard yesterday and gotten sick.

"What's that?" Sunny said, snapping her head toward the house.

"That's Fancy."

She jumped up and started toward his door. "Fancy? Why do you have her? What is she doing here?"

He didn't have time to answer. Sunny opened the door and went inside, her ears obviously pricked toward the barking dog. She bypassed the living room with its heart pine floors and brick fireplace, passed the bright modern kitchen, and wrenched open the door to the laundry room.

Fancy shot out like a maniac, making keening sounds he'd never heard from the dog. Sunny dropped to the floor, and Fancy went nuts licking her.

"Fancy Pants. Oh my gosh, Fancy Pants! Mama missed you. Yes, I did. I missed you so much," Sunny said, wrapping her arms around the dog, tears streaming down her face. She crossed her legs and clasped the dog and then sobbed into her fur. Fancy grew still, almost concerned, her brown eyes shooting toward Henry as if to say, "What is this?"

Henry leaned against the kitchen island and watched Sunny break down. He wanted to go to her, to scoop her up and cradle her against his chest, but he had no clue of what reaction he might get. Instead, he curled his hands into his pockets and waited.

Finally she released the dog and sat back, wiping her face. Her chest heaved and her nose ran, and still he'd never seen anything as gorgeous as Sunny Voorhees David sitting on his travertine tile, crying her eyes out. He pulled the clean handkerchief he always carried from his pocket and held it out to her.

She took it and blew her nose.

"I'm sorry, Henry. I'm just truly, truly overwhelmed."

Fancy danced around Sunny, begging to be petted. Sunny unconsciously stroked the dog's ears.

"I see that you are."

Struggling to her feet, she held the wadded-up, soggy hankie out to him.

Henry shook his head. "No, thanks."

Her face flushed red. "Right. Uh, I'll wash it."

"Just put it in the laundry room," he said, extending his arm toward the good-sized room off the kitchen. A new washer and dryer gleamed beside the large sink and cream cabinets.

She walked into the laundry room and then returned. "Uh, Henry, um, I came out not because I wanted to see the house." Glancing around, she sighed. "It's gorgeous and you're a lucky guy to have this place."

"I am. It's the spot I always wanted, right?"

"Yeah. It is. This is exactly what I wanted."

The unspoken words hung there like heavy fruit waiting to be plucked.

"You were right." Sunny sucked in a deep breath and then pushed her hair back.

"I was?"

"About me running away."

He didn't say anything because he had no clue which direction she was going with this.

"So…" She closed her eyes and whispered, "This is so hard."

He still didn't say anything.

"Uh, the thing is, I've been scared to love. I've been afraid of losing the person I love because I didn't want to hurt again. It's like I'm up to my limit on hurting, you know?"

"I know all you've been through, and though I can't say I totally understand, I've wanted to."

Her face softened. "I know. You've been more than understanding. But anyway, I figured it would be best to avoid any kind of entanglement that might jeopardize my heart. I thought I could come to Morning Glory, do my duty, and get the hell out. It sounded so easy. But it wasn't, because I didn't plan on… on my stupid heart."

Henry felt his own heart surge against his chest. "Well, sometimes hearts have a mind of their own. Which seems ironic considering they aren't supposed to think. Quite the opposite, right?"

Sunny made a strangled noise of agreement. She ran her finger under her bottom lash and wiped it on her shirt hem. "Yeah. I didn't plan on you. Or on developing a relationship with my mom. Or Fancy. Or on any of the other people who cast their nets around me and caught me up good."

At his nod, she continued. "See, when all that stuff happened with Katie Clare, I realized that I had fallen in love with her, with Morning Glory, with belonging somewhere, and I panicked because that felt really dangerous. Sitting there waiting for that ambulance and then waiting in that hospital… Well, it was like experiencing all the losses I had endured all over again. That precious girl could have died because of me. Then when Jillian said I didn't belong, it was like an alarm clanging. I wanted to get out before I got hurt. Or hurt someone else."

"Jillian shouldn't have said that. It was wrong of her. She knows that, but in all honesty, as happy as she is with Eddie, she still has a sore spot over you. She knows that she and I didn't last because I had given my heart to you long ago."

"That's not true."

"Yeah, it kinda is, Sunny." He walked toward her, hands still tucked away because he was afraid to reach for her and have her turn from him. "Thing is, I fell in love with you the moment I met you. I knew even back then that you were the one for me, so trying to make a marriage with someone else work was disastrous. I tried, but like you just said, sometimes the heart has a mind of its own."

She lifted her eyes, and they were so filled with hope it nearly took his breath away. "You're saying you still love me?"

"I'm not sure I ever stopped… or can stop, Sunshine."

Sunny swallowed hard, tears sliding down her cheeks. He was fresh out of handkerchiefs, but maybe he could offer an alternative to the white square. He stepped toward her. "You said you fell in love with my daughter, the town, but you never said anything about me."

Sunny bit her lip. "That's because you're the hardest one."

Henry stopped midreach. "Why?"

"I didn't want to love you. I didn't. I thought we could never have what we had, and you know what? We can't. I was a girl with all these crazy ideas of what love is. But I'm not a girl anymore."

"No, you're not."

"I'm a woman. One who is stupid. So stupid for fighting so hard against my heart. Against you." She bridged the gap between them and reached up to cup his face.

"Sunny," he breathed at her touch. Her cool hands felt so good against his skin, but her eyes delivered something that took his breath away.

"I lied when I said I didn't love you… that I couldn't love you, Henry."

He felt his heart burst. "But why? You know I would never hurt you again. Never."

"I was scared. I'm so sorry I acted like a fool and tried to avoid my feelings. But I do love you. I really, really do."

He wanted to sweep her into a kiss, pick her up and test out the new mattress that had been delivered last week, but he wouldn't until he knew everything.

"But are you leaving?"

"Not unless you don't want me."

"I want you. I always have." He fitted his hand at her waist and lowered his head.

Fancy danced around them, yipping happily like only a dog who'd just realized that everything was going to work out could.

"Are you going to stay with me?" he asked when his lips were inches from her.

Sunny nodded. "Always."

Their lips met then, and the sweetest bliss filled his soul. Sunny had come home. For real. And this time they would claim the happily-ever-after they'd vowed to have in their dream book long ago. As her tongue slid against his and she moved her hand to his neck, something hooked on his ear.

"Ow," he said, breaking the kiss and drawing back to capture her hand. "What's this?"

Sunny blinked and shook her arm. "It's my new bracelet."

On her wrist was a charm bracelet filled with charms. He caught sight of an alligator, a flip-flop, and a red dancing shoe.

"Well, it hooked me."

Sunny started laughing and looked at the bracelet, her eyes crinkling. "God, I think it actually did."

He kissed her hard and then drew back again. "I'm sensing there's more to this story than what you're letting on, and I think I need to hear it."

"Yeah, and I'll tell you sometime, but not right now. Right now I want to kiss you some more and maybe go throw the ball for Fancy."

"That's what you want to do?" Because he could think of a lot of things they could be doing other than throwing a slobbery tennis ball for a cattle dog who sat looking at them with her tongue lolled out, smile in place.

"Well, I have some other things in mind, but I *have* missed Fancy," Sunny said, eyeing their dog.

Their dog.

Because they were going to make this work. They were going to be a family. In this house. On this land.

Where they had always belonged.

He gathered her to him. "We will make throwing the ball like foreplay. Every time we toss the ball, you have to kiss me. And then we'll start taking off clothes. I'm really digging that you're wearing a dress. How do you ride that hog in a dress anyway?"

"I have shorts on underneath," Sunny said, her eyes twinkling. Her hand caressed his chest, and her other hand scratched Fancy behind her ears. The charm bracelet caught in the dying light of the day, and a piece of a puzzle he'd been missing clicked into place.

"Damn it, let's start now," he said, pulling her in for another kiss. She tasted like strawberry lip gloss and forever.

Just before their lips met, Sunny whispered. "We both deserve to be happy. I believe that now. I believe in you and me."

Then Sunny kissed him just as the doorbell rang.

And Henry remembered the sign, the kennels, and that Sunny had no clue about the new space for the rescue. "Come with me."

He took her hand and they went onto the porch to find that UPS had, in fact, finally delivered the sign. With Fancy still running excitedly around them, he pulled out his pocket knife and opened the box. When he unwrapped the sign, he smiled. Holding it up, he turned it toward the woman standing on the porch, glowing like he'd never seen her glow.

"What is that?" She reached out to run a hand over the custom-made sign featuring the logo of the new organization.

"Hop in the mule and I'll show you," he said, taking her hand and pulling her toward where he'd left his ATV.

"I thought we were going to play with Fancy… and then each other."

"We are, but first you have to see this," he said, anticipation welling up to take its place beside the love he'd always carried for her. She was going to love having the rescue less than a mile away.

They climbed into the mule, Fancy hopping up to take her usual place, which was right next to him. The sun was hot, making him sweat. He didn't care. He was as happy as he could ever remember. Sunny loved him, she was staying, and they would be together the way they always should have been.

"I can't believe this," Sunny said, her blue eyes shining with unshed tears. "This is real. You. Me. Fancy. Our house."

As they emerged in the clearing by the pond, the barn sat open, waiting to deliver a sweet surprise. He rode past the water and into the shady building where noisy fans stirred the hot air. He braked and then watched Sunny scan the space, taking in the doggy spa area, the cat room with its climbing structure and air-conditioned cages, the open door that led to the kennels that could house forty dogs.

"What is this?" She turned to him, her eyes wide, her pretty mouth open. "Is this what I think it is? Is this the new rescue?"

"I always said you were the smartest woman I knew."

"Oh my God, Henry. You built the rescue." She jumped out of the mule and Fancy followed her, tail wagging. He watched as she walked through the areas, laughing and crying and calling out things like "This is so cool" and "Oh my gosh, it's perfect."

When she came back to him, her eyes were glowing, her cheeks were wet, and she was smiling. "Oh, Henry, this is so wonderful! I didn't think today could get better, but it has."

The kiss she gave him was as sweet as nectar.

He pulled back and smiled at her. "Oh, one more thing. I couldn't quite figure it out until I saw your bracelet."

The office he'd built for the rescue was cool and dark, a welcome reprieve from the heat. He took the padded envelope from his desk and brought it to her. Handing it to her, he said, "I got this yesterday. I wasn't sure what to do with it, but now I think I know."

Sunny have him a cryptic look and pulled open the gaping edges, allowing a small box to slide into her palm. "Huh. What's this?"

"The note might give you that answer."

Sunny opened the envelope, pulled out the monogrammed stationery, and read the note. "*Henry, I know you won't understand this, but I think this small box could hold the key to true happiness. Take it to Sunny and give it to her before she leaves town. Good luck.*"

Sunny made a face. "Who sent this?"

He tapped the monogram. RRG.

"Rosemary?" she asked.

"Open the box," he said softly.

She pulled the box open and gasped. Inside on a velvet bed lay two charms—one a silver dog, the other a tiny yellow house. "Oh."

"I didn't understand until I saw the bracelet. I guess these are supposed to go on it?"

Sunny brushed the tears from her cheeks. "That's what they are. They're my charms to finish Lacy's bracelet."

"What do they mean?"

"That I have found where I belong. That I'm finally home." Sunny closed her eyes, opened them again, and said, "They mean I'm home, Henry."

want more?

To find more books from Liz Talley visit www.liztalleybooks.com/category/books. Also, don't forget to visit her website to sign up for the newsletter at www.liztalleybooks.com.

Reviews are much appreciated. They help other readers find books they might enjoy (or not enjoy). I hope you connected with my book and will share your thoughts with others.

about the author

Liz Talley is the author of twenty-five heartwarming stories of love and laughter. A finalist in both the Golden Heart and Rita Awards, she's garnered number one spots on Amazon Romance lists and was honored with RT Review's Best Superromance 2014. Robyn Carr says "laughter and tears spring from the pages," and Kristan Higgins says Liz's stories are "written in a warm, intelligent voice." Liz makes her home in North Louisiana with her high school sweetheart, two teen boys, and three dogs. When not writing romance, she likes to read, volunteer, and watch Netflix. You can reach her at www.liztalleybooks.com.

CPSIA information can be obtained
at www.ICGtesting.com
Printed in the USA
LVHW081621280519
619300LV00014B/1084/P